I0604946

# North Star Resort

Russ Vanderboom

**Pepper Seed Publishing**
1902 Pine Tree Trail
Ely, MN 55731

**North Star Resort**
Copyright © 2024 by Russ Vanderboom



This book is a work of fiction. Any references to historical events, persons or real location are used fictitiously. Characters created in the story are products of the process of fiction writing and the imagination of the author. Any resemblance to actual events or persons, living or dead, is coincidental.

The author can be contacted  by email at Pepper Seed Publishing:
RVan@pepperseedpublishing.com .

Cover image by Gabe Horstman

Vanderboom, Russell
North Star Resort/Russ Vanderboom
Pepper Seed Publishing paperback edition
366 Pages cm
1. Family. 2. Boundary Waters. 3. Magical realism. 4. Vision quest.-

ISBN 978-0-9916421-1-3 (paperback)

10 9 8 7 6 5 4 3 2 **1**

*For my family*

*Heal yourself with the light of the sun and the rays of the moon.*
*With the sound of the river and the waterfall.*
*With the swaying of the sea and the fluttering of birds…*
*— María Sabina*

# Open, my eyes

*North Star Lodge*
*Ely, Minnesota*
*August, 1965*

I caved.

Martha covered for me. She settled the children. Dad, slumped in a chair on the screen porch, sunk into the darkness of his own sunset. Ingie lay still on her lounge near our father.

Ixchel found me crumpled in exhaustion and depression. My wizened mentor gazed at me with strength and determination.

"Come join us on my porch," she said to Martha as she gathered me up. She took my hand and led me to the bench on the porch of her cabin.

"It is time," she said. "Sit here. I'll be back."

I sat, motionless. Emotionless. My twin toddlers by themselves were almost too much for me. My sister was more than I could handle. My father was more than anybody needed.

What would I do, but for Martha, my godmother?

What would I do without Ixchel, my teacher?

So great a person, Ixchel. So strong. She stood in front of me when she returned, a steaming cup extended from her tawny hands. Her eyes were dark and deep and inviting.

"We need to communicate," she said. "We are here to see. And to listen."

I accepted her infusion. She went back into the cabin to fetch another cup for herself.

"Where is your white knight now, when you need him?" she said when she returned, sitting on the bench to my left.

"I have no white knight. I have only what is mine."

"Ah! A do-it-yourself white knight. That seems big. Does it not?"

The thought was big. Too big. I snapped my head away, flicking the idea from my focus.

I sipped the hot tea. "Life seems to not be big. Nor small. It just is, and it is mine.'

"Agreed."

I glanced her way. She sat folded up, cross legged, her feet tucked under, her arms folded across her belly.

"Your life is your gift from this world. Is it not?"

All the negative affirmatives, I thought. Where is she leading me?

I sipped. The earthy tasting brew was hot; my belly warmed and the sensation of heat filled my body, filtering down my legs and arms, and spiraling up my neck into my head.

"All that I have is the gift of this world. Time. Life. What more is there?" I looked to her for assurance.

Her eyes lifted, scanning above the horizon. She smiled.

"The perks, my dear." Her compact body shook with quiet humor. "The world snags us in its web of time. It beckons us to reach about for the little perks it offers to make us content. To enable us fully. To give us opportunities to complete our tasks. To be complete."

She leveled her eyes to mine. "To be free."

She nodded toward the tea. "Drink."

The tea was cooling rapidly. I drank.

"The gifts are here for us. Sometimes, we must ask. Other times, they are cast upon us, and we must master them. Sometimes, we recognize those gifts. Many gifts are silent. Invisible. Yet, we can see them, if we train ourselves to look."

I felt a change in my eyes. I heard the clearing of the nightfall. Starlight gleamed like diamonds. Nocturnal creatures moved cautiously in the budding darkness.

My cup was empty.

I watched the ripples smooth to glass on the lake. A meteor cut a burning swath near the ceiling of the sky, a furry tail of sparks spinning off barbs and barbules before fading into the depth of darkness. I chuckled softly. My laughter gurgled deep in my chest. The shooting star's featherlike light tickled my soul.

All about me, I heard sounds like bee wings humming. I looked, but there were no bees.

Before me, the lakefront lit up, thick with color and shape. The pines this side of the lake glowed from within their lodge pole trunks. Their needles writhed like cool green fingers as thin as yarn. Boulders huddled along the shoreline and under the trees, also illuminated from within. They appeared to have gathered as witnesses of the ages.

My vision fragmented: I saw everything in its own compartment. Like through the eyes of a bee, every image in a separate visual cell, bordered by walls like honeycomb. I watched them all simultaneously.

I scanned the panorama. An owl looked down with blazing eyes from within the bursts of pine needles. A martin prowled the shoreline. Out on the lake, a fish surfaced, its signature expanding in a rimmed circle of starlight sweeping across the water.

The buzzing continued.

I focused my ears to locate the source, but it came from all over. I followed it as it moved within, to a place between my ears. It permeated me. And then it stilled.

A doe picked her way among the pines. She lowered her head, looking about. I turned to Ixchel, seated to my left, shaped like an otter sitting upright beside me, awaiting the approaching deer.

I looked into the doe's deep, large eyes. She flowed between the pines. Warmth. Love. She was Martha, and she sat to my right.

I felt the otter's whiskers tickle my ear. She whispered to me. "Consider the night blossoms."

Between the boughs of the pines, in the deep, eternal gaps of space, the seedlings of stars germinated into budding flowers like the trilliums of spring. White petals poured through the pine branches and spilled out upon the lake where they piled like snow.

The doe whistled, and the petals whisked away. My chest heaved with sorrow.

The otter leaned across me and breathed into my ears, and the sorrow softened.

The otter spoke.

"That which was no longer is."

The sorrow lift from my chest.

"That which is, is."

My heart filled with delight, freshness, and peace.

"You are what is."

Joy filled my soul.

"Now, we can find your powers. See."

And in the panorama of my home, I looked into the sky. I searched the many lights and shadows. Space became tiny; I was everywhere at once. And in that space, which was mine, I found strength. Peace flourished.

∞

I awakened as the light of dawn filtered though the canopy of pine. Ixchel sat in a chair near the window, watching out over the lake. I lay under the woolen blankets on the bed in her cabin.

She looked at me with care.

"Good morning," I scrubbed my eyes with my fists like a child.

She smiled. "It is good. A good day to practice. Seeing."

I looked out to the lake. The sky was bright. Puffy clouds reflected off the water.

"A day to see."

She offered me another steaming cup. This time, wisps of mint curled up, opening my nostrils, finding that spot behind my forehead. I sipped the simple tea. Bog mint. We had harvested it from a spearmint variety that grew near the hiking trail along the lowlands of the North Arm. It warmed me; it's fragrance swirled within.

I looked up the sloping lawn toward the quiet lodge. Nothing. Stillness. That would soon be transformed by the magic of my little ones creating their new day. I longed to create with them.

Ixchel cast her probing dark gaze upon me.

"Where are you now?" she asked, stirring a coffee for herself.

"Here."

She smiled.

We rose to meet the day.

I

Book One

# The Ways of Boys

*Tuang es el color de los viajo
a deconocidas tierras y ignotos mundos*

*Tuang is the color of unexpected voyages
to unknown lands and forgotten worlds.*

*— Otto Raúl González*

# Chapter 1

# Father Jack Finds the North Star

*Ely, Minnesota*
*June, 1968*

She glanced toward the gleaming Cadillac as it crunched down the gravel drive leading to her resort. The wooden canoe perched atop the Caddy cast a whimsical sight. She didn't recall seeing many Burgundy red Sixty Special Broughams with cedar strip canoes strapped atop. The canoe was custom made. It had fine lines. She thought it looked familiar.

But the twins had kept her moments longer than she intended before heading to the hospital for her evening shift, so she hustled on toward her old Thunderbird.

The Caddy rocked to a halt and the engine stilled. The driver jumped from his car.

She paused when she heard her name.

"Lynn North?" the driver called, hidden behind his car and its unlikely cargo. He caught her eye as he peeked through the gap between car top and canoe and hustled around the end of the Cadillac.

She could not take her eyes from the canoe "Yes. Can I help you? Are you looking for a cabin? Martha can help you in our office," she gestured toward the sign hanging from the porch roof.

"Miss North?" he asserted; he recognized Patrick's Lynn from the pictures in the albums Paddy had shared. His tone was kind and careful. "Pardon me," the stranger said. "I've been looking for you. My name is Jack Hanley. I'm David Joyce's friend. David, Patrick's twin. I'm looking for Patrick. You do know Patrick, don't you?"

Lynn caught her breath. "Patrick? Yes. I know Patrick." She glanced away from the canoe on the Cadillac and met his eye. "Is that Patrick's canoe? How is he?"

Jack nodded. "Patrick's uncle sent it with me. He thought it would give you confidence in why I am here. I don't know Patrick. Never met him, except through David. I don't know how Patrick is. I thought maybe you could help me find him. Have you heard from him?

Lynn shook her head. She hadn't heard from Patrick in nearly five years. She left him in a way that set limits on both their lives. Yes, she knew when he went to Boulder and played ball. But then, once he was done with football and its publicity, she had little way to know of him. Life became still, absent of her knowledge of him. She wondered often when Patrick might appear back in her life. She trusted he would. She prayed so. He'd find a trail, a clue, that would lead to her. She left him ways by which to start his path to here. Clues. Her family's former address. Would he follow it? She hoped he would. She hadn't expected to leave the old family home in Minnetonka. But if he tried to find her there, he could possibly find her here in Ely. She had wondered how, and when, that would be. And now, it seemed, it had started.

She scrutinized this gentleman keeping her from her work at the hospital. She was drawn to him like an old friend. His long, shaggy mane radiated from his skull like rays from the sun. His eyes were kind and large, widespread, soft and gentle on a face weathered by sun and wind. She noted his bushy eyebrows.

She offered her handshake and a smile. "I feel like I know you, Jack Hanley. Father Hanley," she said. "David's letters. You were his mentor. His guide. He filled his letters with your words of advice and encouragement. Welcome."

She told him Martha would help him settle into lodging and care for his needs. They could discuss matters further when she returned from work, she added. She excused herself; she had to leave now. She was a nurse at the hospital in town. Her patients awaited her.

∞

Martha led him to cabin Number 3. "I'll show you where you can put the canoe. Luther will help you. Have you paddled much? Do you intend to fish? Have you a license?"

Martha struck Jack as one who could read a person with just a glance. She read him like a book. "No. I'd like to, but I've never fished before. Yes, I've paddled both canoes and kayaks."

"We can set you up with a license. Luther can show you everything you need to know about fishing, too. In the morning." She was brief and to the point, but kind.

"Luther's building a fire in the fire ring. You can join us for supper. Beans, hot dogs and potato salad. When the weather is this fine, we often build a fire and cook out. If not, we have supper in the lodge," she said. "Let us know if you need anything else."

∞

After her shift, Lynn returned home. Martha detailed the arrival of the lodger who aimed to stay indefinitely in Number 3.

"He's green. Doesn't know a hoot about the wilderness. He said he's interested in canoeing and camping, but I don't know how fit he is to go out by himself. Luther can show him the basics, but…" She left her judgement dangle.

Lynn nodded. It's not difficult to pick out those with little experience in the boundary waters. Martha's observations didn't surprise her.

"Did you notice his canoe?" Lynn asked.

"Gave it a glance. Looks a lot like yours."

"Identical." She spoke with raised eyebrows. "It's Patrick's."

"The twins' father?"

She nodded.

Martha drew in a deep breath and lifted her eyebrows high. "Well, it's likely he'll be coming along soon enough himself then? Having his stuff delivered?"

Lynn flashed a blush of hope, raising from deep in her neck and chest, and she felt a flutter in her heart.

"We can't say we didn't see this coming," Martha quipped. "So, it begins, does it?"

∞

Ingie identified Patrick's canoe from her perch on the screen porch. She watched Luther lug the wooden boat to the lake front. The new lodger followed behind, a hand gripped upon the stern of the canoe balanced on her father's shoulders. *A challenging one, this fellow,* she chuckled. *Will we have mind games? Most certainly.* She saw it was inviting. Inevitable.

# Chapter 2

# Learning from Luther

Luther was at his best when paddling quiet water or when fishing. His mind purred and maintained track when he propelled his canoe along the shoreline of the bays and islands of Burntside, the lake he knew since childhood. The waters on which he wooed his sweetheart and lifelong friend whispered softly to his heart and brought calm to his mind. At times, he faltered briefly; he didn't quite recognize the island off the bow, or the shoreline of a remote bay. But wasn't it always so? The shoreline changed with the moving sun; shadows tweaked the profile of the granite boulders littering the lakeside, and then the shadows shifted. The shadows changed the appearance of sites that he'd known his entire life. But the changing shadows from the sun moving across the sky was a distant cry from the fog that swooped upon his mind in unexpected ways at unpredictable times.

"Ah, here we are," he said. "We'll pull in here."

His new friend paddling in the bow seat appeared competent enough. And kind. If he suspected Luther was subject to those clouds of confusion, he didn't make a big thing of it. Luther could tell.

He knew at times that he was repeating what he had just said. He did that frequently. He'd go to explain how to secure a hook with a Palomar knot, or link two ends of braided line with a blood knot, and find that he was holding just those ties in his hand, already having demonstrated the loops and pulls that bound the lines and hooks together. This woolly headed friend up front would make nothing of it, or perhaps they would share a kindly laugh. But that was alright. He was a nice gentleman, what's his name?

"Here we are," he said with certainty. "We can pull in here."

His paddling partner glanced back over his shoulder, calling to him. "I see it. On the left."

Luther steered shoreward and they landed the canoe. As the wooden vessel slid to a halt in the sand, Luther's charge stood and stepped out of the canoe, pulling the lead tied to the bow. The canoe settled, half out of the water, on the sandy strip of beach.

"Did ya catch anything, Grandpa?" Ally asked he grandfather.

Luther stepped into the shallow clear water next to the canoe, lifting the stern

"We weren't fishing. We were canoeing. Navigating. And we did a pretty fair job of it." Luther glanced at his paddling companion. At the moment, he couldn't recall the fellow's name, but he gave him a nod of approval. "Got back home, anyhow."

His partner detailed their travels.

"We took the long way," Jack said. "We stayed close to the shore all the way to the point east of the North Arm. Then we turned south and did a bit of island hopping. We went out around State Island, but caught a bit too much wind and waves, so Luther brought us back between Berry and Oliver islands."

"That's quite a paddle," Martha said. "You both must be hungry and thirsty."

"Well, not exactly. We stopped for a break in the lee of Lost Girl island, and Luther caught sight of the islands sheltering Burntside Lodge and figured we might enjoy a cold beer."

"Dad!," Lynn teased. "You're taking our visitors out bar hopping on the lake?"

"Well, we did just that," Luther admitted with a glint of rebellion flashing in his eye. "Just one bar, though. The Lodge. I figured this feller ought to know the highlights of the lake."

"It was a mighty welcomed highlight," Jack agreed. "After paddling three or four hours, a cold brew and a burger was inviting. We sat and chatted without a worry in the world." He cast a knowing look at Luther's daughter. His judgement, he would admit, was little better than her father's, once they sat with a tasty draft quenching their thirst.

"It was a lovely break from paddling, while it lasted. We didn't have a worry in the world. Until we got back in the canoe, that is, and found that the wind had kicked up a notch or two from the southwest. Blew us right past Otter Island before we caught a break and turned north out of the breakers."

"Breakers? You were riding whitecaps?" Martha asked.

Luther sputtered, pursed his lips, and busied himself with the gear from the canoe. "It wasn't all that bad."

"It was a hoot," Father Jack said. "A joyful and exciting adventure."

"I want to go next time," Ally cried. "I love canoeing."

Jack raised his brow at Luther's little granddaughter. "Well, Ally, I think you'd enjoy it, too. Especially if the wind is a tad calmer. You'll have to watch for the right time."

Luther puttered with the lead from the canoe's bow, muttering assurances to himself. The wrinkles about his eyes darkened, and he faltered with the rope.

Lynn saw her father slipping. She often read his moods, and sometimes watched as he submerged into the shadows of the cloud that fogged his thoughts. He was diving now as she watched him, and she went to his side.

"We have hot dogs and beans, Dad, if you're still hungry."

He stood tall and looked about. His gaze probed the fading sky settling behind the ridge to the west. Glancing at Lynn, he flashed a look of annoyance, and then resignation. He was on his way and he knew not where. "Not hungry," he muttered. He fumbled with the tie down for a moment, abandoned it, then shuffled away toward the lodge.

After a moment, Martha rose, glanced at Lynn and followed Luther.

Jack, on the other hand, found a seat on an Adirondack chair and reached for a wire hot dog fork. The sandwich he shared with Luther earlier was long gone.

"You enjoyed your canoe trip?" Lynn asked.

Jack watched the sweat form on his dog as he turned it carefully above embers, avoiding the flames lashing like tongues from the pine crackling in the fire pit. He didn't like blackened barbecue.

"Delightful," he said. "I'm getting quite proficient at map reading," he said. "Sometimes, I'm sure you can understand, that in spite of Luther's confidence, we aren't always quite where we think we are. I'm learning during my many excursions with Luther all about the face of the lake with its islands dotting the surface of these expansive waters."

Lynn chuckled. "It is a big lake."

"Grandpa says there are more than a hundred islands in our lake," Ally chirped.

"Well, we might have paddled the shoreline of all of them over the past couple of weeks," Jack said. "A few times around several of them."

"He used to know this lake like the back of his hand," Lynn said.

"He still does," Jack mused. "He just doesn't recognize what he knows now and then."

He stuffed the dog into a bun and reached for the ketchup.

"So, Jack Hanley. Have you learned enough from Luther to take on this adventure you're thinking of?"

He bit off a quarter of the dog and rolled his eyes as he munched.

"Absolutely heaven," he inspected the bitten end of his hot dog. "And yes, I do think I'm ready to paddle myself around this wilderness. It calls me, and I'd be derelict if I were to drive away in my brother's lavish Cadillac without first baptizing myself in the pristine waters of the Northlands." He bit off another quarter of the hot dog, catching oozing ketchup with a quick lash of his tongue as it drooped from the sides of the bun. He raised an eyebrow toward Lynn. "You know, rinse the dust and dirt from my tired feet and weary soul after my most recent sojourn in the deserts of Asia."

Lynn reflected on the tales Jack had shared around the fire pit or the commons table in the lodge where they shared meals. He proved capable of reading their maps of the lakes and portages. He navigated well. Luther had no qualms about paddling with him. And he had confidence. She encouraged him to plan for his trip. He had made it his quest.

It was Ingie, however, who prodded the padre to reveal more of his self.

"Is a duckshit paddle through the fucking Boundary Waters enough of a test to earn your goddamn kami-sama badge?" Her smile was wicked. Her shoulders jiggled as she suppressed laughter.

He froze with his mouth agape, his hot dog hanging above the chasm of his gullet. He steered his gaze toward the invalid propped up with pillows on the Adirondack chair across the fire.

"Your profanity is charming. I do relish the notion of paddling through the wilds of these Boundary Waters in search of experiences that embrace the essence of being," he said. "Your blasphemy, however, offends my sense of reverence. To be Sama is neither damned, nor is it as trivial as a scouts badge. God invites all to travel the path toward Samadhi enlightenment so that we humble beings can share in his state of exultation." He bit further into his dog. "It's a state of ecstatic being that I seldom glimpse. My quest is to experience that moment"

Ingie wiggled and giggled. She'd shot a round across the priest's spiritual bow. He responded directly and with subtle humor. She anticipated a good exchange with him.

"Her," she replied. She wondered how a man could dedicate himself as a priest and see but a flicker of the moment of exultation.

His brow furrowed in confusion. Then, her comment registered. "If you wish. Her state of exultation. She is Who am." He gulped the dog.

Lynn, however, deflected further conversation between her foul mouthed sister and Father Jack. The children were listening and she knew Ingie got ever more profane as she got wound up in debate. "So do you think you're ready? When will you start on your adventures?"

Jack grinned. "Not for a few days. I think I'll try my hand at fishing again tomorrow, and then go over the maps and select a route with your help—perhaps tomorrow afternoon? Do you work?"

"Here. Not at the hospital. Not until the weekend. Tomorrow would be good, but Martha's the one to give advice on routes. Once we're done with cabins, let's go over your plans."

Jack finished his dog and loaded the fork with another to roast over the scarlet embers.

# Chapter 3

# Wilderness Prepped

At dawn the next day, Jack put in Patrick's canoe and headed toward the islands he'd explored the day before. Luther had pointed out several likely fishing spots. Some were ridges that protruded out from the end of an island, extending underwater with structure where fish sought feed. Others were deep holes protected from the winds in small bays on lee side of some of the more distant islands. Paddling still waters, Jack recognized one of Luther's recommended fishing sites. He hooked and lost a feisty smallmouth, and within minutes felt the impulsive attack of yet another hungry bass. He landed that fish, but didn't get a bite again for another couple of hours at several other sites that were among Luther's hot spots.

Paddling solo was slower. By the time he saw State Island in the distance, it was past noon. By then, he'd caught six nice fish; three plump smallmouth, a couple of decent walleye, and a long, nice-bodied Northern. He looked back toward the resort. It was not in sight. He figured he could make it back in an hour of earnest paddling, so he pulled in his stringer and applied strength to his paddle.

He had the advantage of a tailwind. The return route took only 45 minutes It was half past one as the cedar strips of Patrick's canoe scraped softly upon the resort's fine sands. He secured the vessel and grabbed the stringer of fish he'd brought in for supper. When he looked over the resort, he saw Martha heading back to the lodge from the row of the smaller cabins. The family from Cabin 2 played quietly along the beach near the dock; a slender young woman waded alongside her toddler in the shallows, while an older youngster, a girl of perhaps four, played in the wet sand at water's edge. Luther was no where to be seen. He spotted Lynn carrying a loaded basket of folded bedding to the back door of Cabin 2. Jack went meet her. She may know where Luther was, which would be a help for cleaning his catch. Luther had shown him how to filet both bass and the boney Northerns, but he knew he might need some guidance on his first try.

As he approached the open door to Cabin 2, he spotted Luther strolling across the driveway. Jack waved the stringer with his catch at Luther and headed toward the fish house.

"You get started cleaning your catch," Luther nodded. "That's a nice stringer. I'll help you in a minute, hoisting the gear he was toting to the outfitting shack.

Jack gulped, but set out to the fish house to clean his fish. He was on his own until Luther showed up.

"No surgeon am I," he muttered, cutting along the backbone of a meaty walleye. "Nor butcher!"

He picked his way through the filleting, wondering if Luther would show up. He didn't. A half hour later, with some rough and shredded fillets soaking in a stainless steel bowl, Jack rolled up the skin, bones and heads of his fish, sprayed down the cutting boards, and took his catch up to the lodge for Martha to prep for the evening's supper.

"That's some pretty fancy blade work there, Jack," Martha teased. She held up the backstrap of the northern, sliding her thumb and forefingers along the white flesh. The flicking of bones off her fingers was audible. "We might do best to pickle this fine northern," she said.

"Did my best," he shrugged.

"More practice. You've got the hard part down, catching them. I'd hate to think you'd die choking on a fish bone from your own catch when you're out in the Boundary Waters all by yourself. Practice. You can catch some more tomorrow. Here, I'll show you how to camp fry them. You'll be hungry out there, and you'll want to know how to cook 'em up."

Jack paid close attention as she seasoned the fillets for the evening's dinner.

# Chapter 4

# Campfire Talk

The weather held for the week, Jack caught three more stringers of fish. His fillets improved. The supple white fish meat was boneless and the cuts were clean and smooth. On Friday, the North family clustered around the campfire where Martha tutored Jack on how to cook his catch over an open pit of hot embers. After shore lunch for dinner, Ally and Omie burned marshmallows and made s'mores.

Jack had carried Ingie to the fire ring, where she sat propped in boat seat cushions and life jackets in the oversized cedar lawn chair. Wrapped in her favorite colorful wool blanket, a souvenir from her long past Mexican excursions, her eyes glistened, reflecting the flames from the fire. The twins fed her s'more after s'more, and she reveled in the devotion of her niece and nephew. When summertime temperatures allowed her the comfort of outdoor living, she sat like a queen on her throne.

"Such butt kissing bliss," she decreed. In a lull when the others had dropped their conversations and sat enjoying the twilight and the flames of the fire, she repeated, "Just fucking bliss."

Lynn scrutinized Jack.

"You set now for your paddle?"

He nodded, with a confident smile. "Yes. I'm set. I won't go hungry. I can catch fish and now I know how to cook them. I've practice setting the tent up, and striking camp to load the canoe. I know what gear and clothes to pack. I do have hopes the weather is as gentle as it has been since I arrived. And that the black flies have had their day in the sun. But otherwise, I'm off in the morning."

Martha interjected, "We're about at the end of the black fly season. Mosquitos, however, may suck you dry."

He laughed and shrugged a shoulder.

"It's time to step out into a new world. A trial of sorts to prepare me for my next challenge. And I suppose, all challenges to follow."

Martha chuckled. "Time to forage powers from this corner of the universe, you think?."

"I certainly hope so."

Lynn probed. "So how will these meanderings through the wilderness of our Boundary Waters prepare you for what's next? What is next? Going back to Asia?

A look of remorse shaded Jack's eyes.

"No. I'm done with Asia," he said. "Or perhaps Asia is done with me. I'm to negotiate the resurrection of my career, I suppose. My brother, the reverend Bishop, has arranged a position where I can expound upon the vast experiences of my career in Asia for the benefit of the bright young students at a Catholic university in Milwaukee."

Lynn perked up. "Milwaukee? You mean Marquette? I'm a Marquette graduate!"

"Is that so?" Jack asked.

"It is indeed. I got my R.N. at Marquette. Marquette gave me a wonderful education," she said. "It was really a fortunate opportunity that I studied there. I didn't know anything about it. Just that it was acceptably far enough from home. And my mother considered it a good choice for me. She was right."

"Your mother was an educator, was she not?"

"Correct. She taught art at Macalester."

"She was a darned good teacher," Martha interjected. "Always put her students in a position to learn something of value, each to their own set of gifts."

"Really?" Jack said. "How so? How do you know that?

"She was my best friend. Always. And her students told me so, more or less," Martha added. "Over the years, many of them came to the resort at her invitation. The discussions around this fire ring and the dinner table up at the lodge were filled with vibrant ideas. It was a wonderful time. Her students told me how well she reached them with her insight and knowledge."

"Ah. Insight and knowledge. That is what I need to conjure for my students," Jack said. "There in lies the challenge. What can I possibly teach them from my years of experience in different cultures and communities. How would they ever relate?"

"They might find your experiences spectacular," Lynn said.

"Entertaining, perhaps? But will it give them the stuff that matters in life?"

Jack studied the embers glowing at the base of the fire. Could it be, he wondered, that his tales of tribes and chiefdoms, dervishes and imams, devilry and genocide be something more than curious fodder for the classes of students who he would endow with such foreign concepts. He tried explaining his concern, and the more he revealed, the more excited the women became.

"You have so much to offer your students," Martha said.

"Jesus tits," Ingie exclaimed. "I'd have traded half the fucking boredom-bucket classes in college to hear about how people live in places like you know. Fuck yes, fuzznuts. Tell me about your dervishes. I'd love to spin with those crazy bungholes."

Jack laughed. Ingie's uncontrollable crassness often shocked as much as entertained him. He understood her trial; the brain injury she suffered in the car accident with David's cousin confined her to a body that was broken and a brain that spewed vulgarities and profanity with every thought she uttered. Her traumatic brain injury branded her otherwise sparkling discourse with the vernacular of a drunken sailor. She relied on her sister and Martha for everything to sustain life. Broken, but not defeated, she was a fiery spirit contained in a crumpled, fragile vessel. She lived a zesty life in spite of her limits.

He appreciated her and Martha's encouragement. But his confidence going into his new responsibilities wasn't built on his ambition to be a professor. It was more of a default opportunity. The bishop leveraged old favors to find the job for him. Jack had pretty much walked away from his career, his order, and his profession as a missionary when he decided to leave his post in Iran. The Jesuits were not happy about his decision. He had already caused too many issues for them in his past postings. He'd abandon his work in Iran and Pakistan, and was virtually run out of Afganistan. If it were not for his brother, Jack might not have had any opportunities left from within the order. He just didn't know.

"Well, do you think my students at Marquette will experience nearer to God awareness if I simply spin until I transcend? Would that work for you?"

Ingie screamed. "Go, Beelzubub! Go! Let me see you fucking whirl!"

There were no bounds to Ingie's irreverence, Lynn thought. But she felt concern for Father Jack's apathy.

"Did you lose faith in Asia?"

He dipped his chin to his chest and considered her question. His eyes rolled up under his brow as his gaze met hers.

"It was more than loosing my faith. Or falling short of doing my work. More than the realization that no matter what I did in Iran to counsel and comfort my Armenian parishioners, their lives were framed with the losses that they were left to live with," he said. "And served them, I did. But what became so clear to me was that it was their families that held them together. And the loss of those members of their families that died in the genocide that anguished their souls."

He stared into the embers. He continued.

"They taught me. Counseled me. Showed me how to cope with the loss of family. Of friends. That's why I knew it was time for me to leave the mission. It was I who needed to grieve the only family I have ever known to be true. Not my brother the bishop, or my parents. No. He looks out for me, true. But he probably considers me more of an intrigue than a brother. He thinks I'm his prodigal brother."

Jack stared into the fire, then wagged his head. "The bishop does not know family like I knew David. Patrick's brother. Like a son to me. Like family. Like a brother. David gave me insight to how the love of family is the crux of life. The Armenians knew that, and grieved their loss. My grief is two fold. I grieve for David. And I grieve for the time I lost, oblivious to the essential element of love. Family love."

The fire coughed sputtering blaze from the bed of burning pine embers, and Lynn's family all peered into the heat, mesmerized by the coals and by Jack's admissions.

Ingie was first to break the silence.

"Jesus fucking Christ," she muttered. "You don't think you have any dumb ass lessons to teach those wussies at Mar-fucking-quette? Get a grip."

Jack beamed. Broken as she was, Ingie was refreshing.

"If there was a way, Ingie, empress of wicked-tongued truths and profanity, I would lug you along on this vision quest of mine. You could be my mentor and guide. I'm certain you'd bring me to truth long before I find it on my own."

She snickered. "Piss ant."

∞

In the late dawn light of an early June morning, just before the solstice, Luther and Martha pushed Jack off in Patrick's cedar strip canoe. Two bulging Duluth packs held his tent, sleeping bag, clothes, and a good three weeks' provisions. A tackle box was tucked under his stern seat, and two rods and reels were strapped to the thwarts. They stood on the shore, one looking into distant memories that evaporated in a whirl of thought; the other considering the challenge Jack was about to undertake and the values he may discover along his paddle. She cherished the notion of his inaugural solo journey into the wilderness. She remembered her own solo expeditions into the wilds.

Jack waved to his new friends. He took his paddle and struck deep, powerful strokes in the calm lake waters. As he floated away, he glanced back. His friends watched him, their eyes teeming with hope, caution, and care. He cherished the image. He had learned never to leave without looking back at those who were family to him. He steered the bow south west toward the portage to Clam Lake. He was on his own.

# Book Two

# Sojourn

## Patrick Joyce

*Above all,*
*watch with glittering eyes the whole world around you*
*because the greatest secrets are always hidden*
*in the most unlikely places.*
*Those who don't believe in magic will never find it.*
*— Roald Dahl*

*Chapter 5*
# The Pinnacle

*The Appalachian Trail*
*Blue Mountain, Pennsylvania*
*June 21, 1968*

Here I am, sitting in the dark side of dawn, waiting for the sun to peek up in the east, bringing on a whole new day of I don't know what. More Trail, I suppose. Or maybe I'll savor the solstice all day, right here, on top of the Pinnacle. Some days, I just don't feel like moving on, and that's okay. Moving on to what? I ask myself. Today feels like that kind of day. Just sit back and see what it brings.

It's our birthday today, mine and Davie's. I like our birthday being the longest day of every year. All the days leading up to it get a little longer, the sun gets a little higher in the sky. I've never noticed it as much as this year, though, being out on the Trail from dawn until dusk, every day, rain or shine. The longer the day, the more ground I put behind me.

It's worked to my advantage, too. The shorter days of April meant I had more time at night to rest and recoup after a day's hike. I mean, when I first hit the Trail, I couldn't even go the entire day. I did it all wrong, of course. Tried going ten miles a day right off the bat. Yeah. Ha. Day two, hot spots. Day three, blisters erupting like mushrooms. Day four, bloody socks. Days five through nine, sit on my ass in a soaking spring rain, watching the Georgia hillsides turn blue and green through the mist. Smoking like a chimney. I must have gone through half of what Davey left me in Germany in those four days. I thought I was soul searching. I think now, I was hiding from it. Smoking till I was numb. Smoking until I dreamed of Rosie, telling me I was acting like I had no family.

But I've aired out a bit since then. A bit. Still, I'm sitting here, looking out to the east over the patchwork quilt of the farmland below, lit up all silver by the last rays of the full moon dipping behind the ridge to the west. A soft blue tinge creeps up from the horizon in the east, absorbing the low-lying stars, letting me know that there will indeed be a dawn today. And I can't keep out the thought, wouldn't this be even better if I were high? Wouldn't it be so fucking far out that it would blow my mind? I look around and answer myself, how could it be? How could it be any better at all? It might be. Just light up. Just free up my mind. Fuck. No. Not today. Not my birthday. Not yesterday. Not tomorrow. I've had enough. For now, anyway. It's nice that I can go miles now without thinking about it. Letting it rest. Having it let me rest. Five weeks, I've made it. I don't think there were five days I haven't been rocked out for the past two years. Now I've gone five whole fucking weeks. And yet it still gnaws at me. Not as hard. Not as persistent. But it's there.

I'm anxious for the sun to come up this morning. I want to look at the map. From here, I can see the lights of Allentown, due east. I know the highway heads north from there, then meets the Trail, maybe forty miles from where I sit. I might get off there. It's been almost three months on the trail, and it isn't even my dream, after all. It's Barney's. It's somebody else's. I'm tired of chasing somebody else's dreams.

That's one thing I've realized on this pilgrimage. I don't want to chase somebody else's dreams anymore. I want to make my own dreams happen. I'm pretty clear on that now. After five weeks of fresh air to my brain, I feel pretty confident that my own dreams are sweet. My own dreams are more real. How could I have ever lost sight of them to begin with? It wasn't just the dope. Nope. That didn't help, for sure. But I'd lost focus long before I started the wake-and-bake routine. That's pretty clear to me now. I left my dreams along the way, surrendered to whatever circumstances I encountered. I got used to accepting the limitations of my experiences, rather than exploring all my options.

What do I mean by that? I ask myself that all the time. I've always done it that way. But I want to do something else now.

It's like when I moved to the Dunes, to Aunt Mary's. I just constantly reacted. I figured out everyone else's expectations, and I met them, precisely. I stepped right up to the boundaries of those expectations, and never crossed over them. I responded to how everyone perceived me, a big, dumb jock, and I fulfilled their vision. I knew all the parents looked at me from under their brows, thinking, *this is the son of the crazy woman*. It mattered. I reacted to it. In Indiana, and even more back home in Baraboo, playing ball in Wisconsin, being the star.

That's all I was then: the jock. The running back. I ran to the cheers of the fans. And the fans made me their hero. They didn't want to know about the head inside that helmet, or the heart under the pads, covered by that Baraboo jersey. They wanted to see themselves as number twenty-one. They wanted to project everything they could identify about winning from within themselves, and pin it on number twenty-one, and have me carry the ball for them. And I did, with all my heart. I wanted to do it more than anything, I realize. I wanted to be their hero. I wanted to be my hero, too. But I sold myself short.

It was even worse in Boulder. I mean, that was a full-time job, training and playing at CU. Davey asked how I could walk away from it so easily? Walking away from football was like sucking in the greatest breath of fresh air I'd ever taken. I felt liberated. Free.

Yeah, it took some getting used to. I mean, I thought of myself as the jock, too. It made me wonder, who the hell am I, really, without football? How long had I put all my energy into playing sports? All of my focus? So long that anything really important to me evaporated right in front of my eyes, like the heat waves above the beach along Lake Michigan. Clarity dissipates, and with it, the things of most importance. Like Lynn. I mean, she was like the best birthday present I ever got. Seeing her for the first time on my birthday. Having her for the first time on my birthday. I mean, Lynn —it was meant to be Lynn for me. With her, those expectations, those boundaries, they didn't exist. We just…were. How could I have ever let her out of my life? How could I ever have kept her in my life? I don't know. Were there answers to those questions once, long since evaporated? Will I ever know? I don't know.

From the valley below, the lowing of cattle rises to urgent crescendo as the dawn casts rosy hues in the east. The cows want in. They want to get milked. So they sing. As if in response, Barney, my hiking partner sighs and hums a note, seated on a rock alongside me. He was already up and keeping a vigil, facing east, when I awakened an hour ago. He doesn't sleep much.

We joined paths a few days back, on the other side of the ferry north of Skyland, in Virginia. Together, we've kept a swift pace. Yesterday, we started at dawn, a few miles west of the Susquehanna and covered more than thirty miles to get here in the late afternoon. Over the campfire, we shared a few stories and a little grub, watching night capture the Trail. The moon didn't rise until almost midnight. It didn't get high enough over the canopy to pour its silver light down into our campsite until the very early hours before dawn. Maybe that's what awakened me. Barney was already up, though, keeping watch.

I don't know whether I'll move on with him this morning, if he keeps hiking north. I may just stay here till mid-day, then head over toward the highway. I'll consider it a little more. But it feels like the right thing to me. I think it's time to go home.

∞

By the time the sun breached the sky, my new partner and I were ready to resume our daily routine. I fumbled through my pack, looking for a few breakfast provisions. I watched him stretch, pull on his socks and boots, and roll up his bed with an ease of movement that reflected his experience in the woods. He was traveling extremely light, a skill I'd grown to wholeheartedly appreciate. He had some sturdy hiking boots, military issue, but not like the kind you can get at the Army surplus store. His were jungle boots, the kind with the camouflage sidings, and they were scarred and worn. He toted only a small pack with a few essentials and a bedroll comprising a lightweight wool blanket and a wrap of parachute silk he'd "procured," he said, when he was on active duty. Traveling unencumbered, he claimed. A couple days earlier, he'd mentioned that he'd just gotten out of the service. He'd not said much more.

"Java?" I asked quietly. I'd started a small fire and was heating water to brew coffee.

"I'd be most appreciative," he smiled, drawing his words out like soft, stretched yarns of taffy. He hadn't said a whole lot along the Trail, but he'd loosened up some around the fire each night. I'd immediately been charmed by his southern drawl, the way his words slid right into low, rumbling chuckling and rolling rounds of laughter as he talked of life along the Trail, or his family back home in Georgia.

He offered his empty tin cup, and I poured the hot brew from my cup to fill his. He sipped his coffee, looking out over his steaming cup to survey the farmland below. He nodded, first at his coffee, then at the land below. "Makes for a mighty fine day."

"Yeah," I agreed. "And it's my birthday, to boot."

A pleasant grin spread slowly across Barney's face. He projected his emotions much like he spoke, long and deliberate, complete but with no wasted energy. He extended his hand. "Well, happy birthday, Pat."

I took his hand, which he held firm but not tight. Some men grasp fiercely, clamping down to assert their character. Others offer limp fingertips like boneless trout fillets, leaving me uneasy and alarmed. Barney's handshake was reserved, respectful, defined. It told me that he knew his position in this world, and was comfortable there. His grip was honest and open, inviting but not imposing. True. Last night, by the light of the embers and the silver illumination of the rising moon, he spoke of redefining himself on the Trail. I didn't know what he meant; he already seemed decent and genuine to me. The real thing.

"So how old are you?" he enquired.

"Twenty-two."

"Sweet Jesus," he chuckled. "You had me fooled. I'd have guessed a few years older, maybe 'cause you're so damn big. I'll be twenty myself, come July."

I laughed. "You should have seen me at the beginning of the Trail," I said. "I was a lot bigger. This dirt path has melted forty or fifty pounds of German beer and sausage right off me."

He let his eyes seek the far ridge. Barney often scanned the distance, probing the shadows under trees and alongside rocks and ledges. His eyes moved smoothly, taking in detail I knew I was oblivious of. When he rested his gaze on my face, I felt as if he measured every cell within me.

"I did spot you a couple times, early on," he admitted. "No doubt, you've burned off your baby fat. But it only makes you look older. More mature."

I asked him when he'd seen me, and he explained that he first caught sight of me within a hundred miles of Springer Mountain, sitting in the woods, smoking a joint. So probably in my first week, I figured, right after my blisters had calmed down. A couple weeks later, he'd felt the urge to sit a spell and found himself a place of power amidst a pine grove overlooking the Trail. He set up under an improvised lean-to, taking in the sky. He'd been camped there for three days when I trudged by again.

"You were stepping a whole lot more comfortably than the first time I spotted you tip-toeing off the Trail," he laughed. "But you looked like you were still stoned out of your mind. I'm surprised you got this far without getting lost."

I felt a blush warm my face. I had been that easy to read? Why did I ever think that nobody could tell when I was wrecked?

"Pretty lucky," I admitted. "I've aired it out since then. Haven't lit up in over a month."

Barney nodded. "Me neither." His gaze focused on me another moment. "It was getting in the way."

"Whaddya mean?"

He scanned the horizon again, then studied the ground in front of where he sat with his legs folded comfortably underneath him. He looked as though he could nestle in among the rocks and boulders along the ledge of the Pinnacle and disappear completely. "Means that I started this old Trail in pretty rough shape. I kind of figured I was, just getting outta the service and all. But it wasn't until I heard myself fucking up the peace along the Trail that I realized I was out of control."

"I never heard you," I reassured him. "I can't say I even noticed you. Wasn't like you were bothering anyone. I never knew you were there."

He grimaced, glancing at me quickly, then back at the far ridge. "Wasn't like… noise." He spit. "Maybe inner noise, more likely. I was screaming so loud on the inside, I couldn't suck in the peace all around me. Shit, it's not like I disturbed other hikers. Maybe the wildlife. The deer. Even the fucking birds were scarce, at first. But not the hikers. Hell, there haven't been more than a couple dozen hikers anyway. I don't know that more than a couple even picked up on me at all, anywhere."

I sure hadn't. I wondered why. He'd seen me several times, by his account. I asked why he stepped up and joined me just before crossing the Virginia state line.

"Looked like you were making the walk through to the end," he replied. "And if you are, I thought we might as well get to know one another. I'm figuring on being in Maine by mid-September. You?"

I paused, looking out to the east. The sun had risen, and the day was warming. "Funny you should ask just now. I dunno," I said. "I figured I was, when I first started out. Hadn't really given much thought to not finishing. I figured, if you start it, you finish it." I plucked a stem of mountain grass from a crack on the boulders against which we were leaning. The tender end was slightly bitter between my teeth. "But just this morning, before dawn, I kind of figured that I've done as much of the Trail as I needed to. Like it wasn't really my idea to do it in the first place. I just took someone else's dream, and used it to fill some time, get my thoughts straight. Now, I'm feeling the call of other things. Home. I guess."

He nodded, his gaze measuring me once again. He looked at me with a curiosity that could have made me paranoid, were he not so calm. "What?" I asked, amused. "You're looking at me like you recognize me."

"Naw," he grunted. "Not really. You seem kind of familiar. You talk like someone I knew. You from Wisconsin? You kind of sound like it."

I laughed. "You betcha! That's where I think I'm heading. Get off the Trail up near Lehigh. Hitch a ride to the interstate and turn west. Heading home. I haven't been home in over two years."

He nodded, plucking his own shaft of grass and inserting it between his teeth, twitching it up and down with his lips.

I told him about having been out of the country since the previous summer. He shrugged, saying, "Yeah, me too."

"Oh, yeah? Where?" Would he talk about his service, I wondered?

"The Nam." He looked again to the distance.

I'd suspected as much. But he didn't offer any more.

"My brother's there," I said. "My twin." I grinned. "It's his birthday today, too!"

"That so," he said without a smile. "Celebrating his birthday in the Nam. Happy birthday, bro. Where he's at?"

I shook my head. "Don't know, exactly. He's with the Marines. Someplace up north, I think. Third Recon, or something like that? He says he's in the highlands a lot."

Barney paled in the early morning's light. The blade of coarse grass sticking from his mouth suddenly stilled. He narrowed his eyes, examining me again. "Your brother. What's his name?"

"David," I answered. "David Joyce. You ever heard of him?"

Barney's eyes blazed, still narrowed, glistening in the light from the rising sun. He nodded. "Squirrel," he said. "We called him Squirrel." He leveled his eyes, looking directly into mine. "He was the real thing, man. Your brother, he was there all the way."

He lowered his head, and a tear trickled down his cheek. I felt my heart collapse inside my chest. A great, painful void lurched open within me as I read Barney's face.

"Of all the fucking people in the world to run into on this godforsaken Trail, I meet up with you," he said. "Squirrel's fucking brother. His goddamn twin. He told me about you. Lots of times. Played football, didn't you? He just saw you in Germany, what, at Thanksgiving?"

I nodded. I couldn't speak. The burning in my chest rose to my throat, lodging like a lump of dry, hard bread.

He grimaced again, then softened around his eyes. "He's dead, you know."

I shook my head. I didn't know.

"Yeah," he paused. "I was there." His eyes returned to narrow, angry slits. He rummaged through his pack until he found a baggie with a joint. "I was with him." He rolled the number carefully between his fingers and thumbs. "Yeah. I helped pull him out," he said softly. Then his eyes widened in astonishment. "Man, you better get off the Trail. You best go home. Jesus tits! How could you not even have known?"

Barney—Georgia, he told me, is what David called him—broke camp with me. He stuck his number up behind his ear and trekked along the Trail with it as though it were a reminder. Something he wanted to remember, but not yet touch.

We hiked together to Lehigh, sharing everything we knew about David as we hiked. We covered the forty miles in two days. At the crossing, we shook hands, and I thanked him. He nodded, turned, and walked on up the Trail, heading for Maine. I watched him go. The joint stuck out from under his shaggy hair, untouched.

Then I turned on the shoulder of the road, stuck out my thumb, and caught the first semi heading north to the intersection with the interstate.

I was heading home.

∞

As I rode semis across Pennsylvania, Ohio, and Indiana, or hunkered down in campgrounds and rest stations to wait out the rains that made it so hard to hitch rides, I pieced together a timeline. Davey must have died just about the time I left Germany. I wondered if Eva knew. And what about Mom, and Paddy, and all the folks back home? They had to know already. I tried calling from a couple of different truck stops along the way, but no one ever picked up the phone. I guess they weren't expecting me to call.

# Chapter 6

# Home Again

*North Freedom, Wisconsin*
*June 26, 1968*

No one was home. Walking up the road, I thought for sure I'd see Mom in the garden, or on the porch, writing her endless letter to herself in her notebooks. Or Paddy cutting hay, bundling hay, putting up hay. But there was no one. The hay had been cut and the fields were gleaned. Paddy must have just finished baling the second crop. Where were they? I wondered.

Familiar earthy smells wafted from the double doors at the head of the alley as I stuck my head into the barn and gave a shout. The cattle were all out to pasture. A few sparrows flitted among the leftover grain in the mangers, and a couple of sleepy-eyed cats perched on the sills in the sun. But there was no sign of anyone.

The house was abandoned. The kitchen was immaculately clean, which I guess wasn't all that surprising, what with Rosie and Mom after it all the time. But more than that, it didn't look lived in. The fridge had nothing in it. A box of Velveeta. A few jars of condiments—mustard, olives, mayo, some pickles. In the parlor, the bright June sunlight streamed through the windows. The fields outside bled verdant summer hues. The air was a bit stuffy, and I pulled open a few windows as I wandered back toward the bedrooms.

My own room remained almost exactly as I remembered. My books were there, and the buck Gabriel whittled for me, standing proud on my dresser. The ball from my last high school game, senior year. The MVP award. My jersey, hung on the wall with tacks. Seemed like it should be on my back, over my shoulders, bulging with pads. Not mounted on a wall, like a trophy buck.

The only thing out of place was a large cardboard box, sitting on the chest at the end of my bed. I lifted the flaps and peered inside. Two smaller, open boxes contained books... albums? I picked up the one on top. It looked familiar, but I couldn't place it.

I opened the cover and gasped. The image took the strength from my knees, and I had to sit down on my bed. I was looking at Lynn, sitting atop the tie wall, distracted, looking away. One of the first photos I'd ever taken. I'd not seen it printed before. I turned the page to a shot of me, taken when we first started building the wall. I was looking back over my shoulder, straight into the camera, grinning, as I placed a tie onto the footings of the wall. It was the first tie we had set. She'd focused right on my eye, but the depth of field was deep. Damn, I looked young. And innocent.

I flipped several pages of the album. I knew the photos. They were all here. I turned to the last pages. All of them. The best of them. Some I hadn't seen, and others just like I remembered. I closed the book, and glanced into the box. There were several more albums. The football album was there, and others that were unfamiliar. A stack of loose images was piled below.

Everything. She'd left me everything. Not exactly as I'd once seen it all, with her sitting at my side. She'd duplicated everything, and put the prints in new books. Some of the images were cropped differently than I remembered. And there were so many more.

I remembered Davey telling me about a box he had waiting for me. This box. Lynn's box.

I sat back on the bed, flipping through page after page. When I pulled another album from the box, the pages separated naturally in the middle. An envelope was wedged between an image of her neighbor, Harriet, holding a hose as she sprayed me with water, and a picture of a sand lizard perched on a tie.

The envelope was open, revealing folded pages inside. I recognized the writing immediately, from the cards Lynn had sent me while she traveled the world with Ingie.


*October 5, 1963*

*My darling Patrick,*

*I'm going home, Patrick. I'm going back to Minnesota, to Minnetonka. I am going back to live with my family, to take care of Ingie, to be with those who love me. I'm so grateful that my father wants me to come back. I need my family now, more than I ever have, and they need me.*

*Patrick, I can't tell you how lost I feel without you. I know it was stupid of me to let us get so out of control. I know I had no business getting you so involved with me. I know it, yet I regret not a moment of the time we had together. I loved every moment of our time. I loved how we worked together. I loved how we could talk all night, all day, as long as we wanted. I loved how we could be together and not say a word for hours, just being there, gazing into each other's eyes, sometimes just touching fingertip to fingertip, and feeling One.*

*Was I so wrong, being this much older, to share my love with you? Was I being selfish? I can't think so. I believe what we have, what we had, was real. In the depth of night, I just wonder why we couldn't keep it.*

*I had to let you go, didn't I, Patrick? You have so much to discover, so much to learn. So much to find out about yourself and the world. I wonder what you have before you. I wonder if you will get beyond the jock thing and discover the greatness of your heart and the depth of your mind. I think so. My regret is that I will not be there to share your experiences and all that you will learn. My heart longs to share every moment with you. Every second. Every heartbeat I have, I wish to have with you.*

*So why am I leaving you and going my own way?*

*Because I see no choice.*

*Ingie needs me. She was hurt badly in the accident with Jack. She's still in a coma. If she makes it, she will need help all her life. She will never be the same. Even if I didn't feel some responsibility for her accident, even if it had happened on the other side of the world, she is still my sister. I love her so much. I will be here for her in whatever she needs. So now, I can use this education I earned. I can nurse Ingie, and I will. It will keep me busy and give me a noble, worthy purpose. And it will keep me away from you.*

*I need to be out of your way as you grow, as you conquer your challenges. I know how important football is to you. I so enjoy watching you play and photographing you playing. It is so thrilling to see you play. Patrick, your athleticism is not your greatest gift, but you truly are a gifted athlete. I hope to see you play again and again. I can't tell you how it makes me feel to see you run against a wall of opponents clamoring to bring you down, only to watch you tromp them or elude them! That is just one thing I will miss. There will be many.*

*I will miss your voice, deep, gentle, and sweet. I will miss the way you look at me, your eyes soft and caring. I will miss your touch, your smell. I will miss your presence.*

*This is how I feel about you now. I ask myself, how will I feel in the future? Years from now? I wonder how you will feel about me. I wonder if we will ever see one another again. I write this letter with hopes that we do.*

*Patrick, we must see each other again, at one time or another. I know full well that you will go on and have your life, and that your path may take you places where you will never be able to be with me again, ever, as we have been. I accept that. You must know, though, that I take with me part of you. I will always, God willing, have something of you that cannot be denied. Patrick, I carry our child. And I tell you from my heart, I will love and cherish this child. I am so grateful that I have this part of you to take with me.*

*Some tell me this is a mistake, keeping the baby. Some say the baby itself is a mistake. I admit that I made mistakes with you, that I should never have led you to where we went. I do not know how I could have done differently. I didn't plan, didn't expect things to be the way they were. I regret if I did you wrong. Somehow I think that I didn't. Ultimately, all I did was love you with all my heart and mind and soul. Patrick, if that is doing you wrong, then forgive me. I meant no harm.*

*I hope I gave you something, too.*

*I believe I did.*

*Yours always,*

*Lynn*

∞

I don't know how many times I'd read Lynn's letter when I looked up to see Paddy leaning against the frame of my bedroom door. I'd not heard him approach. I was startled as much by my response as by his sudden appearance. I leapt from my bed and with two quick strides, engulfed my uncle in a bear hug. No sooner had I reached him than I surrendered to the sobs that had been building within me since Barney, or as David knew him, Georgia, told me about David.

Paddy was surprised by my response as well. He took a step back, regaining his balance. Then, wrapping his big, burly arms around me, he murmured comfort in my ear. I felt like a little kid on his shoulder, except I had to bend over to bury my face in his collar. He let me cry, like he'd let a horse have free rein to run itself out. I wept until I could weep no more.

∞

Once I'd calmed down, Paddy herded me out to the kitchen table, and parked me in a chair while he brewed a pot of coffee. He asked me what I knew of my brother, and was fascinated by my encounter with Georgia. He drank in every detail that Georgia had shared with me. What David had been like in the bush. Where they had dug in to observe the trail. How Davey had tried to get to the grenade, but was cut down by the cross fire. Georgia said that one of the first rounds had hit him square in the forehead. Paddy knew from the med reports that David had taken at least fourteen rounds, plus the damage from the grenade. He had been the only guy on the squad who died that morning. Paddy couldn't believe I'd met a guy who was with Davey when he died, who'd actually helped carry him out.

"I'd like to have met your trail partner," he said.

"Still can, I suppose. I got his address."

Paddy nodded purposefully, and I knew he'd look up Georgia someday. I hoped I'd be with him when he did.

After a few moments, Paddy gestured back toward my bedroom. "Seems like you have some business to consider."

"You know what she wrote?"

He met my eyes squarely, a slight frown creasing his brows. "Yep. I read that letter. And I make no apologies for it. I argued that we should've read it long ago, but the women said it was personal for you and we should keep out of it, even if it wasn't sealed. But once they left me here by myself, well, I guess I didn't feel compelled to abide by their ethics. I went ahead."

"Can't say I mind," I confided. "I'm overwhelmed, to be honest. I didn't know…."

"How could you have? She made it that way because she knew it was right. Now you need to reckon what you can do to make it right, as well."

30

I dropped my glance to the floor. I knew what was right. I just didn't know where to begin.

Paddy fetched the coffee pot and refilled our mugs. When he returned to his chair, I asked, "Whaddya mean, left you here alone? Where's Mom? And Rosie?"

He trained a keen eye on me again, measuring what he thought I might know. "When did you say you left Germany?"

"Easter. From what Georgia said, I probably left Bonn the same day Davey died."

"Just a moment." He rose and walked into the living room, where he shuffled through the papers on Mom's old roll top desk, returning with a couple of envelopes. One was an airmail envelope, like Davey had used. The other was white, with fine script inked on the front. The stamps looked European.

Paddy took a deep breath and began telling me all he recalled about learning that Davey had been killed, and getting his belongings, and his body being returned home, and choosing to cremate him, and the funeral on Mother's Day with the kin and friends and the Whitmans. Then, with no further explanation, he simply handed me Davey's letter to Mom. I read, and then I wept again, as hard as I had when he first discovered me in my room. This time, Paddy wept as well.

After we'd calmed ourselves again, he hemmed and hawed and fidgeted for a moment. There was something more, and he didn't know how to bring it up. He fingered the white envelope, then handed it over to me. Inside was Eva's letter, in French, accompanied by a page in Mom's handwriting. Her translation. I read it through slowly, my head pivoting back and forth between the two versions.

"Oh, Eva," I cried. "Eva." I looked into Paddy's face and saw my pain mirrored in his face. "I forgot all about Eva and Davey," I admitted. "I didn't know she was pregnant. Oh, my God." I didn't think I had any tears left, but they flowed just the same.

I felt Paddy's big, soft dairyman's hand on my shoulder. "Well, Patrick, that's where your mother is," he said.

I looked up, confused.

"Elle and Rosie up and flew to Munich. They're with Eva right now. They've been there since late May, and they'll stay to help her with the babies when they come. They wouldn't leave Davey's loved one to be alone."

It was too much to take in, all that I'd read and heard in the past hour. I shook my head. Then it hit me. "Babies? Did you say babies?"

Paddy grinned and nodded. "That's what Eva's doctor thinks. Seems Davey kept the Joyce twin streak going."

"Good ol' Davey. When will they be born?"

"September. Maybe early October," he said. "Davey wasn't in Germany all that long, was he? You can pretty much predict they'll be September babies."

"Wow." I couldn't believe what he was telling me. I was an uncle. Then the thought struck me. I was already a father.

Judging from the expression on his face, Paddy was reading my mind. "You have a lot of thinking to do, my boy. You have a lot of important things to consider. And some decisions to make."

I nodded in agreement.

"First thing you do," he continued, his thoughts right in stride with mine, "you call your mother. She's expecting you." He chuckled. "Damn if she doesn't know you. She said you'd be home by the Fourth of July. And here it is, not even the first. You're early."

He looked at the kitchen clock, calculating. "I think it's about eight p.m. in Munich right now. It'd be a good time to catch her."

It was only the first of several phone calls I was eager to make.

# Chapter 7

# Ely



I found her in Ely.

She met me first with her eyes, dark with caution. Her anxiety was clear, and just. I saw it written on her face, the first thing I absorbed as they approached.

The twins were at her sides, each holding closely to their mother, gripping her hands and examining me shyly.

And the ring, the oval diamond, flanked by emerald green. On her finger, she wore the ring.

I looked from her hand back to her eyes. She read my expression, and all of her apprehension vanished.

∞

During the evening of my arrival, waiting tried our patience; we were doing what had to be done with the family, waiting until at last we found ourselves alone. Together and alone.

The children slept.

Ever-awake Ingie watched the lake sink into the lavender hues of a July twilight. She listened to the loons as Martha read quietly at her side.

Luther wandered about.

Lynn and I left the lodge for the cabin where I was to stay. We were alone, together for the first time in more than five years. We were as we should be. It was solemn, quiet, and a heartfelt, reviving oneness. We gracefully shed everything, every burden and insufferable excess baggage of our time apart. We melded into this moment, this reality of being here, together, now.

∞

She was caring for Ingie. And her father.

She was raising her children. Our children

She was running a business that supported her family, and she held a job as well.

I had forgotten about Ely, until Paddy told me of David's friend Jack Hanley calling to let us know that he, too, had found Lynn in Ely.

Five years had passed since I last was with Lynn. She had mentioned Ely years ago in our night long discussions, wrapped in the warmth of a summer night on the sands of Lake Michigan's beach. Ely, she said. A place where her mother had grown up. A place where she had visited often as a child, spending her summers, growing and exploring in the confines of freedom. A magical place to grow up, Lynn had said. Where she had learned the scope of her adventurous spirit and met her courage and fostered her spunk.

She was grateful for her insight from her years in the Ely wilderness, she said. It gave her the confidence to face the challenges of her family. And their needs.

Now, she confessed, she wondered if she had the endurance to see those challenges through.

# Chapter 8

# The Good Guy List

"I have something," Lynn said. "For you. From David."

The evening sun had set. We settled on the swing hanging from the rafters above number 3's porch roof.

"I was near you in Chesterton, when you endured loneliness by yourself," she said softly. "I won't leave you now. I'm here. You don't have to go through this alone." She paused.

I met her gaze and shook my head, but couldn't find my voice. I looked down at the envelope. It was thick, and had been opened carefully. Inside, my brother's familiar script filled the pages of a letter. I glanced up at her. She nodded, and stayed by me.


*December 24, 1967*

*Dear Lynn,*

*I want to let you know that I did tell Patrick about your albums and letters. Several times, I thought the moment had arrived, but it hadn't, and I waited, until recently. I told him last time I saw him, in Germany. I think it was right.*

*I'm writing this because I don't know if I will be going home. For that, I am frightened and sorry. Frightened that it may happen. And sorry for not having more time. I would like more time to talk with my brother, to tell him things that I haven't had the opportunity to say yet. Which is why, after harboring our secret for so long, I am going to ask you to return the favor. I know my brother, and I know he will find his way to you. He will find your address among your letters, as I did. I apologize for succumbing to the overwhelming temptation those boxes offered, but in this respect I'm glad I opened them. You left him your address, and I found it. And now I can send you this.*

*Another reason I'm glad I read your letters is that it gives me more insight into the love you have for Patrick. And for this I am very grateful. I would like to know you better. I may get the time to know you well. I may not. But I know what you did for my brother. And that gives me an understanding of you that brings me great peace. I know you'll always do well for Patrick.*

*Lynn, I regret laying this burden on you, to give Patrick this last letter. But I have no doubt that you will be by him. And he will need you.*

*Thank you, again, Lynn. For everything.*

*Love,*

*David*


I set the page aside. Lynn put her arm around me and rested her head on my shoulder as we began David's letter.

*Dear Pat,*

*Forgive me for not coming home.*

*I want to tell you what I know about getting through grief. I already know the loss you are feeling. I wish I didn't. I wish it was something we didn't need to know about, being so young. But the good do die young, sometimes. Jannie did. Now, if you're reading this, me.*

*I hope that as long as you live, you find the kind of joy that Jannie did. And that I have, too. Even with the emptiness of growing up without you, I feel joy. It's part of what Father Jack called being a warrior. I think he got it from Rose, although she prefers to say champion, especially when she's talking about you. I'm the warrior, to her. Either way, it's about how we live our lives, with purpose and intensity. With joy. We talked about that a lot on the farm. Lots of crazy thoughts. A lot of our goofy ideas came from Father Jack and Rose. Or through them.*

*The best thing I can tell you about making your way through grief is something that I learned from Jack. It's called the Good Guy List. I mentioned it to you awhile back, when you asked me how I got on after Jannie, but I really didn't explain it all that well. I was still learning how to use it then. And I think you thought I was kind of flaky. Well, a lot of the things we talked about on the farm were kind of out there, but they were good. And the Good Guy List was definitely among the best.*

*The List is really pretty easy. I compose my lists intermittently, whenever I need to. Seems like a lot, lately. Almost as much as after Jannie died. Takes longer now, too, since it tends to grow.*

*Anyways, there are no set rules for who goes on the List—part of the point is to make up your own criteria. Mine includes people who have had a positive influence in my life, or are just decent people. Nice people. I don't look for perfection, or anything close to it. None of us would qualify, if that was the standard. Warmth, kindness, good-heartedness—those folks are in, easy. People I admire, people I aspire to be with, or to be like. People I know firsthand, or sometimes people I don't know at all, whom I've only read about or heard about from a friend.*

*So all I do is come up with these names, and then I jot the list down and reflect on it. I can't say I keep any of the lists after I write them out. Sometimes they get stuck in a book, or a pack, and carried around a bit. A lot of time, I just think the List—I don't bother even putting it on paper. I mean, it pretty much lives in my mind. And heart. I just focus on being cognizant of it. That's why I don't need to keep the old lists. Writing out the lists is like taking in a breath of fresh air and then exhaling, leaving it behind after I've taken in its nourishment. Breathing in, breathing out, again and again.*

*Treat the List lightly, with as little judgmental discrimination as you can. Plenty of good people emerge, and there is something that strengthens my soul to go through and realize how many Good Guys comprise the List. It is a testimony to the goodness of people. And over time, it does tend to morph and evolve, but usually not because anyone*

I let the letter dangle from my fingertips. I looked to Lynn; she was here. Her face reflected my hope, and gratitude.

David's last letter to me. I read it again, and I wept. This time, I wept in the arms of the woman I loved, and she grieved with me.

I slid David's folded letter into its envelope. From its markings, I could see it had traveled. Addressed to Lynn North at her father's home in Minnetonka, it had been returned marked 'addressee unknown." David had the foresight to use his friend's return address, and the letter was returned to Father Jack. Lynn smiled at my puzzled expression.

"I met him, Father Jack," she said. "Last month. He found me here. And he brought this to me."

I laughed. "You met him before I have, then. He called, you know. Talked to Paddy a couple days before I got back home. That's how I got your phone number."

"Yeah. He called from the lodge. I was there," she nodded. "You'll get a chance to meet him. He's in the Boundary Waters. We outfitted him for an extended paddle. He could stay out there for a month, if he has it in him. That would be a lot, for someone who's never done a canoe trip before. He didn't seem intimidated by the challenge. He's on a search quest. He's kind of happy to take it on."

"Sounds like everything David ever told me about him."

"He'll be back. He said he was due to finally meet you. That's his car parked up by the outfitting shed. The Cadillac. Says it's his brother's, the bishop. Besides, he's paddling your canoe."

"Really? My canoe?"

"Jack brought it with him. Didn't Paddy tell you? Picked it up when he stopped by your farm and saw your uncle. Paddy told Jack to take it with him so that I would trust him. It worked. I recognized it the moment I saw it since it's just like mine."

"Paddy didn't say anything about sending my canoe along with Jack," I wondered aloud. "He just gave me your number and told me I'd better call."

"I'm glad he did." She led the way to cabin number 3. "You'll stay here. For now."

I startled, alarmed. I said nothing.

"Don't worry. I'm not going anywhere." She sighed. "I've got no place I'd ever want to go. Nowhere I'd rather be. I've been waiting for you all this time, and now you are here." She folded into my arms. Tears fell easily. She sobbed softly, with no tension. Just release. And joy. I held her until she was spent. She shed the tears of five years of trial. Five years waiting for me.

And now we had each other.

∞

While I played sports and wandered about, Lynn cared for her family. Hers. Ours.

The children were born when I was back home on the farm. David was still at Madison. They were born in March, on St. Patrick's day, 1964. She said she had a real hard time not naming either of them after me or St. Patrick. But, Lynn is neither Irish nor Catholic.

My sophomore year in Boulder, right about the time I was playing my best ball, she recognized that her father, Luther, wasn't making good decisions. Ingie finally resurrected from her two year coma. Luther, had just contrived the deal that would jilt him out of his own company, his own inventions, his own identity. He did it to pay for Inge's needs. They had no insurance to cover her massive injuries. Rehabilitation cost dearly, and those expenses were long with most of the expenses yet to come. It fell upon him to make the decisions that cost him his life's work.

Luther did not understanding the ramifications of those decisions, she saw. They were faced with selling their home in Minnetonka. Luther lost his business and his home all within a year. And he was confused about how that had happened, Lynn saw.

Perhaps she would have recognized his dementia earlier, had not the twins and Ingie taken so much of her attention. She sensed things were different with her father. He was remote. Hidden. She assumed it was concern over Ingie. And of the children. Her father blamed Lynn for both. Just as he had blamed her for much of the impact of Lynn's life on his marriage and family after she was born so long after he had seen his son's grow up and leave home.

In the fall of '66, I injured my neck in a game against Nebraska. The game was on national television. Lynn watched it with her brother, the canoe builder, who was home on leave from his air force base in Colorado. They watched as I caught that ball and plowed into the end zone, and when I didn't get up. She saw the replay over and over again. She shared with her brother that I am her children's father. He held her as she sobbed. It was the last time she had cried, the last time she could cry, she said, until now, in my arms. Our children were two when I was still at Colorado, just finished my career playing with the Buffaloes, blowing smoke, trying to figure my next move in life. She got caught in the whims of the world and embraced the responsibilities of the moment. And she prayed I would find my way to her.

She sold the house in the dunes just about the time I left for Germany. Her mother's trust, meant to provide for both her and Ingie, was exhausted. Lynn could no longer afford to keep her home in the dunes, even with renters occupying the house and paying the monthly mortgage costs. Lynn needed the equity from her home. Ingie needed it. Her family needed it.

They moved to Ely in 1967. Martha was there to welcome them. They occupied the lodge that Martha had managed since Lynn's mother married Luther and moved to Minnetonka. They lived in her mother's childhood home there.

Lynn's eyes were dry as she watched her father descend Jacob's ladder into the torments of dementia. She bolstered her courage to meet her sister's demands and needs. She raised our children. Martha helped her with all. Martha had retired a few years back, escaping the labor intensive business, but they both were grateful for the timing. Martha helped Lynn with Luther, who Martha had known as her best friend's husband for decades. And with her family. She taught Lynn the resort business that would be the bread and butter of their daily lives. She exposed her to the intangibles, the power of nature. She demonstrated how to harness those powers.

Courage, however, was not enough to see Lynn through the challenges she found to be hers. She fell to exhaustion. Exhaustion fed despair. Her soul suffered from unremitting grief. The challenge and joy of raising her children fed her soul, but the test that her father posed consumed. Ingie's needs were compelling and unforgiving; Lynn's daily care for her sister harbored the notion of failed responsibilities. And she was plagued by the recurrent recollection of the love she had lost when she let Patrick meander into the unknown realms of an adolescent quest.

"How'd you ever survive?" I asked.

She leveled her gaze into my eyes. " I couldn't have done it alone," she said. I needed help, and I got it. Martha was here for me. Martha's love kept me from sinking into a dismal depression. Martha and our friend, Ixchel.

"They filled my heart with love while you were away. They tended to the well-being of my soul as I took care of the kids and Dad. And Ingie."

She kissed my cheek. "We are never really alone, if we so choose. And then, one day, as I stood by the kitchen sink, I stopped. It became so clear to me. I saw the challenge as it was, and it was big. I realized , either I do this, or I don't. And there is no room for don't, is there? Not when there is love."

She dabbed her pointer finger at the tip of my nose, then kissed the spot she touched.

I shook my head. *What strength!*

All while I was playing football in Boulder. Or off in Europe. Or on the Appalachian trail. Searching for something to fill my sense of emptiness. My lack of worth. Wandering around, wondering where I belonged in this world.

While Lynn faced reality and came to grips with it.

∞

Lynn's resilience moved me. I kissed her tears away. I felt her surge from within her vibrant body wrapped in my arms. I tightened my hold. I kissed her eyes. And her ears. I felt her desire for me rise, and we made love until we slept.

"It's better now. We are one again," she whispered as she fell into sleep.

Each day, I watched the load she carried, and stepped in to help where I could. We knew how to work together. She seldom asked, unless it was a labor that required braun as much as persistence. But there it was. And I was here to help her.

Her daily life was endless tasks that filled the hours and spilled into the night. I wondered how she had kept at it. She tended Ingie's morning needs, and then the children. If Luther slept in, she had time to tend the needs of the children and Ingie. But Luther slept little. Some days, Luther slept until 8:00 or so. More often, he woke with the sun. And she worked. Her career afforded her family the cash flow they depended on.

I knew I could help with covering expenses and getting the daily needs paid for thanks to David's trust. But I needed more. Something of myself. I looked for how I could be of use. How I could fit into the seamless team work that she and Martha had developed to nurture the young and the broken of her family. I looked for where I belonged.

# Chapter 9

# Luther

When he came for his breakfast, Luther hesitated meeting my glance, uncertain who I was in the lodge's kitchen.

"'Morning, Luther. Coffee? And toast with an egg?" I offered his morning go-to. His brow furrowed, and he mulled the option. Then, without meeting my eye, he nodded. I hatched a brown shelled egg into a cast iron pan where it sizzled and spat.

"It's too hot," he muttered as he sipped his coffee. He stirred it, then took a hearty gulp. With a glance, he frowned. "And who are you? The cook? Where did the old one go?"

"Oh, she's 'round about,'" I affirmed. "Chasing the chicken, I suppose. We're kind of low on eggs."

His gaze hardened. He awaited explanation. He couldn't place me this morning.

"I'm the twin's father. Patrick. The vagabond."

"He's the asshole who knocked up Lynn," Ingie called from her perch on the porch. His eyes tightened and his furrow set deep, he pondered the daily puzzle.

Who was this new person within his household? I was the out of place component to an otherwise normal morning in the lodge.

The twins chirped and laughed in their bedroom. Their noises were joy, filling the cabin with birdsong. His wrinkles softened, and his eyes turned to the sunlight streaming in through the forest. He nodded.

It was going to be a gentler day for him than some. I flipped the egg frying on the range and poured a warmer to his coffee.

He glanced over. "Ah. The bastard who knocked up my daughter."

"Yep. That is me, for certain. Aren't you glad I did so?" I teased as the children scampered to the table to join him. I chanced joking this morning, just by the look on his face. Not like some days.

The twins, on the other hand, observed me with as much caution as curiosity. Alpha, our firstborn, was in all dynamics the leader of the twosome. Quick to observe, she watched out for her brother who tended toward distraction and dreams, much like his father, I recognized. He wasn't a giant compared to his sister, like I was to my twin. Both twins were slight, like their mother. But Omega, my son we called 'Omie', tumbled along in time as though drifting in the current of a pleasant breeze. I could identify with that.

"Want eggs like your Grandpa?" I asked as they climbed up to the table.

"With toast," Ally stated. "And jam. Raspberry jam.

"You want jam on your eggs?" I asked, my eyes wide.

She gazed back with scrutiny. Scrunching her brow above eyes narrowed to a slit, she watched carefully to catch any signs that I was joking. I held my expression, looking baffled and awed. Her brother looked bewildered.

"Jam on eggs?" he asked, looking to his grandfather's breakfast plate. "Gramps doesn't have any jam on his eggs."

As if by reflex, Luther spooned a dollop of juicy red jam and layered it on his remaining eggs as Lynn returned with a tray of Ingie's breakfast dishes.

"Mom," Ally whispered, her pointer finger directed at her grandfather's sticky red, yellow and white fried egg breakfast plate. "Grampa's putting jam on his eggs."

Lynn glanced at her father's plate, then at the children looking agog at the use of raspberries on a nicely fried egg. Shifting her eyes to meet my guilty expression, she wagged her head back and forth.

"So, you challenge the dogmatic with the brink of youthful fantasy. Is that for amusement, or are you testing a hypothesis?" She asked, her face warped in tethered laughter.

"I'll have mine with honey," Martha quipped as she bundled the soiled washcloths and towel used to keep Ingie neat. "And a pinch of cinnamon, please."

"Honey! On eggs? No! You can't do that!" Ally cried.

"Why not?" Omie wondered,

"With cinnamon? That would be awful!" the older of my children argued.

"Nothing more than an egg nog, if you add milk and don't cook the egg," Martha teased.

Lynn rolled her eyes, wiping the jam that had dripped from her father's egg down his fresh shirt. She shot me a look to tell me that the impact of my quips may lead further than I might imagine. I shrugged.

"Jam would be good in egg nog," Omie asserted.

"I'm done," Luther declared, shedding his napkin and pushing from the table. He turned without a glance at any of us and headed outside.

"You're on now," Lynn said. "Keep an eye on him, please. Follow him if he wanders, if you can keep up."

"I'll watch him," Martha offered.

"Patrick offered to keep tabs on Dad, Martha. Thanks, but I think he hopes to gain my father's trust, if not blessing," Lynn replied. I aimed to garner Lynn's confidence as well. Martha cast an eye my way. Again, I shrugged. I was trying. "The kids, perhaps? Are they too much, with Ingie as well, while I strip down number 2?"

Martha smiled gracefully. "Heavens! Looks like I get the gravy duty. Come on, kids. Forget about eggs and jam. Let's make pancakes!" She elbowed me in the ribs. "You'd better have your running shoes on if you expect to keep up with Luther." She chuckled as she turned to the pantry to gather the makings for pancakes.

∞

Martha was right. Luther set a hearty pace. It felt good to have my old, worn hikers back on. I hadn't dusted them off since abandoning the Appalachian trail, and it was a delight to feel them wrapped around my feet like old friends.

Luther would put them to a test, Martha had said, and she was spot on. He set out headed east, then turned north on the Echo trail a mile up the road. His stride was determined, his destination awaited.

You can tell a bit about a man by his stride and the way he takes the trail. Luther knew his terrain. He walked with certainty, his feet taking him where he wanted to go, his mind occupied with certain destinations. Or perhaps, instinct.

We'd gone a mile up the Echo when he stopped, turned left, and inspected the forest from the road. I followed along a quarter mile behind, but he never glanced my way. After considering his choice, he hopped across the ditch and disappeared into the woodland. He was thinking fairly clearly this morning.

I jogged to where I last saw him on the trail and found a cleared path. It looked like a groomed hiking or skiing trail. My old hiking partner from the Appalachian Trail, Georgia, had shown me a few keys to tracking that helped me decide which fork to follow when Luther's path blended into the knee high undergrowth. Georgia had pointed to the tips of leaves turned up trail, tucked in behind other greens in subtle ways that indicated man or beast had passed by. He said he learned tracking with David. They had done it together. They had tracked men.

Luther's trail was bold. He was certain of his way. On other days to come, I'd be following him, a man with less clarity of mind; he would bumble around, make wrong turns or stop, uncertain, pondering unclear decisions. He'd follow paths of instinct or of random wanderings. Today, he headed in a direction with purpose. He followed a ridgeback that strung out along the center of a peninsula that led to an outcrop looking to the south over Pearson's Bay on Burntside Lake where it opened to the ponderous expanse of the lake.

As the trail ended and the outcrop basked in July's brilliant morning sun, I stopped short in the shade of the canopy. Luther sat on a boulder, studying the view, chasing thoughts as they evaporated from his memory. I let him be. On other hikes, I would join him, asking him to share his thoughts. And, as it turned out, memories from this place would draw him back. But this morning, I bowed to any privacy that he found to savored.

Today, he had purpose. I wondered what motivated him. I would need to wait for other hikes to learn more.

# Chapter 10

# Meeting Jack

Father Jack paddled into the resort on an evening in July when the quiet of the lakes hummed in harmony with the loons. He arrived unannounced and unobserved, beaching his vessel, leaving his gear for later. He caught a whiff of something savory drifting down to the lakefront. His hunger urged him toward the lodge.

Luther was startled by the grizzled and weathered traveler who appeared at the kitchen door as we ladled supper onto our plates. The traveler's face caused consternation in Luther's mind on a day when he had struggled under shadows and clouds. But the kindness in the traveler's eyes penetrated his unknowing, disarming him, bringing to the old man's face a look not of recognition, but of safety and joy.

"Got a bowl for a hungry paddler?" Jack asked as the twins burst into greetings that stopped even the loons from singing. He hugged them one against each leg as he walked across the kitchen toward where I stood behind the table.

"Well, the wayfaring pilgrim," Lynn laughed. "I've been wondering when you'd paddle in."

Jack flashed a smile at Lynn, and grasped Luther by the shoulder as he looked him in the eye. Then, turning to me, he held out his hands.

"Patrick," he said.

I nodded. "Father Jack," I said. His gaze felt like a blessing. I took his hands in mine.

∞

The twins tagged along when I went with Father Jack to empty the canoe of pack and gear. Lynn had mentioned how our children had bonded to this lion of a man, totally unintimidated by his shaggy mane and beard. Jack was a mountain; he dwarfed the children who hung on his legs, their little feet perched on his feet, and climbed into his arms as red squirrels scaled a pine. He had a gentleness about him. The twins clung to him.

With the kids in tow, we tipped the canoe over and lugged his gear to Number 3. He'd be staying with me. All the other cabins were occupied. Lynn had shrugged and grinned. "Kind of a bachelor's pad for you two.

Jack nodded his gratitude. "Once again, I appreciate your hospitality. How about I fetch some of my clean clothes, shower up, and join you on the porch

Lynn sniffed the air, chuckled, and agreed. "Excellent plan. We'll wait for you there."

As Lynn left for the lodge with a twin in each hand, Jack stored his pack at the foot of a bunk. He glanced toward me.

"I expect I may be interrupting the routine for you and Lynn."

"A bit, I suppose. Not to be concerned. She's been telling me how much she has been looking forward to my chance to meet you. "

He smiled, dipped his chin to his chest and looked at the wooden planks on the floor of Number 3. "You look more like him than I expected."

I coughed a laugh. "You're kidding!" David had hair like a raven; mine was golden like sunlight. David tipped the scales at maybe 125 pounds, wet, and stood just a hand over 5 feet. I towered over him and carried nearly 100 pounds more.

"No. Really. Yeah, yeah, yeah, David was a shrimp compared to you," he agreed, leveling his gaze directly at me. "It's your eyes. How you look at people. Your children. Lynn. How you see them. It's how your brother looked at people."

I nodded. A lump lodged itself high in my chest. Words didn't come. I felt David, and was grateful for Jack's observation.

He set his bear-paw hands on my shoulder.

"We have lots to share," he said. "About David. About you. But first, I'm going to shower and get respectable. I'll see you on the porch."

∞

Cleaned up, Jack appeared only slightly less wild than when he had sur-prised us at supper. His hair was damp and pulled back into a tail that dan-gled thick and curly down his shoulders. His beard looked more bristly than when dry, and accented the gray in his red brown muzzle. His tanned skin glowed in the soft light from the lanterns lit on the tables between the deck chairs.

Ingie sat upright and stiff. I checked to see whether she was holding her breath. Her lips pursed, the skin on her face drawn and tight as a drum.

Father Jack glanced at her. A sly smile slipped beneath his brushy mus-tache.

"So how has my princess of profanity been while I paddled the pristine waters here in the wilderness?" His eyes twinkled.

Ingie's lips contorted. Her eyes lit with a flare of humor and resignation. He wasn't going to let her off easy. He could have. But he didn't. So she let him have it.

"Just fine, fucknuts," she shot back, her eyes flashing. "And how is the holy duck fucker himself? See anything worth it out there? Did you find any damn peace of mind? Any grace or whatever? Maybe a fuckin' 'ad-vance-to-Samadhi free' card?"

Jack tucked his chin down upon his chest, stifling his chuckle and clamping his lips in a straight tight smile. He turned his gaze upon her and his eyes shone with fondness and care.

"Ah! Feeling tip-top. Well, I admit that the silence of the first week helped cleanse my ears from the barrage of your eloquent diction and warm farewell," Jack quipped. "But then I met some campers. I set up on an island for several days on the north edge of Cummings Lake. They camped on the next island over. A couple young men, new veterans, actually, who were almost as vile as you with their vernacular. Army type. Talking tough, but not as tough as you. Made me think of you, though," he shot her a glance, an eyebrow raised high. "Especially when I told them I was a priest. They couldn't open their mouths to say a word for a whole afternoon. So embarrassed. I don't know why. They got all apologetic around the campfire after we cooked the shore lunch we caught. I told them not to be concerned. Told them about you, and how they sounded like a couple of pussies compared to your lexicon. That put them to ease."

Ingie held her lips tight. Her eyes sparkled. She lifted her fine nose, raised her eyebrows, and nodded.

Lynn and Martha laughed, but Ally took up her aunt's defense.

"Auntie Ingie can't help it if she has a potty mouth," Ally cried. "Those words just pop out."

Jack beamed at the little girl snuggling in her mother's lap. "Is that so, Ally? You think Ingie just percolates profanity with no intent or will?"

Ally grinned. "You can bet your sweet ass."

Jack and I burst out laughing, and Martha wrapped her arms around her torso as tears clustered on her cheeks. Ingie nodded acknowledgement to her niece, and Lynn exploded with shock.

"Ally What are you saying! How can you think it's okay to talk like that?" Lynn said, swinging her daughter around on her lap and looking her right in the eye.

"Oh, Mom. You know I don't talk like that. Too much, anyway. Father Jack is just teasing Auntie. I wanted to give him a dose of his own." There was not a glimmer of repentance in Ally's eye.

Tears ran down Jack's face. I couldn't stop laughing. Martha coughed and sniffed. She got up to fetch tissue from the kitchen and returned wiping her eyes.

Ingie beamed. "Fuckin' TBI," she muttered, giving Ally a nod. She knew her loyalties.

*Chapter 11*

# Gaining Luther's Trust

Sometimes, Luther's morning hikes were less direct, more spontaneous, and whimsical like the flight of a butterfly, dabbling here, drifting there, seemingly nonchalant and meaningless. When we meet up, our chats followed along similar pathways.

Today, he followed the Echo Trail until it intersected a road or driveway, and then after a questioning moment of inspection, he proceeded as he had been headed. He turned abruptly as though drawn by a siren song and took a different route than usual to his favorite site on the point overlooking Burntside Lake.

I thought I could close in without disturbing him. But I snapped a dry twig underfoot and my cover was blown. He swirled on his throne atop his sitting stone when he heard me.

"There are 13 meteor showers, ya know. The Perseids blaze as we sit here," Luther said.

I stopped, looked at the sky. It was brilliant morning. Blue. As blue as the lakes. "Gotta see 'em at night." he stammered. Then, with a lift of an eye, he said, "But they are flying by right now. Or soon, anyway. You'd see them if it was dark." I nodded.

He looked at the boulder across the path from where he sat, then the lake. I took my place on the rock, waiting and listening.

∞

"I had a chat with Luther today."

Lynn glanced up, a strand of Ally's golden braid wrapped around her finger.

"Sat with him?" She looked back to the braid. "And chatted?"

"Don't you always sit with Grampa and chat?" Ally asked, tugging the braid against her mother's grip. Lynn held with authority.

"No. Not without all the family around. Not just by myself. That's new."

Ally scrunched her brow and considered this information.

I could hear Omie in with Ingie. How they prattled on!

"Does Omie know about meteors?"

Both Lynn and Ally looked at me.

"All thirteen major showers. What? Is Grandpa telling you about the Perseids?" asked Ally.

"Yes. All thirteen of the meteor showers, actually," I laughed.

"If it is calm when the Perseids are here, we should paddle out on the lake. It'll be a new moon the middle of next month." Lynn flipped Ally's braid over her daughter's shoulder. Their daughter hopped like a fledgeling to the floor and scooted away to find her twin. Lynn watched her go, then turned her gaze to me. She lifted an eyebrow. "You taught me about new moons. No?"

"Wow." I remembered the night that I had.

"So long ago"

Yes, I nodded. A quarter of my life ago. I shook my head, struck by how much time had passed since our encounter on the sand dunes along Lake Michigan. A chance encounter that revealed us completely to one another, yet predicted the days that were to follow when we no longer would be together. And now, we were passed that hauntingly lonely epoch.

Her gazed appraised me in an unsettling way.

She still had questions.

"What?" I asked.

She tilted her head, looking out toward the afternoon sun hanging high over the lake.

"I see how you work to gain Luther's trust. And the twins', too." She sat on the bedside where her daughter had just left. She set her hand on the bedspread, palm down, patting it twice.

I took my place beside her.

"I see how you look to find the needs of each of us. The keyholes to unlock our trust in you. You do that well."

She took my hand and wrapped it in hers upon her lap. She leaned into me, placing a gentle kiss on my cheek.

"I see how you work to be part of our family here. Your family. And that's as it should be," she said. Her words calmed me. Then, she added, "You open your heart to each of us. Do you open it to yourself?"

Her comment startled me.

"When does your quest come to clarity? When will you see your self as you truly are?"

I sat stunned.

"What do you mean?" I protested. "I am being me. Truly."

"Do you see where you are broken? Have you measured your losses?" Her eyes flowed kindness and care. "We have both grown these years apart. Grown, and broken. And healed—or healing. Me. You. We didn't stop living. We must accept our losses. We grow from the healing of the breaks and losses we have had. The loss of the time we were apart. And what happened during those times."

She stroked my hands with her fingers. Then my face. Her eyes flowed with calm.

"Don't be alarmed. Don't be afraid. I'm not judging. I'm just seeing, and I tell you what I sense when I see your work here. Your contributions. I'm with you now. And I will be with you as you find yourself here. Or elsewhere."

"I'm going nowhere."

"You must, if you intend to be somewhere at all," she smiled. "And it is my prayer that when you find yourself somewhere, you are all together and cognizant of that moment. I hope to see that moment."

Our eyes held. I tried to show my intent. Her words beckoned me to ask her what more I had yet to unveil. That which I felt I had yet within me, but could not reach. What did she see that I could not?

She longed for completeness to unfold within me. She longed for me to be whole, entire, complete.

As did I. But I was cognizant that she saw more than I allowed myself to acknowledge.

# Chapter 12

# The Rescue

We packed our gear in my canoe.

"I'm concerned about Martha." Father Jack said

"Why?"

"Her health. She works too hard just breathing."

"She seems pretty healthy."

"She is. Kind of. She's aging." He stowed fishing tackle under his wicker seat. "I suppose you have to live with the sins of your past."

"Huh?"

He glanced up. "Bet she smoked. You can see it in her skin. And in her breathing."

"Hmm," I set my paddle on the gunnels over my seat. "Ready for a push?"

He settled in the bow seat.

"Let's go."

∞

We traveled west on Crab Lake. It was a pleasure paddling water after trekking over rocks and roots on the mile long portage from Burntside. We hadn't gone long when he called over his shoulder.

"We have a choice," he noted. "There is a prime camp site ahead to the north. It's a point. Lots of privacy, wonderful view of the lake. We can stop there on the way back if we feel like staying on the water this afternoon."

The sun was above us. The sky was clean. We had hours until twilight. A lingering, lavender July evening was in store, but that was for later.

"Let's keep going."

He stuck his paddle and we pushed off.

∞

The embers from our camp fire were still hot after cooking dinner. The sun dawdled at sunset, and we were mesmerized.

"So, what are your sins of the past?" I blurted.

He laughed. "What? You don't think priests sin?"

I flicked a pine cone into the embers. The fire gripped it. We laughed together. He dodged that bullet.

"I was thinking of Martha. Her past sins. Seems like smoking was a sin, in your view. A mortal sin, when you think about it. Whew!"

"Yeah. Whew. Her dharma meets her karma."

"Huh." I nodded. I watched the cone bristle with flame and pondered the message.

"What about Ingie?" Jack stirred the coals.

The sky was deep purple and teal. I stoked a log and banked the embers close in. "Well, she is kinda sick. Already." I glanced at Jack, wondering how much he knew of Ingie's accident. Was he aware of the details of the car accident in which Ingie suffered her traumatic brain injury? Did he know of my cousin Jack's involvement, and his drug and alcohol use while driving? Did he think I was complicit? What had Lynn, or Ingie, told him?

Jack's gaze never moved from his poker stirring the embers. He tossed on another stick of pine.

"Yeah. But it's different. She's healing. She has lots more room to heal lots more. She's young enough. Accidents are a whole different thing. You should know." He pulled off his boots and set his feet on the fire ring.

Yeah. I knew. My neck injury was a challenge. It brought my football career to a screeching halt. Ingie's injury was exponentially more complex. She'd been healing for five years. Slowly healing. In a coma for almost two. She wasn't walking. She had physical therapy every other week, and whatever Martha or Lynn could do with her in between the visits from Derek, her therapist, who drove up from Duluth. She was thin, and she didn't speak without the course swearing of a Marine. She woke up from her coma cursing. It was already family legend. The first thing her cognitive vision focused upon when she came out of her coma was Luther, and she greeted her father lovingly with, "Hi, fuck face."

"Yeah. She's gonna need a lot of work." I said.

Jack kindled the fire and put a kettle on for tea. I dug out a sweater and found mint tea.

"Got any green tea?"

I dug further and found Jasmin.

"Did you have P.T.? After your injury?"

I nodded. Yes. Half a year of P.T. It was the last thing I got out of playing football for Colorado. My farewell gift. Then, I went to Germany. To the University in Regensburg.

He sipped his brewing tea. It was right. He pulled the tea egg.

"Yeah. It was intense," I poked the fire. The embers were dying, mostly white. The big sky in the northwest slowly sucked the last lights of day into the nether beyond the waters and forest. "It wasn't a whole lot different than training and keeping your body functioning to play ball. It took a lot of work. But I was already an athlete. Recovery was hard. I started from a good place. Ingie is little more than a skeleton. She's gonna be a tough save."

"Yep."

She did try. She worked hard with Derek. She tried everything he asked of her. And she cussed him all throughout her workouts. Cussed and cursed. Always with the most profane expressions of endearment. She was totally happy every moment. She loved us all. She was just frail. And weak. And she swore. She could make a Marine blush.

"I think she can walk again. Her arms are okay. She can write." I considered.

"Yeah. But only she can read it."

We burst in a belly laugh. The loons abruptly stopped hooting.

He sighed.

"She's got memory issues."

I considered that notion. I'd noticed.

"Yeah. But not that bad." I shook my head. "I think my memory isn't a lot sharper."

"Well, you spent a good part of your life smashing your head into fast moving slabs of muscle."

"Yeah." I had mulled the thought often. Dharma meets karma.

∞

"I'd like to see Rose. And your mom." Jack said.

A meteor zipped a seam of light across Orion down through the southern horizon.

"Now, where exactly did that come from?" I laughed. David had told me about Jack's tendency to resume a hanging discussion that he'd stored away while he focused on other things at hand.

He remained nonplussed.

"What do you mean? It's straightforward. I'd like to visit with Rose. And Elle. I do miss them."

"You know of Eva?"

"Just that there is an Eva. You know her well?"

I nodded. Eva was on my mind almost constantly. Eva and David. I thought of them as the embers donned thick white cloaks of ash. The moon slipped up over the pines across the bay.

"Amazing."

"What is amazing?"

"That my mother is with Eva."

We considered that notion while we watched a satellite wobble amongst the stars.

∞

In the morning, we paddled west to the outlet from Cummings where a moose wallowed in the shallows. We didn't intend to travel in to Buck Lake,

54

although Jack had several times repeated the details of landing a whopping Northern in Western Lake two weeks prior. Instead, we watched the moose forage.

"Her calf is along the shore to the right," Jack whispered over his shoulder.

The calf was all folded up on itself and looked long and bony and clumsy as it scurried to its feet when we floated by. The mother left her browsing and gathered her calf. The two made speed through the forest away from the lake.

"Wow. That is a big animal."

"There's a bull moose residing downstream near the turn to Western Lake. His rack was a basket that could fit us and all our gear. I floated right by him in the stream. He just chewed and watched as if he had no care on earth that I was imposing on his waters."

"Lucky. I thought they could be mean and cranky."

"To a man of God?" he posed.

"Sheese!"

∞

The loons sang throughout our dinner. The smallmouth were superb, sautéed with onions and fennel seed. Jack traveled prepared. He was a cook. Then the twilight came and the loons sang more raucously than before. An eagle soared the perimeter of the lake. By dark, we slept.

We caught fish at sunrise and lingered long after breakfast, sipping tea, chasing tangents.

"What's your take on Omie?"

Jack looked over the rim of his cup. "Oh, he's a sponge. He's taking in everything. Probably about in twice as much detail as you and I with every glance. Hears and sees everything. Kind of brave the way he's measuring you up."

"I'll forever have an asterisk by my name in his scorecard."

"He's forgiving. He wants you to win."

I nodded. The kettle needed water so I took it down to the lake and filled it. A long thin Northern slithered from the shallows near the landing gravel into the reeds and grass toward deeper water.

The kettle sizzled on the fire rock.

"Yeah. I feel his eyes on me, making his own assessment. Let him make it. Hope I come out of it on the bright side."

"Oh, yeah. You will. He's been looking for you as much as Lynn has. But in a way that speaks to his needs. He needs you to be you. To be his father."

Whatever that means, I thought.

55

"Yeah. I suppose. It'll just take time." For him. And for me.

"Right. Like a puppy."

He took up his book and we fell silent until the sun climbed high and hot. Restless, I tipped my canoe upright and set my fishing gear in place. Jack watched with amusement.

"High sun for fishing clear waters?"

"Yeah. Fishing. Probably not catching."

I shoved off the shoreline and drifted across the breeze rippled surface of the lake. Without the breeze the air would have been on the verge of stifling. The summer sun over the Northlands was serious.

The canoe coasted more than the length of a football field off our campsite. The breeze stilled, and I felt becalmed. I pulled my visor down over my brow and stripped off my shirt. My tackle kit was sparse. I chose a palm sized daredevil and strung it to the line on my pole. I cast it out and retrieved it. Over and over again, I watched the red striped spoon wobble through the sky and splash into the lake with a liquid kerplunk. I cast automatically, like a machine, as my mind wondered back to camp. Then to the resort. Then to Mom and Eva in Munich. And always, to Lynn.

∞

I had wondered why she promoted this excursion for me and Jack. I mean, she was way overloaded with tasks and chores at the resort. And with the kids. And Luther. And of course, Ingie. I argued against Jack's suggestion that we paddle into the BWCA, but she was adamant.

"Martha's here," she said. "We can pick up the slack. We managed alright until you got here, so we can get by for a few days."

I thought my help was becoming more essential, and she read the concern on my face.

"It's not as though things won't be waiting for your return," she laughed. "Sometimes you have to look at the big picture. You have to look at what's good for you, too. What you have left to do."

"What?" I protested. "Maybe I'm doing what is good for me. Being here with you. Helping here."

"You have a place here. You always will." Her fingers smoothed my furrowed brow. "You are needed here. That's not the issue."

"Then what?"

"You are such a heart!" she cried. "You don't see, do you? Your brother just died. Your twin, for God's sake. Have you let that register yet? You've got some grieving to process. You've got some basket case time before you. Go with Jack. Be proactive about it. You'll serve us all better if you heal your heart. And you have to find the breaks in your heart before you can heal them. So pack your gear. You're going."

And that was that. And here I am, throwing a spoon aimlessly across quiet water.

And still I resisted her advice. It was too much of a bite to take. It is impossible to consider this world without David. He will always be with me, somehow. He was with me when I sat in that rail yard in Koln; I felt him and knew he was there, and that was the day he died, and I knew nothing of it. And he was with me for a couple months on the Trail. Almost always, I heard him. I felt him. Sometimes I know I was listening to things he had said earlier, like when he visited Regensburg and told me things that have changed the way I look at what I do and need to do. Like cussing. He told me how Father Jack had made him alert to the significance of his words as the product of his life. A reflection of his soul. And I heard that so clearly on the Trail. When you're talking to no one but yourself inside the cave of your cranium, it's pretty easy to pick up on the profane vernacular spent on denigrating worthy thought. I thought about that and I consciously tried to change that in my life. I found I could take more and more steps on the Trail before I slipped again and muttered something vile, debasing the ideas worthy of my thought. Worthy of my mind. I did so because of David. I wanted David to hear me without the baggage of my locker room lifestyle dangling the f-word between every thing and person and place and action I considered as I tread along my path. Just because of David. And David had already died. He was dead. I just didn't know. He was there, but he was gone. Wasted, his pals would say. But he was with me. I am certain of it. He was no waste.

And Lynn wanted me to figure that all out so that I could be whole again in my time and place. So I wouldn't become a total basket case. She didn't want to lose me again. Lose me! Hardly. The thought made me laugh, and I coughed a chortle that carried loud across the lake to the man reading by the campfire between our tents. Jack looked up. I could see his silly grin flicker across his face. He returned his eyes to his reading.

*I could live with David. David will live in me. He always has.*

But I wondered. *What would I do?*

Lynn had told me, I would find what I wanted to do. Needed to do. Could do. She assured me of it all.

"Remember when I crushed my hand and you had to do all the work on the wall?" she said as we folded the twins laundry. "Yeah. I wanted more than anything to keep on working. But I couldn't, right? So you did it. You picked up the load. I learned something from that," she said, piling the clothing in stacks upon my cradled arms.

"Yeah, but I don't have broken fingers," I argued. "I'm here to help."

"Right. I agree. And I need your help. But that's not all you have to do. You have to find the breaks in your heart. You have to heal. And learn new understandings while you heal. While you grow. While you find strength."

She stopped on a dime, turned, and impaled me with her caring gaze.

"You're broken, you know," she said. 'You lived through trauma to your body and your heart. You body healed, hasn't it? But your heart? Have you found how to heal your heart? In your wonderings around Europe, and your hiking the Trail, did you find healing? That's what I wonder. Were you searching, or where you healing." She tilted her head, giving me a long, probing look. Then she turned into the twin's room.

I followed her. She went on as she unloaded the clothes from my arms into drawers. Omie looked up from the floor where he doodled colors on a tray size chalk board. I glanced at his work; a bird, big with a beak like a raven, soaring above the lake. He had caught the bird in flight.,

"Remember how you couldn't believe how I stepped back from the tie wall and let you finish it? You know why?"

I shook my head. "Always wondered."

"I was keeping so busy doing things to become independent and grown up that I was getting in the way of taking that step of actually accepting being grown up. I was searching. See?"

"Huh?"

She had a gentle, kind laugh.

"With you doing the hard work, I was able to take on the task of growing up. Of becoming a responsible woman. Taking a step away from being an impulsive adolescent." She tipped her face down, but looked at me from under her brow. "It didn't come all at once. And you were there to both help me take that step and complicate how meaningful that step would be. It led to other steps. To where I found new responsibilities. To practice being an adult. To finding powers. To become a total, whole person. To find here now. So there. There it is. You did the work of finishing my dream and that gave me the freedom to focus on what that means and what it meant for me in this little life of ours."

She gazed at me and smiled.

"I wouldn't have been able to do all this," she said, sweeping her hands to take in all around us. The twins. The resort. Ingie laughing with Ally on the porch. Luther, her father, wandering in his demented fog along the lakefront. Me, standing before her, broken beyond knowing what broken is.

"Without that step, I wouldn't have been prepared to accept all this. I had to be willing to find the powers. To see them. To call them. To accept them, like grace.

"Now you have to take the steps that will allow your heart to align with your will and your spirit. To find the strengths and powers that are yours to wield."

Omie looked up from his slate. He shed waves of unspoken kindness and hope unto my soul. He showed me the slate. On it, a man, long, like me, fought a fish from a canoe.

"So pack up," Omie said.

∞

The sun arced straight through the noon hour and now hovered a bit before mid-afternoon. I dipped my hand in the cool lake and drew a drink, then another. Father Jack lay spread eagle in the camp. I wondered if he hadn't had a heart attack, but then saw him swat at a bug. Just napping.

My reel whistled as line spun off the spool. Kerplunk!

I wondered, *what am I doing?*

The crank of my reel stopped abruptly and the tip of my pole bent dramatically toward the surface and held. Nothing moved. I pulled on the crank and lifted my pole, but the line held. Only the canoe stirred as it drifted toward where the line poked into the surface. Snag, I reckoned. I reeled slowly over the place where the shiny spoon got hung up in the log and rocks below. After a moment, though, the line moved slowly away, then stopped again. Current? Didn't seem likely. By the time I gathered as much line as I could, I was in talking distance from camp.

"On to something?" Jack was up, watching my struggles.

"Snagged, I think."

"Looks like a log," he ventured. "Maybe a big old Northern log."

"Dunno. Hasn't moved much."

He watched.

I positioned the canoe directly above the snag, but the line pulled again in a direction parallel the shoreline.

"Your snag is swimming," he deadpanned.

He was right. The line moved away from the canoe, taut, wobbling as the fish swam. It pulled the canoe like a sleigh on ice. I let off a couple turns on the drag until the reel chattered. Slowly, I cranked the reel. The fish continued its course. It had pulled half way back to camp when I saw its dark speckled, heavy shape emerge from the waters below. It caught sight of me as well; line peeled from the spool and the reel screamed against the drag. The fish dove.

Jack craned his neck to see through reflections on the surface. "Can you see it?"

"No," I gasped, clinging to the rod's cork handle while scrambling to let off more drag. The fish slowed, and I drew in more line until it pointed

59

straight into the water below the canoe. Again, the fish started swimming. Jack stood watch. My hands gripped the rod as though it was my lifeline.

I reeled the fish up again as it swam until it reached a point where once again it dove to the depths. It continued its course until I was no more than a short pass to the flats from where Jack stood on the landing.

"It's bringing you home to camp," he chuckled. His eyes were wide as he watched me struggle with the reel. I cranked, and again the fish rose in the water. This time, between the canoe and the landing, the heavy, dark body of the Northern floated near to the surface, exposing its length and girth. It looked like a torpedo.

"Oh, my!" Jack grinned. The master of understatement laughed at his own brevity.

As if overhearing Jack, the fish again dove. The line caught my palm and burned; I gripped the rod with all the strength of my arms and hands.

"So tell me," Jack said quietly. "What exactly are you going to do with this beast when—if— you land it? You expect to eat it?"

I glanced up. His face beamed as if he was witnessing a miracle.

"Get my daredevil back."

His eyebrows arched, and the fish ceased its pull. Slowly, carefully, I tightened the drag and reeled in line.

The sun dropped three quarters down to the tops of the pines as the serpent lazily lifted off the bottoms to the pull of my line, then forcefully dove again to the security of the depths. Jack, after a while, set up on a rock.

"Want me to take your picture?" he asked.

I shot him a look of disbelief. And then I thought about it.

"Sure. My camera is in the right pocket of my pack."

"Yep." He gathered my pack from next to the campfire and dragged it down to his perch on the rocks. In a moment, I glanced up and saw him fumbling with the camera, setting the exposure. I turned my attention back to the fish

It was tiring. When it dove, it was not as emphatic as when it first surfaced and fled. I worked it up part way several times, then let it sink back to the deep. My forearms were tight as cables, and my hands sometimes tweaked toward cramping, but I worked the reel slowly. The Northern ceased pulling. We had moved more than a hundred yards from where I first hooked into it. Jack sat fifteen yards off the bow as he watched from shore. The fish had indeed brought me home.

I cranked line slowly and gently lifted it toward top water, and it didn't fight back. I pulled it to the surface. It floated alongside the cedar strips of my canoe, darker in color, almost black, but complementing the wood tones with greens and browns scales and layers of light, intensely yellow spots stacked in rows from snoot to tail. It was an armor plated, gnarled beast, and its bright, lively eyes took the measure of me and my vessel. I held the tip of the rod up and the line snug as I inspected the fish.

"You've hooked a dinosaur," Jack called.

The width of its head made the blade of my paddle look narrow. It bumped along the side of the canoe, and I could feel its mass through the boards. It looked tired and lazy, and it rolled slightly, as if to level it's eye and get a better look at me. The sun lit its scales. Its tail floated in a fan that spanned wider than my spread fingers. Its gills pumped water steadily and deeply.

My daredevil had set prongs of its treble hook through both the top and bottom lip of the beast, right under the fish's gaping nostril. It couldn't open its mouth with the lure set as it was, which was good for me in that it lessened the chance that I'd be raked by its needle sharp teeth. But it meant that I couldn't let this fish escape without pulling those hooks from the cartilage about its mouth.

I heard the shutter click and glanced up to see Jack concentrating on the image he saw through the lens. He looked over the camera with a big grin, which I saw gasp to a circle of surprise as he watched the fish rise alongside my canoe, just inches from where I sat, lifting its armored head and arching its long, muscled back to muster its strength for yet another dive. I had let the distraction lead me from my focus. The monster on my line gained a sliver of advantage.

The drag, still set hard on the line, tugged the tip of my rod in a complete arc. I reflexively pulled up on the rod as the fish dove. The opposing forces worked only on the canoe, which spun like a roller on the surface of the lake. In a flash, I was under water, working my reel to loosen the drag but holding tight on the rod as line dished out from the spool. I kicked to reach the surface, and gasped sweet air when I broke above the surface. The unmanned canoe drifted helplessly away, and it was clear that my best bet was shore. Keeping the pole tip up and carefully letting line out as I kept tension on the fish, I frog-legged toward Jack, who was wading out to help. He grabbed my shoulders as I reached the shallows and struggled for my feet. Once I was upright, he pulled off his shirt and threw it on the boulders at shore. Then he dove in and swam to the abandon canoe.

I worked my Northern in toward the landing. Before, it was tired. It's last dive had spent its reserves. It was exhausted. In a few moment, I had it reeled in to the shallows at my feet. Jack secured the canoe and joined me. The beast lay on its side on the gravel, its gills heaving and pumping lake as it gasped water for oxygen.

"We have to rescue this venerable one," Jack said. He gripped the fish in front of its tail and tipped it upright. Then he slowly pushed it back and forth, helping move water through its gaping gills.

I fetched my tackle kit and pulled out my pliers. I set to work on the daredevil.

"Did you ever consider cutting bait on this fellow?" Jack teased.

I chuckled. "Not really. I was just worried about losing my lure." I worked one hook from the treble out of the stiff cartilage of the fish's lower lip. With the one hook dislodged, the hook piercing the upper lip slid easily from its hold. I gave a note of thanks to Luther and his habit of filing off the barbs. "I mean, I thought it was caught up on the bottom, until the bottom started moving. And then, when I finally got a look at it, I realized that daredevil had its lips clamped. It wouldn't have been able to eat. Couldn't let that happen."

Jack grinned. "Where did you ever get such a big heart?"

I felt a blush creep up my neck. "Lynn, I reckon."

Jack smirked. "I figured it was your being David's twin. He was all heart.

I nodded. Yeah. All heart. David. My twin.

He worked the fish while I stirred the last of the embers in the fire pit and kindled a blaze. The sun had dipped behind the tips of the trees on the far shore, and the air would cool soon. I stripped down, found dry cloths and went to the lake to help with the fish. I saw my camera on a rock and grabbed it. Focusing on Jack resuscitating the fish, I snapped a couple of shots.

"I think he's going to make it," Jack said. He balanced it upright, then let loose of the tail. The fish hovered above the gravel, listing slightly. Jack clasped it again and continued resuscitating it with gentle pulls and pushes.

"I think it's got you trained. You're its personal masseur now."

Jack snorted. An impish glint shot from his eyes. He addressed the pike, "I baptize you in the name…" His mutters faded into our howling guffaws.

"Have you always been a fisherman? Where did you learn to be a fish lifeguard?"

"Luther taught me."

Luther!

"I didn't know much at all about fishing. Or canoeing, for that matter. Lynn wouldn't let me out on my vision quest until she felt like I had half a chance of surviving. She had Luther teach me."

"You got to be kidding!"

He let the fish free again, stood up stiffly, and gave me a look of affirmation.

"Yep. Luther taught me everything I know about survival here in the Boundary Waters. He's a good teacher. He knows a lot. And he repeats what he knows over and over and over…"

We laughed. The fish dallied at our feet. Jack kicked at it, but it lingered. Finally, with a languid flip of tail, it swam toward the depths of the lake. It stopped after a few feet, checked its balance, and swung its heavy, deep body around, pointing its snout toward us, then gliding into the depths.

∞

Splashes of golden red from the blaze painting our faces, we sat in Father Jack's favorite campsite on our last night, working our fish story over and again. Then, as the flames settled, we fell still.

In a bit, we talked.

He wondered how in the arc of time in which he had come to know David, that I, his twin, had always been away.

I tossed another pinecone into the embers.

"Families get broken up", I said.

He considered, studying the campfire. Then, his eyes shifted up. Our nods met in agreement.

"Did your family break up?" I asked.

He glanced over the flashes of cone fire flame. His lips pursed. His eyebrow raised.

"You asking my confession again?"

I shrugged.

"No. Ok. Simply curious. Yes. Like, what was David like as a brother?" Jack wondered.

My turn to reflect.

"David was like the sunrise. Always, a fine sunrise. He lived early, and he lived with intensity. He burned hot his every moment. He projected an aura that was pure and brilliant, but was not meant to last long."

I paused. He waited.

"David was the sunset."

He looked deep into the embers.

"He was focused." I glanced over. Jack sat upright. His eyes held a keen light reflecting from the flames, and he turned them on me. He demanded more.

But there really wasn't a lot more to David. I shrugged.

"He mastered his moments."

I stoked the embers as he pondered that. The base was hot; flames feathered up in fluid braids of heat that lifted from the dried wood.

"Was he ever not focused?" Jack asked.

"Oh, yeah." I bobbed my head as memories caromed around my brain. David could lose it over a fresh heifer. Or new snow in the morning. I knew him well when he was delightfully unhinged: When he was with Jannie. He was whole then, and he walked in peace with the one he loved. He remained always responsible. He kept us going in the house. Me. Mom. And his farming. He had the cattle and all. But his mind was like a reflection of an August cloud shining off Crab Lake's mirror-smooth surface.

"With Jannie," I grinned. "He came undone over Jannie."

"Yes," Jack smiled. "He did."

"And in Nam," I added, "and in Germany. Totally different David. Still kind. Still fascinated throughout his every waking moment. And with Eva. David found love with Eva. And laughter. Someone he could talk to."

I grinned.

"He was totally oblivious of any possible distraction. The two of them melded their souls."

Jack sat with a dreamlike smile. The notion of David at peace and in love again brought warmth to the priest's kind soul.

Time lingered. The moon dipped below the trees to the west.

"David taught me how to love." I said, looking up from the fire to study his meditative expression. "He taught me not to be angry."

"That's significant."

I chuckled. Significant. Jack's understatement of the day. Significant.

"He taught me to believe."

He shifted. Bending deep from his waist, he leaned his torso low to the ground. His arms and shoulders stretched in a wide ark to the left of the fire where he reached for branches and split wood. He stoked the flames, building a teepee with the fuel. The fire staged a small roar with the wood he stacked in a pyramid.

"To believe. To have faith," he murmured. "And what was that all about? Belief in what?"

I heard my voice say words that came from deep within, but sounded far away. Campfire truths. Thoughts that I had not put to words before. Ideas of how things were, things are, that I had lived by but not identified before. I spoke as if hypnotized, and listened to my heart spill its version of that which carries life across all the instants that rack up in time.

"He showed me how we were one. That no matter how different we were, he and I, we were of the same blood. Of the same family. Of different gifts, different paths, different demands. But the same. That we were both young tigers needed taming. That we were family."

I thought of our family. Of Mother, and felt a deep stirring of old hidden anger. Of her insanity. Of her absence in the institution. Of how my brother covered for her, compensated for the void caused by her craziness.

I thought of Paddy, who was a father to me and David alike.

I thought of how our numbers seemed to grow by accumulating other souls meandering in the same realm in which we tred. Gabriel. Jannie. Jack.

He shot a glance toward me and said, "You sound like David. Like you think like David thinks."

I took that observation and turned over and around like Jack poking at the embers in the fire ring.

"Makes sense," I allowed. "I know two things well. Football, which I don't think about anymore. Much anyway. And Davey's mind. The things David taught me. Gave me. Any thought I have of any value at all probably came at me from Davey's point of view in the first place. And half of all that Davey thought about probably came from you."

He snorted. "We did go round about it. We looked at all his wild ideas, and mine I suppose, from every angle we could think of."

He gazed into the embers for quite a spell, then looked up and asked, "Is David's being gone going to change that notion of oneness?"

I shrugged. Did it matter? I didn't think so. David was gone before I ever knew he had died. But he remained with me. His presence overshadowed his absence. Oneness. It is something that can't be undone. One cannot parse eternity. Oneness is the whole, regardless of how it is displayed. I tossed more wood on the embers.

"As long as I am, I know that David is as well," I said. "I'm grieving him. I miss him terribly. But in the things he shared with me, and the words and thoughts of his letters. I hear his voice. I feel his presence. He is still. He is one with Oneness. And I guess that means I too am one with Oneness, even if I am not as aware of that state of being as he was ." The flames burned strong.

Jack poked the embers. "Eternity, eh? Oneness. That from which all that is can never not be." A silly grin spread across his hairy countenance.

Laughing, I nodded. He nailed it.

I stood, stretched, and picked my way across the rocks of the campsite to the brush. The sky had darkened after the moon set, but the milky way stood boldly in contrast to the blue black veil of the universe beyond.

"Did Davey ever tell you about when he drowned? When we were kids and the beaver dam calamity?"

He nodded.

"Yeah. He told me all about it. We discussed that at length."

"Did he tell you about flying around, above, and all that?"

Jack studied my face. He nodded. I felt the lines of tension that the memory of David nearly drowning brought to my heart. It always did.

"I was so scared," I muttered. "I thought he was dead."

"He may well have been. You brought him back." He rubbed the stubble on his chin and grinned. "Did he tell you about yelling down at you from above?"

I startled. "No. Not yelling. Being there. Above. Watching. What do you mean?"

"If he told you about seeing from above, you have an idea of where his soul was as he watched you look for him in the creek. He told me he felt himself hollering at you. 'Look in the dam, Pat! In the dam!' He said he wanted to push his friend, the little guy who pointed at him, right in the water to show you where he was. But he couldn't do it. So he hollered and yelled, but you couldn't hear him. You know David. He could tell it so that you'd cry laughing."

I smiled. "He always had a way of telling me what I needed to do. I must have heard him somehow." I shook my head. Then the familiar old feeling of nearly losing my brother smothered me with a sense of fear. In a moment, it lifted.

"You know, when I couldn't find him, I felt the greatest panic of my life. The greatest loss. It was so clear to me; I was terrified that I'd be left alone. Without him. It was just impossible.

"And then, when he died in Nam, I didn't have a clue. I felt him with me all along. As I left Germany. As I hiked the trail. Even now. I feel no loss."

He kept his eyes upon me; I felt like he looked through me.

"So that's why Lynn sent me out here with you, I guess. She thinks I need to reconcile the loss of my brother with grief," I looked back into the embers. "I don't feel the need to grieve. I don't miss Davey. He's with me. Always."

Jack nodded, a simple loving expression. Always in contrast within himself, his wild, wind-blown mane erupting like an explosion from his scalp, wrapping around the deeply tanned skin surrounding his blazon eyes, yet his expression glowed like the smiling face of a cherub.

"You are blessed."

Nodding, I accepted his thought.

"It's not so with me," he went on.

"How so?" I asked.

"David was like a beacon of light in my life. A guidepost. He showed me the way more often than I ever helped him. He told me where I stood in this life by the questions he asked, the meaning he sought. He dwelled upon the questions of life that mattered. He was the innocence of youth.

Pure innocent wonder. He directed our thoughts to the essence of meaning. Of the value of our human conditions. Of the why of it all."

We sat, mulling his point.

"What did that do for you?" I asked.

"It taught be to feel being alive. Thinking. Understanding through feeling in my heart. In my gut. Trusting. Of loving. Feeling love."

He tossed his shortened, burning stick into the embers. It blazed in flame. When the flame dwindled, he looked over the embers and found my gaze.

"I felt his loss. I felt it even before he was killed," Jack admitted, his voice struggling to remain even. "When I said goodbye to him for the last time in Japan, I knew with certainty that he would not come home. I was absolutely aware of it. It was inevitable."

"Did he feel the same way?"

Jack studied his hands in the dying light of the falling flames of our campfire.

"I don't know. I don't think so. I think he had hope."

"Hope can be so misleading," I shrugged. "So empty. You gotta have a measure of wisdom to be able to harness the power of hope. I was kinda young to have much in the line of wisdom when David and I lived together. He steered me back on track when I let hope get the best of me, looking for things that were not going to be."

Jack's face reflected his wounds.

"I couldn't even look at him as I drove away when we parted. It was too hard. He was on my mind and in my heart every moment of every day. I, too, hoped. Yes, you are right. There is nothing as empty as groundless hope.

"I knew he'd died, even before I heard from Rose. And I guilted over it," Jack said. "I knew it to the moment, I think. Or very soon after. I think he did a fly by, sort of. I think he visited me as he hovered above us all again. I knew exactly when that was. Easter morning. He came to me. He was there, vividly, telling me it was all right. Not to fear. And it was. From that very moment, I no longer worried. No longer carried the heavy burden of empty hope. It freed me, really. David freed me to think beyond the past and before the future. He set me loose to look at the moment. He did that so very often. I think about it now. I understand it more and more. It was his gift to me."

The embers died and we sat in the light of the stars.

"His was insight into the eternity that the world doesn't acknowledge," he added "Which is why I have such a difficult time doing a daily routine. The world and me, we are out of step. And I guilt over it."

"David always wrote about how your words of advice gave him perspective and direction. He wrote about you in most every letter," I said. I felt a smile forming on my face. "David taught me so much about what is real, what is of value. I think if I have any wisdom at all, it is because David taught me what the value of wisdom is. His letters. He made me think and learn about what is most important. What this opportunity of life means for each of us."

"He taught you well," Jack said. "You learned well."

"His letters," I said. "He wrote like every word counted."

Jack nodded.

The blaze stuttered, then died, leaving only red embers glowing. Jack sighed deeply, and his shoulders slumped.

"I don't know how life can be the same with him gone. Life, to me, was defined by the questions and thoughts that David posed to me."

What was Jack telling me? Was I missing something that was going to catch up with me later? I didn't feel that the world was missing David. Yes, he died. He was dead. He no longer lived.

But he was with me always. Every moment. He lived within me.

Jack straightened his shoulders and looked up into the sky. I could see in the starlight the reflection of tracks of tears glisten upon his cheeks before running into his beard.

"I think he gave me a gift of freedom," Jack murmured. "I think by letting him die in my heart, I gave him freedom of his own."

"He will live always," I said. "In my mind, anyway. In my heart."

Jack turned his kind gaze upon me.

"He will show you how to let him die," he said softly. "He will do so to give you freedom. When you are ready to be free."

∞

Jack gazed into the fire.

I knew what we were to do. I shoved loose gear into my pack and shuttled things down to the canoe. Within the hour, we doused the fire and struck camp.

We paddled quietly. The moon lit the lake as only the moon can, and its streams of silver blue rays highlighted the shoreline trees until we spotted a breach that marked the portage to Burntside. Our work was cut out on the portage. The going was slow with the packs as we stepped carefully on the moonlit trail. We opted to leave the canoe for a second trip.

By the time we traveled the portage across and back and across again, the eastern sky hinted a new dawn. We paddled across the mirror surface of Burntside, meandering between islands, wondering how close we were to the route we needed to follow. By dawn, we saw our bay. We paddled toward the resort. As we cleared the point, I saw her on the bench at the end of the pier. Lynn. Hot coffee steamed from cups beside her. She was expecting us.

∞

After lunch, Lynn took my hand and led me out to the dock where we looked out over the lake. We sat on the dock watching ripples carry mid afternoon light across the surface of Burntside.

"What do you miss?"

I felt my brow furrow. *What did she mean?*

She read my thoughts. "Your life is so different now, isn't it? What was it like? Football Do you miss football?"

I shrugged.

"What do you miss about it?"she asked.

A loon soared as it entered the bay. Fast. Level. Banking to break surface water. Tilting up, slowing, touching down at the very end of an arc of descent along the far bank, then turning toward the center where it skimmed the lake, dragging paddles that lay a sleek silver streak across the surface.

I looked into my palms. *Life. In football. All embracing.* I tipped my head and met her eyes.

"I loved it all." I nodded. "All of it. I even loved the least beast parts of it. Practicing. Training. I liked the training. No contact."

"What were the best parts of it?"

I mulled. "Team. It can be best. Some teams just embrace essence. Some teams have chemistry. The spirit." I rocked my head back on my neck, and rolled it. We smirked over crunching crackles as my head smoothly circled my spine. "And the game. Playing the game. The smell of grass and earth. Sweat. Dust. The contact."

The loon eyed us as he paddled past the pier and entered the shallows over the rocks that formed the bank.

"Sometime in practice, when we gelled, as a team, we moved as one. Like each of us would do precisely all we physically could, in precisely the fastest burst of all out energy we could muster. Each play, in practice or in game time, when we executed a play, like we were all in a zone, together. It was like a ballet. Our timing was perfect. And the only thing that could bust up our play was the zone our foes played in.

"Our zone had to be more perfect than their zone. Sometimes it was." I leveled my gaze toward her. "Lots of times it was. Like magic."

I considered a moment. "Some teams don't have synergy. It can be like total harmony, if it's there. It can be awkward and clumsy, if a team doesn't have it. Frustrating.

69

I looked at her. She was absorbed.

I shrugged.

She nodded. "Magic. The perfect flow of chemistry and physics in the Universe."

I returned her nod.

A second loon splashed from the brush and rocks along the shoreline; it joined its partner for a short swim into the bay.

"There's a nest under those shrubs," Lynn said.

My eyes trained on the spot the second loon had vacated. Nothing noticeable.

"Must be important for a twin. Having team mates."

"Is to me. But I don't miss football. Football was my life, and I had it and loved it. But life goes on. I don't miss it now."

The loon approached the rocks, waddled a few step, and disappeared into the swaths of shadows cutting into the afternoon sun light.

∞

"How about David. How do you feel about David?"

My lips tightened and pursed. I sighed.

"It's like he's still with me. A lot of times. Away, but with me." I wiggled around. The cedar dock bench was suddenly hard and unforgiving. I stood and stepped to the edge, looking down into the clear, calm water.

She waited.

"Sometimes I get angry. Sometimes I can see no reason for why he felt he had to go fight in a war. We talked about it. I asked him once if he thought he could actually kill a man."

One of the loons dove and was under for a long time. The other remained on their nest. I scanned the surface, but the diving partner didn't surface anywhere nearby.

She continued to wait. She was giving me time to figure it out.

"I told him I could kill someone, if I had to," I said. She raised her eyebrows and tilted her head. "I did. Say that. I wanted him to know I understood what he was getting into.

"He didn't believe me. I could tell. He didn't say so, but by the way he answered, he knew what I was saying. What I was trying to do.

I got up and paced the dock. I felt a surge of agitation fueling angst.

"Then, when I got his letters while he was in training, and later in Nam, I could hear in his words as he began to doubt his own convictions. He knew—we both knew he could kill others. Once he wrote about a guy he killed. It was like he was in the process of realizing the essence of the life he had taken. The years of living and experiencing and loving that he snuffed right out of that guy. It was stark. He understood the measure of his act when he was in war. It made him sad. That is when he understood the part of him that really didn't want to kill someone. It wasn't like when he sent his steers to market. There was something good about that act. Something that benefited others, fed others, helped them live. But in Nam, he didn't see it as a sacrifice of good will. "

I was looking deep into Lynn's eyes. She held me bound to that contact.

"He wrote me that he was glad he had me as a twin because it helped him find within himself that element that really doesn't want to kill. He knew me better than I did. It makes me feel both joy and pain that he knew that. I just get angry that he was in that situation to begin with. To go to war."

Lynn's gaze was pure empathy. Her love for me flowed from her eyes as though she saw beyond me, into me, and was fueled by what she saw. Her eyes blazed.

"Yes, I miss him. Like nothing I ever imagined, even having been apart from him so many years," I tried to explain. "I miss him, and I feel he is still with me. There is part of him that only I could know, and he lives within that awareness."

I took my seat beside her on the cedar bench. She slipped her hand into mine. We looked out over the glistening ripples.

Our silence was like a prayer.

# Chapter 13

# Wistful Mist

In the morning, I got back in stride with the Luther watch. Without a bite of breakfast, he strode out of the Lodge, strong and full of intent. By the end of the driveway, he hesitated. I wondered if the fog in his mind had started to congeal.

He rambled along north on the Echo Trail for a ways before abruptly stopping. He looked left into the woods, then across the road toward the lowland marsh. He was lost. I held back, giving him time to find his bearings. He was stuck.

I sauntered up alongside him, scuffling my boots and huffing as if I was winded. He didn't turn his head, if he heard me. His face was twisted, brow furrowed, eyes pained.

"I'm looking for the path to Rosalyn's point," I said "Can't seem to find it. Would you know where the turn off to the point is?"

He thought a moment, his eyes scanning the tree line alongside the Echo Trail. The road climbed a long hillside heading north before turning easterly at the crest.

"It's there," he pointed. "Come along. I think I can show you."

He cast a glance toward me, but I saw no recognition. He avoided eye contact; he knew he was vulnerable. I let it ride. It was good enough that he thought he knew where the path came out on the road. If not, I'd remind him when we got there.

"Go to the point often?" he asked as we strolled.

"A few times."

He glanced over.

"I go there."

I waited, then said, "It's a nice place."

We walked in silence a quarter mile to the path. He looked in under the canopy. The grass along the edges of the bare earth path was fine and dry. He stepped in.

"This way," he affirmed. I followed.

When we settled on our sitting boulders, we looked out over Burntside. I saw the shadow hover over the abyss sinking before him.

"It's slippin' away."

"It always does," I tried to reassure him.

He shot me a searing glare.

"Why?"

I didn't know. It was bottomless, and I watched as he fell into it.

"She was like a meteor," he muttered after a quiet spell.

"Do you think she always will be, like, somewhere? Like, maybe, a comet? Or a meteor? Just somewhere else than here?" I muddled.

He considered it. Slowly, he touched his finger to point above his eye. He left it there.

"My fear is that sometime, maybe soon, she won't be. At all."

"Are you missing her?"

He glanced up. "Always. Sometimes, though, it is like she is here. She is so vitally brilliant it is like the moment grows it's own shadow."

We pondered.

"She brought me everything. She found me, you know. Magic, she was. I didn't find her. I was too blind. Stupid."

"Women are always smarter. They're first. Ahead of us. Then they are there for you. Like your daughter."

Luther startled. He looked up, searching my face.

"Lynn. My Lynn. Your daughter."

His face softened. "She was like her mother, you know."

"How so?"

He tilted his head. "Everything. Her hair. Her eyes. Her voice. Just the way they moved. It was alike." He looked into my eyes, bobbing his head. "They were alike. Gentle. Powerful. Magic, like her mother. She possessed special powers from the day she was born. It frightened me, her powers."

"Why were you so hard on her?"

"Selfish." He twisted the knot, tugging and testing, "Seems like one can't get tired of selfish too soon. It has such diminishing returns. But it's hard to shake selfish. It's like alcohol. If it holds you, you're done. And that's all it is, selfishness. It's just holding on to yourself more than all else. I was selfish."

That reminded me of something Jack had said. I tried to repeat it for Luther.

"Kind of a limiting act of will. You'd think you'd yearn for the satisfying quenching of thirst if you just looked outward toward all that is with us here in this moment. Drink of the gift of others."

"Love."

"Yeah." And then I watched as he fell deep into the fog, mired in the cauldrons of decay within his mind.

"The meteors," he said. "They fly by us all the time. Right now. They always do. They are so fast you sometimes miss them. Sometimes. And then they see like no others."

I listened as his gibberish cycled and recycled.

"Come on," I gathered him up. Then I led him home.

As he shuffled along beside me, the absence of his self-awareness struck me. It was vivid. He was there, but he was not.

I thought of my past self. The way I was. What I had lost and was no more. The focus and cognition of my being. I, the jock. The athlete who spent all my time projecting the aura of a sports icon riding the crest of my own personal 15 minutes of fame, like body surfing the waves along the shores of Lake Michigan. Seeking the endless wave, aware that the hope of an unending gliding surge of power harnessed within the rolling swells of water was vain. All waves inevitably crashed upon the sand or rocks of shoreline. In the dunes, there was immense joy to feel the pummeling curl of breaking waves thundering over me as they rushed me over the sand-bars and shallows into the beach. The reflex was to jump up and throw myself into the backwash of current rushing back into the depths so to gain position for yet another ride atop newly forming waves. Placing my-self into the danger of the water's sweeping power for the thrill that surged waves of adrenalin throughout my body.

On the football field, those surges of the adrenalin were stronger yet, many times so, than the playful crests of rolling Michigan waves. That crashing finale on the gridiron, for me, was more brutal and life changing than any of the spectacular rolling crests of water that spit me out on the sandy shoreline of the dunes. My last play on the altar of the Game of Football left me crumpled, a body suddenly tossed from the divinity of sports and dumped into the common ground of mortals, reborn in a hum-ble, simple construct of human identity. Kind of like Luther, in a way. A life shed of its base identity. Free, in a sense, of the postures and forms of the self recognition that built upon itself moment by moment, day by day, throughout life. I was left with that my twin had given me; I gave thanks for the values, wisdom and love that my brother focused on me as he taught me how to live beyond the tethers of my sports.

Luther tried hard to hang on to shreds of self recognition that revisited whenever the shadows and fogs lifted from his awareness. Luther was a lost soul. His persona dissolved before his inner eye.

Me? Unlike Luther, who was left with a body hollow of the identity which it housed for over 70 years, my sports identity was stripped from my body in an instant, leaving me with self recognition that could heal and grow again. A gift, in a sense. A life freed by the need to adapt to new di-rections, new chances for being. I was blessed, I suppose. That self-aware-ness that I shed like the skin of a snake in the grass of the gridiron left me with a promise of new opportunity for new life.

I glanced at Luther as he shuffled along beside me. He walked in loss.

I felt his loss, and embraced gratitude for life with new horizons. My loss was my gain.

# Chapter 14

# Dialing in to Omie

Omie awaited our return. He often did. When his grandfather stayed away for longer than expected, he cast glances again and again out the screen door and down the driveway.

As I brought his grandfather back to the lodge, Omie asked, "Where've you been?"

Luther remained blank.

"To the point," I responded when the lull stretched too long. "We had a good sit on Grandpa's favorite boulder. You know the one."

"Yep." He watched his grandfather shuffle through the dining room. "I've been there, too."

"Maybe you can hike out there with us next time?" I offered. He turned his face down and hid his eyes.

"Quite a hike today," Lynn said, coming in from Ingie's porch. "Are you hungry, Dad?"

Luther ambled by her. He stopped his shuffle, glanced slowly into the darkened hallway toward the bedrooms. He looked back toward the sunset through the porch screens.

"He nibbled his sandwich late," I said. "And part of an apple. He might not be hungry yet."

"Are you tired, Dad?" She put her hand above his elbow. He turned toward her, wincing. He was uncertain…

"Let's get you cleaned up and ready for bed," she suggested. "Maybe you'd like a bed lunch then before you sleep." She led him, glancing back to me as they entered the darkness of the hallway.

Omie looked up, his little hand offering a drawing. "This is for you."

"Thanks, Om." I examined his art. For a little guy not yet five years old, his drawings were remarkable. He innately captured dimension and depth perception. A loon swimming in the distance was smaller than the paddlers navigating their canoe toward the shoreline. His sun images retained scale against the shorelines and ridges beyond the lakes that were the basis of his artwork. Tucked in among the tall pines along the shore was a furry, large canine shaped animal.

"Wow! This is terrific, Om. This sunset is gorgeous! Is this a dog?"

"Wolf," he said. Omie wasn't one to beam happiness or pride. His face glowed gratitude and humility. His art was based on what he saw; he could draw on paper what Lynn or I might put on film. His hand was measured in the force he put on his chalk or pencils. Lynn saw his talent early, when he was little more than a toddler. While he often used the thick wax crayons that Ally shared with him as they played together, when he worked alone he preferred the colored pencils that his mother gave him. Sometimes, on slate, he turned to charcoal. He loved chalk on slate. His eye for detail was remarkable, regardless of his age.

"Om, help me here," I asked. "What is this?" I pointed toward a pair of streaking lines arching gently above the skyline of the ridge across the lake.

His little finger pinpointed a fleck in the sky. "It's a jet. It was far away."

"Oh, I see. I thought maybe it was a shooting star."

His dark brow scrunched together like a caterpillar.

"A meteor? Grandpa's been telling you about meteors flying around all the time, like in daytime, too. You can't see them in daytime. But you can see jets."

"Jets, eh? I wonder where it was going?"

He took back the picture and held it up to align it against the background of the lake and shoreline across the bay. "That way," he said, pointing south.

"Oh. Maybe it was heading to the Twin Cities."

"Yeah."

"What if it was heading the other way? North? Where do you suppose that jet was flying then?"

Omie met my eye. It was a question that had no bearing.

"Someplace else."

"Oh. Makes sense."

"Like birds. They fly all over. They fly someplace else, too." He glanced out the window toward the bird feeder. A hairy woodpecker chased away a pair of cranky jays and hung upside down on the wire suet feeder. It watched us from its perch outside.

"Windows are for birds to look in," Omie said.

"I suppose they are," I replied, running my fingers through his silky hair.

*Funny, his way of thinking,* I thought. *So fresh. So open. Free.*

# Chapter 15

# Fire ring chats:

# Luther's lament

The flames flickered out above a bed of embers still hot, but cooling to a deep cherry red. I gathered an armload of birch logs to stoke the fire. Twilight dimmed in the crystal heavens; stars sparkled as one-by-one they punctuated the deepening sky.

"Time for bed, kiddos," Lynn announced. The twins stirred, nearly asleep in the golden hue around the fire ring. Slowly, they ambled toward the lodge.

As Lynn led the twins to their beds, I eavesdropped on the conversation between Jack and her father.

Red rays of firelight colored Jack's face as he studied the fishline he worked in his fingers, practicing the knots that Luther had taught him to tie. His busy focus calmed Luther, who struggled with the burdens of his fading past. As he fumbled the braided line, Jack led Luther through his thoughts around the fire ring.

"…It's about how things happen. Could you ever have guessed that things would work out the way they have?" Jack asked.

Luther wagged his head. "Sometimes I try to understand. I almost picture …it." He paused. "What happened? So much pain." He met my eyes, shaking his head slowly back and forth. "So much anger. I almost know what it was. I can almost feel it. It's behind this…fog. But what's left of it is like nothing. Like vapors of gray." He handed Jack a slip of rope. "It's the agony of knowing that I can't remember anymore. Is there going to be none of me here? That's pain. The biggest pain."

He stuck a marshmallow on a fork and turned it above the flames. It caught flame, then burned to a blackened crisp. "I'm so afraid that there will be no me left to be me."

"In my best moments, I am aware that I am living all in one moment," Jack said. "Now. And I see now in one dimension" His words offered solace. "I see now without the feeling of all the old experiences. All the history. The pain. The knowledge of those events, those happenings that brought me to this moment. I don't embrace those moments. Not in this instant. Not now. What happened in the past releases me. Frees me to determine who I am now."

Luther's eyes wandered further into the twilight. He saw the mist rising from the lake. He listened to loons. He melded into the moment. It captured him. The rest was lost to him. He shed it like layers of clothes. The

most recent layers shed easiest. He had no recall of what he had for breakfast. Or what yesterday was all about. Or last month. Or the years since he
worked. Why wasn't he still at work? How much time had been since he
worked? Where was work? What was work?

His loss was a burden, not a liberation.

"I lost it, didn't I?" he said.

"What?"

"Everything." He looked down. "I lost it."

Jack let him consider that moment. Then, bending to look into his face,
he beckoned him. "You still have work in life. Just different." He offered
him the lines. "Please. Teach me. I need to see it again. The blood knot."

Luther stared at the ends of the lines on his fingers.

Jack stirred the embers and stoked three split quarter rounds on the fire.
Within minutes, they blazed.

We watched the flames dwindle. Then the fire turned to coals. I added
another couple of logs.

Luther stirred. His fingers found the line ends. He tied the knot perfectly, and he held it in the light of the rising blaze.

"Now is where yester-moments end. It's where time happens. It is now.
Now is the universal moment of creation," Jack said. "Now is our gift. Our
moment of opportunity. It is when we choose to participate in creation. To
help mold creation's outcome." He looked for the twitch of a response in
Luther's expression, then glanced toward me.

"Right?"

∞

Lynn breathed deep, even breaths of sleep. I slipped my arms from
around her and tucked the covers over her shoulders. She slept on.

I was awake with a notion that my brother had planted in my mind several years before. Jack's philosophical bantering with Luther set me to
thinking about a letter David sent me. It haunted me, keeping me from
sleep. So I got up and rummaged through the stack of my treasured horde
of my brother's letters that I had hauled around throughout my travels.

The one I sought was from the summer of '65. He was home from
Madison and ranting about the craziness he lived in under the mentorship
of Rosie and Jack. I could hear Jack's words from the fire ring working in
David's musings:

*...If there is but one instant, one unique universal now, and everything in eternity is
connected and contained within that moment of now, then time is merely an indexing
device that physics imposes on our perception. A tool to aid us in keeping track of our
sequential observations as we slip and slide upon the warps that Einstein describes as
the bounds of physics captured in relativity. Wouldn't it be something if we could nego-*

He was writing of his thoughts about having shared life with Jannie. The love they shared. Love. Isn't love a fluid grace, a power, something that travels with us through time? Jannie had been dead for almost two years. I pondered that as I reread David's reflections. Love doesn't die with the seconds of a moment. It transverses instants. It permeates the now in memories. It fuels the now of creation. That's what David wrote about. It's what I saw with Jack and Luther this evening. It's what I know of Lynn.

I stashed David's letter and returned to bed. Lynn felt me lean into her and cuddled close. She felt me respond, and from her slumber she stirred. She kissed me, and her hand crossed my belly to where she found me aroused. She drew me over her and took me in.

"Be with me," she whispered. "Always."

# Chapter 16

# Ingie's PT

It troubled me to think I was adding to Lynn's burden by taking from her sleep to satisfy my desires.

"It goes two ways," she smiled. "I've been missing you, you know."

Her spirit fueled my goal of lightening her work load so that we'd have more time alone. Luther was one giant time sink. As were the twins.

And then there was Ingie.

Every morning, while Martha took on the twins and I tailed Luther, Lynn tended Ingie.

She stripped her from her soiled night clothing, bathed her, groomed her hair, dressed her, stretched her sister's stiffened, withered limbs, and cajoled her with humor and gratitude. She massaged Ingie's withered muscles with concoctions of oils and herbs that Martha showed her how to make. To hear the sisters work together was to listen to the songs of angels. One, a decidedly crude and profane angel.

"Gentle, precious bitch! I don't bend that fucking way!" Ingie cried as Lynn pulled sleeves on her lanky arms.

They would laugh, their tones low and private. As youths, they learned to live with the notion of being afterthoughts, late mistakes, unplanned. A burr in Luther's life plan. Together, they were a force that kept Ingie living a comfortable, limited life. They leaned upon each other for meaning as young girls; they thrived to their best ability as grown sisters who needed one another. Lynn provided Ingie with home life. She kept Ingie involved with family and children. She motivated Ingie to find meaning in the cage of her injured body. And Ingie gave Lynn purpose. A special purpose. A mission.

I looked for ways to assist. To intervene, where appropriate. To lift the burden of Ingie-care that could allow Lynn more time with our twins. More time with Luther. More time with me.

"You ought to help with her PT," Jack suggested. It was a notion he hinted at on our canoe trip. And again, with Lynn as we sat by the fire ring. He was right. I had experienced rehab myself in Boulder. I understood how it felt, and how to keep at it consistently. I didn't really know how to put a rehab program together, by any means. But watching Derek work Ingie through the process made it seem fundamental. I approached him about it after his second visit since my arrival.

"How much good is all this workout doing for Ingie," I asked as I carried his gear and walked with him to his van

He shot an appraising eye at me, questioning my motive for asking.

"I've been through PT for a neck injury," I explained.

"Tell me," he said.

I explained the series of ever expanding regiments of motions and exercises I worked though to restore strength and feeling in my arms and shoulders after the hit that left me face down on the playing field. I had to work through numbness. I fought through pain of muscles that were suddenly shut down and atrophied. It wasn't pleasant, but my recovery was pretty fast. I started rehab with a bruised spinal cord, sprained connective tissue and dormant muscles. Rehab was limited more by the neural healing than the rebuild of muscle and tendon. I was different than Ingie.

"I've been through it. But I was healthier to begin with. Do you think what you are doing for Ingie will gain ground? Will she get better?"

"We are scratching the surface with Ingie," he said. "Just to keep her alive. She could so easily regress quicker than we could react. For as infrequently as I can treat her, we won't gain much before some event, some catastrophic bed sore, some devastating infection sets in. She doesn't have the strength to survive that kind of challenge.

"Why? Do you think you can help?" he asked. "Lynn is doing a good job, holding her own. But if you can ramp up the program, Ingie could make much more progress. I can show you what's needed. Can you work with her?"

I nodded. "It's kind of what I was thinking. I mean, Lynn is doing her best with Ingie, but Lynn has a lot on her plate. But if I can do more, would it help? Would she make progress."

He looked toward the lodge. "Absolutely. Everything is additive. It's essential."

Derek changed his schedule so that he visited four times in the two remaining weeks of July. He put me through the program as much as Ingie.

It helped that Ingie revered Derek.

"Oh, you darling dick," she groaned as he worked her legs, one at a time, straightened and lifted them at right angles to her spine as she lay on her back. "You fucking prick! Why are you so wonderful to me?"

"Because you never complain, my darling," he teased her. "Breathe, bitch."

∞

As it turned out, stepping in to work with Ingie's recovery didn't give Lynn much of a break in her care for her sister. And Ingie asserted that she was not about to give up her time with Lynn and replace it with me.

"You can't take Lynn's place, fuzznuts. This is our fucking morning ritual, and it's all ours. Our own little pussy party," Ingie laughed.

"Yeah. I suppose," I countered. "But I think I'm going to step in after your little biscuit and tea breakfast and take over the physical part of your morning. Put you through a bit of gut hardening effort. What do you think?"

She turned her head aside, pointing her nose toward the ceiling.

"You are no fucking white-assed knight to me, bung hole. Do what you will, but if you get even a bit frisky, I'm gonna rip your nut sack off with my fingernails and feed it to the crayfish."

I was able to give Ingie more consistent treatment. And she did respond.

By the time Derek made his last special training visit, we knew the program. Again, I helped carry his gear as I walked him to his van.

"This is real good, Patrick. I'll show you more as she's ready, and you will see her make great strides," he said. Pausing after loading the gear, he looked out toward the lake. "You know, if Burntside was warm enough, we ought to get her in the water. Walking. Swimming. It would be great for her." He shook his head. "I don't think she could handle the cold water. Too risky."

I wondered. "How about a wet suit?"

He laughed. "I want to be around if you try and squeeze her into a wet suit. I can only imagine what she'd call you."

I chuckled. He was right. Fuzz bag was an endearment compared to what she would lay on me if I started pushing her limbs into the confines of a wet suit.

We shook hands and he drove off. He had me thinking, though. I did lots of water therapy in Boulder. It really helped.

# Chapter 17

# Ingie's Pool

As we bundled Ingie up for an evening around the fire ring, I shared Derek's idea about finding a way to get Ingie swimming. Lynn expressed interest. Ingie didn't.

"No fuckin' way. Too goddamned cold," she snapped. And she meant for it to be the end of the discussion.

With all of her deadweight, she was still light as a feather. The easiest way of getting her out to the lake was simply to carry her. As she rode high in my arms while we walked across the lawn to the lake front, she wore an an air of unapproachable celebrity. She was doing me a favor letting me carry her, and she had no ear available to listen to any more about the virtues of water therapy. Some time in the sun, and maybe a  campfire was all she envisioned.

"Maybe it's worth considering," Lynn cajoled, her arms full of pillows and wraps that we used to bolster Ingie and keep her warm enough later as the evening coolness rolled in off the lake.

Ingie raised her noble nose a hitch and chose not to respond.

"You always were the first in the water when you were younger," Lynn said. "You loved the lake."

Nothing. The nose pointed yet higher. She would have nothing of it.

Lynn stepped quickly forward to place Ingie's afghans and pillows on the lounge. I stepped around it, but instead of setting her in the warmth of the woven wrap, I kept walking right into the water. Ingie stiffened as she realized I was almost waist deep.

"The water's lovely," I assured her. "As warm as it gets."

"Don't you dare, ass fuzz," she hissed.

I lowered her quickly so that a she'd feel the drop toward the cool surface waters. She squealed softly, then turned to face me.

"Fish bait. Fucking fish bait."

I laughed, tipped her so that only her feet were threatened to get wet, and dipped her toes into the water.

She arched her back, only to submerge her legs to her knees.

"Son of a bitch! Get me out of here!"

"Toss her in!" Lynn suggested.

"Bitch sister! Don't give this asshole any ideas." She struggled not to laugh.

Dressed in her swimsuit, Ally ran across the strip of sand between the lawn and the shoreline. "Are we going swimming, Auntie Ingie?" Omie followed in his shorts and t-shirt. He stopped short of the waterline, but Ally raced in, spraying her Aunt and me both with splash from the lake.

"Aach! Ummm, fu'ummmm," Ingie gagged, trying her utmost not to curse at her niece.

Ally lost her balance as she ran through the water, slamming into me before plopping into the shallows, only to spray her Aunt with more ribbons of water.

Ingie turned her sharp glare at me and demanded, "Get me the fuck away from this lake."

Jack took in our play as he walked down from the cabin. "Patrick, is she ready for baptism?"

"Never more so," Lynn called.

Ingie moved her nose to within an inch of mine. "I'll feed your balls to the crayfish," she threatened.

I got wide eyed, smiled, and lifted my legs straight out in front of me. We splashed in, hitting off the sand bottom, and I could hear her profanity bubble through the water.

"Mother-blub-fucking cock-blub-sucker," she laughed as she broke surface. "I can't believe you goddamned dunked me, piss ant!'

The sun had warmed the shallows all afternoon and the water temp was pleasant. I made no move to lift her out.

She propped herself up on my half submerged body, gripping my t-shirt to keep from slipping under. I gently lifted her enough that she settled down.

"Not so bad, is it?"

"You dick."

"Hey? What's that? What's that warm water?"

"Piss on ya', bastard!"

"Oh, man."

Om stood his ground on the sandy beach, but Ally wanted to play.

"Come on, Auntie! Water fight!" She wound up and splashed a hearty spray of water, all of which missed Ingie but hit me directly in the face. Ally at first looked wide eyed, but then thought it even funnier that I was the target. She wound up and let me have it again.

Ingie relished the idea as well; she reached out and wound up, but her weakened arms didn't get much lift on the splash. So she grabbed me by both ears and pulled down with as much tenacity as she could muster!

I went under, but I brought her down with me. Again, she blurted her finest profanity through the bubbles of the lake.

We played for a few moments more. Then I scooped her up and lifted her out of the water. Interestingly, her body relaxed in my arms, and she rode more like a rag doll than the prim princess that sat haughty in my grip on the way down from the lodge.

Lynn met us at water's edge with a blanket for her soaking wet sister. I turned her like a baby as we wrapped her. Already she shivered from the cooler air. But the smile on her face revealed the pleasure she had from our play.

"Take me home, buttfucker," she commanded. "I'm wet."

"You know, you're about twice as heavy when you're all wet," I teased her. "And now we know you kinda like the lake, don't we?"

"Up your ass."

"Come on," Lynn said. "Let's get you dried and changed before you're chilled. Witch sister."

"Bitch sister."

As we headed to the lodge, Jack set kindling in the fire ring.

"I'll have it roaring by the time you bring Princess Profanity back for the evening."

∞

Ingie sat regally upon her pillows, snuggled in sleeping bags. She beamed, and her smiling face reflected the golden hues of the blazing fire.

"So, now we know we can get her wet and she really won't castrate us. What's our plan to get her back in the water?" I asked.

"I rather like your methods today," Martha quipped.

Ingie turned her royal nose toward Martha, but held her thoughts.

Jack studied the flames, a pressed lip smile indicating his approval of the project. He offered nothing of strategy or tactics that assured Ingie would ever get back in the lake.

"Auntie Ingie will get back in the lake," Ally burst. She gazed at her aunt, eyes glistening. "We had fun playing in the water?"

Ingie shifted her gaze toward her niece and lifted her eyebrows. Her smile warmed her niece's expression.

"She won't go," Luther said. We looked to him to explain.

"It's too cold. The lake. Warm today cause it was still, and the sun beat down on it." He shifted his eyes from the fire to the sky. "Too cold more days than too warm. I wouldn't be jumping in the lake very often. Maybe some days. Not today. It's night now." He looked back up toward emerging stars. "Maybe there will be meteors."

Omie shifted in his lap. The youngster looked up into his grandfather's face. "There are always meteors, Grandpa. Sometimes you just don't see them."

86

I marveled at Om's reason. And his special way of seeing eye to eye with Luther.

"Dad's right," Lynn said. "Lots of days this time of year might be inviting to us, but it would be too cool for Ingie in the lake. It will be entirely too cold in just a few weeks. The lake is not the long term solution to hydrotherapy for Ingie. Besides, she's such a spoiled witch that she'd want something more like a jacuzzi."

"She'd' like that. It'll be nice and warm," I agreed. "Maybe too shallow to do any standing leg work."

Ingie stirred. "Sister bitch. I am not fucking spoiled. And quit fuck-mouthing me right in front of me. Don't call me 'she'. Assholes."

"They have a big walking tank down in Duluth. Derek told me about it," Martha said. "Big enough for two people to walk in. One right behind the other. And they walk against a current."

"A tank?"

"Yes. Stainless, I think he said."

"Yeah. We had some heat therapy tanks in Boulder. Most were like single person jacuzzis. That would be neat to have one to walk in. What, did they pump water through it?

"Must be. Derek didn't say."

"Hmmm." I wondered whether we could buy a tank like that for Ingie. Or have it made.

"There are some hot springs in Montana," Jack said. "Not too far from of Yellowstone. North of the Tetons. The springs aren't real big where the water comes out of the earth. But it's warm. Warm enough to sit in under the stars, even in winter. Especially in winter. It's really neat. And the water flows out of the springs into a basin maybe twenty feet downstream. It forms a little pool where you could stand and warm yourself in the flow. Very nice.

"Sounds like it."

"It was all rock."

He looked over at Luther. The old man gazed off into the twilight, while his grandson watched wide eyed, his mind imaging a hot springs bath in the rocks of the mountains. Luther looked into a distance all of his own.

"Luther," Jack called. "What were you telling me about digging a hole in the ground here?"

"Can't be done. It's the stone here. Ledge rock. Greenstone. It used to be a mountain. Higher than the Himalayans. Old stone. You can't dig in it. Its rock. Hard rock. I chipped it once. Used a hammer. It bounced back at me. Could have killed a dog. It felt like it exploded, and it was big. Loud. I thought it was a canon." He fixed his gaze on the fire and lost himself.

Jack turned his eyes from Luther to Lynn. Her eyes studied her father. She followed every word he had said. She watched him, her son sitting on his lap.

Martha broke the silence.

"We could blow a hole in this rock that Luther is talking about."

Lynn lit up.

"We can!"

The face I knew only too well, Lynn's optimism face, was shining right at me.

"Can we?" She laughed at her doubt.

"Whoa!" Ingie spat.

"I say, why not?" Jack said.

"How?" I asked?

Ingie's eye's sharped to a razor slit reflecting the gleam of the flames.

"Get the fucking Bass Brothers."

# Chapter 18

# The Bass Brothers

After her dunking, Ingie warmed on front of the fire. I carried her in to the lodge before twilight set in. Martha offered to take on Ingie's care once we returned to her quarters, but she took a quick detour to the office as we crossed the Lodge commons.

"I'll give the Bass Brothers a ring," she said, her tone a warning to keep from me whatever they shared about Ingie's friends. I heard her dialing as I carried Ingie down the hallway.

"Who are the Bass Brothers?" I asked.

"Martha's nephews," Ingie said dreamily. "Brian, Dunkirk and Teddy." Her eyes sought out the teal and blaze sky that painted the western horizon. She said no more, and I let it be. I placed her in her recliner next to her bed where she'd wait for Martha's help. Her head lolled back lazily, her eyes rolling around the room until they focused on my face.

"You are a wonderful fucking prick, after all," she said. A long, sweeping smile spread across the stunning beauty of her face. Despite the scars from her accident, she remained hauntingly beautiful. Her dreamy gaze wandered back toward the lingering sunset and she sighed peacefully.

"Need anything?"

She wagged her head once, and shooed me off with a languid sweep of her finger tips. I left her waiting for Martha.

∞

I met the Bass Brothers, Martha's nephews, Brian and Dunkirk Devis, the next afternoon. We were toting the makings for dinner down to the fire ring when they pulled into the resort in a hot red GTO. Hard jawed and wirey they moved with ease and efficiency. Between them, there wasn't a pound of fat. Neither came close to being as tall as I, but they each struck me as the kind of ally I'd want on a team. Tough as Army mules.

Brian, the younger and a real talker, gave me a handshake that was earnest and firm. Dunkirk, or, Dunny as they called him, squeezed till my fingers went numb.

"Pleased to meet you," Brian said. His cadence was snappy and direct. His words came with a riveting gaze. "Lovely Lynn's long lost lover. Where the hell have you been, boy?"

Dunny spat a laugh. Lynn gasped.

"Mind your tongue," Martha snapped. She shot the boys a heated look, but they burst out laughing.

"Just wondering, Auntie. Who in his right mind would leave a woman like Lynn and go off to where ever?" Brian's smile sealed any doubt in my mind that although he was direct, he spoke in friendly jest.

"You're right," I replied. "If I'd have been in a right state of mind, I'd have been here with Lynn all along. But I wasn't. That must qualify me as a dumb shit."

Dunny threw back his head and croaked a guffaw. "I'd say," he seconded my notion.

Lynn sidled over to me and wrapped her arm around my waist.

"You boys mooning over never winning my affections?"

"Only mooning around here is this one," Brian quipped. "He stuck his bare ass out the window the other night as we drove by the Olsens outside the Steakhouse," he nodded toward his brother. "Nope. Got over you a long time ago. Too old for us young boys anyway."

Martha shot her nephew a fiery gaze. "Dunkirk, you bared your butt right downtown? You bone heads better not be bothering Sig Olsen. Or Elizabeth, for God sake."

Dunny sneered sheepishly, and dodged his Aunt's stern reprisal. "Damn Sig Olsen will be the death of resorts like this one. Where will Lynn be then?" he snorted, but left the thought as his aunt narrowed a threatening gaze at him. He turned his attention back to his smoldering adolescent dreams about Lynn as he disagreed with his brother's opinion. His words rolled out as though lubed in heavy oil. "Yeah. You worked your spell on me. Oh, I still have a crush on ya. Even if you are too old."

"What!" Lynn exclaimed. "You're just a few years younger than I am, Dunny. Why, Patrick here is younger than you." She set her eyes on his brother. "I believe Patrick's younger than both of you."

Their faces sagged.

"No!" Dunny grunted.

"Well gol' damn, Lynn!" Brian burst. "If you were gonna rob a cradle, why not mine."

"You boys are better off with Ingie anyway. You love her more than you love me. She's waiting for you. You'd better go give her your righteous adoration."

Dunny looked toward the lodge, but his brother held his ground.

"Oh, hell. We won't get any further with her than we do with you," he said. Turning to his aunt Martha, he wrapped an arm about her shoulder and smacked her a loud kiss right on her cheek. "What'dya say, Auntie? Is Ingie calling us out here for love or money?"

"Money. We got a job for you. And she's too smart to get caught up romancing either of you anyway. Besides, she's all soft on Teddy, looks like to me."

"Teddy! Damn! Has he been by, casting his spells on her now?"

"Well, more so than the both of you. He's in with her right now."

"I'd of guessed. Well, let's go try and save that poor soul before the two of them get themselves all tangled up in a big mess."

They let themselves into the lodge, and in a moment we heard Ingie's commotion taint the air.

"Jesus tits! It's a fucking convention of the Bass Brothers! Praise God and shit not the Pope!"

Martha rolled her eyes, but a sliver of a smile brightened her face,

"Kin," she muttered with feigned disgust, and followed their path into the lodge.

∞

Martha's nephews blasted ore in the pits between Babbitt and Virginia. Dunny was the brains of the blasting; Brian the logistics guy who carried the gear and oversaw peripheral safety. Dunny was the techie, the blasting engineer. The brothers joined us at the fire ring that evening to consider the plans and roast hot dogs. Brian chewed on a hot dog while Dunny mulled Ingie's proposed project.

"You want to blow a hole in the shield and carve it out like a holding tank for water, deep enough to walk in. Is that it?" He rubbed his clean shaven chin with a calloused miner's hand.

"Fucking right," Ingie chirped. "'Cept it'll be an ass kicking big basin into which you'll build a tit-lovely pool.

Lynn passed the boys a couple cold Hamm's and shared her concerns. "It can't be just a hole. Ingie's going to need heated water. And we have to pump the water to make a current that she can work against. And it would be great if you could kind of taper a ramp into it. She can't just jump in and climb out."

"Not yet, anyway. We'll roll her in. Or she can roll herself in." I added. "But we don't want it too big. Maybe longer, and no deeper than chest high."

Brian sneered. "Your chest or mine?" I had at least eight inches on him. So did Ingie.

"Right up to the top of my fucking boobs, donkey dong," Ingie laughed.

"I best take a measure," Brian offered. Dunny flashed him a look that indicated that he might be the one to take on that job.

Teddy, big quiet Teddy, however, slammed that idea shut. "I think we will be able to provide you with the appropriate measures." Fire swam in his dark eyes, and his tight lipped grin closed any debate.

Dunny furrowed his brow and chugged his Hamm's.

"We can probably set the charges in at an angle, like a 'v'. That could keep the blast from making too wide a hole." He studied an image formed in his mind. "The taper might be tricky. And we'd most likely have to come back with a jack hammer to shape it up right. But, yeah. It's doable."

Jack reached for another dog and stuck it on his roasting fork. "When can you do it?"

He knew Jack was near the end of his summer. "Soon enough you'll get to see it.

"I'd kind of like to watch this operation."

Dunny pursed his lips and nodded. "Hard part is the prep. Gotta drill the granite to set in the charges." He looked at his younger brother. "Whaddya think? Four loads in two rows, angled in at maybe a slant like so." He held his arm at a cant pointing toward the moon overhead.

"A little steeper," Brian suggested. "Maybe 35 degrees. And six sticks. Easy. Maybe even a couple more for the ramp."

Dunny considered his brother's advice. "Yeah. Okay. Might be a little hot with that much stick. Definitely going to have to come back with a jack hammer." He looked at Jack. "You can work an air hammer before you leave. What, two weeks? We can drill this weekend and it will probably take every bit of it." He glanced over to Martha. "It's gonna be a big boom. Have you got the cabins full?"

"This week. Not next. Other than Jack here."

Dunny looked back to Jack. "Prep this weekend. Blast the following Saturday. That work for you?"

Jack grinned. "Wouldn't leave before it."

"How about you, Auntie Martha?"

"We're good at the lodge. Guests coming in on the 7th, but quiet until then."

"Won't be quiet with us around. How about you, Lynn. You want us to give this a try?"

"Yes," Lynn was quick to respond. More cautiously, she added, "How much will this cost us?"

Brian filled in the logistics. The dynamite wasn't all that expensive, but caps and wire would run the bill up higher. They'd need cover fill to dampen the blast. And a back hoe to clean out the hole. Then, maybe they could use Swanson's compressor and hammer. "He'd rent it at the very least, unless he's got it out on a job. All total, couple hundred in materials and supplies. Labor is love. Me and Dunny, and Teddy too. We're in love with Ingie. And you, too, Lynn. We'll do it just to be near the air you breathe."

The group chortle sounded like a cough from the choir. I thought I caught a blush creeping up Lynn's cheek. "It's covered," I whispered to her. Her eyes gleamed.

"Let's do it," she said to the boys.

Ingie was ecstatic.

"Ah, my own fucking Bass brothers! You make me so goddamned happy."

∞

Teddy drove his old International truck up to the lodge the next afternoon. The box was loaded with heavy metal tools, hosing, gas cans, chisels and chains. He was dragging an air compressor. He parked by the stairs to the porch, stretched to his full height as he got out of the tiny International cab, and looked in toward the office.

Lynn saw him arrive and was on the porch before he could unfold his long and sturdy body.

"Hi, Teddy. Getting started already? No work today?"

"Got the evening shift. Gotta go in at three. The boys said it'd be good getting this job started ASAP. Thought I'd get things set up." His words rumbled coming from deep in his massive chest. "We can't do all that Dunny's talking about over one weekend. We gotta get it going." He looked across the parking area toward the lakefront, and then toward the woods along the drive,

"Where are you thinking of building Ingie's pool," he asked.

I joined Lynn as she left the porch and led Teddy toward the sauna building at the east end of the row of cabins, sixty feet or so from the lodge. I could see Teddy sizing up the work space and the placement of the buildings.

"It's going to be tight."

I had the same concern. "Do you think we can blast here? Without damaging the lodge or this sauna? Or any of the buildings?"

Teddy shook his head. "Dunny can. He can blast anything, anywhere." His white teeth sparkled against his dark skin, and his sharp eyes flickered. "But this will put him to the test.

"I'll pull the truck over here," he said. "The boys will be out this evening after work to figure everything out. I'll talk with them after my shift so I can get it going tomorrow. We'll need all the time we can find if we're going to drill the charge shafts."

"Are you a miner, too, Teddy?" I asked. He'd been by visiting Ingie a few times, but I had never really got to know him. Lynn told me Martha's

93

nephews had been friends with Teddy since grade school, and she considered him family. Like another nephew. When the boys were youngsters, Martha hired Teddy's folks, Bess, her cousin, and her husband Eino, each summer to keep the resort going. Teddy and her nephews spent their vacations climbing the bluffs and gorges away from the lake, and paddling canoes across miles of boundary water hunting and fishing. Martha kept Teddy and the boys busy with chores to earn small change for fun money, but they spent most of their time doing all of the adventures they'd likely reminisce about later in life. They got their nicknames from their many fishing trips; they were masters at bringing home bass and walleyes that kept their families fed.

Lynn remembered them from their early years at the resort, and on a few occasions was put in charge as their babysitter when Lynn's folks joined Teddy's folks in town for a fish fry. She remembered how they tormented her. And how they teased Ingie, who was closer to their age. Lynn had never gained the upper hand on the three boys. Ingie had controlled them from the first. Now, Teddy towered over Lynn, and had me by two or three inches. A big, powerful man, I took for granted that he and the boys worked together. He looked at me, though, as if I were ignorant.

Lynn chuckled. "Teddy leaves the mining for Dunny and Brian. He works at the hospital, where I work."

"I'm a nurse," Teddy said. "I take care of people."

Lynn explained further. "Teddy's a veteran. So are Martha's nephews. They all went in the service right from high school. Dunny was an engineer. He learned explosives in the service. Brian, too. Teddy went into the Navy and became a medic." She smiled fondly toward him. "He was the smart one of the three."

Teddy stood stoically noncommittal. "Just didn't want to blow things up, like Dunny. Or shoot anyone." He looked far away, across the lake. "The VA put me through nursing school once I got back."

"Well, can I help you unload the truck?" I asked. "You're going to have to be moving if you have a three o'clock shift."

He parked the truck near the sauna, and we placed the compressor to the side with the drills, hoses and hammers that had been piled in the little truck's box.

# Chapter 19

# Blasting Ingie's Pool

*Early August, 1968*

It took all week to prepare for the blast, and Dunny inspected the wiring a last time before they were ready to set the charge on Saturday.

He had planted the loads in the shafts that Teddy, Jack and I had previously drilled into the shield granite plate. There were a dozen holes. Wiring laced the shield face. It looked like a big game of connect the dots done with red and black wire dipping in and out of each hole. Dunny liked what he saw, and we loaded buckets with the dirt that Teddy had delivered during the week. We covered the wiring and blanketed the blast area with the pile of fill dirt. Spread out, the dirt wasn't quite as impressive a mound as it had been on the truck.

"Gonna be enough?" Teddy asked.

Dunny growled his reply. "Hope so."

"I'll get more."

Dunny hesitated. Then he gave the go ahead. "Should be good. Might use more on the ramp part, but it's a shallow blast with lighter load there. It's about right."

It was noon when we cleared the parking area. Lynn took the kids down the lakeshore where they could see the blast from a safe distance. Martha joined them with Luther.

We moved the cars and Teddy's truck out near the road. Jack swung the Cadillac around the sauna and outfitting shed and parked next to Cabin 3. Teddy brought Ingie out, and we set up cedar chairs well back from the blast, but closer than the shore.

"Tell me again, how are you going to blow this fucking hole, donkey balls," she glowed when Dunny retreated from the blast site to where the detonator was strung.

"Nope!" Dunny shrugged. "You're gonna blow this mother."

Ingie squealed.

He pointed to the box set on a picnic table.

"You're going to switch the right lever here when we get ready, and it's gonna pump a jolt of current along that line to the charges. The four inside sticks form a 'v' at the bottom of the drill shafts. The four corner shafts go straight down, but the two on the end by the sauna are a lot deeper than the two at the opposite end. Then there are the two light loads that went in shallower, and a shallow angle. Thank you Teddy," Dunny acknowledged.

Drilling the shafts at 30 degrees down from horizontal had been a task that left Jack stiff and soar, and blistered my hands and tightened all the muscles from my shoulders to my finger tips. I had to ice my neck for hours after that chore.

But Teddy persevered quietly till the shafts were positioned to break the granite in a thin plate where the ramp would lead to the deeper pool. The v would blow granite upward, the corner blasts would square out the corners and define the walls.

"That's it."

Ingie beamed.

Jack asked, "Is that engineering talking, Dunny? Or hope?"

Dunny had a peaceful little smile on his face, and he glanced over to Jack, but didn't reply.

"I've seen Dunny practice a bit of engineering over time, but he's been kind of sketchy on religion," Brian said. "I don't think he's practiced using much hope lately."

Jack laughed. "Confidence fosters optimism. Let it blast."

Leaving the kids with Martha and Luther, Lynn joined us at the detonation table.

"Is all that dirt gonna blow away with the blast? I'd love to use it in a garden by the porch." She pointed toward the office entrance.

"Should be fine for that," Brian said. "It's just gonna hold rock down so it doesn't fly about and do some damage."

Lynn furrowed her forehead.

"Ready?"

Ingie smiled wide. She nodded to Dunny.

"Well, then here. Just turn this handle down."

We watched Ingie set her hand on the lever and followed her gaze as she looked toward the blast site. I caught the movement of her hand as she dragged the switch toward her; the instant swelling of the mound of dirt over the blast site with an immediate *harrumph* pounding from the muffled blast looked surreal. The soil surged up, loosening like a blanket shaken from the edges. The blast, though dampened by the soil containment, pressed heavily against my ears.

From the stirred cushion of dirt, a round of stone popped up as if it had been launched. It flew high and fast in an arc over the roof of the sauna, sailing like a flying saucer right toward Cabin 3. As it cleared the roofline of the sauna, the disc-shaped granite tumbled like a tiddlywink. It sailed over the sauna roof shingles, but an instant later, a crash of broken glass and bent metal boomed from between the cabins.

The kids viewed the entire trajectory from the vantage of the shoreline. They screamed and scurried, joining us as we ran toward the sauna. Teddy swept up Ingie, and she road in his arms like an empress surveying the battlefield after a great war.

I scanned to see whether the flying rock had damaged either of the buildings, but it had not. Through the windshield of Jack's Cadillac, however, I could see something dark and wrong in the back seat. I looked over just as Jack reached the other end of the car. He set his hand on the fender, tenderly, as to heal a wounded soul. His shoulders sagged, and head dipped. I could hear his sigh across the length of his car. His brother's car. He looked so guilty; I could imagine the words he was telling himself.

He bent forward, peeking into the broken rear window. The rock, nearly the size of a manhole cover, sat comfortably on the lavish red fabric, bedecked in shards of shattered window like diamonds. Jack picked up a crystal the size of a quarter. He glanced over at Ingie. She wiggled and shivered, a grin from ear to ear. He smiled. Ingie glowed.

"Can I be the one to tell the fucking bishop?" She squirmed, laughing.

Jack raised his bearded chin up over his head, his eyes squeezed closed, and he burst with a belly laugh to match the blast that launched the projectile into the Caddy. He stepped toward Dunny and clamped his big paw on the engineer's sinewy shoulder.

"I was hoping this kind of thing wouldn't happen," Dunny muttered. He looked sheepishly at Jack. "Guess I oughta practice religion a bit more. Build up my hope."

"You couldn't do that again if you blasted a hundred times!" Jack cried. "What a shot! It was made to be!"

Dunny kicked the dirt, shrugged, and laughed. It looked to me that he was considering his odds of duplicating the blast and it's launch. The look he gave Jack told me that he thought he could do it.

Instead, he looked at Ingie. "She's the one who blasted it. It was her shot."

And Ingie squealed like the children.

# Chapter 20

# Elle's Note

We worked hard and long to remove the rubble from Dunny's blast hole. First, the soil had to be moved to Lynn's garden along the front of the office. Then, we lifted, dragged, pried and pushed hunks of ledgerock ranging in size from hardballs to a couple chunks that were twice as big as the saucer sitting in Jack's brother's back seat. Some hunks were small boulders. As we cleared the blast site, Dunny's skill showed more and more evident. The blast created a trough a good fifteen feet long and eight feet wide at the top. The lakeside end of the lengthy hole was tapered, graduating from a depth of six feet or so to just a few inches at the entry point.

By noon two days after the blast, we had stacked the rubble in a curved wall around the mound of dirt for Lynn's garden. Teddy and I shoveled and swept the fine debris from the blast hole. By noon, the hole looked convincingly like a pool.

"There's plenty of room for the plumbing," Teddy observed. We discussed how we would place the pipes to move water at a measured rate, like a current, from the deep end of the pool toward where the grade rose from the floor to the surface. We'd put in forms to pour concrete, install the plumbing, and mount the pump and heater that would provide both challenge and comfort for our Ingie. On her cushions and wrapped in her warm shawls and blankets, Ingie supervised the progress from a lounge chair we set alongside the trough.

"Better be fucking bath-like in that water," she quipped. "Hot chocolate! I wanna bathe in fucking hot chocolate!"

Teddy was on it.

"We'll rig a safety check valve up at the pump," he gestured to the stone at the deep end of the trough. "Ingie doesn't put out during her rehab, we flip the valve and she gets a blast of lake water. Keep her honest."

"Assholes. The both of ya."

"We're on to you," Teddy said. "No more Princess La La. You're gonna work."

∞

By mid afternoon, the pool site was prepped for fine chisel trimming of the sides and bottom. Teddy promised to be back in the morning with tools.

"Ah, the fucking Bass brothers," Ingie said between sips of lemonade. "What would I do without them?"

"You'd be a lot more bored," Martha ventured. "Those nephews of mine are a story. Both of them, and Teddy too."

I thought about it for a moment. The three were pretty much inseparable, except when they were at their jobs, or when Teddy was with Ingie.

Martha explained the boys as she watched Lynn and the twins walking from the mail box. Ally carried a small bundle of mail, while Omie pranced out ahead, holding an envelope high, keeping it safe from whatever grounded perils he might imagine. "Those three have been a gang of trouble since they were knee high,"she continued. "Worried me near to death before they ever came to the age of reason. Then they were relentless. Surprised we got them all through alive."

"Why are they 'the Bass brothers'?" I asked. "I thought you were talking about Dunny and Brian when you called them that. Teddy too?"

"Yep. All fuckin' three of them." Ingie quipped, glancing side-eyed. "Guess they goddamned know how to catch fish."

"Shenanigans," Martha said curtly. I noticed a mix of humor and disgust in her reply, but I got the distinct feeling they were skirting an issue to which I was not privy.

Ingie fidgeted and snickered as she put an end to the subject. "Anything worth a shit in the mail?" she asked Lynn.

"There is for Patrick," Lynn smiled. "Your mom wrote."

"Wow," I took the traveled envelop from Omie..

"Before you get into what your mother has to say, can you give me a hand with our pampered one?" Martha asked. She turned to Ingie. "You need a lot of work "

"Glad to. You gonna douse her mouth out with something stringent? Kerosine, or turps?" I swept Ingie up and spun her around and rocked her up and down, all while she hollered oaths and curses aimed at me, as though I was definitely no white knight.

∞

Leaving the twins playing croquet on the lawn, Lynn strolled over to join me on the swing hanging on the porch of Number 3.

"How's your mom?" she called from the steps. Then, examining me with the eye of a nurse, she asked. "Is everything okay? Are you okay?"

I didn't know. I knew the feeling of not remembering to breath. It was a reflex for me. I'd learned to cope with it. To control it. But Mom's note came out of nowhere. I had no inkling. It was like a baseball bat to the gut. I glanced up.

"Jesus, Patrick. Are you okay," she knelt by my arm. "You're pale as a ghost."

She hugged my shoulders. Her breath was warm in my ear.

"Breath, Patrick. Inhale."

She helped me lower my head to my knees. I broke into a cold sweat. I inhaled. The air was sweet with Ely summer.

I dangled my hands low, between my ankles. The letter fell to the ground. I breathed. Lynn's hand gently, softly circled a spot between my shoulder blades.

I reached down and lifted the letter. It fell open as I lifted. The first paragraph below the crease caught my eye.

*So the best way, the easiest way, the quickest way for us to get everything documented for Eva's immigration is for you to come here and marry her. Will you do that?*

I handed Lynn the note. Her eyes widened as she inspected the ornate, precise loops and squiggles of my mother's script.

"She wants us to go to Germany," I said. "And she wants me to marry Eva."

"Germany?"

"Munich."

Lynn focused on the content of my mother's letter. After reading through it, she started over on its first page.

"Well, that's an idea to consider."

I shot her a look.

"She wants me to marry Eva."

"Yeah." She shifted her eyes from Mom's letter to me. It felt like she was grabbing my heart through my eyes and taking my soul with it. "For good reason." She read further. Mom had written three pages. She had been meticulous.

"She's thought of everything."

I winced. "Not everything."

"Yes. She has."

She turned back to the first page and trained her eyes below the crease."

"Goodness."

I waited for her thoughts.

She smiled as she read it again. "Wow. Wild. Zany."

She flashed her riveting caramel eyes. "I've never been to Munich."

"Are you serious?"

"Why not? She is asking to see her son. And his family. And it sounds as she may need help with Eva" Lynn smiled. "I've never been to Germany. Neither have your children." Her eyes flashed again as she drank in the humor of it all. "If you're gonna be a bear, be a zany old grizzly."

*Wow!* I thought. *Wow!*

"What about your resort?" I asked, gesturing toward the line of cabins filled with summer tourists. "Or Ingie? And your dad?"

"The season's over in two weeks, when the schools open up down in the Cities. Ingie's good. Stable. Martha has been after me to take a break for two years, for heaven's sake. She can handle Ingie, especially with Teddy around so much." A fleeting frown wrinkled her forehead as she considered Luther. "I'm more concerned about leaving her with Dad, but we've discussed it more than once, even before you came back. He's worse now, but she assures me that she can handle him. Teddy loves Dad and would help with him, too."

She paused, considering. I could see her muster determination.

"I really want to go. The four of us."

I nodded. She stood before me, certain, unwavering. I could only smile, as much from gratitude as from appreciation of her spunk.

Lynn pulled a porch chair over close. She lay her palm on my forearm and snickered. "Who would ever have thought?"

"My mother."

"I mean, in this way. For things to be like this?"

I looked into her glowing face. She stared out over the lake.

"It's crazy."

"Yes. In a curious sort of way."

I breathed. She smoothed the hair on my arm.

"I only want to marry you."

"You haven't asked me, yet."

"Will you?"

"Yes. Of course. It feels like we already are. I thought we'd get to it sooner or later. Just a matter of timing. Getting our ducks in a row." A tear welled, then started a course down her cheek that splashed on our arms. "You know, Patrick, what a crazy, tangled life we have woven in the time we have known one another. Not at all conventional. Nothing socially 'normal' about it. We can't expect life to unfold like a typical storybook for us. It hasn't from the day we met. From before we ever knew one another. Everything we ever did, ever were, was meant to lead us together. How we take advantage of that which was is meant to take us to that which is now. How we act now will build upon all that, and be the foundation for what we are when time has moved on to the new moment of now. That's how it is."

My face was twisted in consideration of her perspective. She laughed, patting my arm.

"Good thing we did. Procrastinate. Now we can do this." She looked square at me. "If we are going to do this, we may as well enjoy the good we can do in the process. What a hoot!"

On the lawn near the beach, the kids idled in their play. Summertime is so kind for children. Their perspective becomes the open world. We dallied as the children kept to their games and imaginations. Our imaginations whirred like tops, spinning madly. We let them whirl.

I sat back up. I felt the color come back in my face. The cooling breeze evaporated water from my face. I breathed.

"That was quite a spell."

I shrugged. "Yep."

"Come on."

"What?"

"The office. We have to phone your mom."

# Chapter 21

# Essential Journeys

The hot afternoon sun lingered high in the western sky as Omie stood along the shoreline, gazing toward the point guarding the bay. His arm floated up, his finger lifted toward a canoe rounding the head of the point. Father Jack paddled in from camp after his last overnight camping before leaving for his teaching appointment.

"I was wondering where he was," I sighed, "when I needed him most."

Lynn chuckled. "Like he's been called."

We turned toward the shore where Luther waited and Ally and Omie played in the sand near the canoes.

∞

Toward evening, we gathered around the fire pit. The blaze was crisp and crackling. The Bass Brothers had arrived. They fed the fire with logs that they split again and again. Dunny and Brian prattled nonstop as they worked the good dry pine, and it spat as it crackled. The kids hustled from the shore to the fire ring while Jack and I tipped the canoes for the night and gathered the paddles and gear. By the time we joined the fire watchers, Ally was snuggled securely in her Lynn's arms, and Omie was perched on Martha's lap, her arms around him.

Ingie sat enthroned on a chair in the golden hues of the flames. Lynn sat shoulder to shoulder with her sister. They shared a joyous, dreamy expression.

Jack sat by Luther, listening. Martha was telling the tale of her escape into the boundary waters after her husband's death.

I'd heard the story before, but it was an abbreviated version told by Lynn. It was about Lynn's mother's best childhood friend, Martha, whose new husband died just weeks after they married. He and his father were killed as they flew their resort's float plane north to pick up clients waiting on Pickerel Lake in the Quetico.

Now, Martha shared her memories of her story of redemption.

She and Lynn's mom, her best friend, had paddled deep into the border waters northwest of Ely, then turned east, portaging and paddling, putting the world behind with each stroke. They set out with few provisions and little gear. A single fishing rod and a handful of lures and tackle. Everything an old tackle box kicking around the bottom of a canoe might carry. They shared a pup tent, little more than a canvas tarp that kept them dry but was no barrier to biting insects. They took the supplies that John, Martha's husband, had prepared for a weekend camping trip planned for when he was to return from his fateful flight, but the girls stayed out in the wilderness for seven weeks.

"It was after John's funeral," Martha explained. "There was little to nothing for me back here. There was less than nothing. The emptiness of lost love." She glanced over to Lynn. "Except the presence of your mother. She figured she'd just come along with me. So we paddled away and didn't look back.

"Folks said they figured we were crazy, and I suppose we might have been, except it seemed to us, or to me anyway, that we were doing the right thing. Surviving." Her gaze across the blistering fire, glanced my way for an instant, then she toward Jack, and finally to Luther. The old man sat with a lackadaisical grin. His brow relaxed and his eyes looked young again. The words of her story took him back to a time when he knew the value of courage and honor. He remembered her story, and was part of it, and her telling took him into that reality.

Martha told of black flies and summer weather, of dawn's crystal light, and the cool taste of the waters rinsing the salt from her lips. She spoke of Lynn's mother. Of the healing heart that her friend offered to Martha as she struggled to stay afloat. Of frogs and crayfish, and walleye-thieving snapping turtles.

"We were doing a crazy trip to keep from going insane is the way I think of it," Martha said.

"What's the insane, Auntie?," Omie asked. "And why were you going there?"

She smiled, gathering him close.

"The insane, is it? Well, Omie, it's a way of thinking, that's what insane is. It's not all that good a way to think, or that healthy, but sometime's it's the only way a soul can see things."

"Why?" he pursued.

The shorter of the two Bass Brothers spit into the flames, glanced over at Omie and said, "'Cause that's sometimes the best way to see at all, youngin'."

Omie frowned. He didn't grasp the rationale.

"Sometimes, everything you do doesn't seem to have any bearing on what is happening. Like you don't have much control of all that is going on in your life," Martha said. "That's the way it was for me in those days, honey. And your grandmother wouldn't let me go off on my own. She kept me safe. She was like my guardian angel as we paddled the northern waters."

Omie folded into her, and she held him close.

"Like my angel-titted sister," Ingie snorted, gazing keenly at Lynn. "Fuckin' New Zealand! Whew!"

Lynn pursed her lips in a smile that told she held secrets. Her travels with Ingie had tested her skills at keeping Ingie safe from her younger sister's zany antics.

Martha chuckled. She knew of their trip. And she identified with them.

"Exactly, Ingie." Martha said, slowly ruffling Omie's thick mop of hair between her fingers.

"We'd have gone hungry, if it weren't for your mom. She was persistent."

"She often said she learned how to fish out there with you," Lynn said.

"She could catch 'em," Martha said. "But there were a few times it took her a bit longer to bring in what our stomachs needed. We did alright with berries. Loads of raspberries. And more blue berries than we could eat. But there were stretches where I think we would have eaten the next fish raw if it took much longer to catch it. We ate more crayfish than I can tell.

"But sometimes, it didn't matter that we were hungry," Martha looked down into Omie's sleepy face. "Sometimes we just paddled. It was summer, you know. Long days. There were days we were paddling at dawn, and paddled and paddled and paddled. Sometimes, we might portage, but we were on the big waters near Ottertrack and Sag. We didn't hurry. Sometimes we looped back, just to see a bay under different light. That's what we were looking for. Seeing it again, under a different light. It was magic. Your Grandma showed me the magic of the moment. The power."

"That's where we screwed up on our trip," Ingie muttered. "We weren't looking for the goddamn light. Or the magic. Least ways, me, bitch."

Lynn lay her head on her sister's shoulder.

"I was."

∞

Jack stirred.

"Sometimes it seems like the light just isn't there to be found." His tone was subdued. I could have missed what he said entirely, but he looked up from the embers and restated his thought.

"Sometimes, it is just dark."

I wondered where he was in his mind and heart. He gazed long at Ingie. Then he rested his sight upon Lynn, and finally Martha.

"I know where the dark is," Luther muttered. "Dark is real, too." We waited, but he said no more.

"Nothing can steal the light from your heart more than losing your loved ones," Martha said. "Darkness has its own powers."

"Heart of darkness," Teddy said. "Losing family."

His tone caught me; I was surprised by the sharp pain that rustled my heart. I'd not felt it for weeks now. Noticing Lynn watching me helped.

105

Jack said,"When I was in Iran, I was working with those who had lost family. The Armenians."

"They are a sad lot," Martha interjected. "My heart goes out to them."

"Who?" Dunny asked.

Jack leveled his gaze on Martha's older nephew. "A people. What's left of them. From western Asia. They were killed by Turks in the dying days of the Ottoman Empire. It was genocide. Families were slaughtered. Almost a couple million people died. It was dark."

"What were you doing, working with them?" Lynn asked.

"Pastoral work. I was assigned to a parish in Isfanan in Iran. Many of the families had immigrated to Persia from the north during the genocide fifty years ago during World War One. The souls of those Armenians were healed somewhat after five decades, but their scars were thick. Nothing was forgotten. When you have that great a scar, it affects how you see the light of day. Or, the darkness." He again trained his gaze on me.

"And then David died."

"Heart of darkness," Teddy repeated. "Is that why you came back?"

Jack nudged the embers and added a couple logs. "Nope. I came back because I was empty. How could I help them, give them what they needed, when I had nothing left. I was looking for something to fill me."

"Did you find it?" Ally beamed. Her smile cast sparkling light, reflecting rays from the fire.

Jack returned her smile. "I think so. I'm still looking. You have to keep looking for the angels in your life. Angels are a transient gift."

"They are," Martha nodded. "Your grandmother was an angel in my life. We talked of it often. She would laugh and say she found herself being like an angel to me as we paddled that summer. It would have been a bleak, frightening trip for me, if not for her. She found ways of keeping us in the light. When things were darkest, she conjured a spark that lit the world back up. She kept me in light."

Jack dropped his chin to his chest. "What a gift."

"One I can never be too grateful for."

We mulled the notion, each of us in our perspective. The fire died to embers.

"The dark isn't necessarily a killer," Teddy said.

"Shut up," Ingie blurted. "The dark can suck the fucking life right out of you, if you aren't careful."

"Who's not careful?" he said, leveling a look as if to warn her.

"Oh, Jesus," she muttered.

"You can heal in the darkness," Teddy said. "It may be that you need to be in the deepest realm of darkness to find where the light is."

"Or isn't," Jack shot back. "It's like knowing which way to go to surface."

Teddy bobbed his head. "It can be more."

Lynn agreed. "Darkness can lead you toward healing, if you let it."

Martha hugged the sleeping Omie in her lap. "Lynn, you sound like your mother."

"She taught me."

"Me too."

I felt my head swiveling around like a tetherball. "What's healing? How can you go about healing?" I asked.

"I don't know," Jack sighed. "I'm not there."

Teddy stood. He stretched his arms into the stars; he towered into the night sky. His silhouette carved darkness into the cast of the Milky Way. He sucked in air, his chest expanding like a blacksmith's bellows. He grunted and growled as he expelled the spent air in his lungs. When he finished exhaling, he farted like a buzz saw barking from metal caught in the grain of a sappy pine log.

Startled awake, Omie clapped.

"Magic!" The Bass brothers chimed together.

"Jesus shit!" Ingie howled as we all broke into guffaws.

"Nada," Teddy grinned. "Just warding off dark spirits that we call with this talk." He tossed several sticks of pine onto the embers.

"I know dark spirits," Luther piped up. Then, squiggling his nose, he asked, "Did someone fart?"

It set us off again.

I held my sides, laughing. Tears streamed down Jack's cheek, leaching into his shaggy beard. Lynn rocked Ally in her lap, and Martha settled Omie who had startled at the roar of his friend.

Martha's nephews rolled in the dirt around the fire ring, screaming, laughing, praising the spirit of their brother, the medicine man. "One after the other, they leapt to their feet, spun and twisted, dancing around the fire to the rhythm of their chanting and laughing. Ally jumped up, dancing like a rag doll in the golden flashes of firelight. Omie joined her, mirroring her moves, their arms pointing high toward the stars, their legs swaying like reeds in the wind above water. Soon, we each held our place in the dance that circled Teddy, who hovered above the flames in the fire ring, yielding an imaginary whip that crackled above our heads like the pine logs spitting in the fire. Only Luther sat in reserve.

"Pagans," he spit. "We are a family of pagans."

∞

When we settled, Martha offered to take the kids to their beds. Ingie asked to go up to the lodge as well; she complained that the chill of the night was reaching her bones. She shrieked as Teddy swooped her up and tossed her over his shoulder like a sack. The Bass Brothers delivered their profane princess to her domain.

Jack stoked the fire as Lynn and I settled into the comfort of the sand and logs around the fire ring.

"I have news," I offered after the bustling energy from our departing family settled into a calming lull.

"News? What's that?"

"I'm getting married."

Jack's eyes sparkled as a wide grin spread across his wooly face.

"Well, congratulations!" Jack looked first at me, then Lynn. "I've been wondering when you'd come to this. Have you set a date? Are you looking for a minister?"

Lynn smiled, wagged her head back and forth like it was on a swivel. "Don't look at me for the details. It's not my wedding."

His brow scrunched like a shoe brush, he turned his stupefied look toward me. I shrugged, winced and shook my head like Lynn.

"Yes, indeed, I'm looking for a priest," I said. "Got time to travel before you start your job? Want to go to Munich? Lynn's looking to be the maid of honor, once she meets the bride."

Jack looked resigned. Perhaps the chants and dances had tipped his sense of reality toward the surreal, and now he groped to understand. I glanced at Lynn. She took my mother's letter from her hip pocket and handed it to Jack. '

We watched Jack read Elle's note.

"Oh, my," he gasped. He looked up from the letter. "Does she mean this for real?"

"What, Jack, is 'real' for my mother?" The rage I held for my mother heated up within my chest.

Jack glanced at me with a measured eye. "You pissed?"

"Trying not to be." I fumed.

His head continued to wag to and fro.

"Unbelievable."

"Exactly."

Looking at Lynn, he asked, "How do you feel about this?"

She looked at me. "Not angry. Not at Elle. She means well, I'm sure. It's just so unexpected. Zany.' She sighed, shrugged and looked up toward the sky.

"I am willing to bet that it will never come to pass. We called Elle this afternoon after Patrick got her letter. She was evasive, I'd say. Like she didn't know if her idea would really work. She's been helping Eva meet with an immigrations agent at the U.S. consulate in Munich. Things are developing, but Elle is leaving nothing to chance. She thinks having Patrick marry Eva to allow her to immigrate is a way to resolve the problems they've been encountering. She thinks."

Jack examined Lynn's expression. He saw her confidence, kindness, and perhaps amused wonder.

He sifted his gaze to me.

"Lynn knows what she wants," I shrugged. "She sees it as an adventure."

Lynn explained. "I have been blessed with an interesting life. This will be one more zany aspect of it. Taking my children to their father's wedding. I always wondered how they would imagine us getting married. This will truly expand their perspectives."

He looked at me, but said nothing.

"Do bigamy laws apply internationally?" I grinned.

Horror convulsed Jack's expression.

"Yes. But, you'd have to marry Lynn as well, for that to be the case."

Lynn grinned as I kept a strict poker face for Jack's behalf. "Want to live on the wild side? Maybe Jack should marry us now?"

Our mountain man spiritual mentor shook his head and muttered, "Unbelievable. Elle! What are you thinking?"

∞

We all sat exhausted as the embers died in the fire ring. Jack, too, was spent from his day paddling topped by the emotional drain of my mother's plans. He drifted off toward number 5, a cabin vacant due to a cancelation. I was glad Lynn and I could be together and alone.

We fell onto the bunk and curled our bodies like spoons as the cool evening air rolled in from the lake. All was quiet. I felt Lynn shiver and twitch, and I wrapped my arms tightly around her. We fell deep into sleep.

Light from the waxing July moon spilled into the cabin window, waking me. I was alone and surprise. Lynn was no longer in my arms. She'd slipped away. I sat up, looking about. There, through the window, I saw her silhouetted in soft moonlight, her eyes scanning the surface, illuminated by rays reflecting off the placid water. She stood on the dock with her arms to her sides, her palms lifted toward the light, as though she gathered energy from the blue. I headed to the shore.

The wooden dock rocked with my steps. She held her pose. Her face was a portrait of peace, joy and understanding, yet a single tear crept down her cheek. I watched as she let it run its course.

"What do you see," I asked as she shifted her eyes from above to the reflection of the moon off Burntside's mirror. "You're crying."

She tilted her head. Her smile flickered.

"I scry," she whispered. "It is my prayer."

"Huh?" I asked. Scry? Prayer? I said nothing, waiting.

After moments, a gust riffled the surface, like the breath of a baby.

"I don't see." Her voice was kind. Her eyes remained on the silver band of moonlight reflecting on the lake. She watched, reading the ripples as they smoothed. "I scry."

She turned her eyes to mine.

"Let me show you."

She placed me before her, away from her, my face to the moonlight. I felt her warmth on my back. She moved my hands, lifting my arms from my sides. She cupped my fingers. My hands felt like baskets filtering the silver glow.

She wrapped her hands about my belly, fingers laced where my ribs met my abdomen. The world cleared and darkened. I gazed into the reflection of the moon upon the water. Time poured into the blue white light.

She whispered, her breath warm on my shoulder. She said things I didn't understand. Words. A language. But different.

The moment was flush with magic.

I saw that we were one, Lynn and I. She showed me that which is in the moonlight. It told me of our love. Of joy. We had one love, she and I. Of that she was certain. She moved her hands, her fingers drawing in the shining silver light on the waters.

"It's not a destiny," she said softly. "Not a fate. It just is, an instant of creation and a moment in which to commit intent. It's prayer, and that's where our power abides."

I watched, and our lives unfolded from time and spilled into our being in the blue crystal waves of moonlight.

She her fingers slide down the skin of my belly. She lay me down, placing me on my back on the dock. She sat upon me. The moon lit her face, her laughing eyes flashing silver.

I felt whole. We felt one.

# Chapter 22

# Perseids

I heard Omie's plaintive call as he and Lynn struggled to keep up. I let my paddle skim the water and we drifted across the still surface, Ally's paddle gurgling and setting swirls along the sides of our canoe. A loon surfaced just a paddle's length from the tip of the bow; the bead-like eye of the bird scanned us curiously. From near the shoreline, the loon's partner sang its song. With Ingie tucked in among blankets and pillows propped against the front thwart, Teddy smoothly paddled their canoe straight and swift. Martha navigated her craft in loops, with Luther churning the waters from the bow seat. They made wide circles about our canoes.

No one else on was the lake, so we dawdled when it came to lighting our bow and stern lights. As we drifted slowly to the middle, the placid surface reflected the skies. The planets emerged, then the stars from our galaxy and beyond. Omie spotted a satellite wobbling across the face of the Milky Way. A loon called, and Luther answered. He was a good mimic. Occasionally, the shadow of a bat darkened the reflection of the stars on the lake's glass smooth surface. The air carried the fragrance of Burntside's water. "There's one," Ally whispered. I'd caught the meteor's bushy tailed reflection on the lake, but it was gone before I could see it in the sky. Shortly, another flash trailed a long, thick track, the reflection interrupted only by the body of our canoe as the meteor crossed directly overhead. Ingie giggled. From across the water, Omie purred his praise. "Awww. Neat."

Martha kept count and claimed that 37 meteors blazed tracks across the sky in the first hour of deep darkness. Some were short and furious. Many tracked in lazy streaks across the entire sky, laying long fuzzy swaths of brilliant white, like sparklers. Their reflections hovered over the shadows of the depth around the canoes.

"They're like twins," Ally said. "One in the sky, one on the lake."

"Twins aren't reflections," Omie said. "We are different. We don't look like we are looking in a mirror."

We pondered the twin images. David came to mind.

"My twin, your Uncle David, was like these meteors," I said. "He blazed across the sky, and everybody noticed him."

"Did he leave a reflection?" Omie asked.

I felt a lump build in my chest. Lynn spoke for me.

"Patrick's twin shed his light on everyone he encountered. He made his mark. He lit up everyone's heart, including mine."

We watched another tandem meteor-reflection.

"He lit the way for me as I grew up," I said. "His was a fast, bright burst of light that climbed across the highest sky."

The twins made no reply. Ingie hummed. In the distance, Martha urged Luther to take up his paddle.

"Time to go in," she called. "The mosquitoes found me."

"You let Dad take you too damn close to the shore," Ingie muttered.

"She's steering," Luther grumped.

We joined Luther in dipping our paddles into the lake, but our pace was slow and graceful as our necks craned up and our eyes looked into the soul of the universe.

Book Three

# The Heart of Bavaria

## Patrick Joyce

# Chapter 23

# Traveling to Munich

*Late August, 1968*

Ingie's pool took shape during the middle of August. By the end of the week, Teddy and I had plumbed the heater, the pressure jets, and the return flow piping. The forms were set and on Thursday we poured concrete to enclose the pool. On Friday, we added the deck surface area. On Saturday, we broke down the forms and honed off the rough areas. I felt guilty that we had not completed the project when it was time to leave for our trip to Munich.

"Not to worry," Teddy assured me. "Dunny will help tile the deck by Monday. We'll have the pool lined in a week. My buddy Aaron is planning to hook up the electricity. If this weather holds, we'll have the walls framed and the roof shingled before you get back." He looked at me through narrowed eyes. "You really gonna get married? To someone besides Lynn?" He couldn't contain his grin. He'd asked me that same question no less than a half dozen times since we shared our plans with him. "Dunny's ready to cover for you, ya know."

I shot him a glance filled with dread, and he just laughed.

∞

Jack packed up and headed toward Milwaukee on Friday. He was scheduled to start lectures at Marquette the first week in September. But he was adamant that he should and would 'tie the knot' for me and Eva—if that were to come to be. "For David's sake," he said.

Our plans were to meet at O'Hare on Thursday where he would fly with us first to New York and then to Munich for a five day weekend. After he did the deed, he'd fly back to the States on Labor Day and be ready for his classes later in the week.

We lined up on the porch to watch him drive away in his brother's Cadillac, a gaping void where the rear window once was. The disc shaped slab of granite that demolished the window remained in the back seat. Jack was certain his brother would find it amusing; he was also hedging that the rock would support his otherwise incredible explanation.

The twins tried their hardest to talk him into staying in Ely. He had connected with the children, as well as with their mother and aunt. Ingie demanded to be with us as we sent him off.

"Fucker can't just drive off without a goddamned good-bye," she muttered.

We were all touched, aware that a powerful force was about to leave a void in our lives.

I noticed Luther. He dipped into silent depression. I wondered whether he sensed the loss of one more meaningful icon slipping away from his life.

Jack looked back through the broken rear window, waving, hollering a hearty farewell.

"See you in Chicago!" he called.

∞

Our plane passed to the north of Chicago, swooped out over Lake Michigan, tipped its wings sharply, and turned back westward in its final descent into the airport. Our beloved Indiana sand dunes lay along the strip of beach to the south of Lake Michigan. I nudged Lynn, pointed out the cabin window, and our smiles celebrated the memories we had formed on those beaches. Then, as the plane flew toward the runways of O'Hare, we passed above the lakefront of the Windy City.

Cars crawled along Lake Shore Drive. Masses of people filled the greenways and parks north of downtown. The streets were filled with traffic, and police and emergency vehicles clustered at many intersections near Lincoln Park, lights flashing, busy people streaming like ants between the cars and trucks lined up on the roadways.

"What a mess," I said. "The convention."

"Yeah," Lynn agreed. We had paid some attention to the political process in Chicago, but from the peace of the northern woods it was like a remote, surreal world to us. Now, with the teeming crowds and flashing lights filling the streets below, it appeared even more unreal.

In moments, we had passed over the city and felt the bumping of tires on the runway. We had just over an hour to move the kids from a terminal serving domestic travel to the international hub. We scurried, excitement palpable, Omie's calm almost unnerving. I watched him like a hawk, wondering whether something might catch his eye and draw him off path. In a blink of an eye, he might wander off. When he gently reached up and took my hand, I felt a rush of security replace my tense concern for traveling among so many strangers with our kids.

We arrived at our gate in the International terminal with time to spare. I noticed Lynn craning her neck, searching the crowds. I, too, looked through the busy throng. Our glances met, and she frowned.

"No Jack."

I nodded, then glanced at the time on the register above our check in desk.

"He has time."

Within minutes, the airline begin boarding the plane. With our kids, we were among the first to board. We settled in. Tending the twins, we occasionally looked toward the incoming line of travelers.

No Jack.

The line of people headed for Germany thinned. Attendants hustled about, several times stopping by our seats, inquiring about the children and cheerfully bantering with Ally who considered the entire commotion something of entertainment designed in her best interests. She showed the attendants her secured seat belt, introduced Molly, her rag doll traveling companion, and exuded all the confidence and charisma of a world savvy traveler.

Lynn looked at me above the heads of our children. I shrugged. Jack was not on board.

They closed the plane's heavy doors, locked them tight, and we settled in for the ten hour flight to Munich.

We didn't see Jack in Chicago like he promised.

∞

The twins slept. I dozed, but lightly. When, someplace above the dark Atlantic ocean, rippling light reflected off its expansive surface under a starry sky, I opened my eyes, feeling Lynn's presence as I often did during the years we were apart. I turned to find her watching me. Looking at me as I slept.

"What?"

Her smile was kind. "I can't believe I'm taking you to your wedding."

I dropped my head back against the seat rest. I felt a smile grow across my face. Turning to her, I said, "If my mother's crazy idea were ever to happen, which is most unlikely, I'll ask my new wife's permission to take you to my wedding bed. You can be her surrogate. She's too far along with this pregnancy for any sort of wedding night hoo-rah! She has no business having sex." I forced a haughty grin. But my face fell flat, and my tone swelled sober. "It's not my wedding. It's David's. I'm just the best man, standing in. If it happens."

Lynn looked impish.

"So, Mr. Best Man. Whatcha gonna do when the good Father says, 'You may kiss the bride'?"

I cocked my smile to one side, and raised an eyebrow to the other.

"Well, I guess I'll have to give Eva a big one right on the smacker. Whaddya think? Eva's French. Suppose I should slip her my tongue and give her a French kiss? Gotta do it right."

117

She laughed quietly, tipping her head back, looking at the ceiling of the cabin. Then she tossed it right back at me. "You should. Right in front of your mother."

"My mother!" I gasped. She laughed again. We settled into our seats, our slumbering children between us. Our hearts fused in our eyes.

"You know. This one's for David. And for Eva, because Davey can't do it himself."

"I know. You are the only one I know who could do this and be true to yourself. That's why I love you."

"When will you marry me?" I asked.

"As soon as you get your divorce."

I coughed, choking between a laugh and an exasperated swallow.

∞

We dozed again as we crossed the black expanse of the Atlantic. I woke to see dawn sneaking out from far across Europe. Lynn slept, as did the twins.

How could I be taking her to my wedding where she would be a witness. As would my children. Zany.

Her eyes fluttered awake; she found me watching.

"How can I possibly be bringing you along to my wedding? And not be marrying you?"

She watched my eyes. Then smiled. "I'm here to witness your wizardry."

We flew on toward the Alps.

The children woke and we tended them. The stewardesses were a wonder. They pandered to the twins and made the the trip easier for all of us.

We landed well after breakfast. Ally gave each of her new attendant friends a hug as we stepped into Germany. We were in Munich.

For my wedding.

# Chapter 24

# Eva and Elle

Eva met us at their door.

I swept her up in my arms as tears poured from my eyes. I saw her last in the Etage, the floor on which we lived in separate apartments in Regensberg. She had been standing by the pigeon holes where we picked up our mail, reading David's most recent letters. Now, she was in my arms and we wept and laughed and hugged tight.

My family watched us. Lynn! She stood by my side, our twins tucked close, her hands on the shoulders of our children, each with an arm curled around their mother's legs. They watched with wide eyed curiosity. I pulled them into our embrace. "Lynn," I blubbered, "and our twins. This is Eva." I sniffled through a wreck of introductions. The twins looked up at me in wonder. Lynn covered for me.

"This is Ally, and Omie. We are so happy to be here. Patrick has told us so much about you!"

Eva's grace and composure emerged through her tears. Her English as faulty as I remembered, she greeted my family. Still in my arms, she reached a hand to the top of Ally's blond curls. Her kind eyes settled on Omie, and he returned a shy smile. She stepped from my hug and wrapped her arms around the twins and their mother.

"You welcome here," she stuttered. *"Herzlich willkommen! Ich bin froh, dass ich sein kenne."* She knelt to look at each twin at eye level, wiping tears as she smiled widely into their beaming faces. She shifted, balancing to stand. I gripped her elbow and helped her to her feet. She stepped into Lynn's waiting arms and, like sisters, they hugged

"I wait long with you to talk." Eva said softly into Lynn's hair, her tears streaming down her cheeks. "Patrick tells me of you. And David. He tells me of you both," she said, breaking from her embrace but focusing solely on my beloved. They hugged while I knelt by my children, taking one in each arm.

"We are here for you, Eva," Lynn spoke softly. She stepped back but kept Eva's hands in hers and her eyes locked onto Eva's. I knew well the peace that Lynn gifted with her gaze.

Mother was nowhere to be seen. *"Eva, wo is meine Mutter? Ist sie nicht heir? "*

"Your mother is away. Suddenly she goes. Vamos, she say. Moments before you come." She shrugged and grinned, her English rough but her smile heartwarming. "It is your mother, no?"

I laughed. In our long talks after David had left, she had asked of our family. My description of my mother was candid; I had not considered them meeting, much less living with one another. Even when Eva suggested the notion of life with David and all the hopes and plans they had shared, Mother did not seem to be a player in those dreams. And now I was in their apartment in Munich. Their apartment. They were sharing life together under one roof. Whimsical winds of fate brought them together. And now our family was here as well.

Except Mother was missing. Eva shrugged, a comical little grin on her face. *"Die Elle. Sie ist eigenartig. Gespannt."*

*Flakey*, I thought.

∞

She showed us our room. Tidy and compact, so European, we would be crushed together in a bed not much larger than the cots in Number Two cottage. When we had our bags unpacked and our clothes put away in a great wooden armoire, we came to a communal pause. Omie candidly wondered, "What now?"

Ally replied, "I'm hungry." As if her plea was answered from somewhere above, Eva knocked at the door.

"We have bites to eat," she said. "Have you thirst?"

The kids whooped and hollered, rushing past Eva toward the snacks in the living room. Their enthusiasm drew a wide smile across Eva's face. Her eyes sparkled. She looked lovely, and Lynn told her so.

"Danke,"she said, glancing from Lynn to meet my eyes. "I am loved. David. His mother. And now you."

I felt warmth spread up my face, and returned her smile. "God, Eva. It is wonderful to see you." I slipped my arm around her shoulders, and Lynn put her arm around her waist on her other side. We strolled toward the clamor the twins raised as they selected their *Kuchen* and *Keksas*.

"What's this," Ally asked, eyeing a small dark pastry.

*"Franzbrotchen,"* Eva replied. *"You like…Zimpt?"* She looked to me for help.

"Cinnamon, Ally. Try it. You'll probably like it."

She snapped up a bite, and her eyes lit up. Omie was more circumspect. He pointed toward a wedge of creamy cheesecake topped with glazed apple slices. He glanced up warily.

"That's *Kasekuchen,* Omie. You'll love it."

He took a bite and studied the flavor melting on his tongue. A shy little grin flecked with cheese bits showed his approval.

We joined in, sampling the selection of *Mohnkuchen, Pfeffernusse,* and other German treats.

"Umm! This is good!" Ally smiled.

"That is *Bienenstich*," Eva said. Again she looked to me for help. "Bees," she hinted.

"Bee sting. Careful, Ally! There might be a bee in that sweetie."

She examined the pastry momentarily, glared happily at me, and chomped another bite. "Yummy," she muttered through a mouthful.

Eva motioned toward a pitcher of milk and glasses. "Have you thirst?" She asked the children. Ally howled approval, while Omie gazed up over Eva's belly, smiling timidly. He nodded, whispering "Yes, please."

We watched the children respond to the sugary snacks with a surge of energy, enthusiasm, and questions for Eva. I helped in the translation, but my replies were really a shorthand abbreviation of the answers Eva offered.

With the kids' full of milk and cakes, the toll of long travel settled in on them. I noticed Ally's eyelids looking heavy, and then Omie dropped his head on his folded arms, an unfinished marzipan bear half eaten on his plate.

No sooner had Lynn settled Ally on a day bed and I lay Omie on the sofa in the sitting room than they were sound asleep. A minute later, I heard a thunking click of the door latch. Mother had returned from her errand.

"Oh, my! They're napping!" She couldn't help herself; she leaned over first Omie, then Ally, viewing her grandchildren for the first time. She held herself back. She wanted nothing more than to give them each a kiss and a hug.

"Lovely!" She whispered, nodding, taking Lynn's hands in one of hers. "Your darlings are just beautiful!" She stood above them, smiling eyes, holding in her other hand uprooted plants with roots still clinging to soil and lengthy stems with lush green leaves showing little sign of wilting. Her fingers were muddied, her nails lined with soil.

"These were prime for harvest," she said. Scrunching her nose, she whispered, "I didn't want to chance anyone else finding them."

Lynn smiled graciously, put her arm around my mother's shoulder and casually lead her out of our suite. We closed the French doors behind us and joined Eva in the main sitting room.

"You return," Eva said. "And with more of your herbs"

Mom met her gaze. Her eyes glistened as she continued her head nodding, now directed toward Eva. "I should get them into water quickly."

"It's good to see you, Mom," I said. "I was surprised you weren't here when we arrived."

She lifted her eyebrows. "I think I panicked! I found these prime for picking, and I threw myself into them and forgot all about the time."

Eva chuckled and rose to embrace Mom, addressing her calmly in French. After a word or two, they giggled like school girls.

Mom looked back toward me with apology.

"I thought perhaps it would be too much for your little ones to meet me and Eva at the same time. I thought perhaps you should all meet together, first," she said, waving her hand toward the three of us. "You young ones, meeting first."

Lynn kissed her cheek. "You are so thoughtful, Elle! So gracious and kind."

Mother beamed. "You three will be friends for life," she said, still holding Lynn's hand with her earth caked finger. She led her to Eva. "*Comme des soeurs*. Like sisters."

∞

I wondered why I was here. The urgency I felt upon reading the letter from my mother calling me to Munich in order to marry my brother's love was nowhere evident as we sat and chatted in Eva's living room. I was inclined to let the matter rest. It was as though we had been invited for a casual afternoon tea. Had we not called across the Atlantic to determine my mother's state of mind? Was that the last we were to discuss about the state of Eva's immigration plight? Hardly. On that call, Mother had hemmed and hawed and denied anything seemingly real. We came here to Munich to determine what the problems and solutions actually were. And now, it was a topic not to be discussed at all! I distinctly felt that Mother was avoiding the more compelling discussion of Eva's immigration, and her proposed plans for my wedding. It was unsettling. Lynn's glance let me understand that she, too, wondered about the absence, or, rather, the avoidance of discussion on the matters that drew us to Munich. We waited. It would come.

∞

Our children awakened with the vigor of those who were a half a world out of sync with the time of day in Munich. Their enthusiasm sparked a few moment of family commotion but coincided with the end of Eva's day. She was weary. She bid us a good evening.

122

# Chapter 25

# Eva the Teacher

In her room, Eva settled in the rocker at the foot of her bed. The children chirping like birdsong drifted in from the living room. Eva smiled, savoring the music of their little voices.

She heard Patrick's deep voice quietly but assertively discussing issues just out of the range of hearing. Elle's replied in a tight, high-toned voice, but with muted words exchanged with her son.

Eva understood. They had years apart to address. Elle had shared her concerns about the son she didn't raise. Eva was relieved to have withdrawn to her room. She knew their discussions were about her. And her immigration.

Her hand drifted to her violin. She had set her heirloom on the side table next to her chair. She placed it under her chin, its delicate neck extended away, fine under the touch of her fingers. She let the horsetail tickle lightly upon the strings. A short stroke across first the A string and then the full compliment of her instrument's strings satisfied her; her instrument held its tone. She closed her eyes. A melody rose from her fingers dancing gently over the violin's taut strings. Bach's song was a delicate lullaby. His music lay a message of peace upon her soul. It was simple. And sweet. As the melody rose to song, Eva slowly opened her eyes.

Standing before her, silent and wide-eyed, Ally stood in wonder. Her skin glowed, her eyes shimmered. She watched Eva's fingers play upon the strings.

Eva lowered her instrument, holding Ally's gaze

Neither had words. Neither could understand how to say what they felt.

"I teach French to you," Eva whispered. "And German."

"Will you teach me music?"

∞

I watched as Ally gravitated toward the sounds flowing from Eva's room. She'd left her door ajar and our daughter was drawn like a butterfly to nectar. She stepped unbidden into Eva's bedroom.

Mother was explaining herself to me, her efforts to urge the immigration agents at the embassy to move Eva's paperwork forward. Her life in Munich. Her life without Rosie.

"Mother, why am I here?"

She streamed ideas in reply. Notions she had been mulling over as she awaited our arrival. She started with Eva's immigration. How could she get Eva and the babies, her grandchildren, to America? She said she felt stymied by the process and was uncertain of when or if Eva could return with her to the States.

I held my hands out to halt Mom's spiel. I couldn't help but smile. Mom. She was the same. More complex, more of the world, but the same. She feared anything she could not control. But she was stronger. Stronger than the fears that had so destroyed her in my youth.

She looked at my hands, then my smile. She shrugged.

"Mom, Ally's gone in with Eva. Excuse me a moment while I check on her," I shrugged. "I hope she isn't bothering Eva."

"Nonsense. Eva is drawing the child to her with her music. She's playing the Minuet," Mother said, her voice nervous. "In G. It's her way of bidding good night. It's enchanting."

How did she know it was the Minuet? Eva had touched her. She waved me on with a flip of her fingers. "Get your daughter. She's a sweet one." She got up from her chair and headed for the kitchen. "I'd like some wine. A glass of white. Would you? Or Lynn?"

"We would, indeed. Do you have red? I'd enjoy a Burgundy. Or Syrah, if you have one."

"We are tapping into our landlord's cabinet. He has it all. Go. Retrieve your little one." She squeezed past ignoring my bewildered expression, and disappeared to a closet where Herr Professor Kramer kept his wines.

I slipped though Eva's door. Ally stood before her, mesmerized. She was wrapped in Eva's arms, Eva's violin snug on Ally's shoulder. Eva carefully coached Ally how to handle the precious violin. With her own lithe fingers, Eva gently set Ally's tiny fingers on the strings just below the figurine of a woman carved in the maple scroll. She carefully bent Ally's pinky above the A string. She carefully moved her bow across strings and softly purred an A. Tapping Ally's pinky down onto the taught gut, she jumped the note a step and drew the bow again. Ally beamed.

Ally lifted her gaze to meet mine.

"She's teaching me music, Daddy."

I wanted to cry. Instead, I laughed. *"Was würde Jacob sagen?"*

*"Er würde mich dafür loben, dass er unser Kleines Mädchen unterrichtet habe."* I asked Eva how the maker of her violin would react to a child learning on his lovely instrument.

Her smile conveyed her confidence that Jacob Stainer would have approved.

I looked at my daughter. "Ally, you played lovely notes. Let's tell your mom about what Eva's teaching you!"

Ally carefully handed Eva her violin. "Thank you."

Eva lay her finger on Ally's sternum. "Danke." She flipped her finger to her own breast. "Bitte. Welcome. Danke. Thanks. Bitte, welcome."

Ally kissed Eva's cheek.

"Danke."

Eva nodded.

# An English Gardens Picnic

Mother opened a Rioja Gran Reserva. Stunning. The Professor's wine closet was indeed worthy. It seemed odd that I was sipping wine with my mother. I had never seen her consume alcohol. Ever. Maybe, I wondered, it would loosen her up and she'd discuss the issues of this marriage idea and Eva immigrating to America. She hedged around the topic before our happy hour. Now, with Lynn and the twins playing on the floor, Mother and I sat on the sofa sipping our wine. Eva had closed her door. It was late in Munich, even if the kids and I felt like it was mid-afternoon Minnesota time.

Lynn busied herself, cutting slices of cheese, breads, hard sausage, and fruits, prepping a bed lunch for the kids and us. She kept the twins occupied nearby, searching cabinets and drawers in the kitchen for utensils and plates for evening snack.

"Where exactly are we with getting Eva's immigration permit? And this marriage idea?" I asked. If I wasn't direct, I was not certain we would get to the matter at all.

Mother sipped her Riesling. She shrunk with each sip, her shoulders curling forward as she arched her spine down to her waist.

"Well, I have been to the consulate," she mumbled. "There are several options, and I've helped Eva complete the appropriate forms." For a moment, she watched the children at play. Glancing toward me, she nodded at our children. After another sip, she lifted her shoulders. "When Rose and Paddy called on Tuesday, they said Father Jack was traveling with you."

The deflection was effective. My concerns for Jack continued during his absence. "We thought he was. He didn't show up for the flight from Chicago. I don't know what to make of it. His intent was to help resolve Eva's immigration process. And this goofy marriage idea."

Her eyes flashed about as if looking for escapes.

"Yes. Jack is a maverick in many ways. You never know what priorities he might come up with to change his plans. I was relieved when I first heard he was planning to be with you." She set her empty wine glass on the end table.

Lynn and the kids joined us, carrying plates filled with tidbits for an easy meal. We nibbled and chatted, letting the pertinent issues rest until we could continue without the children listening.

"You know, Mother, I don't think I've ever seen you drink before. When did you take up tipping back a glass of wine?"

She laughed, a tinkling little noise, then blushed. It struck me as another first; I have no previous recollection of my mother blushing.

"Well, it was Rosie and Eva's doing. I can say the same thing about Rose. I had never seen her take a drink, either. But Eva offered us a nice Rheinhessen kabinett soon after we moved in with her. My, goodness, it was refreshing. Such a dear! She hasn't had a sip herself since I've been with her. The pregnancy, you know. But she assured me that the wines she has offered are worthy of the gods, and I believe her. It's no wonder the Greeks revered that Dionysus fellow!" She gave me a knowing nod and I wondered if the small portion she had just consumed had her tipsy. I reached for the bottle and offered her more, but she quickly covered her crystal. "Heavens, no. Enough!" she exclaimed.

I was amused, but I was also anxious. "What about these plans for Eva?"

Mother stood, straightened the wrinkles in her skirt, and dismissed the topic. "We can review them fully in the morning. You may still be on a Minnesota clock, but it is late here in Munich. It is time I go to bed." She nodded, then turned to her grandchildren playing on the floor with their mother. "Goodnight, little grandchildren. It fills my heart with joy to have met you. Thank you, Lynn, for bringing them and my son here to Munich." She nodded again to Lynn and went to her bedroom.

Lynn smirked. "Whatcha' know?" She was talking Minnesotan smack again. She did so when she observed me in a pickle.

I shrugged. Nothing. I knew nothing. What more could I do?

∞

When we woke late Saturday morning, mother was preparing a basket of treats for a picnic in the Munich's signature park, the English Gardens. Eva had gone to meet her students.

"She can meet us at noon," Mother reported as she poured coffee for us. "She has only two students this morning. We can join her at the Garden. It's very close. If we hurry, we can check the potatoes. They are certainly ready to harvest." Her expression bent toward the mischievous. "We should dig them on the equinox."

I sighed with exasperation. The equinox was three weeks away. I ignored any potato harvest talk, more concerned with Eva's work load.

"She's teaching? Violin, of course. Does she have many students?"

"Too many students, I'd say. She works a lot. She gives individual private lessons on Thursdays and Saturdays. And she has classes at the Institute of Art on Mondays, Wednesdays and Fridays. She lowered her voice, confiding one of her secrets. "I planted potatoes in the park. Among the flowers. And garlic." She put her finger to her lips, a warning to keep her secret.

I cringed. I didn't think I want to know about Mother's clandestine crops. It was something she couldn't help herself with, I'm certain.

"Whoa! That's a lot of work for Eva, seeing how far along she is with her pregnancy." Lynn said.

Mother looked at Lynn. "Yes, indeed. She said she will work right up until she delivers."

"When is that?"

"Well, any time, really. We think she's due the second week of September or so. David left her on December 10, so..." Mother left the thought dangle. We all did.

∞

We met up with Eva as we made our way to the gardens.

Omie spotted her when we were still a block from Konigstrasse. "Eva." He murmured.

We moved as a group with the kids questioning everything along the way. Elle asked Eva, "Will we walk far?" The French captured the twins. Their eyes widened in curious awe.

*Allons-nous marcher loin?* Are we to walk far?

*Le jardin de la bière chinoise. Chinisescher Turm. Si je peux aller aussi loin, ces deux peuvent certainement"* "Eva said, laying her hands on the kid's shoulders. Just to the Chinese Tower. If I can make it, these two definitely can.

*Peut tu?* Can you?

*Peut-être?* Maybe?

We strolled on. The lush gardens invigorated the twins. They set our pace. Mom and Lynn chatted as we walked. Eva and I dropped back at a slower pace, but we seemed to catch up every time the twins' curiosity slowed their progress. Or when Mom got sidetracked with things growing in the flowerbeds. She showed the kids where she had potatoes planted in some plots, and herbs in others. She was always on the lookout for medicinals. Kneeling along the grass border of the plot, she probed her fingers into jumbled vines and pulled up a couple potatoes. The kids marveled and were alongside their grandmother in a flash. But she hurried them off down the walk, looking slyly around the park to see whether she had been observed.

"We'll come back when more potatoes are ready to be harvested," she told the twins, each carrying their first new potatoes as they followed Mom toward the Chinese Tower. Inspecting the soiled spuds my children trea-

128

sured, I recalled the times my brother and I spent in our North Freedom garden, digging new potatoes. I chuckled at the twin's excitement.

Eva and I searched for words as we first started strolling. Then she asked, *"Wei hast du gehort?"* How did you hear?

How did I hear? I whipped my head around. I winced, then smiled. She was asking about David.

"On a trail. On a hike. From a stranger I met while hiking. He happened to know David. A coincidence. It was like a miracle."

She smiled. *"Konnte es anders sein. Vielleicht wie ein Zauber."* Could it be otherwise? Perhaps it was like magic?

We chuckled.

I told her of David's friend, Georgia. And of leaving Germany. I apologized; I was more than rude to not see her before I left. But she got the note explaining my departure from Regensburg, and she was now more interested in my having met someone who David lived with in Vietnam.

*"Und wie hast du von David erfahren"?* After telling her all I knew from Georgia, I asked how she had learned of David.

Looking up from under her brow, she said *"Deine Mutter. Sie bestätigte was ich befürchtete hatte."* Mother had delivered the news to Eva!

Eva told of waiting for David's next letter.

"There were two that arrived after I came here to work. They are addressed to you. Maria keeps them with some of my belongings that I left in Regensburg when I moved here."

She spoke of the drawn out, desperate anxiety that gnawed at the joy of her pregnancy and the anticipation of raising their children together. Hope waned.

She mustered enough courage to follow up on a lead given her by the conductor of the Regensburg orchestra, her friend Franz Meier.

She wrote to Franz's friend, Professor Kramer in Munich. Professor Kramer invited her to *das Hochschule fur die Musik unt Theatre.* He listened along with his wife as Eva played her violin. He requested several pieces that she played impromptu. Partita no. 5 in D, 1 Allemande. Partita no.2. All Bach. Her specialty. Her strength. He was delighted, as was his wife Helga, who taught cello and base at the *Hochschule.*

Professor Kramer told Eva that he sought someone of her skill to instruct his private students during his upcoming sabbatical at the Curtis Institute in Philadelphia, he explained. Professor Kramer met with Eva and offered a job filling in for him while he was in America. The new work started in May and would continue until he returned next summer.

Eva arrived in Munich in mid-May, settled in the Professor's home, and busied herself with the onslaught of new students to teach her love of the violin. The Professor so appreciated her ability that he suggested to his department head that he allow her to mentor a number of the students at the college that he had been mentoring. They needed to work with someone during the summer. That extra work load kept Eva occupied and focused, all the while she hoped against hope that a letter would arrive from David.

And then, my mother came into Eva's life.

'*Ein Geschenk des Himmel*,' Eva said. "She was a Godsend when she arrived. She and Rosie." Her face softened as she mentioned Mom and her best friend. Rosie, I thought, was indeed Mom's best friend. And maybe David's, too.

I wanted to hear more. But we had fallen too far behind the family moving ever on toward the *Chinisescher Turm* within the English Gardens. With a laugh, Ally danced back to us, falling in alongside Eva and taking her hand.

"Do you want me to carry your violin for you," Ally offered.

Eva understood. But she held her encased instrument firmly, like a hug. "Danke," she smiled at Ally. Then switching to English, she offered her more. "Thank you. But I like to be holding my violin."

Ally didn't know that no one carried Eva's violin. I never had. David, perhaps, being an exception. She did let him play it. At least once. I was there. And then, last night, she let Ally hold it.

We caught up with the others and Eva begged off.

"Elle, I now know. *Der Chinesches Turm* is too far. I walk enough." She placed a hand behind her back and arched.

The kids were glad to hear it. It was picnic time. I carried the basket toward a grassy little hill with a bench. Eva and Mom sat on the bench. Lynn and the kids and I set up the picnic on a slope rolling down to where Mother and Eva sat. I grabbed the kids and rolled them, first Omie, then Ally, down the slope. We repeated the fun several times, then switched roles. The twins urged me to get in position at the top of the little hill, then pushed and shoved, but couldn't roll me over. Lynn, who was snapping pictures as we played, chided, "You stubborn oaf! Get the anchor out!"

So I rolled, the twins thinking it was the best fun ever. At the bottom of the slope they piled on and I squirmed and wiggled as they did their best to keep me grounded. But I emerged from beneath them, roaring as I picked them up, one on each shoulder. I stalked over to the bench. The twins' faces lit with amusement; Eva and Mom had encouraged the kids to somehow gain control and tame me! It was not to be—until Lynn hung a half sandwich over my roaring mouth.

“Hmmm,” I muttered. “Perhaps more tasty than a twin or two.”

“Let us down,” Ally laughed. “Beast!”

Omie rode out the struggle with a quiet grin. As I swung Ally down from my shoulder, I felt his little arms cling close to my neck. I left him up. He rode contentedly on my left fore arm as we went to our picnic.

# Chapter 27

# Life in Munich

Thus our extended stay in Munich was defined. We played. We read and we drew. We walked the city, exploring parks, searching for herbs and potatoes that Mother had clandestinely planted and cultivated all summer. We took in the museums. Eva took us to a matinee opera at the Prinzregententheater a few blocks away. We shopped, both for the essentials of food as well as for the luxuries that big cities afforded us rural travelers.

We just never discussed directly any sort of plan for Eva's immigration to the States. It was a subject that Mother deftly deflected. When the conversation seemed about to take hold, something intervened; the bell would ring and a delivery would arrive. Omie would howl after a fall as he chased after his sister. Eva's midwife, Vidya, *die Habamme*, would arrive for Eva's pre-birthing work out of stretches, breathing, and meditations. The tea kettle would sing. It would be time to repeat Eva's yoga routines. If nothing else, Mother would recall something of critical importance and run off, not to escape our conversation she assured us, but to resolve the impending issue.

One afternoon after Eva returned from teaching, the twins and Mom were preoccupied with a craft project. Mother was elbow deep in paper mache and the kids were in it to their shoulders. They were making something that looked like a lump with a hole on top.

"Are you to yoga?" Eva asked. "Vidya is to come soon."

"Absolutely," Lynn replied. She glanced at the mountain building project in the kitchen. "Oh, boy. The twins are a mess. I better get them cleaned up before Vidya gets here." She got up and drifted into the kitchen, discussing with Elle the project's progress and prognosis.

For one so far along in her pregnancy, Eva sat lightly on a stuffed chair alongside the sofa on which I was stretched.

I asked her in German. "What were you practicing this morning?" She had played something by Bach, a piece I was certain I had heard before.

"Partita. Zwie. D minor."

"I love it."

She smiled. "*Doch. Ebenso.*" She settled back into the softness of the pillows. She relaxed, sinking into her yoga demeanor. She switched back to English. "Are you to make yoga?"

I nodded, "Do. To do yoga. Or to practice yoga."

She nodded,

"Eva, where are you with immigration?" I blurted the question that was at the center of my family's presence in Munich.

"Waiting," she reverted to Deutsch. "Up to date with forms. Everything is current, until there is something else. Or medical reports. Or a new form. And of course there is the pregnancy. But it is well."

I considered it. After a moment, I asked, "And in your head. How are you thinking about it. And feeling."

She thought, and she glowed. "It is hope, is it not? Hope can be of lovely light colors, when it is worthy and focuses on something pure. As is this. David has given me family. It is a dream. I have always dreamt of family." Her gaze pierced me, then turned toward the sounds of the twins and their mother drifting through the hallways. "Family," she said again. "So I hope. And I wait. It was explained to me, this be lengthy process. I wait." She looked toward the hallway where we heard the children welcome Vidya. "And I do yoga."

I nodded, resigned, The details again eluded me. I sat up.

Time for yoga.

# Chapter 28

# Regensburg Revisited

Eva suggested a trip to Regensburg. She had papers, some letters, and books that she'd left behind when she moved to Munich and some personal thing she hoped with our help she could retrieve before delivering her babies.

"Eva, dear," Mom said. "You could go into labor at any moment. This is not the time for travel."

A whimsical smile sprouted across Eva's face. "Perhaps, that be best to make this go," she said, lifting her belly with both hands.

We laughed. Both mother and Lynn nodded with understanding and empathy. And both warned against the trip.

But Eva was determined. She wanted all in order for after her delivery. The nursery next to her bedroom was prepared; the cribs were lined with clean linen and warm woolen blankets. The nursery cabinet held neatly stacked diapers, towels, and garments that Elle and Rose helped her buy in the months when her energy levels were high. Not that she had slowed down much. She continued her work schedule and perhaps even increased the time spent in yoga and meditation. All was in order, but she tended to the details over again. She was nesting.

And again, mother and Lynn understood her need to have everything in place for the arrival of her newborn. But they argued against her travel.

"Too risky," Mom declared.

"Elle's right," Lynn added. "Would you like your children born on a train?"

Eva pursed her lips. "No. Okay. I just want my things from Maria."

I gave her an option. She stays home, I go to Regensburg and retrieve what she needed. I didn't mention the letters from David she had mentioned. But they were on my mind.

"Is Regensburg far?" Lynn asked. "Is it something we can do in a day trip?"

"Two hours in train," Eva said. "Less."

"We can do that, can't we?" Lynn posed. "There and back in a day. About like going from Ely to Duluth."

I considered it. Sure. Easier than a trip to Duluth. We wouldn't have to drive. Taxi to the train station, Munich's *Bahnhoff,* and a two hour train ride. Taxi in Regensberg to the apartments on the Etage where Eva had stored her belongings with Maria, her closest friend and colleague in the University chamber orchestra. Grab a quick lunch along the way. I'd made the trip a dozen times during my days in residence in Regensburg. We'd even have time to tour the city for an hour or two before catching the return train that evening.

Mom's eyes widened. I recognized an old expression that, as a youth, I had seen in her too often. She appeared to be almost overwhelmed.

"Yes," I answered. "We could do it. We could take the twins, too."

Mom's face visibly softened.

"Well, they could stay with me for the day. I think that would work if it allows you to move around more easily."

"Not necessary," I assured her. "I'd like them to see Regensburg. I'd like you to see Regensburg, too."

Mom shook her head. "I've seen Regensburg. I searched all over that charming city, trying to find Eva." She demurred. It was clearly a relief that the twins would go with us; but she had no inclination to go along, however-er. "Not this time. I will remain here with Eva. Another time, perhaps."

Eva looked relieved.

"Vielen Dank," she said. "I be thanks."

Ally chuckled. "You mean 'I am thankful', Eva."

"Doch. Thankful. I am thankful."

∞

In the morning, we boarded a train headed north to retrieve Eva's things from Regensburg.

The kids were fascinated with the train ride. We piled into an empty compartment with no time to spare before the train glided out of the *Bahnhoff* at precisely the scheduled departure time, and within minutes we watched Bavaria whiz by. The conductor opened the door to our compartment and the twins looked up with a start.

*"Reisepass und tickets, bitte,"* he said, his Bayriche accent rumbling like the gnar of a bear. He checked our papers, punched our tickets, and nodded as he passed our papers back. He raised an eyebrow in salute to the twins, who gawked wide eyed at his uniform. He bowed his head and left us to ourselves.

Omie turned his eyes toward the window and was silent the rest of the way. Ally chattered joyfully; her curiosity blossomed.

When we stepped off the train in Regensburg, I reached for Omie's hand and helped him jump the final step to the platform. He glanced up gratefully, and I swung him up onto my arm. He was like a little monkey sitting on a limb. He liked perching on my arm. He was slight, much like Davey. He could ride around on my forearm like he was in an easy chair.

"Who is that man?" Omie whispered as we passed the conductor helping people step down on to the concourse from the far end of our car.

I looked about, but there was no one conspicuous person who I thought he was referring to.

"What man?"

"The man who growled. The soldier."

I followed his gaze to the conductor.

"Oh! The conductor. He works for the railroad. Did you like him?"

Omie's eyes narrowed to slits. He shook his head.

"He looked at me funny."

I asked him what he meant.

"He looked from behind his eyes."

An involuntary shiver swept me. What could Omie have meant? My son perceived things that might otherwise be unnoticed. I knew that asking might not lead to an answer. Instead of probing, I tightened my grip on his little body perched on my arm. I love the way he leaned close into me, like I'm his security blanket.

∞

We did a mini-tour of some of my favorite spots in Regensburg. The Kaffee and Kuchencafé, and the farmers market by the Danube. I showed Lynn the concert hall where David and I heard Eva give a perfect performance. And we walked past the Old Stone Bridge to Adolf Smetzlerstrasse and my old apartment.

"This is where I lived when I went to school here in Regensburg," I told the kids. The door to my apartment building had an unusually high knob. The twins looked up at the door with the elevated lock and handle.

"Can you open it?" I asked them.

Ally jumped toward the handle but missed by half a foot. Omie just glared at the odd placement of the hardware.

"David said this doorknob was too high for him when he first came to visit me," I laughed.

Lynn considered the notion. "David visited you here. Amazing."

I nodded.

The bell was clearly out of reach to the kids. I reached up to ring it. In a moment, I heard the clomping of footsteps pounding the old wood staircase. The door latch clattered and the heavy door swung back. There stood Uli, my closest friend from my time here at the University!

*"Der Patrick!"* he cried. *"Servus! Komm bitte rein. Und ver hat dich dabei?"* Hello! Come in! Who do you have with your?

136

I wondered why Uli greeted us with German when his Oxford English was more polished than my American, but I shrugged it off. It had been months since I'd seen him, but it seemed like years. So much had happened since I'd left Regensburg.

"Lynn, this is my good friend Uli," I directed my comment to Lynn. Turning back to Uli, I returned to German.

*"Das ist meine Familie. Die Liebe meines Lebens, Lynn, und meine Zwillingkinder, Ally und Omie."* This is my family. The love of my life, Lynn and my twin children, Ally and Omie.

*How could this flow so easily from my mouth!* I wondered.

Switching to English, I added, "Now if you wish to dazzle my family with the Queens lovely English, they will very much enjoy speaking with you."

Uli beamed, shaking his head.

"My good chap, it does seem as if it's been a while since you took your leave of us, but certainly not long enough to raise a pair of vigorous twins. How could this be?" His eyes couldn't help but wander to Lynn. Beautiful Lynn.

"Come in! Come in!"

We climbed the stairs to the Etage as I gave him the micro-version of our history, and told him of our visit to Germany on Eva's behalf.

"Yes, indeed," he said. "Maria explained that you are with Eva these days. This is good, is it not? I am sorry for your loss. Your brother was a bright spot here in the Etage. His time here with Eva."

"Yes. David." I nodded. And winced. It had become reflexive. "And now, it is good to be with Eva again."

"Come. Maria waits. She is so excited to see you. We have Eva's things ready for you to take to her." He opened the door to the Etage and the voice of a woodwind poured out. Maria was greeting us with a melody I remembered well. She honed her mastery of it during the my months living in the Etage. Her favorite song. Tipping her head right and left, she peeled the scales and measures, crouching all the while, playing at eye level with the children. She mesmerized them with her spell. Omie studied her fingers. He tipped his head, listening to the sound spilling from the woodwind. After a couple minutes of the piece, she rested her clarinet, and aimed a great smile toward the twins.

"Chromatic Fantasy. Bach. Johann Sebastian,"she said. 'He wrote it to delight you." She spoke softly, intentionally to the twins.

They were wonderstruck.

"Patrick, it is good to see you again," she said, rising up to meet us. She gave Lynn a particularly warm smile and took her hand. "When she called to tell me you were to visit, Eva told me very lovely things about you, Lynn. Her new sister, she says of you. I feel kin to Eva, as well. Welcome, sister. Such lovely children you bring to visit us!"

We ate more *Kuchen.* We drank more coffee. Uli pulled out a bottle of schnapps, and he and I downed a requisite *gemutlich* portion. We shared our updates; Uli and Maria were to be married later in the fall. They had both finished their last term and were soon to be relocating to Bonn. They had missed saying farewell, and were glad now to have a chance to visit and send me off again. Which we did in due time to catch our train back to Munich, several boxes of Eva's belongings in hand.

"Perhaps we will see you soon. After the babies come," Maria promised when we left them.

∞

The kids slipped into the magical slumber of exhausted children before the train had rolled out of the *Bahnhoff.*

"Do you supposed we stunned your friends," Lynn chuckled.

I watched her smile widen and her eyes twinkle. She was so tolerant of my behavior during my absence. Every time something from my past few years came up, she showed ample curiosity but never jealousy. I cringed nonetheless. My relationships with others while in Regensburg prior to my return to America would have given no clue to my having a family. I mean, I didn't even know! The memory of my life in the Etage must have strained Uli and Marie's notion of what my life had been all about.

Lynn spread her sweater over Ally, and used my sweatshirt to cover Omie.

Germany was a blur of late summer green outside the window of our compartment. Omie lifted his lids half way, not enough to see more than a split image of his mother nestling him close. Then he fell back to the deep slumber. Ally was gone, deep into dreamland.

Lynn looked across the seats, her eyes soft with the smile she so often had for me.

I spoke, hoping not to bluster.

"Uli and Maria were quite more than shocked, even though Eva warned them. I don't blame them. Sometime I'm shocked at how I took such a tenuous route back to you. *'Given our own devices, the human soul tends to challenge itself unnecessarily with foolish and difficult tests frivolous to the essence of good sense.'* I believe that is a direct quote from one of David's letters. He had been writing of us. Or at least, of me in the context of us."

138

Her eyes sparkled joyfully, then softened suddenly to melancholy.

"Did you ever wonder about my time away from you? Of how my days and nights were?" she asked.

"Of course." I looked again out at the passing German countryside. Then back into her gaze. "Every day. All the time. Every day. And at night. Especially at night." I could taste the bitterness of my jealousy. Nights and days when I wondered who may have had my Lynn. And my taking others in her place in hollow pursuit of pleasure. Almost like revenge. I had wasted so much of myself in spite of the love that was true. "Tell me."

She moved her foot in the space between the seats of our compartment, hooking it around the back of my calf. She rested the top of her foot against the warmth of my leg.

"It was worse at first. It was chaos, with Ingie. And then Dad, and losing the house in Minnetonka. My life was a series of decisions about questions and crises that I had no say in. No control over anything.

"I never bothered with even the littlest personal decision. What to wear that day. Whether to go to a movie. Or who to be with. All the day-to-day decisions—I just didn't have time for them. It was all life and death, every moment, a right now reckoning. I accepted the decisions I had to make without fretting on the missed alternatives. I did what I had to do when it was asked of me. Then the twins came along. Oh, it shook me to my soul when Dr. Franklin told me they were twins! Two children! I never considered it. I never had time to. The decision was made for me. I focused on Ingie. And Dad." She gazed at me for moments.

"The World, Patrick. It broke me. I could not handle all it tossed at me."

She was so brave. I told her so. She lifted an eyebrow and shrugged.

"It wasn't a matter of being brave," she said, turning to glance at Germany passing outside the compartment window. When she turned back, she locked eyes with me. She tilted her head and smiled. "I didn't need bravery. I needed you. And the thought of you sustained me. I believed in you, Patrick. I knew you. I trusted you would find me. Believing in you gave me faith in myself. And that held me over. That, and the care of my friends, Martha and Ixchel. When I bent, when I broke, they saw me through. Saved me, really. My soul, anyway. They showed me the light. They showed me how to see. How to look and and how to gaze into the matrix of that which is now and yet to be. How to scry. And how to cry."

With a tilt of her head, she continued. "How to live my life as a prayer. That's all. To live as a prayer. For others. For Ingie, and Dad. Our kids. You."

That set me off balance. I thought of Lynn always. But did I pray for her? Did I even know how to pray?

"Just breath," Lynn said. "That's all it takes, if you set your heart to see-ing."

When we talked about our time apart, or the meaning of our being, we inevitably ended by sharing love. I wanted her so much at this very moment, it hurt.

She smiled and the twinkle sparkled again in her eye. She could feel my need. She teased. "I want you."

I dropped my head back against the tall seats of the railcar. "Never more than now," I muttered.

She chuckled. "So you know now what it was like for me during those years. I wanted you, always. But it wasn't the right time. I had to wait. It was like an incantation from all the universe, set upon me. On us. We had to let it form. To develop. To see whether our wills were aligned. Melded togeth-er. To know it's perfect conjuration. It was ours to determine. Ours."

She rested her eyes on me. "And here we are. Wanting one another above all."

I moaned, and she laughed aloud.

"Remember that summer, how I would drop you off at your Aunt's house and we'd plan to meet later when the time was right?"

"Yeah." I thought of that often.

"Later."

# Chapter 29

# Prelude

The twins were rested by the time the train rolled into the Munich *Bahnhoff.* We piled into a taxi and headed back to Eva's.

The drive was short, and in minutes we poured into Eva's apartment with bluster and enthusiasm. Ally proudly carried a satchel with the papers and documents that Eva had left with Maria for safekeeping. Omie carried a box wrapped with gift paper featuring butterflies and bees flitting above a canopy of sunflowers. Maria had trusted Omie to deliver the baby presents to Eva, and Omie carried them with the air of a dedicated soldier. Lynn and I carried Eva's storage boxes

We were all shaken by Eva's appearance. Pacing from living room to kitchen and back, Eva walked with Vidya at her side, her arm tucked securely in the crook of Vidya's elbow, her violin in her other hand. Her face was tense, her gaze steady and distant. With little more than a nod and a salutation, they strolled on with purpose.

"Hello," Eva nodded. Vidya greeted us with a simple, calm glance.

Mother trailed Eva like a lost puppy. She detoured toward us at the door.

"How was your trip?" Elle asked, distracted.

"We rode the train," Omie offered. "We ate cakes all day. I have a box for Eva from Maria."

Eva glanced back over her shoulder as they trudged on.

"She's had contractions now for six hours, but they seem to be weaker and longer in between," Mom said. "Vidya thinks it's a false labor."

"I went through two false labors before these two came along," Lynn said. "They weren't ready, I suppose." She put Eva's box on top of the one I set down. She joined the pacing pair.

Mom shrugged. "What have you got there, Ally? More of Eva's things? Let's take them into the library, please, until a better time."

We stacked the boxes in the library. Omie hung on to Maria's gift and fell in behind Eva and Vidya as they passed back through the vestibule on the way to the living room. Eva appeared less tense.

"Please forgive," she said. "I contract when you arrive." She turned to Omie. "What have you, Om?"

He whispered as he held out the package. "From Maria." Having delivered his charge, he clasped his hands and watched with anticipation for Eva to open the box.

But Eva looked at Maria's card first, which gave explicit directions to wait until the births of Eva's twins before opening the gift. Omie was taken aback. He had done so well caring for Maria's present. He had not considered that it may not be opened immediately. His sense of gratification was put on hold.

Lynn took Eva's elbow, walking and chatting. Later, Vidya checked Eva one last time before leaving and assessed Eva to be no further dilated than when she had arrived around noon.

"Good practice, is it not?" she declared. "We will be ready."

Eva gave her a grateful but disappointed smile. I had not seen a hint of Eva being impatient about her pregnancy before this false alarm. We felt Eva's fatigue.

Mom made a hot soothing chamomile and mint tea that we shared. The rigors of the day caught up with us. Eva showed the most wear. She sipped the tea and remained quiet, listening to the twins' account of our day trip, asking questions of what they had observed in Regensburg, and about their meeting with Maria. But before long, she begged leave and went to bed.

In her room, Eva picked up her bow and played her violin, but briefly.

Mom followed suit. Then the twins climbed into bed shortly after, the boost of energy from their naps on the train thankfully short lived.

# Chapter 30

# Touching Home

Lynn and I were alone.

She bore an expression of curious concern.

"I wonder how Ingie and Martha are doing at home?"

I thought she might be getting homesick.

"Call her," I suggested. "What is it? Noon in Ely?"

I led her into the Professor's study and took up the phone to ring an operator for help in placing the cross-Atlantic call. Once the phone at the resort rang, I handed her the receiver.

In a moment, her eyes lit up, her smile spreading.

"Martha, it's Lynn. How are you?

She listened, nodding, her smile totally conquering her face. I could hear Martha's muffled voice sharing the news back home. But her words were indistinguishable. I waited for Lynn's replies.

"Teddy's made that much progress? Wonderful!" Again she listened and her brow crinkled. "Does he think it will be soon? Oh, dear. I bet Ingie is as impatient as a ferret." Martha's reply made her laugh outright.

"And you? All is well?" She listened for several moments, interjecting an "Oh," and a "Really?"

Nothing tests one's patience as much as being the eavesdropper on a one-sided phone conversation, listening to the 'ohs' and 'ahs' of concern. Lynn ignored my questioning looks, turned away. Torture. I had no choice but to listen to the relatively meaningless side of a conversation

Lynn's tone brightened as she turned to answering Martha's questions about our visit to Munich. She told of our trip to Regensburg, and of the days we walked the old city in Munich, touring museums, parks, and the *Konditories* and *Cafes*, while Eva worked, meeting us at various places after her lessons were done, Lynn shared the details of our living situation.

"It's really a big old house that Eva has for the duration that Professor Kramer is in the States," Lynn explained. "It's his family home. He was raised here, and lives here with his wife." Their home, like most in the inner wards of the city, were crushed under carpet bombing during the war. Their stables, which had become their garage and were the workers quarters before the war, remained relatively unscathed behind the rubble of the home. The Professor, then in his early teens, was away, having reported for conscription. He returned a few days later, refused for service to his country due to his malformed foot. He limped, and was deemed unsuited for duty. The clubfooted violinist was the only youth to be turned away for duty that particular day. His presence at the military receiving quarters saved him from the bombs that killed his parents and destroyed his family home. Only the lightly damaged garage remained, and over the years he built it into a fine home. Now, in his absence, Eva occupied it. Eva and her new family.

"It's large. There are only two primary bedrooms, but there is an office, a library, a study, an aviary on the roof, if you can believe! Patrick's mother raises herbs up there, and she feeds her bird friends," Lynn told Martha. "We are very comfortable. The Professor and his wife are on sabbatical. They were in Michigan all summer, and just now are heading to Philadelphia where he will teach."

She explained how the Kramer's had asked Eva to reside in their home while they were away. They had arranged for maintenance, but assured her they would be grateful if she lived in residence to oversee that all was well. Eva had admitted that when she had appeared for her interview with the professor, he had at first been unaware of her pregnancy. After his wife sensed Eva's condition, she and her husband were adamant she "take refuge" in their home from where she could concentrate on her students until she was ready to give birth. He was elated that her skills were such that he felt confident about her taking on his students, and considered it appropriate that she use his home while they traveled the U.S. It worked well for all.

"Oh," Lynn dropped her tone. She listened. "Wow. Teddy is with her now? Ok. Tell her we all miss her. Especially the kids. I'll call her tomorrow, Ok?"

She listened to more, nodding, humming her acknowledgement of the messages Martha was sharing. Then she choked a laugh.

They said goodbye.

Lynn turned her gaze to me.

"Come on. This day is running out of time." She caressed my neck with the sweep of her fingers as she headed to our room.

She never stopped talking the entire time we made love.

She recapped her perspectives of our day. The trip to Regensburg. The train. Ally's exuberance. Omie's wonder. My friends, and their curious awe when meeting our family. Uli and Maria had looked at each other's astonished expressions as I explained that I, too, was surprised by the twin's being in my life. But I assured them that my heart was always driven by my love for Lynn. They smiled, but their shared glances revealed their surprise in the contrast of my present situation compared to my life at the Universitate in the last year.

Lynn had been something short of smug as I made my explanations. Maria nodded and accepted what I told them, steering our conversation back to English and glancing over to Lynn every time I shifted into German to offer explanations. Uli however was hopeless; his face revealed awe, amazement, and a profound sense of humor over my predicament. It was clear that I had lived a free spirited lifestyle during my time at the Regensburg. I found myself constructing my explanation as cleverly as possible, without embarrassing Lynn as well as not alerting the twins to the relationships I carried on before reuniting with their mother. Lynn saw, however, that I had other women in my time away from her. And those women, particularly one woman, was well known to Uli and Maria. Lynn read right through the veiled explanation. She was amused.

"I loved meeting Maria and Uli," she said. Her voice changed to taunting. She turned me over and straddled me. "They led me to think that you may have had way too good a time here in Germany."

I cringed.

That became her tease. We were entirely entwined in our loving, moving, caressing, thrusting, pressing into each other. She drove me wild with every motion of her body. She worked her tease, and she let it go. She moved on.

"Sounds like Teddy is courting Ingie. Martha says he's there every morning before work. He's loved her since they were children."

I groaned. She moved in a rhythm paced by her thoughts.

"She's missing the twins."

"Martha?" I gasped. My mind lagged behind our passionate dance.

"Well, yes." She moved slowly, pressing her hips into me, squeezing her legs into my sides. "Yes. But Ingie." She gasped, then sighed. Her thoughts spiced her moves. She set her hands alongside my neck and dangled her locks across my shoulders and face.

"And Luther."

Synced. We were in sync. I moaned. Quiet, she let her movements take her.

When she spoke again, her voice was but a whisper. "Teddy's at a standstill with the pool."

The thought registered. I asked, "A problem?"

She folded down upon me, her arms cradling my head, the heat of her breasts warmed my chest.

"Pump and motor." She pressed against me. She paused. "Backorder." She pressed a last time, gently and slowly, with after tremors.

Stilled, she blanketed me. Her deep breaths were a whisper in my ear. Feeling myself still part of her, I pulled the cover up over her back and held her as we slept.

# Chapter 31

# Chaconne

E va's warmup sang like wind chimes stirring in morning quiet. I listened as her fingers limbered over the violin's taut gut. She'd run a riff, then pause. I pictured her adjusting the tuning pegs. She'd strike a note, then adjust, then hit it again. Seldom could I hear the difference her adjustments made. She buried herself in Bach. She worked her fingers gently into the melody. A minute or two into the piece, she paused, returned a measure or two she had just played, first tweaked a trilling high, and pause, then the measure again. The trill tightened. She pressed forward with it. Her notes where crystal. Her music flowed like honeysuckle on a cool evening breeze.

I knew the twins listened to her play as well. I'd hear them soon. The patter of their little feet on the hardwood floors first to Eva's room, then here to us. To roust us. To claim their morning dose of family. Of mom. Their mom, who's sleepy head rested on my chest, her body wedged snug to my shoulder, warm between my arm and chest.

Eva stroked her violin to Bach's *Chaconne*. I knew this piece. She had told me about Bach's tombeau that she mastered in the months after David left her in Regensburg. They had played it together often while he was with her. It was not until after he returned to duty that she gained a degree of perfection over the timbre of every note, every measure, till she was satisfied to have reached her aim to perform the *Chaconne* for David. She explained how she teased the up-tone melody that bantered with the play of Bach's deep, base reply. She saw David in every note, she said. She heard the melody plead with him to return to her, to live, to survive. It was the last piece I heard her play before I left for the Trail months ago. She had imprinted it in the melancholy of my memory, and I had walked the mountains of the Appalachian Trail to the agony of its conflicting debate. Now, however, in her mastery, she commanded all that I could imagine emotionally knowing or feeling, listening to Bach's lament. She was thinking of David. I too thought of my brother, my twin.

Lynn sniffed and I saw tears.

"Are you okay?"

"Yes," she said. "It's Eva. She breaks my heart when she plays this."

I kissed her tears and she started, seeing my smile.

"What?"

"Like sisters. *Tu es comme des sœurs.*"

She laughed her tears against my chest.

Eva had played the *Chaconne* often since we'd been here. I told Lynn how she practiced it with David when he was with her. He had coached her on tones and lingering, inviting inflections she might play into a chord, or even single notes. She had sought perfection on the piece, playing it over and over again. She had mastered Bach's commemoration to love and loss that she now played magically. Each time, it was perfection. Sometimes when we listened to Eva, Lynn's gaze caught my eyes. Her expression told me, she knew Eva was playing with David in mind. And in her heart.

# Chapter 32

# Jack Arrives

Eva's final note lingered as the chimes for the door rang. We had a visitor. The patter of little feet sped by outside our bedroom door. We were spared for the moment from the expected intrusion of the twins; instead, we were called to rescue any visitor from the zeal of Ally and the inquisitive peering of her brother. But before we could jump into our jeans and pull on shirts, the squeal from the twins had us both grabbing our robes and rushing to the raucous greeting going on in the vestibule. We found the twins chatting merrily, nestled comfortably, one on each of Jack's thick arms.

Jack greeted us with a big grin.

"Mommy!" Ally cheered. "Jack's here!"

We stood shocked. I had given up on him a few days after we had arrived from Chicago. He hadn't been in touch with Martha, nor had he communicated with Rose and Paddy as of last weekend when I called them. Now, here he was, big and burly, a grin the size of Burntside Lake.

"Nice to see you," I greeted him.

Lynn gave him a wide-armed hug that enclosed the threesome, her twins and the big bear sporting a roman collar.

"Good to see you, too," he laughed. "Wasn't sure we would, this side of the Atlantic.

"Had us wondering," I nodded. "What, got waylaid?"

"Something of that sort," he said, and I looked twice to see the rush of a blush rise on his cheeks above his beard.

"Must be good," I laughed. "You're embarrassed about something."

"Later," he said, glancing around. "Is Elle here? And I'd like more than anything to meet Eva."

"She's in there," Omie said, pointing over my shoulder to Eva's study, where she had just finished playing.

He carried the kids as he headed toward the study. Eva met us at the door. She glowed. I'd seen her transcendent expression often when she practiced. Her glowing, however, flowed from a truly happy face; her smile was grateful and welcoming, and she leveled her gaze at him as though they were old friends.

*"Pater Jack, der Priester,"* Eva greeted him. *"Der beste Freund und Mentor meines Mannes. Ich bin so froh sich zu treffen."* Father Jack, the priest. The best friend and mentor of my man. I am so happy to know you.

*"Meine Leibe Eva, Ich freue mich Sie kennenzulernen,. Wir haben beide gesegnet, David in unserem Leben gehabt zu haben."* I am pleased to meet you, Eva. We both are blessed to have had David in our lives. He took her hand with his from the arm supporting Ally. The twin spun into Eva like a little monkey, wrapping her in a hug.

Jack spoke German! I felt my eyebrows rise. I was stunned again. First he appears, then he speaks German. "I didn't know you knew German"

"You never said anything to me *in der Muttersprache*"

I guess I hadn't. The notion never occurred to me.

"Well, welcome!" Lynn said, helping Eva with her load of twin. "You have much to tell, and much to explain," she teased. "But first, Patrick and I will get properly dressed. Have you had breakfast?"

Before he could answer, Mother stepped into our circle. She said nothing, drying her hands on a dish towel, smiling happily at her friend, Jack.

"Elle!" Jack cried. He swallowed her up with his free right arm and hugged her tight, with Omie caught up in the squeeze. Omie's eyes grew great and round, and he watched with interest as Mom and Jack shared welcomes.

"Oh, Jack! So good to see you," Mom's muffled greeting came from within the wraps of Jack's bear hug.

"We welcome to you, Father Jack," Eva said, switching to English. "Have you hunger? I do! Come, let us break fast.'

"I've got things about ready," Elle said from deep within Jack's hug. "I made plenty. Pancakes. It's a good thing you are here to help us eat them, Jack Hanley."

She stepped from his embrace, taking charge of her little grandson, his eyes like big polished buttons, his eyebrows at full mast.

∞

"We missed you in Chicago," Lynn said as we mowed through Mom's stacks of pancakes.

"Ran into a diversion of sorts," Jack said. He sipped on Mom's rich black coffee and sighed. "I was on my way to the airport. 'Chicago's finest' found grounds to detain me for a few days." He went back to his coffee.

"Chicago's finest?" Lynn gasped. "What, were you arrested?"

He smiled sheepishly. "I was. It was not intended."

Ally looked at Jack with the widest of eyes. "Father Jack! Did you get thrown in the slammer?"

The burst of our laughter caught Jack up short. He gulped a swallow of coffee and it went down the wrong way. We laughed, he coughed. In a moment, we were settled back down.

150

"Yes, I admit," Jack eyed Ally. "I got thrown in the slammer! Now where did you hear about people getting 'thrown in the slammer', Ally?"

She beamed. "Auntie Ingie says that Omie and I should get thrown in the slammer all the time. Auntie has extra words for when she's talking about the slammer." She beamed.

"Well, she's probably right in what she says about the slammer. But I have never before spent a moment in the slammer," Jack noted. "And I don't intend to repeat myself. I just got caught up in the moment."

"And what, may I ask, were the grounds that the Windy City's finest considered strong enough to put you in the clink?" I asked.

He shot me a look from the corner of his eye. He turned to the young ones and said, "Close your ears. Go on. Cover them." He waited for Omie to cover his ears with his hands, and motioned toward his sister, who muffled both her ears with the press of her palms. When Omie had also complied, he quickly muttered, "Resisting arrest. Striking an officer."

My mouth hung open. I glanced at Lynn. Much the same, but a lot more bug-eyed.

He shrugged. "I hit him, the bastard." After a pause, he added, "As Ingie would say."

He told us all about the activity in Chicago for the 1968 Democratic Convention. The protests in Lincoln Park. "They planned some singing, is what I understood. Protest songs, and the like. Well, it got out of hand. When the police came. Well, I have never before in my life hit someone." He shook his head. "Never. Not even when I was a youngster and my brother the bishop bullied and tormented me. But Chicago's police were turned loose, and I happened to be in their way. They were shoving and pushing me, and I nearly fell underfoot. But I landed a pretty good haymaker on one gentleman in blue," he grinned. "And the party was over for me."

Lynn was laughing. "So you chose a cop. A Chicago cop. Nice. A bit dramatic, maybe. But nice."

Even Jack burst out laughing. Eva smiled; the mirth was contagious.

The twins unplugged their ears to hear the laughter. Ally blurted, "Why did you hit the policeman?"

We burst out laughing again.

When we caught our breaths, Father Jack reached over to Ally's nose with a stout, long pointer finger. He flicked her nose. "You were listening." She squirmed, smiled and laughed as she settled on her mother's lap.

"Yep," Ally confessed, beaming, looking ever so much like Lynn would have at that age.

# Chapter 33

# Immigrations at the Consulate

Over more coffee or tea, we discussed the day's plans.
Eva had no lessons scheduled, but she did have her regular appointment at the Consulate for immigration matters. I perked up when I heard that.

Mom shrunk even smaller than she was and pulled her cup up close to her face. She looked like she was hiding; she dwindled to almost nothing behind her cup of tea.

I snapped to attention. I could feel my eyes widen as I thought of the implications for Eva. The pancakes suddenly stuck in my gullet.

"You're going to the consulate?" I blustered. I had been so discouraged by the lack of information about Eva's immigration that to all of a sudden be privy to a glimpse of it was, well, breathtaking.

Eva blinked. "Yes. We meet. It is time. There will be forms. More forms."

I glanced at Mom. She was hiding entirely behind her cup and the creamer, which she had pulled before her to expand her tea cup sheltering fence.

Jack eyed my mother. "What is the status of Eva's immigration? What are the options? Any progress?"

Lynn chimed in, "Where are you in the process of going to America?"

"I say, it is much wait. Wait, wait, wait," she said. "I fill out new forms. I do as they ask." She shrugged. "We will see."

Mom stayed mum.

I asked. "May we go with you?" I checked Eva's gaze, and turned to Lynn. "Both of us?"

Lynn asked, "The twins?"

From behind her cup, Mother spoke up, "I'll watch them."

Eva frowned. She looked at Mom and asked in French, "*Tu ne viendras pas ave moi?* You won't come with me?"

Mom shrugged. "*Laisse Patrick et Lynn vous accompagner.*" She looked at me. "You go."

Jack looked first to me. Then to Eva, he said in French, "*Puis-je venir? J'ai déjà aidé avec des questions d'immigration. En Asie, mais toujours dans les consulats. Ou ambassades.*" "May I come along? I have helped with immigration matters before. In Asia. But always in Concilates. Or Embassies, he repeated in English.

Eva nodded. *"Je vous serais reconnaissant."* I would appreciate that.

∞

Catherine Reichle at the consulate was welcoming but stiff. She expected Eva and Mom. She asked if Elle was well. Eva nodded, explaining that my mother was tending her grandchildren. Ms. Reichle turned her focus on me.

I introduced myself as my mother's son. I spoke English. She had addressed Eva freely in German, and some in English. She looked at me, then Lynn, then Jack.

I introduced each of them.

"And your relationship to Eva? she inquired.

I sucked air deeply. Then sighed.

Jack intervened. "We are her friends. Her family." He left his words hang. "We hope we can help in getting Eva passage to America."

Eva explained that we came to help her understand what the next steps would be. And that we filled in for Elle. Mom had been her advocate. *Yes, I* thought. *This had Mom's fingerprints all over it.*

Ms. Reichle looked to Jack. "Are you family or friend?"

Jack locked eyes with her. "Friend. Friend of the entire family."

She shifted her attention to Lynn. "And you?"

"Friend," Lynn said simply.

Oddly, Ms. Reichle skipped over me.

"Eva," she said. "You look quite ready to have your babies."

Eva smiled, and Ms. Reichle returned the gesture. They sat and chatted about her pregnancy and the impending birthing. They stuck to English. She asked how Eva was doing with her pregnancy. Eva tilted her head and said, "It is long. I labor yesterday. All day." She held a hand to her back, shaking her head. "It is soon. Not yesterday. Soon. Babies will come."

"And how are you related to the father," Ms. Reichle abruptly asked of me. Her tone was frank, but not unkind. "David," she stated as if to proclaim that she knew more that I expected.

I held her gaze.

"My brother," I said. "These are Joyce children. Eva's babies are Joyce children," I replied. I saw Eva marvel, then frown. "They are my family. David's children. My twin brother."

I glanced over at Jack. His head was tilting back. He appeared to have been blown by a straight-line storm. I thought he would keel backward.

Ms. Reichle had a funny little smile.

I returned one of my own.

She returned to Eva.

"We will need another physical exam for you, Eva. After you deliver. And one for each of your twins."

She glanced quickly to me. "Congratulations—on your growing family." She held her gaze.

I tipped my head. My smile was genuine. "Thanks."

She nodded.

Then, she went over several forms with Eva, explaining, requesting, outlining demands. Eva listened intently. When she finished, she again turned to me. Then to Lynn and Jack.

"May I see your passports? Please?"

"Of course," I said. We pulled out our documents.

She read each, then turned to make copies in a machine behind her desk. Nodding, she returned our documents. "Good. Thank you."

"Eva, Next week? Monday? Will that work? I expect that we will have your records from France that we have been waiting on."

Eva's whole body lifted. "Yes. If I am not having babies." She absently patted her belly.

Ms. Reichle placed her hand on Eva's arm. "You will be a mother by then. Let me know if we should delay that appointment."

Eva thanked her, and we left the consulate.

*Chapter 34*

# Elle's Journaling

Mom and the twins were discretely scrounging through flower plots in the Gardens when we caught up to them before noon at our meeting spot. When we got there, Mom joined Eva and they strolled arm in arm to the nearby bench and sat together in the sun. The twins ramped up their energy and challenged Lynn, Jack and me to a game of duck duck goose. We switched to straight out tag, and then, finding a bit of slope on the nearby rise, we rolled down the little hill. Jack pretended to get stuck, but the kids already knew that trick from the times they lured me into their rolling game. It was worse for Jack. He was so ticklish he couldn't bear their little fingers probing his ribs. He rolled like a log down a ski ramp.

Lynn avoided the grass rolling game by resorting to her beloved hobby. She grabbed her camera and chased us around, getting in position to catch us in the midst of our play.

I glanced over to see Eva resting her head on Mom's shoulder. She slept peacefully. Mom sat still and upright like a sphinx, but still able to write pensively in her current journal. How many of those blank books had she filled? Many.

*September 7, 1969*

    *I see him now, my oldest son, Patrick, and I understand. I should have named him Michael, after his father. He looks so much like him. I don't know if I could have told the difference. Or maybe it's just time that blurs my memory. Time, and all that has happened during its passage.*

    *I see him now and I watch him move like his father moved. Gracefully, with strength and poise. The swagger of a champion. He has always been a champion, a fighter. Both of my twins were fighters. This one came out on top, though. He came out alive. He chose his battles. He is a winner, of life.*

    *I see him, and he looks at me and smiles, and he looks so like his father. He sounds like his father. He gestures like his father, and his expressions unfold like Michael's did. He is more than his father, though. More than his father and his brother both. He came back to her. He came back to her and stayed. To her and her children. His children. His twins. He's a good man. He has a place on the List. They all do.*

    *I see him now, walking hand-in-hand with his twinnies, his little ones. He between them, his huge hands swallowing up their little mitts. She, before them, looking through her lens. She has done such a fine job of mothering them. Much better than I did with my twins. I look into her eyes and I see strength and grace, and I am grateful. She an-*

155

swers my gaze with kindness and openness. I sense she is fond of me. And grateful. Goodness, she hardly knows me! But she is so candidly grateful. She has told me so. Grateful for her Patrick. And she directs her gratitude toward me. Heavens. Patrick is hardly my doing. She had as much to do with bringing him up as I did. More, perhaps. I abandoned him. Left him for the struggles of my illness. Such a tragic waste of time. His and mine. But he has thrived, in spite of my cowardly mothering. Perhaps because of it.

I see them now, Patrick's family. How that little girl loves him! And her brother adores him! How well she raised them, to never lose faith in their absentee father. She left him, too, didn't she? For so different a reason. How loving she was, to grant him the freedom to grow, and discover, and choose. How rewarding that he chose well. Chose correctly. Such a risk! Such a gamble! Yet there she is. There they are. I don't know how she lived with it. The fears would have smothered me. They did smother me. I let them bring me to my knees. I felt myself succumb. Such a tragic waste of my time. And theirs.

Ah, well. I tried. Can worse be said?

I see them now, and I see my daughter, her head upon my shoulder, snoozing in the warm Munich sun. We bask in the sun as we sit upon this park bench, watching my surviving son and his family playing on the grass. My little French-speaking German daughter. I am so grateful that she has opened herself to me. To us. To become part of our family. How trusting she is. How helplessly, hopefully trusting. My, she is big. I see myself in her, and her in me, once upon a time. Once, so very long ago. But not that long, I suppose. Twenty years, and then some. Just half my life, so far. Half my life ago. Her twins must not wait much longer to be born. They must give her some relief. Will she ever know relief? I wonder. If I can be of any use to her, I hope to bring her relief. To free her of worry. Of fears. I hope that I can be of help to her.

Rosie writes that we need to come back to the farm. Me. Eva and her babies. Patrick and his family. All of Michael's family. Eva will come, I know. I sense it. She seeks to live among David's roots. Perhaps it will come to be. Let her give these children birth, and we shall see. In the meanwhile, Rosie and Paddy can build upon the time they have together. It is meant to be. I can see it, have seen it for years. I am grateful. Imagine, two of the first of those who grace my List. And now they are together, as one. They who were the first with whom I shared the List. And they believed in it. Added to it. Yes. Life and love blend back into one another, if you let them linger long enough. I am grateful.

Oh, dear. My little Eva is stirring. And dripping. I believe it is her waters.

So it goes.

# Chapter 35

# Eva at the Edge

As I watched them, Eva startled. She drew her head up, a picture of surprise. She looked to Mom, then bent over to view her feet. Or perhaps, under the bench. I tried to focus. Mom suddenly stopped writing. She tucked her journal in her handbag and turned to help Eva. After exchanging a few words, she turned and called to Lynn. Then to all of us.

"It's time," she said in a clear, unalarmed voice. There was certainty in her tone. So unusual for Mom. "Come. We could use some help. Lynn? Can you come?"

Lynn hustled to their aid. Eva showed a measure of confusion. Sliding over to the edge of the bench, she looked down where she had just been sitting. She didn't appear afraid, but perhaps bewildered. Something unexpected had happened, but it was not unexpected at all. She had started labor for certain. Mom announced it to all.

"Eva's water broke," Mom cried out. "Time to go."

We walked at Eva's pace to the south edge of the Gardens, passed the Consulate where we had met with Miss Reichle just an hour or so earlier. Jack hustled ahead and flagged a taxi, which was waiting for us where Prinzregentenstraße grew out of Von der Tannstraße. Eva got in, along with Lynn and Mom. The twins wanted to ride along, but I tried to persuade them we could hike to the house on Possartstraße in little time, and maybe find some ice cream along the way. As we watched, Eva, Mom and Lynn drive off, and Ally put her foot down.

"We should take a car," she demanded. "They might need us." She crossed her arms with an expression so stern and demanding that Jack burst into laughter. A smile spread across my face as I beheld the stubborn little girl who was my daughter. *Why fight it,* I thought.

Jack hailed another taxi. We arrived back at the Professor's house in minutes. Ally spilled out of the car and ran to the Professor's door with Omie following. Jack and I finished tipping the driver, and hurried in to see the status of events.

Eva seemed comfortable but restless. She had rang up Vidya, her midwife, and was explaining her condition.

Twenty minutes later, the bell rung. Vidya had arrived.

"So, it is a good day to give birth," Vidya said as she hustled into Eva's bedroom. "Let's see were we are, my dear," she greeted Eva. She faced us with less than a smile and an arched eyebrow. We were to leave.

"Once her waters are broken, there is no turning back," she noted as she ushered us from the room. "We have work."

We retreated to the study. The moment was foreign to us all. Omie sat in a deep, stuffed chaired, looking out the study door toward Eva's bedroom. He said nothing. Ally fell into a stream of unanswerable questions.

"What are they doing? Will Eva be okay? How long until the babies come?" She asked. "What's going to happen? Can we see her? Why is Vidya keeping us out?"

I had no answers. I felt like I was caught in a vortex. *Who knows?* I wondered.

Jack, however, was in full command. "Eva will be fine. Vidya is helping her. It takes time to give birth to babies. They don't just pop out. So what do you want to do? Any board games here? Monopoly, perhaps? A deck of cards? Do you two know how to play 'Fish'?"

∞

Most of the hour after Vidya's arrival was consumed with preparations for birth. Once Vidya had assessed Eva's progress, we mobilized. Elle sent me on missions to fetch towels and linens that lay folded and covered. I was to bring them into Eva's room. Mom was well rehearsed. She moved about on autopilot. The twins tagged along with Lynn and me as Vidya examined Eva, but, with the exception of when Vidya shooed us away, they remained with Eva. They shunned Jack's invite to play games and dedicated themselves to Eva.

After we'd organized the birthing layout, we gathered with Eva, who sat in her plush cushioned chair with Lynn and Mom on one side, and our twins, Jack and me on the other. The midwife was looking at Lynn. Vidya said, "you will coach her." It was not a question.

Eva heard it and agreed. She had known she could depend on Lynn all along. Elle knew as well. It was in her eyes from the very first. Mom had trained with Eva. But she did not want the responsibility of attending the births of her grandchildren. Eva's false labor had convinced her so.

It all seemed so natural. Everything was falling into a rhythm. With the twins at her elbow, Vidya consulted with Eva in German, gauging Eva's progress, timing the gaps between Eva's recurrent and building contractions, and chatting with the twins in English, explaining that Eva was laboring in childbirth and what the children might expect to see or hear. After the first hour, all was in place. Vidya suggested we distract the children. We and the kids were welcome to check in as we would at any time. But Eva needed to concentrate, and Lynn needed to focus on her role in Eva's children's birthing. We were unceremoniously booted out once again by a strict and explicit midwife.

Which left the twins to me. And Mom. And Jack.

How does Jack always seem to show up at the right moment? Even if it's the wrong time. Late. Jack lived in late. He told me once, when we were paddling back waters of the Boundary Waters, that he preferred living in late mode. He always felt he was more of a reactionary type of person than one with the reflexes and instinct to respond to the immediate.

"I have mulling in my genetics," he had said. "I need a moment or two. Then I can best react,"

I thought about that as we distracted the twins with play and reading and games and a walk over to the ice cream store. Occasionally, when we checked in again with Eva and Lynn, we could see the women working at a pace that was consistent, persistent, and patient.

"How is it?" I asked in a break right after a contraction.

"Good. She is strong," Vidya commented, stroking Eva's shoulder as she rested. "But she just starts with her labor."

Lynn kept eye contact with Eva, holding her hands. I could see them breathing together, as in our yoga. "We are fine," Lynn said, glancing over first to me. Then to the twins, she said, "This is how you were born. Just like this, how Eva is working to bring her babies into the world." Omie watched wide eyed. Ally narrowed her eyes. There was something about the process that raised the hackles on the back of my daughter's neck.

Eva smiled. She was breathing easily but with a purpose, and was strong. Her smile was not weary. She conserved her energy. Drawing all she could as she met our gazes, one at a time. And then back to Lynn. Suddenly, she bent forward, wrapping her arm across her belly.

Vidya inspected her watch. "Okay. *Genug.* Enough. you are off. It will be time again soon for Eva to work. But you can come back. Do come back."

# Chapter 36

# Standing with Eva

We did come back. The twins remained curious about Eva and this birthing process. They had become so fond of Eva. Attached. Like friends. They fed off the friendship their mother had found with Eva. Eva drank from it. Ally held her hand. She watched Lynn and her new friend. Something about Eva's condition alarmed Ally. I found it curious. The call of the maternal in such a little one!

∞

In lulls, Lynn and Vidya sometimes chatted. They asked questions about each other lives.

"The yoga," Vidya asked. "You practice?"

Lynn nodded. "Not much. But some. With my sister."

Vidya tipped her head. "What yoga you do is good. I think, Patrick knows more, but practices less."

She was right. I had probably learned more poses than Lynn knew during the years since I added yoga to the training I did for football. At Colorado, I met a fellow student, Rebecca, who practiced on the mats in one of the workout rooms where I stretched after workouts in the summer. She became my personal yoga mentor. She was a graduate student who had practiced yoga for eight years. She taught well. She led me through the challenges of downward dog, warrior pose, the plank and all its variations, and dozens of other poses. Rebecca took me in and out of a torrid but short sexual relationship, and we remained friends and yoga partners for the two years I played ball at Boulder. And then after I got hurt, she took it upon herself to bring me back to health. She helped me stay healthy when I played, and her instructions during rehab contributed to my rapid healing. I stayed up with yoga when I got to Regensburg. I did some light practice, inspired, I suppose, by Eva. Yoga was my introduction to Eva. We sometimes practiced with Maria and several of the residents in the Etage. But I practiced less often; I partied more and forgot about yoga, discipline, training, things that had ruled my life in football. I did pick up yoga once again on the Trail, but I was lax.

And then I started practicing again with Lynn and Ingie. It was a kind and gentle return to the discipline.

I agreed with Vidya. Lynn knew fewer poses, ones that applied to Ingie's healing. They didn't do more than a several sitting poses. And child's pose. A lot of reclining breathing practices. The pranayama was helping now; she and Eva synched their breathing as the contractions came on. Even the twins, who were used to practicing with Lynn and Ingie, joined in the sessions Vidya led. Omie was a crack at it. A real breather.

Now, as we visited the team of women working with Eva's labor, Omie perched on Lynn's lap and the two of them focused solely on Eva as her contractions built in intensity and frequency. Omie said nothing, but his eyes locked into Eva's and he shared relaxed control over each breath, his little stomach bubbling out under his t-shirt, his face flushed but soft, his shoulders loose. He seemed to be willing her to share in his controlled breathing, filling his lower lungs first, then expanding his chest and lifting his shoulders and ribs to complete the inhalation. His little body sagged comfortably after softly expelling each breath.

Eva shared his gaze at the end of a set of breaths until the contractions once again waned. Then, a smile displacing any tension held in her face, she reached out to our little guy, stroking alongside his eye, thanking him.

After several contractions, Lynn wrapped her arms around her son, kissed his head above his ear, and murmured something just for his ears. He turned his eyes to peer up into her face, and he slipped down off her lap.

"I'll be back," he assured Eva, and he ambled over to where I watched, slipped his hand into mine, and we set off to find Jack or Elle, and found them with Ally.

∞

Eva picked up her violin and played between contractions. Soft, merry lilting melodies. Or earnest, driving themes. Sometimes with vigor, sometimes touched with melancholy. She played. She gauged each breath. She rested. And she labored.

After one short piece by Bach, Eva set the violin aside and rested. Omie returned and sat on my lap in the big stuffed chair.

"I hear what you play, and nevertheless, it is beyond my imagination how you create such sounds," Lynn whispered.

Eva looked to her, questioning.

Lynn explained. "I understand the instant of artistic creation. Of when you reach down into your soul and all of you gathers to make something rich and beautiful, and it is art. You create sound that you hear in your mind and make into music.

"I," she continued, "create through my eyes. I do not hear to create. I listen and I enjoy, but I do not create music. I create through how I witness the light and the shadows, and I compose what I create when I see though the lens of my camera."

Eva turned Lynn's words over in her mind.

"I weave sound waves to music. You capture light waves into pictures. That is creation."

She held her belly, feeling the contraction of her muscles move the contour of her womb.

Lynn set her hand atop Eva's fingers.

∞

Elle and Jack chatted. At their feet, the twins played quietly. I'd had few moments when all were content in how they were sharing time during this wait of Eva's labor. I thought of Lynn. She had so easily taken on the mantle of the doula. Lynn and Eva were in tune, total sync with one another. I could feel their bond; it was tangible. It touched my heart,

I wondered about these babies ready to be born. We had discussed them in the Consulate. Ms. Reichle had gone through documentation from Eva that confirmed that her babies were children of a citizen of the United States. Something akin to a blush had shaded Eva's face. She nodded. And we had moved on to other items to be addressed, particularly regarding medical exams

In her labor room, I heard Eva and Lynn working together through several cycles. With the kids busy at their grandmother's feet, each leaning against Jack's shins, I sauntered to Eva's room as she finished a sonata between contractions.

They met me with their eyes as I leaned into the door jamb. The moment of rest allowed them to relax. They were chatting. Their smiles were inviting.

I joined them by Eva's bed. Lynn softly kneaded the sole of Eva's right foot. She seemed to anticipate every need that might occur. If, during a lull, Eva frowned, Lynn asked if her back was in pain. Or whether she'd prefer having her neck rubbed. Sometimes it was simply skimming her fingertips over Eva's scalp. It was a touch that Lynn liked as well; I'd done that caress for her often. If Eva asked to sip on ice, Lynn had it there for her. They worked as if labor was a dance.

I could see fatigue in Eva's face. But she was strong. Her eyes were bright with determination.

"What was that you just played?" I asked.

She glanced at the violin, her sole heirloom that shed light on an element of her family's past. She had used the violin in France as a child; she never questioned it because it had been made available for her to learn. Eight years later, it had been bequeathed to her upon the death of her mother. She learned of the gift at the same time she learned that Sister Alma was her mother. She was told the history of the violin and how it fell to her ancestors. And that as the only member of the youngest generation of her family, she was its sole heir.

*"Chopin,"* she ran her fingers on her violin's face. *"Dritta Nocturne fur Klavier. Erinerst du dich?"* Do you remember?

*"Doch"* Yes, I remembered. I'd heard the Nocturne last in Regensburg. We had been lounging with David in her apartment. It seemed like yesterday. *Yesterday so long ago,* I mused.

Lynn simply tipped her head. "All's well with the kids?"

Again, I nodded. "Playing. Getting tired. But they are doing well. You?"

She nodded. Affirmative.

"How do you know what Eva's needs are all the time?" I marveled. Sometimes, Eva didn't ask, and Lynn was there with a solution to what appeared to her was a need. It was cosmic.

"I had a good doula when our twins were born. Martha was there for me," she said. "I remember how Martha helped me and I try to do the same. I've been through this. I see where Eva is. I just look at her and know. Or she tells me."

They shared a glance.

"Do you think we not know the other?" Eva teased.

I shook my head and wandered off to play with the twins.

# Chapter 37

# Laboring On

Eva's contractions quickened. Early on, she had eight to ten, occasionally 12 minutes between the successive contractions. During the lull, she played her violin. Sometimes she played short works. Or she might clip off a longer piece after a likely measure. She may play four or five minutes of a partita, then quiet her instrument and resume her work. As the contraction waned, she tucked her violin back under chin and continue the piece, often precisely where she had left off.

∞

Omie turned his head from his sketching, drawn by the lure of Eva's music. Bach's partita no. 3 pealed off her violin's taut strings. Bach's whimsy caught Eva; her fingers danced along the neck of her violin. I watched her through the doorway, pacing about her room as her music flowed. She'd play for several minutes. She played the partita at a clip.

Omie got to his feet and followed the music to the her room. I followed after him to the door. As I stepped behind him, feeling him lean back into my legs and wrapping an arm around my knee, I notice Lynn. She was ebullient. As was Eva, who suddenly winced. She abruptly ceased playing. Then she set Jacob on the bedstead and carefully positioned herself on the recliner. Their locked eyes. Vidya sat in an overstuffed chair alongside Eva's bed, examining her notes. She spoke without glancing up. "Six." She, too, wore a look of disciplined expectation. All was going well.

Omie sidled up to Eva's recliner. "Can I come up?"

"For a minute or so," his mother said. She lifted him carefully, setting him alongside Eva.

He examined her face with the gentle trust of a child. She gave him a smile.

"You make pretty music."

"You do too. Music of your own sort."

He slid over the side and planted his feet. Looking back over his shoulder, he nodded. She laughed.

And then she winced.

∞

"She sweats." Omie said as I carried him out to join his sister and grandmother.

I hadn't focused on that. But he was right. The braids of hair that were pulled back on either side of her forehead had darkened, and tiny beads of perspiration gathered below her hairline. She worked harder. But she didn't seem tired.

∞

As her labor intensified, she sometimes skipped playing. She might simply hold her instrument. Or sip water. Or walk a slow track around the apartment.

But over time, the intervals narrowed. She sweat more freely. She'd cast herself on the floor on all fours, arching her back gently first in cobra, then slowly into cat. Lynn and Vidya set Cushions to bolster Eva's weary body.

"Slow easy breath," Vidya encouraged. "Manage the exhale."

Eva succumbed to child's pose. Lynn placed bolsters under her head and arms; Vidya tucked a small one under her belly. She'd get up, sit on a chair of air with her back tight against the wall, Lynn on one side, Vidya or me on the other..

Lynn and Vidya kneaded the muscles in her back, across her pelvis, and along her spine. At times, her body writhed.

∞

Sometimes, she'd sing,

It reminded me of Jannie's mother. Helen Whitman would bring her daughter Jannie and and David to play lovely notes as she softly sang to lead them into a sonata, a concerto, an Air. I quivered to think of Jannie now, at this moment that David's Eva worked to give birth. *It all rolls in together, into one*, I remembered. He had said so, in a letter.

Eva's contractions were relentless. She endured them for perhaps a minute or two. It seemed long to me. When it let up, she visibly relaxed. She breathed. She played. She'd be calm. She prepared; she resumed her work. She breathed through the pressure of the contraction. Then, as the contraction waned, she tucked her violin back under chin, touched the horse tail to the strings and her violin wailed.

∞

She played her final piece of the day as the afternoon sun sank deep in the west over the English Gardens. Shadows darkened the room. She left the lights off, preferring the dim twilight glow. It eased her work as her labor gained momentum. Her contractions were regular now, and strong. She went through a half dozen cycles, each five to six minutes apart. Time evaporated with the onset of each new constriction.

By the dark of night, Vidya checked Eva's cervical dilation.

"You are there, Eva," Vidya advised her. "Work with your contraction. Don't force them. As they build, push. We'll help you."

Eva grimaced. Lynn watched.

165

Jack and Elle payed a visit to the labor room. Ally followed. She had been uncharacteristically intimidated by Eva's labor. She walked alongside the furry mountain of a man, her hand clinging to his tuber-like fingers.

"All is well?" Jack inquired.

Eva nodded, her eyes focused on something unseen.

"She is good," Vidya said. "Strong. In control."

Eva glanced at her doula. Their eyes held. Her brow furrowed, she inhaled sharply, and went to work on her next contraction.

Ally lead her contingent out to the quiet of outer rooms where she waited.

∞

The urgency of Eva's contractions ramped up. She sat back into her reclining chair, body focused. Lynn paced her breathing, blowing sharply between panted inhalations.

"Your lips," Lynn noted, touching Eva's cheek. Eva responded; her pursed lips softened. Sweat beaded on her forehead. Lynn dabbedEva's brow with a linen cloth. As the contractions built, Eva moaned. Lynn brought her back into a patterned breathing. Vidya stood behind her, whispering, her fingers softly soothing Eva's temples.

"Need you push?"

Eva shook her head. "It's all here," she said, dragging her fingertips across her lower belly. "It is pressing so much here."

"Eva is okay, Oms," I reassured him. "She will be done soon," I said. It was more hope than certainty. He returned his watch on Eva.

She writhed with the onset of yet another sharp contraction. It made her cry out.

"Manage your push," Vidya said. "Let it build."

Lynn moved her face close to Eva's, breathing even, whistling sets of panting exhalations. Eva's eyes darkened, her brow tightened. Sweat dripped from her nose; Lynn dabbed it gently with the linen. Eva gasped.

"*Drüken,* Eva," Vidya urged. Push!

Omie sat upright on my lap.

I watched Lynn's tears spill down her cheeks. Her eyes remained locked with Eva's.

"Awwa," Eva cried, then stifled her gasp. She looked to Lynn and they resumed their synched breathing.

I marveled at Lynn's total focus. Her fingertips stroked the back of Eva's clenched fists, then worked into her fingers to relax her hands.

Vidya took position before Eva.

166

"*Es ist gut, Eva. Ich sehe einen Kopf. Ihr Baby krönt.*"

Eva took on a new set of rhythmic, staccato breaths. Lynn paced her. They sounded alike. Vidya encouraged her to push.

"*Jetzt, Eva! Drüken!*" "Now, Eva! Push!"

'Breathe," Lynn said. "Softer. Regular."

"*Mon Dieu,*" she murmured between sets of hearty huffs. "*Mon Dieu!*"

"Yes," Vidya said.

Their voices sounded muffled, distant. I felt like I'd walked into a baseball bat. I couldn't find my breath.

She cried out.

And again.

"*Drüken!*

"Breath!"

It seemed dim. Hazy. Like looking at a huddle from below. All the faces. From the ground. Up into the sky.

# Chapter 38

# Eva's Twins

"Hi, eye!"

It was Omie. He was propping my right eyelids open with his pointer and his thumb. He looked down into my face with his warm, chocolate eyes. I heard the scramble of feet approach, and then Jack leaned his bushy mug over Omie's back, hovering above him.

Jack swept Omie off my lap and pulled me forward by the collar of my shirt,

"Sit forward," he said. "Put your head down." He pulled my legs straight and helped me lower my head. I was bent like a noodle.

I heard the noises of the women forming crisper, clearer sounds. They worked on. Eva cried, a piercing, anguished cry.

"Is she having her babies," I asked, my words thick, stupid. My head rocked back and forth as I struggled for thought.

"The first is born. You missed it. You fainted."

"Oh." I wondered if it were a boy. I sagged.

With his long reach, he slid the leg of the overstuffed chair near Eva's bed next to me. With one swooping lift, he slung me onto the cushions and shoved my head further between my knees. Omie stood alongside, his little hand gentle on my shoulder.

I glanced toward Lynn. She briefly looked my way, her brow furrowed. Then she turned her attention back to Eva, who grimaced, propping herself up on her elbows, her knees spread apart, her breathing heavy and rushed. Lynn toweled the sweat and tears from her face. Eva's eyes clinched tight; she growled and cried as she pushed.

The light about her dissolved as I fainted once again.

∞

*"David hatte richtig,"* Eva raised an eyebrow. *"Du bist so ein Stiefmütterchen."* David was right. You are such a pansy.

Vidya chuckled, as did Jack.

A pansy. Eva, who has just given birth to not one but two babies, impaled me with a look. I had no retort. I shrugged. David had called me that when we were together in Regensburg. We laughed hard as he explained to Eva the idiom. He'd called me a pansy when I stated a case against walking across town to join our friends at a restaurant. I wanted to take a taxi. At the time, the taunt brought on tearful laughter. Now, it seemed even more appropriate.

*"Doch. Ich gebe zu."*

She smiled, one of her babes at her breast.

Vidya and Lynn swaddled the other.

"Your boys are healthy and spunky," Vidya assured her. "Perhaps more vigor than their uncle, is it not so?"

Lynn held the other infant in her arms, swaying like a reed in a breeze.

"Oh, Uncle Patrick is strong enough. He just forgets to breath when he gets too excited." Lynn quipped.

I wondered which of the brothers was older, like me. Or younger, like David.

"Which is the first?" I asked. "Who's older?"

Eva looked at the child at her breast.

"This one. Jacob."

"And the other?'

"David.'

I nodded. It was so right.

# Chapter 39

# Onward

Days passed in a flurry of diapers and details.

Eva bounced back, albeit at a measured gait. She had ample help. Mom asserted herself into the mix with meals and care that paced us all. I'd never seen her so involved. It was heartwarming, in a weird sort of way. Lynn tended to Eva and the babies, but in ways that involved both our twins and me. As a family, we worked well together.

Jack wanted to stay. He offered a hundred different reasons to avoid returning to his teaching job. He could see it was not a good fit. He'd left Ely just in time to arrive in Milwaukee to meet his students and teach his first class. He arranged with a graduate student to take the Thursday discussion while he made his way to Germany, stopping briefly in Chicago for the protests in Lincoln Park. He hadn't expected the events in Chicago to get out of hand.

He missed his flight and spent a miserable night in jail. The bishop intervened on his behalf to free him after his altercation with the police. But he'd been issued notice: his brother would not support anything more than the temporary teaching appointment he'd been offered at Marquette. After several weeks of teaching his class, his department head had called him in. It was made clear to him, his class was to be discontinued. He was on his own. He hopped on a plane to Munich. He really had nothing to lose.

"Can you go back to your order?"

"Marquette is part of my order." Jack ran his fingers though his hair. "It doesn't seem likely."

I couldn't understand. "How could the Jesuits just cut you loose?"

He fixed an eye on me. "If they don't find work for me, it is as much a message as a predicament. Even the Jesuits have bounds." He leveled an honest eye on me. "I haven't been a stellar Jesuit."

"I thought Jesuits were famous for being cutting edge," I said.

He shrugged.

"What'cha going to do?"

Mom listened as she folded laundry. Lynn caught my eye. She glanced between Mom and Jack, then back to me. Was she sending me a signal? I wasn't sure what she had in mind.

Jack fretted. He was in a quandary.

"I have a friend in Guatemala. A Maryknoll. He could put me to good use."

Mom frowned, shaking her head. "Why would you go there?Guatemala is not a peaceful place. "

He shrugged. "It seems peace is not what is calling me at the moment."

She shook her finger at him. "Jack, your head is so far up your ass, you can't see for the crap in your eyes."

We stood in shock, looking from one to another, and then, as if orchestrated, at my mother. Our laughter rattled windows; with the babies sleeping in the room down the hall, we squelched our outcries. Our focus turned to the little woman standing boldly before the bear of a man with the bright red face.

She pursed her lips.

"This family has lost too much to war." She shook her head and narrowed her eyes. "Sometimes, simple is the sane solution. You don't have to jump from one fire into the next. You just have to back off and accept what you are given."

"Well, Elle, you have a point. I just don't see what that solution is." Jack said.

"Maybe the message from your Order is the answer to your predicament," she challenged. "Maybe it's time for you to be on your own. You have more to offer the world than the limited opportunities that your Church is allowing you."

With a blush that crawled crimson up her neck and flushed across her cheeks, she gathered up the laundry, shot Jack a glance that made his face flush, and headed into Eva's room with her arms loaded with the baby clothes.

Jack looked bewildered. Then, a smile snuck across his face. He's decided to stay on with us another week.

∞

Eva was up and about the next morning. She tired after walking her sons, first Jacob, then David. She played for a short while, then napped. By noon, she was up again, in time for her midwife's visit. Vidya hugged Eva and kissed her cheek. "Remarkable," she said. 'Truly remarkable." Eva smiled. She took up her violin and played as her children snoozed by her side.

Mom made sandwiches. She had discovered decent Munich bakeries with their heavy oval loaves of rye and barley. She set a stack of halved sandwiches on a platter for us. Carrying a tray with a steaming pot, a couple of cups and a pair of sandwiches, she beckoned to Lynn to join her for tea.

"I'll be up in a little while," Lynn promised. "I told my sister I would phone her today." She missed Ingie and looked forward to the call home. They talked for half an hour. Then she quietly took the stairs to the rooftop sanctuary.

∞

They nibbled at their sandwiches and sipped the warm tea as Elle trimmed the deadheads from her flowers. Neither offered small talk. Lynn wondered why Patrick's mother had invited her to her private domain.

"Your children are delightful," Elle said. "A pleasure to have around." She left the thought hang.

Lynn sipped her tea. "They are a blessing," she replied.

"You've done well, raising them. Alone, I might add. I know what it is to raise children alone." She glanced over to Lynn, her eyebrows arched.

"I haven't been alone," Lynn said. "I've had my friend, Martha. She was my mother's best friend, and now she is mine. She loves the children. I'm so grateful. And now, Patrick is with us…,"she let the thought hang. "It's like we are complete."

Elle nipped a withering sprig from a basil plant and sniffed it.

"You have much to be grateful for," Elle agreed. "But from all you'v said, plus what Patrick tells me, you have shouldered a lot of responsibilities with your family. Your sister. Your father."

She tossed the basil into her compost bucket and left her thoughts out there for Lynn to respond, if she chose.

"It's Martha's gift to me. I couldn't do it without her. It would be too much."

Elle nodded. "I understand. Sometimes it's too much." She put her shears in its place among her garden tools and turned to face Lynn. She sat, perched on the edge of a garden chair, her spine straight and her hands folded on her lap.

"And what of Patrick? Will he be a blessing, or a…," she paused to consider, "… a project?

Lynn found Elle's question peculiar. *Project*, she considered. Why would she call her son *"a project?"*

Before she could respond, Elle continued.

"When my husband came home from the war, he was different. He had left a part of himself on those islands in the Pacific. He never filled the void that had opened in his soul.

"Patrick didn't have to go to war. To serve. But his brother did, and David was such a big part of Patrick's life. David was a big part of all of us."

172

Elle paused, sniffing another sprig of basil. Then she said,. "I see my older twin, Patrick, and I wonder. Is there a part of him that is now a void. He's had so much in his life that he has lost. His football. His brother. Me, during his youth…" She paused, and then turned her gaze to Lynn. "Thank goodness he has found you again."

Lynn looked at her hands on her lap. Patrick's mother had identified a concern that frequented Lynn's thoughts about Patrick.

"I think he will come through alright," Lynn said. "I don't think he knows exactly what grief is, regarding the loss of David. I trust he will be solid. And honest with himself."

Elle scrunched her face into a look of doubt.

"I hope he can. We all must learn to be whole again, once we are broken. For Patrick's sake. For yours, too. And your children."

They sat sharing silence for a moment, and the quiet worked to bring them close.

"Lynn, I was not the mother that my children needed. I don't blame myself. I don't know how I could have escaped from…it. My illness. I don't know how I got there. It was the World. It broke me. It shakes me still. But it was not my children's' fault. Or mine. We all had to live with it, though. Have patience with Patrick. He means well."

Lynn smiled. "Of course. I understand, and I am just glad Patrick is back in my life," she said. Her smile dissolved, however, and a shadow crossed over her eyes.

Elle, I understand what you went through," she said. "I understand about when all the world caves in on you, and about having no hope. No spirit. I understand."

Elle peered into Lynn's gaze and saw a woman who's honesty flowed from her heart though her eyes.

"Share with me," she invited her son's loved one to trust her. "I don't know what I have to give, but I hope that what I have will help."

Elle's offer hung above them. Lynn smiled, nodded, and said, "I'm grateful, Elle. I know I can come to you. And I will. As I learn what I need, about Patrick. I will come to you for help. Thank you."

∞

I finished reading Ally's favorite story for perhaps the tenth time. She looked up from my lap with a measured gaze.

Ally watched over me, her father, like a mother hen. She was determined to prevent any further fainting spells.

"You don't have to worry," I assured her. "I don't usually faint."

"Then why did you faint?" she asked.

I rolled my eyes. "I don't know, Darlin'. I didn't expect to. I'd probably not have been in Eva's room when she was having her babies if I had known I would faint."

She scrunched her nose up into a button. "I didn't want to be there. It was hard."

I said gently. "It was beautiful, in a way."

She shivered, looking away. "Not as beautiful as the stars sparkling on the lake at home."

I agreed, thinking that my daughter may be getting homesick.

She climbed up on my lap with *Die Häschenschule,* one of the books she and Eva had picked up at nearby book store. "Let's read," she said. She amused me with her interest in the story's stern, straight-laced teachers and fastidious students. She preferred *Martine,* a French storybook that Mom read to her frequently. I couldn't do French justice, so she brought her German stories for me to read to her. I wondered at how easily she was taking to languages. Eva had promised to teach her German, and Ally pressed her to help her learn French as well. Ally was like a sponge soaking up water.

As was Omie, but in a different, subtle way. While we read, Jack taught Omie the basic moves in chess. He didn't have to repeat whether the bishops could only travel diagonals, or the knights hopped their two plus one routine, sometimes hurdling over other pieces like a steeplechaser. Om marveled at the queen and her mighty power. But the king stumped him.

"Why is he so slow?" Omie worried. "He can only go one step at a time."

"Kings are best at leaving the work and danger to their serfs and subordinates, " Jack offered. "Are you thinking it has to be equal?"

Omie frowned as he marched his players about the board. "Doesn't seem right."

∞

Naps. Reading. Shopping at bakeries, grocery stores and market stands. Gelato at the stand on the other side of the little park across. Wine in the Professor's study. We maintained a simple routine after the birth of the twins. Except, of course, the babies, who followed their own sense of rhythm. Jacob and David. My brother's children.

∞

Later that morning, Lynn found me idling through the writings of Sigrid Olson that she had brought along from home.

"Your mother is up in the aviary," she noted. "You should go to her. She asked for you. Go. Talk with her."

174

I frowned. *Why?*

"Jack and I are taking the kids for ice cream." She pointed toward the roof. "Go to her."

"I'd like some ice cream."

"Later."

*Oh*, I thought. I headed up to the aviary.

∞

Mom pitter-pattered among her herbs, clippers in hand, trimmings caught in her garden basket. Her head tipped upward, her eyes followed the flight of fine little winged birds with blue heads, a strip of black through their eyes, and a white strip across their wings. Several of the chickadee sized birds fluttered about the aviary. One little fellow perched on mother's extended hand, picking seeds from her palm.

"*Blaumeise*," Mother said softly. "They visit me often."

"Your friends.:"

"Yes. They trust me." Her eyes glistened as she shrugged her shoulders. "It took them a month to do so, but now they feel free to perch on my hand and peck for seeds. But they really love spiders. They didn't take to landing on my hand until I offered spiders to them. Now they eat seeds as well."

"You fed them spiders?"

"Yes. It was creepy."

She struck me at times as a curious girl. As the bird perched on her fingers, her nose just inches away from the little bird's beak, she examined its fluff of golden yellow down that covered its breast and back. Gently moving her free hand toward the bird, she stroked its blue and black feathers just under the pointed, rice sized beak. The bird tucked its beak under Mom's finger, prodding her to scratch the back of its sky blue head.

Then, lifting her hand gently toward the open windows above, she set the bird to wing. She watched it fly to the opened glass panes above, then turned her gaze to me. I had never seen my mother at such peace.

"And to think I worried that the nuthatches and chickadee's back home would peck your eyes out when you and David were children!"

"I believe our local birds and wildlife were justified for their fear that we might harm them." I answered. "Not the other way around. Except for those red-winged black birds. They terrorized us."

"Only if you threatened their nests," she said. "Then you had to watch out! They might peck your eyes out!"

I laughed as her face opened up with wary caution. I was not conditioned to see her with such a wide array of emotion and response in her expressions. Her face was young with feelings. Young, and happy. I was drawn to her.

She motioned toward a chair nearby, and I pulled it over to the table on which her potted herbs grew.

"How is it for you, to suddenly having a little family of your own?" she asked me.

"It's good," I said. It was easy to say, but the words carried a feeling of comfort. And fullness. I could honestly say it is good and feel no reservations. It seemed right.

She nodded.

"You seem so happy here, Mom. I think it's fair to say I've never seen you happier. Even more than after I got home from Aunt Mary's."

"You seem happier, too, Patrick. But if I may say, your life has seen some turns. No more football. No more college. Will you ever go back to finish college?"

I shrugged. It was not something I had focused on. Jack had asked me. And Lynn wondered as well. But I saw no clear path to returning to college just to take courses. I didn't know. I didn't even care. I didn't see a purpose. It was not what motivated me. I told her so.

"What does?"

I searched for the words.

"Home."

She looked surprised

"Not North Freedom, particularly," I explained. "Having a home. Family. Lynn. The kids. It blows me away every day. They make me feel like I mean something real."

I shrugged. "It's good."

She nodded. Then she looked into the pocket of her gardening apron, shuffling through several seed packets and papers. She pulled out two envelopes, read their addresses, and offered them to me.

"These were among Eva's papers that you brought from Regensburg. She asked me to give them to you." Her hand trembled as she held them out to me.

Letters. From David.

"Oh," I muttered. It caught me off guard.

I held the letters loosely. I looked at the postmarks. Early April. Then again in later April.

I held them in my lap, uncertain whether I should open them in front of Mom. When I looked up, she held her eyes on my face. She read the torn and tired emotions that David's death left on me. Her face, too, reflected her anguish.

"Okay. Let's see what he left for us."

The first April letter was brief. David simply assured us he was still alive. He'd been in camp for most of a month. Khe Sahn had been under fire throughout all of February and March. He felt imprisoned.

*…We pretty much hunker down and try to stay out of it all. Pretty hard to do, but it's all we can do. I haven't been in the boonies for weeks. We can't get out like we were doing before these ramped up attacks that started in January with the Tet offense. It is withering. I'd much rather be in the jungle, staying down and snooping around, trying not to be noticed. This isn't much of a life. But it is all we have, and I find it remarkable that these guys who live and breath this fire infested life in wet, dirty sloppy trenches and behind walls of sandbags still find things to be amused about. Every morning after Colors, we get a fresh barrage of Vietnamese 120 mm mortars right through camp. Douglas, one of my buddies from the bush, puts an offering of his K-rations on the bags up top of the trench wall, begging the guys launching their mortars to please, please please, do him the favor of taking out his daily beans and eggs. But they always miss, and he always bitches them out for being such bad shots. He shouts down to the perimeter for the front liners to let Maggie's Drawers sail, letting those distant gunners know what a lousy job they are doing. Then Douglas moans and groans that he has to eat his damn breakfast after all. He cracks us up. Thank God for the crazies.*

*Not much more to say. Except how I miss home. And Eva. And you. Tell Eva I love her. And I love you, too.*

*Bro*

The second letter was longer, and David wrote that much had changed for him and his fellow Marines at Khe Sahn. The siege had ended early in the month, and he had been out on recon for one long stretch before returning to the camp. He expected to head back out within a few days. His tone was different. More confident, but more cautious. He felt free of the shackles that the siege had on the base. But the boonies held perils; their probes into the thick mountain jungles led to more encounters with the enemy than what he had experienced before his time with me and Eva in Regensburg.

*…I am glad to be in recon, rather than humping these hills in platoon or company force. The guys up above keep sending orders for my Marine buddies to go out and 'clean up' any lingering enemy troops in the area. Like the brass think the NVA just climbed back in holes and are licking their wounds and finding their way back home. They are*

*hard to find, but they are out there in places that are to their advantage. A few nights ago, a company of Marines moved in parallel on trails up the opposite hillsides of a valley. The Vietnamese hunkered down beneath the trail lines until our guys were strung out and exposed up above. Then the gooks opened fire at our Marines on the trail along the opposite hillside. Well, those boys opened return fire big time—right at their buddies on the other side of the valley. Of course, those guys opened right back up. The gooks got us to fire on ourselves. Seven dead. Nine injured. It's crazy. Just crazy. My recon squad and I were a couple clicks up that same valley. We had been plugged in for several days and observed more enemy troops moving both days and nights than we had since the siege was broken. When the fire down the valley opened up the other night, it was the deep stubborn bark of AK47s that we heard first, but only a few of them. Then a whole bunch of M16's popped off a couple thousand rounds in about four minutes. All aimed at their Marine buddies on the other sides of the Valley. We heard it where we were hunkered down. We could see tracers and explosions lighting up the night. Maybe a mile down hill. Eerie. Listening to our buddies shooting our buddies.*

*In the boonies, I key into the sounds of the jungle. Especially at night, but daytime, too. I don't rest in the jungle, but I can kind of relax. It's a comfort to know I am doing what I can to be undetected. It's so much more relaxing than squatting in the trenches in Khe Sahn, hoping random incoming wasn't gonna do me harm. It's our job in the jungle to be quiet. To be invisible. It means concentrating, but it's like we have some element of control over our well being. Our outcome. It's easier to trust my buddies here in the brush, because I can see and hear how good they move, or hunker, or evade when we sense danger. In Khe Sahn, it was insane.*

*What more can I tell you? It's something I am glad that you will never endure. Remember how you used to tell me how you thought you could enter combat, you could take a man's life if it was necessary? I know you were trying to help me keep my courage about going into the Corps and all, but neither of us could really discuss that concept because we didn't know diddly about what insanity it all is. All the rules and conventions of civilization are left behind when you enter War. There are no rules, no morals, no sense of guilt. There is really just survival. You do everything just to survive. You don't hope to survive; hope is empty when it comes to combat. You just act on survival instinct. You turn yourself loose to the instinct of defending yourself and killing others. That's why those boys down the valley the other night shot each other up without even thinking about what they were doing. Instinct. Survival. It doesn't depend on morality. You can be brave, and you can fight courageously, but really, you just have to be lucky to survive. And if you do, you have to live with it. What have we done? We stuff it someplace to figure out later. You just tuck it away, keep on truckin', and live with it. And pray that it all gets evened out over time. And that you can begin to forgive yourself.*

*These men I serve with. They are like family to me. We care that much about each other, because each other are all we have over here. It's like having a bunch of other guys who are like you. I care about them. My brothers. They come into my life in a flash, and sometimes they leave in a flash. But to know them, to think of all that they have lived through just to get to be here in this insanity of war, and that we have each other to look out for and worry about and care about, that is our morality. That is our moral touch-stone. We can get mad and yell and bitch about one another, but not when we have to depend on the next guy when we are in the fire zone. No. We have to trust them each to be like a brother. I think about you, my brother, my twin, and am ever grateful. You taught me what a brother can be. You are the best brother I can imagine. I watch the guys here act with each other like they know what having a brother means. I think about the VC and the notion that they have brothers back home. And sisters. Parents. And they are here just like I am, because the notion of Nation dictates our presence in the insanity of this war. I wonder about that a lot. Why do we maintain this notion of War as part of our civilization? What is the point? Where does it take us? I would be satisfied to just be with my brother, my family, rather than live this life in the brother-hood of soldiers. My Marine brothers. They mean everything to me, and I can't do with-out ever having known them or the reason we are here together. But I wonder, why?*

*Crazy. Isn't it?*

*I gotta go. I've laid too much on you. I'm sorry.*

*I envy you every moment you have with my Eva. Tell her I love her. Take good care of her. And Mom. You're a great brother.*


*Love,*
*David.*


Neither Mom nor I could talk. She shed a few tears and sniffled, wiping her nose and drying her eyes with a wrinkled tissue. I sat, stricken, unable to say a word. David lived in the words he had written to me. I could hear his voice. He lives on in me. And it crushed my spirits to think of the life he had in those days and weeks before he died. I could see no sense in it, but had to accept it. Life is not crazy, or happy, or sad. Those are attributes we blame life on for the times when we hurt. Life is life and it comes with all the jolts and disappointments, the beauty and surprises, that make us feel. We interpret what the day brings us, and we assign judgement to what we observed. It doesn't enrage me that David died in a life of insanity. Crazy is as we make it. My trust is that he will live on, for at least as long as I carry the memory of my twin, his words, his acts and intentions. No one knows my twin as well as I. He lives in me. So be it.

∞

Mother sniffled, coughed, and set her hand upon mine. I looked into her piercing gaze.

"Can you grieve your brother?"

I shook my head. "I miss David. I always have when we were apart. Knowing that I will not see him again? Yes, I'm sorry for that. But David lived in me. Lives in me. Still does. It was how he embraced life. How he did things. Everything. He lived the life of the grizzly. He gave his all to us. To me. To you. That was his life, and we can't just leave him behind. Time marches on, but he will march right along with us. We really don't have much to say about it. He gave us that. I cherish that. I honor it."

She looked bewildered. Ashamed. Regretful.

"What?"

"I let him down. Let you both down. I regret that. I'm sorry."

I slowly shook my head, keeping my eyes locked on hers.

"You lived your life as only you could. You have nothing to regret. You are our mother. You did your best. My friend Teddy says sometimes you have to live in the dark side to heal, to see where the light is and commit to seeking it in your life. Look at you now, here, healthy, able to help David by helping Eva. You have purpose."

She twitched her head on her thin neck, shocked by my thoughts.

"Do you think David forgave me for…not being all you boys needed as a mother? Do you forgive me?"

My brow furrowed reflexively. I pondered a moment the notion of forgiveness.

"No. I can't say I forgive you. I never thought I needed to forgive you. My hope was that you forgave me. For all the anger that raged in me. For how selfish I was, asking more of you than you could give. I have not forgiven you. I have no reason to forgive you. You gave me life. You gave me a twin brother. Now I see you, how strong you have become. How healed. All I feel is grateful."

I shrugged a shoulder.

"I've had a good life. A very interesting life. It is the life you gave me. Thank you."

She looked timid like a kitten.

"That's odd. I felt guilt all these years. Like I needed forgiveness for being away when you needed a mother." She looked up to see the *Blaumeise* flutter amongst her plants.

"Do you think David forgave me?"

"David loved you. I love you." I said no more.

We sat quietly for moments. Mom reached for David's letters, and together we read them again.

# Chapter 40

# Homeward Thoughts

"I 'm thinking it's time to go home," Lynn said.

"Is something the matter?" I asked.

We lingered with Eva at the table after breakfast. Jack sipped yet another cup of coffee. The twins busied themselves, Ally reading from her library, Omie at his drawing. He looked up from his art. "We need a campfire," Omie declared.

"And the lake," Lynn added. "It's time. Ingie needs us. She needs the kids. It's been more than a month. We need to go home."

She was right. Our stay in Munich had grown long. I took stock of the weeks that had slipped by so quickly and the joy we shared with Eva. And with Mom. Now, with Jack.

He'd committed to returning to the the U.S. in a few days. He scheduled a flight for Tuesday, the day after Eva's next appointment at the Consulate. He suggested that with the experience he'd had working with his parish people in western Asia who sought to gain entry to America, he may be able to facilitate some of the requirements and forms necessary for Eva to immigrate.

Eva thanked him, but shook her head with resignation. "This immigration process is long," she said. "Many steps. Many forms. It will be long."

"We'll see," Jack tried to assure her.

"And you," Eva said, leveling a kind look toward Lynn. "Are you missing home? *Deine Schwester?* Your sister? You leave soon?" She held young David, who had just finished nursing. The pint sized babe snuggled in a ball tucked in under Eva's neck as she patted his back.

"Soon. Yes." Lynn said. "A week or so, perhaps. I want to be sure you are back on your feet and everything is going smoothly. You and Elle," she said, gesturing toward the nursery where Elle walked Jacob. "We'll help you with the babies until then."

Eva glanced toward Elle with her firstborn, strolling around the nursery. "Your mother is a gift," she said. "Maybe David sends her."

The lump in my chest burned with sudden, fierce intensity. I swallowed once. Then again.

"Breathe," Lynn smiled.

I inhaled deeply.

"Not to worry," I laughed. "Just thinking about David."

She nodded.

The immigration issue was on the table and I didn't want to let it slide by. I was about to question Eva when young David burped his feeding, spilling milk down Eva's blouse. She was up and away before I could utter a word.

∞

We ignored any further immigration discussion until Monday, when it was time for Eva's appointment at the Consulate. At first, she suggested she cancel her time with Ms. Reichle.

"It is much to do for me," Eva explained. "So soon. Too much." She drew young Jacob to her shoulder. "Next time I go. Not now."

Jack, however, put his foot down.

"We can't seem ambivalent about pursuing immigration," he argued. "The government has to be convinced your request is your priority. Perhaps if I meet Ms. Reichle, we could keep her focused on your case."

"I'll go, too," I assured her.

Eva looked resigned. "Yes, This is helpful. *Danke.*"

# Chapter 41

# Patrick and Jack at the Consulate

We walked to the Consulate deep in thought. Within sight of the Consulate as we stepped out of the park, I asked Jack what he intended to say.

"I'm going to listen. It depends on what she says. Or asks."

We crossed Königinstrasse.

Jack hesitated at the door of the Consulate.

"If she asks, the truth is generally the best response. No padded answers. So we wait to see what she asks. Or tells us."

∞

Catherine Reichle, the Consulate Affair, asked us again how we are family to Eva. She sat us down in her office and before she had taken her place behind her desk, she asked us to explain our relationship to Eva. She didn't ask about Eva and the babies.

Overall, I thought Jack handled himself well. He looked her in the eye and said, "Patrick is closer to Eva than I. Perhaps he can best explain how he knows her."

I gasped. Not a big one, but I inhaled just a bit too fast. I believe my face was in full blush. My skin felt warm. Too warm. Hot. I shot Jack a glance. Did he really throw me under the bus? There was nothing smug in his demeanor. He apparently thought it best for me to explain why we were here on Eva's behalf. I pulled out the letter from my mother that I had brought with me and held it before me. I told the truth.

I told her of knowing Eva in Regensburg before she met David when we studied at the *Universität*. And of our lives among the group at the Etage. How we practiced yoga together. And listening to her play her violin. And of her reading my brothers letters that arrived from Viet Nam. And of my brother finally being able to visit. And staying. My twin meeting Eva. And of them playing music together. And of them being lovers.

I teared up as I thought of David in Regensburg. I took a deep breath. She waited. I continued.

I told of David's death. I told of learning that Eva was to be the mother of his child—of *his children*, *twins* like their father. And me. "They are the children of my brother," I told her again. "I am their Uncle."

My voice faded. I had no more words to say.

She met my gaze, and turned to Jack.

He began, "I know Eva because I know David. Knew David. I know Patrick and his brother—his twin—because I have known the Joyce family

183

for years. They took me in as a friend. As part of their family. I have been part of the Joyce extended family. Their mother, Elle, has been a friend for years. So has their uncle, Paddy, who raised the boys like a father after his brother, Michael, died, leaving Elle to raise his sons on her own. I have had my hand in helping Patrick's mother raise her boys. It has been my privilege."

He paused. She waited.

Jack said, "I have come to know Eva because Elle called us to Munich to give Eva our support. She is part of the Joyce family now. She is a Joyce mother."

She waited a moment longer, all the while leveling her gaze upon him.

He returned her gaze and shot her a question.

"Is Eva facing obstacles to her immigration?"

I couldn't have been prouder of Jack. His question startled me, perhaps even more than Ms. Reichle.

She tilted her head and took his measure.

"In spite of the closeness, and earnestness, of your association with Eva, I don't believe we can discuss that." Her voice was not unkind.

Jack nodded.

She looked back to me.

"David was your twin?"

"Yes. I'm the older."

"I am sorry for your loss." Her voice was kind. "It is hard for family to lose one to their service. It just doesn't seem fair, no matter how brave our soldiers are. Our Marines."

She knew David was a Marine. I wondered how much Eva had disclosed about David.

"My husband was a Marine," she offered. A shadow passed over her eyes.

*Was.*

David *was.*

Her eyes remained leveled at me.

"Was?" My voice shared my condolences.

She simply nodded. Then, shifting from her professional voice, she added, "It is hard to lose a husband. You have to be so very brave, going on. Eva is very brave, isn't she?"

Her change in tone touched me; her words were heartfelt..

"*...to lose a husband...*" Her words snagged like a feather caught in a web.

Jack stirred in his chair. It made me think of letters from David when he described his good friend Jack 'de-transending'. Grounding his being after a saunter among the cosmos. *"Mien Mannes,"* he mumbled. He lurched, like he was jolted back into his body.

"Eva? Brave?" Jack asked. "To have lost David?"

She glanced toward him, but addressed me.

"Am I to understand that you intend to be father to your brother's children?" She frowned in confusion. "To take Eva as your wife so as to take care of David's twins?"

I didn't know how to answer. I clutched Mom's letter tight in my grip. We sat, the three of us, exchanging glances. I held out my mother's letter, my summons to Munich.

She gave me time to form a reply. Jack took a breath and was about to offer his thoughts; with a simple gesture, raising two fingers from her hand nearest him on her desk, she signaled him to refrain. To allow me to speak.

"I will always care for my brother's children." I held her gaze. "And for Eva."

She leaned back in her chair, folding her fingers together with her elbows on the arm rests, her head facing up, looking toward the distance above the ceiling. Jack rustled; he wanted to make a point. Her index finger held him off again. She pondered her thoughts.

"Eva's children will be U.S. citizens." Her tone was straightforward.

"They are U.S. citizens," Jack responded. "She gave birth last Thursday."

Ms. Reichle set her chair forward, looking first at Jack, then me. A broad smile fixed upon her business face.

I nodded. "Twins. Boys. Like David and me."

"All is well? Eva?" she asked.

"Yes. All is well. Eva's fine. She's remarkably tuned in to what she is doing."

"Yes, she is. Has she told you why she intends to immigrate?"

It was a question I had not asked. It just seemed like the right think to do. The twins were, after all, David's children.

Jack ventured a guess. "To raise the children as Americans?"

"Perhaps," she replied. "But there is more to it. She told me that she wants her children to have family. After meeting your mother and her friend, Rose, she feels that she has more chance of providing a family for her babies if she immigrates to the U.S."

"She is right," I asserted. "We will look after them. We'll all raise them. Just like my family raised David, and me."

She appeared to weigh my pledge.

"I am glad to see your support for Eva. She will need advocates when she get to America."

*When she gets to America!* So there was no problem! She was going to be able to immigrate.

"So Eva can go to America!" I blurted. "That's terrific! Soon?"

"That depends on what you mean by soon," she said. "It's complicated. She is a French national, so we have to obtain documents from France and that is adding to the delays we have had. But Eva is the mother of your brother's children. A foreign national married to a U.S. citizen who is a service member has certain advantages toward immigration. David's children are U.S. citizens They need their mother."

*Married to a U.S. citizen??? Lose a husband???*

"David married Eva?" Once again, I blurted, but this time there was little wind in my voice. I was shocked.

"You didn't know? She didn't tell you?"

I shook my head. She hadn't said a word. More shocking, David had said nothing about it. I was stunned.

So was Jack.

Ms. Reichle rifled through a folder of forms on her desktop. She looked briefly at a document, then passed it to me.

The document trembled in my fingers. Ornate, old German script in dark ink proclaimed the marriage of David Michael Joyce and Eva Maria Baron. The wedding took place in Absam, Austria, December 9, 1967. I shook my head. *Where was I?* Off with Courtney, my old girlfriend, I recalled. I missed my brother's wedding. I had traveled to Bonn with Courtney in early December. When I got back to Regensburg, David had returned to the Marines. He was on his way back to Viet Nam. I missed him. I missed his wedding.

Ms. Reichle spoke slowly as she detailed the complications of Eva's application to immigrate.

"Their wedding was in Austria. In a small town, Absam, near Innsbruck. They went there because that is where her violin was made. And her family came from there. Their trip there requires documentation verification of another order. So we have your brother, a U.S. citizen in the service of the United States Marine Corps married to a French national in a wedding held in yet another country." She went on, discussing sponsorship and employment for Eva, health documentation, and a bundle of other issues that she and Eva were working through. It began to buzz like the noise of hummingbirds in my ears.

"Mr. Joyce," she called to gain my focus. "Your intent to care for and provide for Eva and her children…can you explain please what you intend to do? Is it your intent to marry Eva?"

I met her piercing look. I took in a deep breath. I stuffed Mom's letter back in my pocket.

"It is my intent to do whatever is needed to bring Eva and her children home. If marrying Eva makes the happen, I will do just that." I listened to my voice say what my heart was telling her. My mind was in disbelief.

"Let me explain," she responded. "We are well on our way toward processing all the documents required for issuing Eva's visa. Your intentions are good hearted — does Eva know about this???—but may make matters more complicated than they already are. If you, the two of you, file for fiancee status, we will need documentation of your relationship. You will need provide assurance of your marriage in the United States within six months of her entry to the country. Or, if you choose to marry here in Germany, that will impose certain restrictions on the privileges she has as the wife—the widow—of a U.S. serviceman who has died in the service of his country, but who remarries before immigrating."

She let the thought rest a moment. Then she leveled her most appraising eye toward me.

"Mr. Joyce, may I ask. Is this as much your idea to help Eva as it is your mother's?"

Jack boomed! His outburst made me laugh outright. He held himself to get in control.

"You know my mother then?"

She smiled. "We have had many discussions. She has many questions. She is Eva's most loyal advocate. I think she wanted to magically make it happen for Eva."

I glanced over to Jack. His barrel shaped torso heaved up and down as he stifled his amusement.

# Chapter 42

# Campfire

When we got back to Eva's apartment, Jack pulled out the large tall votive candle he procured from a church we passed along the way.

"We need a campfire tonight!" he proclaimed. The kids went nuts.

"I will draw a fire pit," Omie offered.

Jack sought out Elle to help prep for the campfire.

I found Lynn.

She was with Eva. Her look told me. She already knew.

"They're married." I was startled by the mix of excitement and astonishment that laced my voice.

Lynn nodded. Her smile was kind. She lay her hand on Eva's shoulder. "She told me. Just now, when I asked her about you mother's suggestion."

Eva's eyes showed her sadness, but they were dry. She had married my brother and he had died.

I marveled that I had been unaware of either event.

"I didn't know."

"Yes. So I thought."

I didn't ask her why she had not told me.

"Does Mom know?"

"I tell her."

"I see." I took her hand. "I'm so happy. I'm so sad. I love you both so."

She nodded

We three hugged. And cried

∞

Mom lit the votive candle campfire. We filled the living room. We propped Eva every which way with her babies cradled in her arms in the big stuffed chair we pulled out of her room. Lynn and I shared a loveseat to Eva's right. Jack pulled one end of a long sofa out from the wall to tighten our fire circle of furniture in the room. Omie had set his slate with his drawing of a fire pit—one that very much resembled our pit along the lakeshore in Ely—at the center of a plush, tight knit carpet. Jack placed the candle on Omie's rocks and handed a box of matches to Ally.

"Will you give these to your Grandma to light the fire?" He asked her.

Mom struck a match and lit the candle. The flame took. As we watched the flashing tongue of fire in our lakefront fire pit, we sat quietly for moments, absorbed in the golden flickers from Jack's votive candle.

Our chitchat stemmed from small thoughts.

Ally joked that s'mores might be difficult to melt over this blazing candle.

Jack said he was glad there were no mosquitos.

Mom whispered, "Isn't it lovely!"

Eva watched the candle throw flashes and shadows about the room. "I have not ever to be with campfire." We turned as one to gaze at her, sitting with her babies in her arms. Mom went over to her. Eva offered up young David. Mom carried the babe back to her place next to Jack on the long couch. Ally tucked in beside her, and they looked lovingly into the curious dark eyes of the newest Joyce family member.

∞

Eva asked, "What is this like to live where your home is?"

"I've told you about the farm." Mom said "Well, right now it's fall. Maybe the peak of color. The trees may be ablaze with reds and browns and gold in between the green of the pines. It is rich and warming, though the chill in the air tells all about summer fading."

"*Herbst*," Eva mused. "Autumn."

"Ely is golden in Autumn right now," Lynn said. "Goldens with tamaracks and aspen, and green from the pines."

"And blue from the lake," Ally added. "And from the sky. And white from the clouds."

"Or gray," Omie joined in. "We have campfires even when it is gray. If there is no rain."

"It's like here; it gets dark earlier in the afternoon as fall arrives," Ally observed. "So we burn the campfire earlier."

"Yeah," Omie said.

As when we gathered around the fires on the shoreline at home, we sat transfixed, staring at the blaze, a single flame dancing and swaying atop the candle on the rocks of the fire pit drawn on Omie's slate.

"Sometimes the fire gets hot on my face," Ally said. "Mommy asks me if I am too close to the fire."

Jack asks, "Well, are you?"

Ally snickered. "Not now!"

"I can feel the fire. It warms my face." Omie offered.

"Don't catch your hair on fire," Mom piped up from the sofa. Omie hitched back away from the flame. His nose remained within a couple feet of the candle. His face reflected the gold of the beeswax flame.

"It feels good."

∞

The candle burned down the length of the flame into the wax.

I wondered what Jack was thinking. He had slid off the couch cushions onto the floor next to Omie.

Eva's eyes flickered in the candlelight.

"I wonder. David. How he thought…about…," Jack muttered. He swung his mane as he tipped his head. "I wonder about David."

Mom leaned forward from the sofa. She put her hand on his shoulder. The twins each found a place on his lap as he sat cross legged, leaning back against the front of the sofa.

"David is alright with it. Facing life as it is. Life, and death," Mom replied. "Sad. But alright. David was born wise."

Eva's eyes sparkled as she looked to Mom; a tear formed.

*Oh*, I thought.

"Who is 'he'?" Omie asked. His sister was near slumber in Jack's hammock of an arm.

"Your uncle. My twin."

Omie's gaze turned to me. "You. A twin."

"My brother, David. Your uncle."

Omie's campfire candle flickered and flashed across his face.

We all pondered our own thoughts.

*How could she think David's dying was alright by him?* I wondered.

∞

Eva asked, "Why does your brother not tell you of our marriage?"

I considered her question.

Lynn had thought about it. She explained David. He wanted to introduce his wife to each of us. He hoped he could do it in person. He never considered the awkwardness that might pose, or the pain, or anxiety, if he could not be there. He would not consider the notion that he would not be back to her. He could not. She was his hope.

"I agree," Mom said.

I could see that. Would it help Eva, though, with her grief for my brother?

∞

The flame fed from a deep pool of molten wax gathered in the core of the candle.

"You knew David?" Eva spoke to Lynn.

"Yes. We met. On two occasions." Lynn reflected on those occasions. "Enough that I trusted him completely." She glanced toward me. "He held my message for Patrick in a secret promise."

190

"Two times?" Eva considered.

"Once, on the farm. When I stayed with you," she looked to Elle. "And again in Baraboo, when I watched your football game," she turned toward me.

"I saw you at that game. I was sure it was you."

Her eyes narrowed with her smile. She knew I had seen her.

"I told David that night. I saw you."

"Yes," Mom said. "Paddy and Rose were certain you were there, too. I didn't see you, though. They kept pointing toward where they thought you were, but I never found you. Too many people."

My jaw dropped. So did Lynn's.

"You never said a word," I said.

Lynn was astonished. She questioned Mom. "Why does this make me feel so awkward? What were you thinking?"

"Young people," Mom said. "They don't know the power of the magic they wield. Sometimes, the goofy things that young people do happen so fast that by the time you think to react, it's all over. We didn't know why you were there. But I didn't think you meant to hurt my son." She glanced toward me. "David never gave a hint. We thought it was goofy. Kids do goofy things. These twins, anyway." Mom gestured toward me. "We learn to just let it be."

Eva looked across the face of the family of which she was now a part. We laughed, we blushed, we shared discoveries from times we had together. I watched her turn her gaze upon each of us as she held young Jacob in her arms. I watched her fall in love.

∞

We explained to Eva the ramifications of Lynn's visit to Baraboo and her surreptitious meeting with David.

"David holds secret so long?" she asked.

"Yes. He never told me that Lynn had entrusted him with photos and letters to me until we were together in Regensburg," I said. "He had stored them in his closet until he felt it was right to tell me about what she left me. She made him promise to keep it secret."

"I remember." She said in German.

I didn't want to dwell on then. Instead, I shifted the focus to her. I answered in German.

"Why do you name your first born after your violin? What will you tell him when he asks why you named him after a violin?"

Her gaze fell upon the baby in her arms. Then she looked up to me with an amused smile.

191

"It is not I who call my violin by the name of its maker," she chuckled. " It is you who call it 'Jacob'."

"Me?" I was astounded. "When did I name your violin, Jacob."

She laughed.

"In Regensburg. When I told you, and David, how my violin has come down through my family to me."

I felt my brain spinning. *Jacob is Jacob because of me?*

'I do like that you call it Jacob," she smiled. "It is so American of you. No one would christen a violin as you did."

I have been befuddled before. Eva had me befuddled now. Hadn't David shared naming the violin with me?

"Didn't David call Jacob by Jacob?"

"Not that I recall. Not when I was present."

Had he with me? I couldn't remember

"What's he saying?" Mom asked Jack.

"He named Eva's violin Jacob. It's a nice name."

Eva agreed. "My violin lives as Jacob Stainer now."

"Hasn't it always?" Jack asked. "Once a Stainer, always a Stainer.'

We all thought about it, losing ourselves to the flame of the campfire. A third of the candle had burned; a deep well of liquid beeswax fed the flame of soft gold. The kids little faces basked in the light it cast. My kids faces. David's babies faces were surrounded by swaddling and absorbed the more scarlet rays from the candle. They lay in slumber in the arms of their mother and grandmother. Ally sat by her mother cross legged on the floor. Omie tucked himself in between Jack and Mom. He inspected baby David's sleeping face as his grandmother slowly rocked side to side.

"What's Stainer?" he asked.

"My violin is a Stainer. It was made by Jacob Stainer. So it is a Stainer."

"Not a Jacob?" Omie pressed.

"Ya. Jacob *auch.*" Eva assured him.

He pursed his lips

"Are you going to let Jacob sing again?" he asked.

"*Doch.* After baby sleeps."

Omie sprouted a contented smile.

I examined Jack's noncommittal expression. "You know about Stainers?"

Jack emerged from where he dwelled when he considered that which he didn't know.

"I know of them. You told me."

I hadn't recalled telling him about Eva's violin. "When?"

Jack doesn't emerge all at once. He may have slipped back to where he went. He remained silent.

We fell back into a revery deep and secure.

∞

I asked Eva, "What are you going to play?"

"Chaccone."

The candle drank of it's bottom third.

The kids slept lightly.

The babies stirred. They were waking.

"How about the Air?" I asked.

Mother sat upright. David squirmed in her arms. He yawned and mouthed the air.

Eva smiled. And nodded. Jacob looked up into her face from where he lay on her knees. Eva kissed her babe and passed him to Lynn before taking up her violin.

Her fingers tickled the strings on her Jacob Steiner violin as she made it sing Bach's Air.

∞

By the time her bow swept slowly across Jacob's strings in the final measure, Ally had climbed up on my lap, her legs crossed, her head leaning back against my chest. Omie stared, mesmerized, leaning against his mother's knees, peering into Jacob's face, then following Eva's finger's on Jacob's neck.

As the gentleness of the Air settled our hearts, Jack stirred.

"So you thought that Patrick would marry Eva to help her immigrate to the United States." He turned his burly face to mother.

Eva turned to Elle as well. "Est-ce vrai?" she asked. *"Is this true?"*

Mother raised her eyebrows to full mast. She pursed her lips.

Jack's laugh startled the infants.

I shrugged. Mother. What more can you say?

Lynn shifted young Jacob in her arms, returning him to his mother after Eva set her violin aside and took young Jacob to her breast.

Elle handed David back to Eva as well.

"Well," Elle began. "I thought we may have to do something to help Eva get home to America."

I gasped. "Well, calling me here to Germany to marry Eva was a pretty dramatic measure!"

193

"I thought it might help. " Mom shrunk back into the sofa. "And I didn't actually know you would." She shrugged, her expression looking elvish. "It was a test."

I sat silent, flummoxed. I glanced over to Lynn, who beamed, enjoying my predicament.

"You did well, my son," Mom said. "You acted on your love of your brother. I am proud of you."

"His brother," Lynn said. "And Eva. Patrick loves them both." She turned her gaze to Eva. "This is Patrick's heart. It is why I love him. He is so kind. So loving. He would have done right by you, Eva. In the spirit of his brother, he would have done right by you."

"And by you?" Eva stirred. Lynn's thoughts disturbed her. "How could Patrick do this act to you. It is not right."

"He means well. Could worse be said?" Jack offered.

I struggled to turn my thoughts into words, but my thoughts dodged anything resembling coherence. "How could I do such a thing to you?" I repeated. I watched Lynn blur as my eyes teared up.

"Well, you didn't have to, after all," Mom said. "Miss Reichle told me it would take longer if you were to marry Eva. So it wasn't going to happen anyway."

I flushed with rage toward my Mother as I used to before I ever left home. "You knew?" My voice was too loud, too strong. The children startled. "And you let me bring my family all the way anyway."

Mother stood her ground. I had never before seen my mother do so.

"Certainly. It was a bit of a shock to learn you were planning to travel so soon after you got my letter. But I saw no harm, especially when you brought Lynn and your children along. How could you possibly marry Eva when you traveled with your family?" She bore an expression of benign innocence. As never before, I could see something very lovely about my mother. My laughter startled the children, as well as Mother. Jack chortled along with me.

"You're nuts," I told her. "You know that, don't you?"

We chuckled.

"I am aware," she smiled.

∞

In the moments of quiet that followed, I idly asked Eva, "You knew nothing of this?"

"I did not," she said. "I wondered why Mrs. Reichle stressed the importance of not re-marrying when I had not asked about it." Her eyes turned to mother, and her look was filled with love and humor. "I did not consider this line of questioning. Do you really think I could simply marry my husband's brother?" Her tone was so kind that mother simply shrugged.

"I thought it was worth considering."

"What of Lynn? And my children?" I posed.

"Patrick, I sometimes don't think in as straight a line as you do. Or as David did. You're right. I'm still kind of crazy."

"Pleasantly so," Eva added."You mean well always."

Jack intervened. "Elle, you are the kindest soul I know. And you have given your kindness to Patrick. Being kind sometimes leads to an imbalance for how you treat yourself and others around you. My question is for Lynn. How could you let this go on?"

Lynn stared at Jack a moment. She stroked the head of her daughter, asleep at her side. She looked first at Eva, who watched her with an open expression, full of wonder and fear. Then she turned to me.

"It all seemed too fantastic. Unreal. There was no magic spared in all of this. I looked for strength in it. I looked away from hope. Faith. Those empty powers that lead to despair or contempt. I know I will never lose Patrick again. That was real for me. I believed that. In spite of his love for David, I trusted Patrick." She then turned to Elle. "You asked so much of your son. He is a good man. You have done well."

"As have you," my mother replied.

∞

After a moment, I looked into my mother's eyes. I saw no fear. She was all present.

"Why do you think it was okay with David."

She shook her head. .

"He knew what is here now. He has for so much of his life."

∞

As the campfire waned, the twins had dropped off to sleep. All the twins. We bundled them off to their beds. Mom blew out the flame. Jack helped Eva from her chair, then carried it to her room. Then, by happenstance, we all met in the hallway outside the study as we made our way to our rooms. Jack reached out with the arm span of a bear and gathered us in, first Eva, then Elle, and me and Lynn.

"It is blessed to be among this Joyce family" he said.

I nodded. Eva hummed a note of agreement. I felt Lynn's head lean into my shoulder.

Mom whispered, "Amen."

195

# Chapter 43

# Reconciliation

In the morning, we sent Jack off in a taxi to the airport. His absence left an immediate void in our *gemutlich* familial community. The twins missed him dearly. Eva was quiet all morning after he drove off in the shiny Mercedes. Lynn shed a tear as he hugged her goodbye. So did Mom.

As for me, I felt a lump of concern nestle in my gut. I worried about what Jack was returning to.

We stayed on in Munich another full week. By then, Lynn and the twins longed for home. I did as well.

We confirmed our return plane reservations for the end of the week. Mom protested only in form; she knew we were due to leave. She had no qualms about being Eva's primary support and advocate.

On Friday, as we packed our bags in preparation for our Saturday morning departure, Mom found me with Lynn in our room. The twins were busy tending to Eva and cooing with her babies. Mom quietly closed the door as she entered.

"I'm very proud of you, my son," she said.

"You didn't really expect I would have to marry Eva, did you?"

"I didn't know. But it seems to me, you would have, would it be necessary. That is you. You are here because that is what you do. Meet the needs of others. You always have, when you could.

"It's your temperament. If others ask too much of you, or you see what is demanded as something you cannot provide, you get frustrated. Angry. Hurt that you feel you are falling short of what is expected of you. I asked you to accept me as I went crazy, when you were just a boy. You didn't accept that. It was too big. Your anger showed I asked too much of you. Of any of us. That became the heart of my hope during those years of insanity. Your anger, your intolerance of my illness. You showed me better. You demanded better."

She paused, reflecting. Her eyes fell under a momentary shadow, as though a cloud passed over.

"I didn't realize that asking you to help Eva get to America was too much. But then, I don't always think well, do I? I just knew we could do, must do, something to help Eva with her new family. David's family. Our family," her eyes brightened. "There are ways to help her find her new home with us. And for a moment, I thought that the fastest way to help Eva was through you. You are a good guy, Patrick. So I asked. But I knew deep down that you would forgive me for asking so much of you. That, too, is you. You are a great forgiver. I trusted you would forgive me." With a nod like a bird pecking for grain, she dismissed me.

I was spellbound.

She directed her gaze toward Lynn. "You are a most remarkable person, Lynn North. I am grateful on behalf of my son that you are in his life."

Lynn drew Mom into her arms and hugged her. "I'm proud of your son, too," she said. "I hope, though, that you will not try marrying him off to anyone but me in the future."

We laughed. It was a good laugh, a laugh so good it would hold us until we were back together again, at home. On the farm. The whole family together again in North Freedom. All of us, except David.

Book Four

# Patrick's Quest

# in the

# Boundary Waters

*There is magic in the feel of a paddle and the movement of a canoe, a magic compounded of distance, adventure, solitude, and peace. The way of a canoe is the way of the wilderness and of a freedom almost forgotten. It is an antidote to insecurity, the open door to waterways of ages past and a way of life with profound and abiding satisfactions. When a man is part of his canoe, he is part of all that canoes have ever known.*
*—Sigurd Olson*

*…Heal yourself with the kisses that the wind gives you and the hugs of the rain. Stand strong with your bare feet on the ground with everything that comes from it…*
*— María Sabina*

*Chapter 44*

# Boundary Waters in October

The lengthy, lingering August daylight had long since waned by early October when we returned from Munich to our home on Burntside Lake. Now, a few days later, October casts deep and chilling shadows that sting skin as the penumbra grew longer and sank into the darkness of night. Sunsets are shorter than before we left for Munich, and start much earlier in the afternoon.

The autumn sun now hung low over the southern shore of Lake Ogishkemuncie and peered from over my shoulder, as I paddled my canoe to the north west. With a couple short portages between the small boundary waters lakes Jenny and Annie, this day's paddle would easily get me to Eddie Lake, where I planned to pitch a camp. A slight southeasterly breeze at my back nudges my canoe across Og's big lake surface. Here I am, paddling toward the quest Lynn so encouraged, whatever her reasons. As the rhythmic splash of paddle on water marked the passing of the morning, I reflected on how I came to be here in the wilderness.

∞

Our jet from Munich was no more than half way across the Atlantic, but Lynn had already renewed her encouragement for me to 'find my soul' in the Boundary Waters.

*Find my soul?*

"What makes you think I don't know where my soul is?" I asked.

"I know you, Patrick Joyce. We may have been apart for too long, but I know you deep down into your heart. That's my gift in life. I know you."

I laughed. "You know the boy I was when we built your wall. When we were together in the Dunes. When we worked our mischief together, sneaking around so that my Aunt and Uncle were clueless to the freedoms we took." I shook my head, but I wasn't disagreeing with her. I admit, I think she knew me better than I knew myself. I winced, however, when I thought of the paths, the wrong turns and missteps I took in the years that passed since our time together.

She leveled her gaze, looking down her nose down at me from above the rims of her reading glasses. I squirmed, but the warmth of her gaze assured me of her love.

"So what did you learn on your trek through Appalachia?" Lynn asked. She saw me speechless. Flummoxed.

*Where did this come from?*

Her smile was kind. "Really. I'm curious. How long were you out there? A month? Two?"

"Twelve and a half weeks. Eighty-eight days."

"Tell me about your hike. Your trek. Was it a pilgrimage of sorts? What did you find along the way?"

I stirred my thoughts and feelings. It was easier to deal with what was going on at the moment than bringing up the difficulties of paths already trod.

"I knew I had to find you."

Her eyes flashed and her smile broadened "Well, that may have been an answer to my prayers," she teased. "Something more, though. What did you learn about yourself?"

"What do you mean," I dodged her question. Since I left the trail, life wound up so quickly that I didn't have a lot of time to analyze my journey. My pilgrimage. I knew what she was asking, but I didn't have a ready answer.

I measured my response. How much had I understood about the unraveling of my thoughts as I walked those hills and trails? Loose ends. I had a handful of frayed, loose ends.

She waited.

I came up blank. I looked squarely into her inviting eyes. I shook my head. It was more like a tremor.

"I don't know. Just about the time I figured out that the trail had given me all it could and more than I thought I needed, I ran into Georgia and found out about David," I confessed. "My world turned upside down all over again."

She nodded. "We'll fix that. You have David in your heart. Plus you have your mother to figure out."

"My mother," I groaned. "There is no figuring out my mother. She's just barely got herself figured out."

She leveled her discerning eye upon me. I shivered.

"Your mother is doing quite well,"she said. "She is comfortable in her own skin, with her own unique ways. You might have to figure out a bit more about how to accept her without asking her to change into someone she is not. She was broken badly and she fixed it. She is who she is and it is working for her. You have been broken, too. Have you fixed yourself? You have work to do there, Patrick. Your mother, and your brother. They wait for you to find comfort in your own skin."

She rummaged through her satchel, retrieving a paperback she had read during our flight from Chicago to Munich. She handed it to me. Another Listening Point book. "Start here. Consider listening to the quiet of the wilderness. When we get home, we'll get you out into the Boundary Waters. It will be like a renewal for you. Paddle the waters. Cleanse the soul." Her gaze pierced my heart. Her smile spread across her face, then she leaned over to plant a kiss on my ear. She picked up her book and returned to her reading.

I read Sig Olsen's *Singing Wilderness* until we landed in Chicago. The next day, October 5, we arrived in Ely. We had been gone 40 days. Almost seven weeks.

∞

I was home just four days before I plunked my butt on the seat of my canoe and paddled away from my family at Seagull Lake.

Lynn didn't miss a beat when it came to organizing my trip. She recruited Martha and Teddy to help gather the essentials for an extended paddle. We stuffed two Duluth packs with food, a sleeping bag, tent, rain gear and rain fly, fishing tackle, route maps, and all the sundries essential for a solo trip into the wilderness.

Teddy went over each item, which pocket or compartment it was in, and why they were so organized.

"You've got two compasses," he showed me. "Keep one in your pocket. I like it in my shirt. Easier to get to and it won't just slip out like it might from your pants pocket. The other is in the map case, which is in this pocket," he said, opening a long side compartment on the green canvas pack. "In case you lose the first one," he grinned.

He showed me the fishing gear in a box stuffed deep under the sleeping bag and tent. He went through the smaller pack carefully. It included the kitchen gear and food, first aid, a flashlight, matches, candles, and some clothing. The rain fly, he observed, was the last item packed. That way, it was on top of all the other gear and was the first item out in case it was needed to protect me from rains as I set up camp.

"If it is nice, the rain fly might be all you need for a night, as long as the weather holds," he cautioned. "You may plan to stay at a site only one night. If it looks dry and the wind is down, you can get by with the fly. There won't be any mosquitos," he grinned. "Just wolves," he deadpanned.

The packs weighed less than 40 pounds each, and he showed me how to fit one on my back and one on my chest so that I could carry both at the same time with the canoe on my shoulders as I portaged. I wondered about that; wouldn't it be easier to just double back and make two round trips on each portage?

"You be the judge of that," Martha advised. "You might find it easier to do one trip on some portages. And if you're looking at weather or daylight getting short, you may want to save time."

Teddy added, "Watch the sky. Feel changes in the wind. Always, day and night."

I nodded, considering all their advice, and wondering once again just exactly why I was heading out into the wilderness this late in the fall. Nights were distinctly chilly; the leaves were gold on the aspen.

Teddy inspected my expression. "Best time of the year to be out in the wilderness," he assured me. "Absolutely."

Lynn nodded. "I wish I was going with you."

"And remind me," I pleaded, "Why is it that you can't?"

"Your twins, my father, and a wild woman I may or may not claim as my sister. Plus my job."

"Right," I allowed. "And with all that, you prefer I'm not here to help?"

She simply nodded. Case closed. No more arguments or appeals.

"Now, let's go over your maps once again. You want to know your route as much as possible. It will help."

Explaining what I could expect of the portages and highlighting good campsite opportunities, Lynn voice twinkled with excitement as she drew out the proposed route for my trip.

"It's a good route, with a number of portages," she said, drawing her finger along the pencil path through both big and little lakes of the boundary waters. "But none of the portages are too long, or steep. You'll have time to follow this route and make good time till you get to Moose Lake here, off the end of the Fernberg. We'll pick you up there at Latourell's outfitters. You can call from their lodge when you get there," she said. "If you follow this route and stay on these marked campsites, you'll do fine. You will paddle into Latourell's in two weeks. Fourteen days."

I focused on the route she showed me. More than a dozen lakes, strung out along a path that twisted and turned and wound through forest littered with hundreds of other lakes and rivers. I felt intimidated.

She noticed.

"You'll do fine. Just take your time to read and know your route. It's a good one. You'll want to know your route as thoroughly as you can. It will help."

*Only if I can stay on it,* I reflected.

∞

That night, we loaded the canoe on top of the old van we used to taxi summer customers and campers to and from Boundary Waters access points. My gear went in the back end. The next morning, October 9, we left home at the crack of dawn. Martha stayed back with Ingie and Luther, while Teddy, the twins, Lynn and I climbed in the van for the ride to the Gunflint Trail end of Seagull Lake. After a merry and hearty picnic, we loaded the canoe. I climbed in, gave Lynn a loving kiss and a look of bewildered disbelief that she was sending me off on this mysterious voyage.

Then, I paddled away from my family and friends. A quarter mile off shore, I looked back. They stood watching, the twins gathered about their mother's legs, Lynn wrapped up in her own arms, and Teddy standing tall and strong, a look of determination urging me on. Omie raised his little hand, palm toward me. I felt both grateful and wistful for their send off. I rounded the north end of Three Mile Island and headed into the maze of islands clustered in Seagull's northern waters. When I looked back, they were gone.

# Chapter 45

# Wandering Wolves

I had started fairly late to expect that I'd reach Og before twilight, and I didn't really want to pitch camp in the dark. The waters were calm, and the breeze remained at my back for this first stretch of the route. I meandered through the islands on the north end of Seagull until I reached the portage to Alpine. My second portage into Jasper Lake took less than a half hour. Jasper lay like an emerald in a setting of deep green forest; I was tempted to set camp on Jasper's inviting shores. All of the sites were vacant. I hadn't seen a soul since I last glimpsed my family on the shores of Seagull hours before.

My progress was steady, but paddling solo is slower than when there is a partner in the other seat of the canoe. There was no workhorse in the bow to power stroke my cedar strip canoe, and while I worked diligently at my j-stroke from the stern, I tended to zig-zag more than Teddy or Luther when they paddled solo.

"Dodging subs?" Teddy teased during one outing when we both commanded solo canoes. His boat sailed like an arrow, straight and fleet. He crossed to the portage on Burntside that day in three fourths the time it took me to complete my left-right course. I shook my head.

"What do you mean?" I asked.

He waggled his hand back and forth. "Diversionary tactics. Dodging submarines?" he laughed.

I found a suitable island campsite a third of the way down Ogishkemuncie Lake, the long, narrow lake dotted with numerous islands, many with inviting and vacant campsites. Og was a particularly beautiful lake, even after the grace of the lovely lakes I had paddled through. I saw why Og was Lynn's favorite. I'd paddled and portaged the 12 miles in just under seven hours under clear blue skies on calm waters. Less than an hour had been portage time, so I knew my paddling was slow but deliberate. I was glad to pitch camp while the October sun sank into the southwest shoreline.

The sky was clear and the stars brilliant, but with a full belly and a long day's paddle behind me, I was tired. I slipped into a deep sleep and woke only when the sun was peeking over the east end of Og.

∞

Over my second cup of coffee, I took out my route maps. Martha knew these waters better than anyone, Teddy assured me. She had suggested working my way toward the South Arm of the Knife. She'd marked a favorite campsite on a crescent shaped island at the west end of the Knife's bulging east end.

"You'll find refuge there," Martha had told me with a leveled gaze.

*Refuge,* I thought. *Refuge from what?* But I nodded my head, acknowledging her helpful advice. Her gaze filled with humor, she continued.

"Beyond this campsite is Isle of Pines," she said, sliding her finger to the left through the narrows to the west. "It's just a few miles. Maybe a half dozen. When you join up with the main body of Knife, here, it's not all that far." she pointed on the map, "You'll come across a big island, Robbins. Just to the west of Robbins is Isle of Pines," she noted, moving her finger west. "If you're lucky, Dorothy will have some root beer brewed and bottled. It's kind of late in the season, but you'll appreciate sipping on Dorothy's hearty root beer."

She leveled her eye on me again. "You might want to put in time on the South Arm of Knife Lake. It's the most peaceful place on the planet.

As I read the maps, I knew I could make it to Martha's recommended camping site on Knife within the day. But I wondered, *Why?* I was in no hurry. I was due to meet Teddy at the west end of this route after 14 days. I'd be almost half way there if I hurried along to sip root beer. I decided to stay the day.

∞

By mid morning, I was bored and antsy. My island was little more than a rock with a stand of pine. Summer campers had pretty well picked over the firewood. But the sun was warm and the breeze remained calm. I sat against a log next to the cold fire pit, reading Sig Olson and wondering, what the hell did this romantic do to fire up his adrenal gland?

∞

By noon, I had to move. I set Sig aside and hopped in the canoe to gather some firewood on the nearby shoreline. I had chosen an island short of halfway across Og and only a hundred or so yards from the southern shore. With a bundle gathered in the bottom of the canoe, I paddled along Og's shoreline. I strung a daredevil on my fishing line and cast out, away from shore. Before the spoon could drop to rocky bottom, I took up my paddle and set a course parallel to the shoreline. Within a short distance, the tip of my rod swung wildly back toward my lure. I brought in a nice northern, maybe 24 inches, a couple pounds. Perfect for dinner. I let it flop about on the bottom of the canoe among the kindling for my fire. Soon, it too stilled like the wind and the lake. My lazy paddling was the greatest display of energy under the sun, which sluggishly continued it's descent toward the southwestern horizon. I was in no hurry to get back to my campsite. I'd be there all night long. At that moment, I knew I'd move on first thing in the morning. The stillness of Og felt a bit stifling.

∞

With a belly full of fish and a fire of dry kindling sending sparks up toward the Milky Way, I settled back against a log and wondered just what the fuck I was doing here, sitting on an island, alone, away from the ones I love. Away from Lynn.

And wondering why she thought this was going to help me? I kind of resented it. I mean, what was wrong with me that I needed to 'cleanse my heart and find the core grace of my soul." I heard myself grumbling about it and shook my head. I wanted to put my bad attitude aside.

I thought of Luther, too. Luther, in one of his more lucid moments, which were ever more fleeting since our return from Munich. He'd looked into my eyes with his hazy gaze as he sat nearby while we packed my gear. Nodding his head, he said, "You'd best mind her. She's got a head up on you."

Teddy snorted a laugh. Martha took the map packet from Luther; he'd been unpacking items as quickly as we'd placed them in their assigned compartments.

"Luther, how is Patrick going to do this trip if you pilfer his supplies?" Martha's tone to Luther was patient and kind. She gently took the maps from his grip. He stared blankly at her, questioning all that she said.

"I'm so afraid," he told us once as we lazed around the blaze flashing in the fire pit, "that I won't be me much longer. That there will be nothing left of me for you to know who I am." If his worry hurt her, Lynn concealed it. She encouraged him. "You will always be you, Dad."

But me? She sends me out to the wilderness to find my soul? To learn who I truly am? *What's with this?* I wondered

I stirred the embers of my little campfire and considered its warmth. The fire kept me company. How strange, it seemed, to not have anyone with whom to share my campfire. I considered stoking the scarlet embers with additional twigs and branches, but why? I wondered. Why, other than the warmth on my face. Campfires were conducive to stories, jokes and confessions. Here, on my little island in the waters of Ogishkemuncie, my stories would lay fallow. No one to share my jokes. My confessions would be for naught.

I let the embers die.

Before long, the sky opened up. Stars beamed in concert. The Milky Way commanded all above, and her reflection saturated the glass surface of Og.

I felt small.

But not alone.

And then, wolves began to howl.

Their chorus of melancholy cries tore at my heart. So forlorn was their plaintive cry. It sent shivers across my skin; a tightness formed in my core, about my ribs.

They were close. Probably along Og's southern shore. Maybe a couple hundred yards, or even less, from my island campsite.

I wondered, could they swim? I shook my head. Can dog's swim? Would a wolf swim? Most certainly. Does a bear shit out here? Did I really want to think about bears? Wolves were enough.

I considered stoking the fire again. But I let it rest. I wished my shore-line companions to the south would cease their racket.

And then they did just that. They were still. The silence brought peace. I watched the stars as they rolled across the skies until I fell asleep.

# Chapter 46

# Chasing Thoughts on Eddy

The sun broke across the eastern horizon as I put in my canoe, heading west toward the portage into Jenny and Annie. As I neared the west end of Og, three silent grey bodies emerged from the morning shadows along the shoreline near the landing. They watched as I paddled, then slipped into the darkness of the woods just a hundred yards from the portage. I paused on the portage. Wolves wouldn't bother me, would they? Luther said not. So did Martha. I'd be lucky to see them, they said.

Teddy smiled when he heard their advice.

"What they're telling you," he said, "when the wolves show themselves? Pay attention."

Well, the wolves howling kept me up a good bit of the night, but they had been as quiet as shadows this morning. I looked along the stretch of shoreline to the south. Nothing. Quiet. Had they shown me anything?

∞

The morning was soft with long rays of autumn sunlight as I paddled into Eddy. Couldn't have been nine o'clock yet, and the October morning sun slashed into the shadows along Eddy's western shore. I pulled into a bay near the portage and looked for the campsite Teddy and Martha had mentioned. Teddy said the gentle rise from the waters edge made for beautiful sunset watching, and that fishing in the bay was generally good. Smallmouth. Large northerns. I didn't really need large northern, but I was counting on catching fish. It would be a necessary protein source, and as I looked at the camping menu we prepared, I thought it was a bit light. I'd be hungry if I didn't catch fish.

"Don't worry about that," Martha had said. "It's fall and the fish are feeding. You'll catch plenty." She looked at the map and pointed out a bay on Eddy' southeast end.

"Lynn's mother and I stayed on this bay for almost a week, toward the end of our trip. Caught fish every day. Enough to eat. You won't go hungry. You'll be just fine."

I hoped she was right, and soon after setting up camp, I was trolling a line behind the canoe. I had lunch, and dinner as well, on the stringer in no time. I paddled back to camp and busied myself with gathering wood for the campfire. By noon, I had a nice wood pile and set about to make a fire to cook the three smallmouth bass. I cooked up the six nice filets, ate four and saved the others for snacking later. I cleaned up the area and stored my provisions. Martha said I might be greeted along the way by a late feeding bear looking for that last meal before hibernating. I wasn't concerned at the moment, so I left the food pack leaning against a downed log and found a comfortable sitting place along side. I looked about. The sky was blue, the breeze chilly. I felt the sun warming the side of my face and shoulder. And I looked about.

Nothing. Not a movement in sight. Not a bird in the trees. Just the shadows of pine needles creeping under the sun as it crossed mid-day. I was left with my thoughts.

∞

I wondered where to start. I didn't want to grumble about Lynn's rationale for the urgency of my paddling pilgrimage. I had been over that enough. There was no answer to that internal discussion.

I did wonder about the wolves. I'd abandon the island safety of my last site and now realized that no lake served as a moat to separate me from wild creatures. I recalled the intense reaction of the hair on my neck during the howling last night. What could I do about wolves? Nothing, I suppose. Is that their message? I could do nothing about them. I was probably lucky to have heard their woeful song during the night. And to have seen them this morning. What were they telling me? *Be careful?* I don't know.

I watched as a gentle breeze rippled Eddy's placid surface. It was soothing.

With a bellyful of bass, I slipped into deep sleep, toppling over beside the log where I napped.

When I awoke, the autumn quiet reigned. A young loon had taken to Eddy's surface, and it dove and floated with its own quiet purpose, but didn't call out.

I noticed the left over fish fillets had disappeared from the rocks surrounding the fire pit. I looked around for evidence, but found none that indicated what kind of company I had in my camp. A bird? Maybe a Gray Jay? They were bold when it came to sharing food and scraps at the resort. They'd arrived from the north a week or so earlier. Martha pointed them out, saying they'd flown down from their Canadian summer homes. Had they robbed me of my afternoon snack? I'll need be more careful next time.

Oh, well.

I was left again with my thoughts.

I shrugged.

What was I going to do with all the time during the next twelve days? I couldn't imagine.

I dug out the blank journal that Lynn gave me for the trip.

"Jot your thoughts," she'd encouraged. "Any thoughts. Little or big. Complete ideas or just fragments of thoughts. You'll find they will add up. Like the strokes of paint on a canvas. This will help you. You'll see."

I opened the journal. On the second page was one word printed in Lynn's fine script: *Grace*.

*She's so cosmic,* I chuckled.

I turned the page. The blank paper glared at me, daring me to enter something worthy, valuable, meaningful. My mind was as blank as the surface of the page.

I put the tip of my pen to the page and watched, with no small horror, my first entry: "I have no thoughts."

∞

My time on Eddy Lake lasted for two more days. Eddy was a lovely, peaceful lake. The weather remained mild, although ice did form on the water I left overnight in my cooking gear. I dipped into the dehydrated stores that Martha sent along. Jerky by the handfuls. Fruit. Nuts. It was enough, especially with a couple more smallmouth that I caught from shore.

On day two at my Eddy campsite, after coffee and breakfast, I sat against the log and looked at the entries I'd made in my journal. Still pretty limited. I decided to grab thoughts that flew through my mind and enter each on a page spread, with the words describing the idea on the left side page. As I fingered through my progress, I read the ideas waiting substance.

*Job.*

*School.*

*Career.*

*David.*

*Mom.*

*Lynn.*

It went on.

*Ingie.*

*Luther.*

*Mom* (again. I must have forgotten I'd already considered her as a topic to address.)

I realized that most of my ideas were people. What was I thinking?

I remembered something David wrote that Jack and I had once discussed. Philosophers don't mire themselves in discussion of things. Objects. Artifacts of the day. There is no gravity in the mass of things. Only want and desires. Too many people are consumed with things and the trivia of the day. Or people. Insightful, wise people may have meaningful communications, but generally, discussions about people often never rise above anything more than rumor. Or locker room talk. "People-talk" too often generated nothing that fueled the ideas of determination, admiration, aspiration, value.

It is not the quality of an individual's beauty, power, or wealth that nourishes the soul of society. It is the appreciation of wisdom and worthy thought that feeds the soul. One must leap to the insight of great minds to latch on to the true fertile sap the runs up the stems of hardwood thought. One must aspire to be inspired.

So I concentrated on several key philosophers whose thoughts and philosophies were inspirational to me. I assigned them to a page of their own in my journal.

*de Chardin (David and Jack's favorite. And Mom's. And Rosies', I added below the page title.)*

*Ghandi*

*Neitzchi, the fucking Kraut who just about ruined my mind in Regensburg.*

*Kant, the fucking Kraut who salvaged my mind and soul in Regensburg.*

*Ann Rand*

*Einstein*

*Buckminster Fuller*

*Aldo Leopold. (Lynn and I enjoyed reading him when we were in the Dunes.)*

*…*

I glanced at my list. Still more people. It was daunting and obvious. I didn't know much about how people thought. I considered that point for a moment. Then, I added a couple more names.

*Vince Lombardi*

*Mohammed Ali*

*Bobby Dylan*

*John Lennon.*

Who was I kidding, I thought. I'm dumb as a bolt. I don't know what I think myself, much less of people who I may have heard about.

What am I going to do?

Georgia?

I wonder what he's thinking. Is he off the Trail? Should be.

David.

What's it like *to know*, without even thinking?

∞

I listened to a pair of owls calling across the lake as the stars gleamed above.

The realization that my education had done little to discipline my ability to ponder and ruminate and act like a real thinker left me feeling, well, withered. I can accept it; I was in school as a jock. To play a game. I fed off the cheers and adulation of fans. But not to think. So I guess I really haven't failed in life. Just in sports. I came to a screeching halt in my life as a player. It was an energy draining, body-damaging, mind numbing existence, being a college football player. Or even a high school football player. I wasn't expected to ponder and probe the better notions of the mind.

So I didn't.

Where does that leave me now?

David.

Most of the truly rewarding concepts I had considered were due to their presence in the many letters my brother had written to me over the years. It was like my schoolwork and homework; David did the heavy thinking for me. But he did always try to share some of the knowledge he so rabidly consumed. I considered the many ideas he had shared with me. Ideas and concepts about values. About life. About death. And the meaning of both.

I realized how grateful I am for my brother. He shared with me his deepest thoughts. He taught me things that amused him while he was milking his cows. Like the earth spinning like a gyroscope. And gobs of frozen ice in Greenland and Alaska balancing the earth as it spun. Wondering about that while wadding gum on his most valuable toy and making it change its wobble. Hours, he would feed me random thoughts that meant something. Spoon fed me his considered values. It was so easy to take in those lovely gifts. David was the heart of whatever family I had, and he gave me what I needed to be whole.

Now, I felt, being whole was there for the taking. David taught me family, but David is gone. I know what to reach for in this life; I know what family means to me. Lynn. Our kids.

I want to live in a way that honors my family. And keeps us together.

# Chapter 47

# Winds and Waves on The Knife

In the morning, I was too restless to linger longer in the placid peacefulness of Eddy. I struck camp, paddled to the portage and put in on the crystal waters of the South Arm of the Knife.

The day had assumed a facet of my restlessness. Dawn was late and dark; a thick ceiling of clouds rolled in over night, carried in by a sharp, raw wind that came directly across the length of the South Arm's big body of water. The lake was choppy when I put in, but not beyond what I thought was safe. I paddled straight into the wind, heading toward the large, crescent shaped island at the far west end of this stretch of the South Arm.

The band of clouds hung low and dark above the western horizon, and the rate at which it barreled down on me sent a chill down my spine. The deep gray cloud ran the length of the horizon, churning and rolling as it advanced. The wind at my face was already stiff; choppy waters rolling toward me foamed with breaking crests. The wind took on a tone that deepened and ramped in volume. I dug in and paddled deep and fast, but it felt like I was being pushed back toward the portage from Eddy. I put all out. Slowly, stroke by stroke, I paddled closer to my island goal. When I finally broke into the bay formed within the pinched ends of the crescent isle, my cedar strip canoe cut through the wind blast and on to choppy but somewhat calmer water of the lee. I was groping for my breath, but I kept digging my paddle into the deep water of the bay.

Within a few minutes, I paddled my canoe to shore. I stepped out, grabbing the leather shoulder strap of a Duluth pack and swung it over the wooden gunnel of my canoe. With a paddle in one hand braced on the wet rock and the heavy pack in the other, I stepped cautiously on the landing. The wind gusted with anger. I turned back to retrieve the rest of my gear as a tremendous blow pushed me from behind. I looked to see the wind catch the canoe's bow, turning the boat sideways where the force of the gust caught across it's length. It launched the craft back into the choppy waters of the bay. I ran toward the unmoored vessel, but the wind was strong and the canoe lightly loaded. It was 15 feet off shore by the time I got to water's edge. I stepped quickly into the shallow edge waters but my next step took me to a deep drop off. Instantly, I was underwater. I found footing and pushed off toward the surface. My face broke the waves and I gasped in all the breath I could before I sank back underwater. My legs felt heavy with the weight of my boat shoes, but I lunged upward and bobbed at the surface.

The canoe had blown another ten yards off shore. I slashed the water with sloppy swimming strokes. A surge of panic gripped my chest and rose to my throat as I chased my boat. With every stroke, the distance to the canoe got wider. I swam after it regardless.

*If the wind just breaks…* I thought as I swam. I looked again and the boat was easily thirty yards away. I glanced back to the island, surprised to find that I was now almost a hundred yards off shore, almost to the end of the lee's calm. I looked back to the canoe. It was bobbing atop the breaking waves.

The wind had beat me. I gasped and coughed up the lake that I'd swallowed in my desperate attempt to reach the boat. I bobbed and tread in the choppy surface, my head turning first toward land, then to the boat, and back once again to the island.

I floated on the surface of the chop, gasping, slowly kicking and paddling in a backstroke to the campsite landing.

# Chapter 48

# Assessing the Obvious

Black clouds that rocked and roiled above Knife Lake's surface waters brought rain. It poured. Drops as big as pigeon eggs pounded the rock shield on which my campsite lay, hitting the granite with noisy splats and bouncing back up into the deluge.

I was amused. As amused as I could be, given the moment. The rain was warmer than the lake water that saturated my cloths. It felt almost good. I shivered nonetheless, hastily tearing through my one salvaged supply pack. I had grabbed the pack with the rain fly, spare clothes, a hatchet, a folding camp saw, matches, several portions of dehydrated food, and my sleeping bag. I shook and shivered. I had work to do.

Although the storm weakened to a steady rainfall, I figured the rain fly was the first essential task on this crisis agenda. With shaking, shivering fingers, I tied cord from eyelets along the edges of the fly to pines and saplings lining the perimeter of the campsite. The wind softened to a gusty breeze; the fly danced, suspended from the trees. It sheltered me. I dragged the Duluth pack into the shelter, stripped off soaking clothes, dried myself with a t shirt, and scrambled into a set of clean dry clothes. I felt the warmth immediately, but my shivers continued. I needed a fire.

I found my poncho in a side pocket on the pack. With that for cover, I grabbed the hatchet and set out to find kindling. *How will I ever get wet wood started?* I found a toppled aspen along the edge of camp. I hacked at it's smaller branches, breaking off four and five foot long ends. After collecting a bundle, I returned to the rain fly. I broke down the wood into one and two foot pieces. Crazy, I thought when the stack of kindling piled up less than knee deep. You think you've cut a whole pile of wood, but when you cut it and split it, the pile shrinks tremendously. Always does. I looked at the little stack of sticks and headed out for another load. The next stack was thicker in diameter and would give my fire some mass to warm me.

I just had to get it burning.

My hatchet was sharp. I used it to cut wedges from some of the thicker diameter kindling. It seemed fairly dry once I cut off the wet surface. I cut a bunch of the kindling, enough to give the fire a decent chance of burning. Then I cut fine chips and shaved long strands and slivers. Once I had enough, I built a wooden structure of many layers shaped in boxes and rectangles. I'd warmed up considerably with the dry clothes and the work I'd done to bring in firewood. But my fingers still fumbled as I struck a match and hoped for it to blaze. It did, and I carefully tucked it into the shaved kindling at the bottom of my fire. I held the match until the heat from its flame seared my fingers. But the fire didn't take.

I stuck another match, but the wood didn't take the flame. I grabbed my pack and looked for paper. There wasn't much. I looked at my blank journal. No, not the pages that Lynn had given me! I couldn't do it. I found a roll of toilet paper, tore off a half dozen sheets and crumpled them into a balls. I struck another match and the flame blazed. I held it into a fold in the toilet paper sphere. It caught. I placed it carefully into the chopped kindling. The paper produced a weak flame, but it was enough. The wood chips took the flame.

I sighed deeply. I watched as the flame crawled though those chips and I added larger sticks until I had a blazing fire. It cast warming rays on my face and I held my hands to it, rubbing, flexing my fingers, shivering. I had fire.

∞

I heated water and added dehydrated soup. It filled me with delicious warmth. I was tempted to down another helping, but no. I had let my boat float away, and in my boat was the pack with most of the kitchen stores. I licked the flavor off the metal cup in which I had made soup. I licked the spoon until no flavor could be tasted. Then I assessed my situation.

I had no canoe. I did have a paddle, but the spare was still lashed to the thwarts in my free-floating boat. As was my fishing rod. I had my life vest; I was grateful for the warmth it provided during my dash around camp to set up shelter. It would dry: the rains had stopped.

I had several dehydrated meals. Another couple of packets of soup. A bag of jerky, maybe half a pound. A bag of granola. Maybe 12 ounces. Same amount of cashews. I love cashews. I could eat them all now. But I can't, really. Can I?

I had two more apples tucked away in a side pocket on the Duluth pack. Four candy bars. Two oranges.

That was it for food.

Two, maybe three days of light nutrition. If I stretched it.

I was going to have to get my canoe back.

The darkness of the storm sunk into night as I mulled over my situation. I had clothes to stay dry. I had a bedroll to keep warm. I had much to do in the morning.

But I was just beginning to feel warm to my core. I stoked the fire, climbed into my bag, and watched the dance of the flames until they surrendered to the glow of embers.

I fell into a restless, troubled sleep.

216

# Chapter 49

# Teamless

The sun rose into a pure blue sky as the morning unfolded. I'd had breakfast. One of the apples. And some granola.

I sat contemplating. I climbed the bluff at the south end of the island. My eyes combed and probed every conceivable mooring spot across the lake for my free floating canoe. Perhaps it had somehow lodged itself on the far side, in the lee, of those little islands. Maybe it was snagged somewhere along the shoreline.

I couldn't see it.

The sun over my shoulders eased the early morning chill. I hung my wet clothes to dry in the sunlight, but the cool air wasn't going to help. I figured I needed a whole lot of firewood to keep me warm and help dry my soaked gear. I set to work with my hatchet and folding saw.

The pile of wood next to the fire grate mounded up until I had what looked like a loose face cord stacked chest high. By mid afternoon, I was hungry as a wolf. I could have eaten half my food stores and was tempted to do so. I allowed myself a pan of chicken noodle soup and an orange. It wasn't enough, but it quelled my hunger.

I climbed the bluff above my campsite on the far end of my island. Ledge rock soaked the sun's heat on the exposed bluff, and I found a hollowed seat that was made to fit me. I was inclined at first to have a post lunch slumber, but the meal in my stomach wasn't heavy enough. I couldn't just snooze away the day; rather, the seriousness of my predicament was foremost on my mind. I guess I'd have to put off finding my soul, I reflected. The thought struck me funny. *Sorry, Lynn. Can't find my soul at the moment. Have to work on saving my ass.*

But the humor of it all dissipated quickly. I realized I was doing something I generally avoided. I was worried. Normally, I worked around anything that might be worthy of worry. I ignored it. I trudged on without resolving my concerns. Worry implied resolution through embracing responsibilities. It hit me like a cold fish in the face: I was irresponsible. The most responsibility I'd taken on was to play sports. I hadn't done a whole lot in my life that required acting responsibly. I didn't need to. Pretty much everything was done for me. Davey had seen to that. He made so much money that I didn't have to answer to anything. Just go with the flow, not needing to answer to anybody. Just playing. Games.

Oh, I suppose I was responsible to my team. My football family. Football. You hurt to play the game. Sometimes, it hurt so much that I could hardly move. But I had to live up to the loyalty my teammates deserved.

And I did. Till it all came to a relatively painless end. So painless, at first, that it seemed anticlimactic to have it be the end of my athletic career. A neck injury. Couldn't feel a thing. If you're going to get hurt, best thing is to have an injury that keeps you from feeling any pain. However, the aftermath, the rehab, was no bowl of cherries. But it wasn't like I was screaming and crying from the intensity of it. It could have been worse. And it did give me an out from any further routine pain the sport caused. It was simple. The man in the white coat read the verdict. "This is serious. You need to consider your days playing football are over." Hmmm. *Consider it?* I had wondered. I suppose it would have been irresponsible to ignore his advice.

I shook my head to clear my mind. Why was I thinking about football? I took the man's advice. I stepped away from the game. Walked into a world where responsibility fostered self motivated. Motivation. What was the source of my motivation, I asked myself. To what end was my motivation devoted? Ah, I thought. Therein lies the crux. I wasn't very motivated because I had no source, no goal, and no accountability. I just wandered. First across Europe. Then the Appalachian Trail from Georgia to Pennsylvania. Walking along, never blazing trails, just following ghosts along well tread paths. Rarely leaving the trails—except unintentionally. Just taking wrong turns. Getting lost, really. Wandering around, lost. The thought struck me funny. Maybe this is what motivated Lynn to send me out here to the wilderness. She sensed I was lost.

An eagle soared high above the lake, wings still but for inflections in the wind, tipping its beak first right, then left, watching the surface below. I watched for minutes. It was a lovely sight.

But my thoughts beckoned me to return to them.

I felt the anguish of losing Lynn when we were torn apart in the Dunes. Twice we were forced apart. First by her choice; she ran from the young me. It was so hard to figure. Harder to accept. I somehow understood her logic. She ran away so that we could survive. We were doomed in those days when we were so young. Our love would have been squelched by others. We were the right people at the wrong time. She was so brave. So bold. She did what she needed to do to save us from ourselves and the hungry slaves of righteousness that prowled society. She acted with responsibility. I was shattered. I had never felt so lost. It set a low watermark for me in life. I remember it well. I couldn't understand it.

The eagle turned its beak downward, taking a steep angle toward the waters below. It flattened its course as it approached the surface, tilted its wings to catch the wind, and kipped its legs forward, talons out. As it dipped, the sharp claws of its talons swung down into the water just below the surface, its body jerking with the weight of its target, but never ceasing its flight, digging its widespread wingspan into the wind, lifting a long, gleaming fish above the lake with every flap of wing. The Northern was stiff, its body paralyzed by the talons piercing its back.

What a change of perspective, I thought. From water to airborne in seconds. I savored witnessing the eagle hunting. I sat motionless, long after the eagle cleared the bluff of my island and disappeared with its meal. I thought of hunting with David. Of helping him drag his venison from the woodlots and hedgerows on the farm.

As the sun set and the air chilled, the fire warmed me. Its flames soothed me. The smoke from evergreen branches lulled me. It was like the smoke streaming from a censer. Aromatic pine awakened longings in me for my family. Foremost, Lynn. And then, David.

David. My lost twin.

His memory ripped into me again like a dull blade. Oh, how I missed him! I felt anger flashing through me. Why did he go to war? Why did he have to die? Was there no other way?

I'd grappled with these questions. Too often. In ways that always left me wanting. But never answering. Never finding peace. Just empty words tasting like dry ash. There was no justification to explain away the loss of my twin.

I felt my face tighten, my lips purse tight, my eyes squint. I felt my anger. There was no answer for the loss of David. There never would be.

Why? The heartbeat of despair was most intense when considering David. It grated on my soul.

So, like any irresponsible man, I buried it. Left it encased in a bitter bile that would never be swallowed. I rejected even the thought.

I scrambled to my feet and grabbed kindling from my stack of wood. The embers were low but hot and the flame took off quickly. I meandered to the edge of camp. I rearranged the wet gear to dry the other sides and then walked down to water's edge. I couldn't sit back by the fire just yet. The scent of the evergreens threatened to snag my thinking in ways that spun my head around.

# Chapter 50

# Introspection and Determination

I scrambled back up the bluff in the fading twilight to scan the lake again for sign of my canoe. Nothing. Too dark to see the far reaches of the Lake.

Back in camp, I made a light dinner. Cashews. Jerky. I made some orange drink from a can of powder. It was sweet, but not satisfying. Shortly after I drank it, I craved water to quench my sugar driven thirst.

I stoked the fire, a bit alarmed at how much kindling the fire consumed throughout the day. My gear was drier, but had a long way to go. I figured I could gather more wood in the morning. Something to keep me busy. I took a seat by the fire and let its flames mesmerize me.

I started by worrying. Is this day six of my planned two week excursion? Maybe day seven? I had enough food for maybe two days, eating as lightly as I did today. I was getting hungry. Really hungry.

The fire was warm and friendly. It just couldn't talk back. No stories to tell, no jokes or anecdotes. No advice. What truths did it share with me? I was missing the lakefront campfires at the resort with Lynn and the family.

Omie crossed my mind. Our trip to Munich brought out a lot in him. He was fascinated by the city, by Eva's music, by his grandmother. But most of all, I felt his trust in me grow.

He is a funny little guy, I mused. Remarkable with hand drawn art, he was slow to talk. Not that he couldn't. It was as though he chose not to. Sometimes, when I'd ask him a question, he'd respond by drawing a picture that explained his answer.

"What did you do this morning?" I might ask. He'd turn to his chalk board and sketch an image of his grandfather fishing from the dock.

"Did you go fishing with Luther?" I inquired.

"No," he said softly; he was proficient at one word answers. He altered his picture, showing Luther with a fish on the line hanging above the dock. "Grampa."

"Oh. Grampa caught a fish. What did you do? Watch?"

He shook his head. No. His was a world where the past was trivial. A reference library. He lived pretty much in the now, and if the previous instant of now was mundane or, worse, boring, he let it slip by. He took his chalk board and erased his image of his grandfather and took himself to a different place, a different time. His drawing took the shape of a flower blossom, unfolding into a mandala of petals and patterns. I'd let him be.

He'd been much more conventionally conversational on our visit with Elle and Eva than he is normally at home. He loved them both. He was drawn by their warmth to reveal his inner workings. His drawings still reflected the impact of the birth of Eva's twins. He drew them often, at least daily. "Cousins," he confided to me. I often ask him to show me which one was David or Jacob. He was confident with his answer each time.

I missed the little guy. I had grown to enjoy the warmth of his little body sitting cross legged in my lap as he drew. His trust in me was satisfying and soothing.

And now his trust for me grew. I was pleased. Happy.

The thought left me quiet. Thinking in terms other than words. Almost like pictures. Visions of things beyond words.

As the embers died and the evening darkened into a star studded night, I felt aware. I wasn't certain of what. Just of being there. A bit chilled. And tired. I gathered my sleeping bag and stretched out on the soft earth along the top edge of the ledge rock.

Day six, done. I slept soundly, listening to distant howls of my friends the wolves. What were they telling me?

∞

There was no sign of the canoe in the morning. The lake's mirrored surface remained like glass well into daylight; the wind slept late this morning. The sun brought warmth and encouraged optimism, but the whereabouts of my canoe remained obscured.

I was hungry. I kindled the fire and made one of the dehydrated meals. I ate another third of the jerky and an apple. It was the biggest meal I'd had in three days and I felt satisfied. I considered what I planned for the day and knew I'd need the energy.

After breakfast, I packed the granola in water tight plastic, and took an orange. I changed into some of the still damp clothing that I'd tried to dry the day before. It wasn't bad, just damp. And it smelled smoky. That was okay. It would be getting wet again soon.

I nabbed a plastic liner from the Duluth pack and stuffed it with dry socks and a sweatshirt. I figured I'd be cold before the day was done; the lake's crystal waters had lost the warmth of long summer days. It felt like the chilly waters of Lake Michigan in early summer, with temperatures hovering in the 50's.

Over a cup of tea I studied my maps. The northern shore of Knife Lake's South Arm faced south. It's slopes were steep and wooded, rocky and jagged above the shoreline. It would be a tough hike. A mile to the east, the shoreline came to a point. I figured that perspective may give me a chance to see where my canoe had lodged, or was still floating about. I doubted it had sunk. Lynn and I followed her brother's directions in constructing the cedar strip canoe so it had enclosed baffles in the ends filled with fitted blocks of styrofoam. It would be hard to sink. And the Duluth pack with all my gear was strapped in under the canoe's forward thwart; all my gear was wrapped and sealed in heavy plastic bags. They should remain buoyant. Even if the canoe had capsized, I still might be able to spot the amber colored cedar hull floating in these clear blue waters. Especially if I climbed higher on those north shore bluffs.

But first I'd have to get wet. It looked like a good hundred yards, maybe more, between the north end of my island and the lake's north shores. After packing up, I hiked several hundred yards across the island to the point. Looking at the span between the island and the land to the north, as I edged out on the point, I realized the span was more like 150 yards. Oh, well. I stripped down, putting my shirt, pants and jacket into the plastic bag. I'd have to keep it overhead for the clothes to remain as dry as possible. I kept my boat shoes on, and I wore my life jacket both for safety and for warmth. The rocks along the shore were big and slippery. This was no place for bare feet.

With my clothes parcel under one arm and a long walking stick in my other hand, I stepped into very chilly waters. It took my breath away. Every step deeper was gasp-worthy, but the drop off was steep. I was soon free-floating, struggling to keep the bundle of plastic wrapped clothing above the surface. I wasted no time; I kicked hard and stroked with my right arm as I balanced the parcel as well as I could above my head. That forced me under about every ten feet or so, and the cold water felt like it shrank my skull and compressed my brain. I focused only on getting across the gap between island and mainland. Half way seemed long. Three quarters and I was breathing hard. My legs and arm were cold. My muscles seemed numb and stiff. I was determined; I closed in on the north shore and soon it was only 25 yards away. I could see the huge boulders littered beneath the crystal water along the shoreline. I pushed with my legs, and stroked with my arm, and pushed again. Each stroke brought me closer, but it seemed the distance closed by smaller increments with every kick.

And then the rocks below the water were directly beneath me. They were huge and still and remained below the length of my body. My feet didn't touch when I tried landing on them. It was hard getting back into the rhythm of the kick/stroke that had worked to get me that far. Only a few more yards remained, but my momentum was broken and my legs hung heavy toward the bottom. I felt myself sinking.

And then I felt hard rock against my leg. I kept stroking, trying to keep my clothes dry. My feet searched for bottom and found slippery rock. I pushed myself ever more toward the shoreline until my knees scraped rock. I was close; I tossed the plastic wrapped clothing toward the shoreline and it hit and lodged among the craggy rocks. I grappled with slippery boulders as I dragged myself onto land. It was difficult to use my muscles in ways other than I had in my swim from the island. Cramps knotted my calves and my biceps ached. My knees rubbed submerged rocks along the shoreline, and my fingers felt stiff and weak as I grabbed at the dry boulders on land.

I pulled myself out of the water. The rocks were cool but the rays of the sun felt warm even as the air evaporated the water from my skin. I shivered, then shook almost uncontrollably. I focused on moving my fingers to pull the tape sealing the plastic around my clothes. The improvised pack had worked well. I pulled out my shirt, the top garment, and it was wet from seepage. But not bad. I used it to dry my head, then my torso, and finally my arms and legs. The sun was kind. I slipped off my boat shoes and sat naked on a broad flat boulder facing directly into the sun. My shivers subsided with each breath. I turned around like a chicken on a spit, cooking each side in the warmth of the sun. The rocks along the uneven shoreline made it difficult to move around, but I tried nonetheless to dance about, working blood back into my chilled arms and legs. The thought flashed through my mind that I might be quite the site if someone witnessed my naked dance on Knife's craggy shoreline. I thought how I'd welcome it if someone came along at that moment. To find me. To help me find my boat. To save me.

I realized as I worked my stiffened limbs into dry clothes that I'd made a key mistake. I had neglected to pack matches. Had I done so, I would have gathered dried windfall and driftwood and made a fire to warm me more thoroughly. It lodged in my mind: Don't get caught out here at day's end without fire. I simply had to make it back to camp before dark. The sun was already a quarter the way across the southern sky. I guessed it was near ten o'clock. I had perhaps seven hours left before sunset to recon the north shore in hopes of locating my canoe. And the thought lay heavy on my mind. Even if I did spot my vessel somewhere on Knife's now placid waters, it would need to be near the shoreline. I reflected how I would need make the return swim to the island and back to my camp later that day.

It took a while for my muscles to limber up to hike along the shore. It wasn't easy hiking. There was no open trail. Every step was deliberate. Rocks, trees, underbrush. The impediments of the wild. By noon, I was maybe half way to my objective. I stopped on a particularly large boulder that jutted out its watery shoring and served as an elevated perch a dozen feet above the water's surface. A breeze had kicked up and ruffled the lake. The two islands east of my camp were now either south or slightly south east of my vantage point. I could see the lee side of the island. Nothing there. No canoe. Nothing but wilderness.

After searching every visible detail of the lake, I lay back on the sun heated boulder. The sky above was blue, as true a blue as sky could be. Clear. Sunny. Inviting. I closed my eyes. The sun shone red through my lids. I felt my body relax, surrender. I was no longer cold. The climb along the shoreline warmed me.

I hadn't found my canoe. But in the moment, I didn't care. I basked in the sun. My body soaked in the rays, warming even more than from the hike. A breeze wafted across the waters, picking up coolness from the surface, washing my skin with freshness. I slept.

A bird screeched, loud and alarmed. I opened my eyes and the daylight made me wince. I sat up and heard the bird again. An eagle soared above. Was it for me that it cried? It swooped in an arc high in the sky above the lake. I wondered if it was the raptor I had watched yesterday. It saw me move about and tipped its wings, altering its bearings further east to the far end of the lake.

I looked about. Still nothing. No canoe.

I looked up the north embankment. Tall pines and rocky terrain stood bold in the sunlight. The sun had moved markedly across the sky. I must have snoozed for nearly an hour. I needed to move on.

I changed my objective. I knew I could not reach the east observatory point and still return to my island and the warmth of a campfire before nightfall. I climbed off the boulder onto the shoreline and headed uphill. The hillside was steep. I grabbed the trunks of pines and birch trees clinging to the slope. Each step was a step up. My footing was fairly secure, but occasionally loose rock tumbled down the hillside. It felt like a mountain. Steep and long. I climbed and climbed until finally I reached a little outcrop from which I could see across the lake. I turned to look again for my canoe.

My observatory was perhaps a hundred feet above the lake's sparkling surface. Maybe more. I felt high above the water. Knife Lake looked like a glistening diamond in a setting of evergreen. The sun shimmered on ripples riled by the breeze and the sky saturated the lake's surface with forget-me-not blue. I inspected every inch of Knife's surface, looking for a hull or the concave hollow of my cedar strip canoe.

Nothing.

I looked further. I watched the movement of ripples crossing the water. I felt a surge of sadness. I longed for my family. I sat in reflection of the lake's beauty and pondered the love I felt. It was sad and it was heartening. I mustered strength from it. I had to find my canoe.

I could see my campsite from my perch above the lake. It look small and far, and I knew what it took me to get this far. I guessed it was nearly two o'clock. I had maybe four hours until sunset, five at the most until twilight gave way to night. I shivered involuntarily remembering my swim from the island this morning. I wanted to be back in camp well before dark.

I made good time across the face of the hill. Deer traveled across this slope enough that I found a path that made for somewhat better footing than along the shoreline. I made it back to where I stashed my plastic pack liner and life jacket. But other than taking it back to my island, I wasn't about to strip down and stash my clothes to keep them dry. I hoped they help keep me warmer than this morning's trip. I slipped the padded life jacket over my shirt and looked for a way into the water. I spotted a log near my crossing point and pushed it to see whether I could dislodged it and use it to float across to the island. It wasn't difficult to set it free, so I launched it and grabbed hold. I wondered if it would slow me down in these cold waters, but once I got it moving I made decent time across the straights. I did feel somewhat warmer than I felt this morning, and it was nice to be buoyed up so that half my torso emerged above cool waters. I kicked for all I was worth, but the morning's swim and the long hike on shore took their toll. By the time I neared the island shoreline, I was spent. I rolled off the log and onto the rocks that I had left hours earlier. Again, my chilled muscles cramped in my thighs and calves, and my fingers, cold through, were difficult to bend as I clawed my way onto land. I scuttled over boulders on all fours, trying to warm my limbs, anxious to get back and start a fire. The hike over the last couple hundred yards to camp was a tough trial. I had no energy, and my muscles were useless.

In camp, I stripped down, dried off, and wrapped up in my warmest clothes. My body was chilled enough that I didn't find immediate warmth once I dressed. I felt a moment's panic as I gathered kindling for a fire and my fingers shook and cramped from cold. I struck a match and it broke. I tried again with the same result. The snap of the match sounded loud and cruel. I nearly cried.

I sank to my knees at the fire ring and crouched down over the kindling. Bracing my arms on the grate over the fire, I concentrated with all my might. Slowly, deliberately, I struck a match. It took. My entire forearm trembled as I reached to put the match to kindling. I thought I'd lose the flame from my shaking, but it held. The kindling took the fire and spread. In moments, the fire blazed, and embers formed from the heavier branches.

I sat, looking into the fire. I hunkered down close. The heat met my face. I thought of Ally telling of how she liked inching up the campfires on the beach at the resort, feeling the heat of the flames on her face. I leaned forward and welcomed the fire's warmth on my face.

# Chapter 51

# Prey

A rising moon backlit silhouettes of rugged pines fringing the horizon at the east end of the lake as I sat in the light of my fire's flames. I was content. I had eaten another dehydrated meal that I reconstituted in boiling water, and a candy bar. I'd had three hot cups of tea. I held the warm metal camp cup of a fourth brew of tea as I contemplated the results of my day.

I had failed to find my canoe.

I was in dire straights.

I had no ideas. No thoughts. I was in a muddled place. I didn't know what more I could do. I had little food. I had no means of getting away by the routes we had planned and studied on my maps. I looked at possible ways out through the forest, but I was caught in a maze of islands, lakes, and forest covered lands. There was no direct way out from the Knife. I'd run into other flowages and lakes if I traveled through the woods. Or bogs. And I really had no supplies to make the trek across land through these rocky, hilly woods. Quite simply, Inge would have told me, I was fucked.

I sat calmly, inspecting the fire. I wondered if I made a big enough fire and generated enough smoke that someone might see and come help? Would someone come and find me? I considered the distance from where I put in on Seagull. Probably 15 miles as the crow flies. Smoke from a significantly large campfire would probably not be noticed by anyone downwind of the prevailing winds from the west and northwest. Maybe if I burned the forest on my island. Maybe. It struck me as a dumb thing to do. Irresponsible thing to do. Desperate thing to do. But wasn't that me? Desperate?

I was spent. The day had depleted my energy. I felt no pain. I was calm. I set aside the cup of tea that no longer warmed my hands. I wrapped up in my sleeping bag and watched the flames of the fire dwindle. The coals glowed, then darkened. The moon climbed up toward the milky way

I watched it all.

∞

In the morning, I ate an apple and the last of the granola.

I checked the horizons. No errant canoes floating anywhere.

I lit a fire. Tea was soothing, but I was soon hungry. I tried to ignore it.

I watched. I saw two immature loons practice their take off. They needed work. Like me, I reflected. And laughed. Me and the loon adolescents.

The eagle soared in the sky. The loons disappeared. I don't know where they hid. Maybe under my canoe, where ever that was.

A high overcast, dull gray sky eclipsed the stunning blue of the days before. It was sad. It brought a degree of chill. I missed the sun almost immediately. My body felt the loss of its warming rays.

Nuthatches and chickadees combed the island about my campsite. A Gray Jay visited; its partner soon joined . They perched on rocks about the fire ring and cocked their heads, searching about for scraps and tidbits. I had left none. I watched as they flew across water to the forest. There was nothing they needed that I could offer.

At midday, I rekindled the embers and boiled water to brew more tea. I had just a few more teabags. I decided to reuse the one I'd dunked several times yesterday. The tea was getting quite weak. Pale, actually.

As the sky yielded to an opaque screen of high clouds, the wind shifted. A south wind blew gently across the lake. I watched the current of ripples scramble and churn and straighten themselves out. The bay to the north of my camp ruffled in disgust. It preferred the calm of being in the lee.

I did too. The breeze added to the lack of warmth and sent a chill across my shoulders. I felt my store of energy evaporating. I was hungry and I was cold. I ate my last candy bar.

I thought of Lynn. I thought of how often over the years I wondered about her, thinking I might never see her again. Wondering if I would. I wondered if she would be disappointed with me for the predicament I was in. I haven't had much time to 'find my self' these past few days. Distracted. Busy. Oh, well. I wondered how I could make up for lost time. It struck me. So much of my life was lost time. Time that I was off balance. Adjusting to the most recent catastrophe of my life. Mom going nuts and abandoning us. Getting booted off my high school football team in Indiana. Being involved with my cousin Jack's death simply by being associated with Ingie, and Lynn. Boulder. Seems like so many things I did would build up and begin to amount to something and then BAM! It would come down in a Big Collapse. Football in Boulder. I was doing so well. I wonder where it would have taken me? And then it was gone.

David. Gone. All gone.

How many times do I have to leave half of myself behind as I shuffle through life? How many times? What will be left of me when all else is pared away, hunk by hunk, time after time? Will I be less than Luther?

I shook my head. My thoughts were not helping. I needed help. I didn't know where to look for help.

I just knew, I had to get back to Lynn. *She is the world to me, my North Star, the love of my life*, I thought. *I have to get back to her. And to our kids. How? What was I going to have to do to get home to Lynn?*

As a weak, pale sun hiding behind thin clouds dipped down below the bluff to the southeast of camp, I felt another degree of chill set in. My wood pile was okay; I'd have enough for the night and in the morning. But the clouds gave me concern. I spent a couple hours making more firewood. You can never have too much firewood. I stacked it up and placed pine branches bushy with needles on top to protect them from rain, if that developed. I hoped it wouldn't.

When I returned to my stony throne by the fire ring, the sky still held late afternoon light, muted as it was by the cloud cover. Once again, I scanned the lake, the shoreline and the islands. No canoe.

Movement, however, caught my eye on the bluffs along the north banks near to where I had observed the lake yesterday. I squinted; the day's waning light concealed detail among the trees and rocks of the hillside. But in a second, I caught movement. Several deer scurried along the trail I had taken back on my return trip. Their movement was fleet and troubled. I watched them run half the distance to my island in seconds. The lead doe stopped, looking back over her shoulder as two smaller deer barreled by her on the path. I could see her chest heave as she sucked in the cool October air and then exhaled heavily. Her ears focused along the path behind her, then she swirled around and bounded again toward the west. I looked back along the path and saw motion, low and even, at first one, then another, and then several more dark, low slung bodies, loping evenly in a steady pace on the trail of the deer. Wolves. a pack, pursued, not a hundred yards behind.

The deer raced forward. As she bound ahead of her young ones, she faltered. Somehow she caught a hoof under a root or rock, tripping up and tumbling. She scrambled to her feet, but her injury was obvious. A foreleg swung useless, broken. She was lame. Her young ones again sped by her. A couple hundred yards east of the tip of my island, they split up. The smaller deer slithered through the pines toward the top of the ridge. The doe bounded downhill toward the shoreline.

The wolves split as well. The lead and two long bodied animals turned to their left and cut across the grain of the forest to close the gap to the doe. The remainder of the pack cut up the slope after the pair that struggled uphill.

I watched in wonder. Except for the tumble of rock loosened by the hooves of the fleeing deer, the chase was silent. I thought I heard an occasional gasp or cough from the doe as she headed west. She closed her distance to the north tip of my island. When she reached the boulders lining the shore, she leaped into the water and angled toward the island. The sound of her huffing carried across the bay; her gasps where hard and frantic. Her eyes were wide. She swam the straights quickly, climbed on to shore and bound on her three good legs up the hill to the highlands above my camp.

The wolves plunged in to the lake without hesitation. Their swim was determined and deliberate. I felt my own eye's widen as they emerged from the water and sped up the hill after the doe.

With the chase now confined to the island, I reached for an armload of kindling to build up my fire. Soon, the flames were high and flashing. Twilight took hold of the sky and the forest on the island darkened.

In moments, I heard brush snapping and swaying above the camp. A series of plaintive bleats stabbed at my heart, and the thrashing of beasts in the undergrowth indicated that the chase had come to an end. The wolves remained remarkably quiet, but for the gnashing of teeth and the ripping of flesh. The doe cried out again, bleating like a ewe, and then all fell quiet.

Twilight harbored just a portion of the day's last lights. My camp reflected the golden hues of the fire. I listened and looked, but all was obscured.

And then, they howled. At first, one yipped and yelped, unable to contain it's excitement any longer. Then, a low, guttural moan built into a howl of wonderful upward cascading victory. A second voice joined in the howl, then a third. They held their rising tones for seconds before letting their song descend to a whisper. Their refrain rolled into another chorus. Their song reverberated the quiet air above the lake. It was haunting.

In a moment, a group off in the distance, perhaps above and over the ridge to the north, howled in answer. Their joy was clear. They cheered their family members. They would eat tonight.

After several rounds of howls, the wolves in the north grew still. Those behind me turned to business. I listened to the grunts and heavy breathing as they tore at their kill. The sound of flesh sloshing in their jaws was close. I wished I could watch.

I heard the sound of a body splashing in the water to the island's north. More splashing followed. The air had grown so quiet that I once again heard huffing as the wolves swam to the island.

I was on the island with a pack of wolves. They tended their kill less than a football field away from my campsite. I listened to their yips and grunts as they gathered around the downed doe. They feasted until night covered all outside the globe of light cast around my camp site from the fire that I stoked high. The tear of tendon and hide and the crunching of bone told a tale of feast for the pack.

I listened with wonder. Awed, definitely. I listened until all grew quiet. The last sounds were of heavy footed beasts slithering through the woods away from the kill site.

I stoked the fire periodically through the night, nodding at times, jarring myself alert with vigilance every time I dozed. I paced the area within the range of my fire's globe. I maintained the vigil until dawn lit the sky in the east with dull gray illumination.

# Chapter 52

# Feast

I waited as the morning brightened to a dark gray. The skies looked heavy and ready to rain. I soaked my well used tea bag in hot water and sipped the weak infusion until I was ready.

I left the camp site and climbed the hill toward where I last heard the wolves gorging on their feast. They were closer than the dark of night led me to believe. Perhaps the woods muffled their gluttonous feast. They were but fifty to sixty yards when their gnashing and tearing divided their prey.

I was surprised at the remains of the doe. Her face and nose had been chewed, and her neck. Her hindquarters were all but gone, one leg ripped completely off. The other stripped and dangling. Her viscera was devoured. No liver or heart could be found. Most of one shoulder had been chewed, but not entirely. The other was relatively untouched. The backstrap along its spine on that side was unscathed beneath its skin. There was meat under the remaining hide. I dug my knife from my pocket, flipped a blade open, and carved out seven inches of intact ribeye from under the shoulder blade. I peeled off a couple un-chewed chuck muscles. Perhaps I could have salvaged more, but the hair on my neck did that involuntary stand up trick and I felt a shiver down my spine. I wondered if I was being watched. I backed out of the kill site and hustled down the hill, watching over my shoulder the entire way.

I was hungry. I hustled to build up the fire. From the last packet of soup I took the salty dehydrated broth cake and rubbed the meat. When the flames died down and the embers cast good heat above red coals, I cooked the venison slowly and thoroughly. I hadn't eaten much venison since my days on the farm when David provided ample stores of deer meat. I remember liking it; deer was lean and sweet. I kept the ribeye turning as it sizzled above the heat.

As it cooked, I looked around and above the campsite. I hadn't seen or heard any of the wolves since their feast. If they were still on the island, they had ceased their eerie howling. If they left the island, I missed any splashing or swimming noise. I assumed they were still nearby. I hoped they were satisfied with their fill. Luther had told of how they could eat 20 pounds at a feeding. This had been a very large doe. If only seven wolves formed this pack, that means they could have devoured 140 pounds. Judging from the remains of the carcass, that was entirely possible. Not much left. I hoped they didn't begrudge me my few morsels.

When the meat was cooked through, I bit into it with the gusto of one of the pack. The salt of the soup mix did the meat justice. This venison had a distinct piney, cedar tinged accent, not like the sweet alfalfa fed venison that David harvested. I didn't mind. To me, it was wonderful. Like the wolves, I gorged. I ate the entire ribeye. I cooked the chuck but left it to cool on the fire grid. I had been hungry, and I'd be hungry again if I somehow didn't get off this island. I saved the meat for later.

The day remained gray and the skies were heavy. I leaned back against my sitting stones and watched until the embers died. Twice I got up to fetch water from the lake. I was thirsty. Returning to the stones, I leaned back, ready to submit to post gluttony torpor. My eye lids drooped, my thoughts dissolved into near dream like images. I fought sleep because I reminded myself there was a pack of beasts around. Then I chuckled, thinking their torpor was probably more severe than my own. I fell into a deep, exhausted sleep.

# Chapter 53

# Harbinger

When I woke, the day was no brighter than it was earlier this morning. An afternoon sun slid like a silver disk behind a pale sheet of high clouds. A wind had kicked up and carried a chill. I blinked away my sleep and stretched. I was cold. I needed a fire.

Movement to the south caught my eye. On the bluff to the south of my camp, a lone wolf stood firm, gazing to the east out over the lake. It's dark saddle covered its spine and matched the mottling on its ears and face. It was a stately beast, ignoring me completely, peering into the distance across the expanse of the South Arm.

I froze. It didn't dawn on me that the wolf most certainly knew of my presence. It didn't matter. I hunkered down and watched it, hoping to be inconspicuous, unobserved. My intent was idle, though. The wolf indeed was aware of my presence. After watching intently to the east, he turned his gaze directly toward me. It's golden eyes penetrated mine; I shivered but couldn't turn away. The beast broke it's gaze, turning to view back across the lake. Then, it slid quietly into the forest.

I shook uncontrollably. I was cold from my uncovered nap under the cool gray skies, I felt nauseous. I wondered if it was the venison. I took a breath, then another and the nausea left me. I glanced back to the bluff, but nothing was there.

I rebuilt the fire. With an armload of tinder, I stirred the embers and revived the very few remaining coals. It was satisfying to save and extend the fire that I'd burned all night. As the flames grew, I stepped back and stretched. My eyes widened and I started with a jolt, however, when I spotted something on the surface of the lake to the east of my camp.

I strained to see the floating object. A smooth, rounded shape bobbed above the surface. It was the color of cedar, but it didn't have the lengthy profile of a canoe. My eyes watered and blurred as I tried to see the mass in the water.

It was a ways off. Halfway to the end of the lake, almost even with the rocks from which I viewed the lake on my search three days prior. I shrugged off the thought of duplicating that effort. I had neither the energy nor the time. It had taken a whole day, and already it was well after noon.

I could do nothing but fixate on the drifting object.

By twilight, the floating thing remained to the east, several hundred yards south of the north shore and probably close to half a mile from my camp.

By dark, I shrugged, wrapped in my sleeping bag under the rain fly, and surrendered to deep sleep.

During the night, I woke up just once. The wind had kicked up. It was blowing now, steady and strong. It came straight across the lake from the east.

∞

At daybreak, I turned uneasily in my bag. A steady cold rain fell. I gave thanks for the cover of my rain fly, but I wondered how I would fare in this changing weather. The mild October days had been a comfort I took for granted. I didn't want it to change. But it had turned. I felt like it was suddenly sliding into early winter. At dawn, the rain tapped on the rain fly like it was frozen. Probably sleet. As the morning brightened, I could see it was rain, but barely. It was cold.

I thought about my gear. Most of my heavy clothing—the wool socks, sweaters, and knit hats—were packaged in the Duluth pack cruising around in my lost canoe. My rain gear. My tent. If this weather keeps up, I could really use my tent. The rain fly was keeping me dry for now, but it did nothing for the cold. Damn.

I pulled my sleeping bag up around my neck and curled up to keep my body's heat close. Rain dripped from the flap of the rain fly. I was glad I'd done my work in setting up the rain fly so that the area it covered remained dry. I wondered how long I could stay dry. It was hard enough to keep from getting cold without being wet as well.

As the morning light brightened, the rain slowed. The breeze from the lake was stiff; I watched choppy waves bounce and dance toward the island. I scanned the waters to the east. The floating object my friend the wolf watched yesterday afternoon was nowhere in sight. I was stiff. I was hungry. It was time to get up.

The rain dwindled to a mist. I put on my life jacket for warmth, but I shivered nonetheless. My fingers were stiff and clumsy and it was difficult to sort through the twigs and small kindling I had stacked under the larger pieces in my wood pile. Most kindling was wet. I took out my jack knife, opened a blade and started to whittle from a round branch. My hands did not work right. I found the hatchet under the rain fly and set to hewing dried shards of wood to get a fire going. I would need a pretty hot nucleus of fire to get the rain soaked tinder to burn. It took me a while, but my efforts helped limber my stiffened hands and warm me up. After not too long, I had fire. I piled wood in a teepee shaped cone and let the flames grow until I could feel heat on my pant legs. My hands stung as I held them above heat. I thought of my gloves tucked among my cold weather clothes in the pack in the canoe. I looked reflexively toward the lake. Nothing

234

broke it's ruffled surface. I felt my face tighten. I fought the feeling of disappointment.

I looked to the bluff where I had watched the wolf. What had he been watching out on the lake? What was that floating object. My gut told me it was my canoe, although it was too far down the lake to be sure. Nothing else had appeared on the surface of the lake since I got here. Could it have been a dead animal? A moose? Maybe. A dead floating deer would not have been big enough to be the object floating so far down the lake that I saw after the wolf had shown me where to look. What ever it was, it was big. Too smooth and oval to be a floating tree. Perhaps a drowned moose. Likely? No. It looked more like a capsized canoe hull viewed on end from down the keel line. Light brown, the color of cedar. Like my canoe.

I stood with my back to the fire, soaking warmth up my legs and back, as my eyes combed every inch of surface waters to the east. The surface churned, but the chop was not too rough. The wind had calmed to a gentle, cold breeze. Rain fell gently but steadily. I couldn't see my canoe. It was lost.

I wondered, *am I lost?*

My stock of wood was dwindling. I took the hatchet to the windfall above the campsite and dragged down several long limbs that I cut up to keep the fire burning behind me. The exertion of chopping coupled with the heat of the flames helped. I stopped shivering. When the first pile of sticks were stacked, I fetched more branches from the pines and aspen toppled on the hillside above. But when I'd hauled them in to camp, my energy was gone. I was running on empty. I left the wood lay.

I cut the remaining venison chuck into a half dozen strips and heated two long pieces on rocks next to the flames. The meat was savory and satisfying. I chewed every last bit of flavor from each bite before I swallowed. The venison sat heavy in my stomach. I was hungry, but the meat helped. I needed water to quench my thirst. No tea bags remained, but I decided to heat water to sip anyway. It would help keep me warm.

I took my metal cup to the shoreline. Ledge rock wet from the rain was slippery. The rock along the waterline was treacherous. My legs felt tired and weak from my work on the wood. And from hunger. I crouched slowly, carefully keeping the soles of my shoes firm on the slippery footing. As I dipped my cup into Knife's crystal water, I glanced toward the point where I had swum to the north banks. Darkened waters lapped up along the brown and beige boulders lining the shore under the overhanging forest above the bay. There, poignantly perched against the rocks and out of place, bobbed my canoe, hull facing up, rolling gently as the wind urged it westward toward the island.

# Chapter 54

# Redemption

I cried. I shouted and cried and ran across my campsite to the forest leading to the bay. Branches and undergrowth tore at my face and arms as I dashed into the woods, forcing me to slow and watch my footing on the slope above the waters. I picked my way across the island to where I thought the canoe lodged against its shores. I heard the bumping of the it's hull as the waves bounced it on the rocks. A thick mantle of underbrush formed the border between forest and bay. I broke through to the shoreline boulders. My canoe sat snug along the shore.

I slipped and slid into the water, moving too fast for the footing on slick boulders. It didn't matter. I'd get wet righting the canoe, turning the vessel upright in the shallows of the bay. I pushed it off the rocks to thigh deep water and maneuvered it so that I could grip it mid-ship at its gunnel. I lifted; the canoe rocked but was carrying water and was laden with heavy, probably saturated gear. I rhythmically rocked the boat, each time pulling higher on the gunnel until I felt the momentum was right. I heaved as hard as I could lift and the boat spun over as if an axle ran down its length. Upright, it lay deep in the water. Half a foot of lake water flooded the bottom like ballast. I looked at its content. The Duluth pack was sodden, sitting a third submerged by the water in the canoe. The extra paddle remained strapped to the forward and center thwart, but my fishing rod was missing. Oh, well. I had tackle in the Duluth pack. I could rig a jig. I needed the protein.

The lead rope drifted from the ring in the bow plate. I pulled it in and led the canoe along the shoreline, picking my way along as I slipped on the bottom. I considered hopping in the canoe to paddle it back to the landing below my campsite. But with it so low in the water, I figured I'd roll it back over trying to get in. I trudged on, making decent progress across the bay and was soon back to my campsite.

I slipped and landed on my butt in a few inches of water when I pulled on the lead to land my canoe. Everything was slippery. I crawled on all fours, clinging to the rope, until I stepped onto flat rock. With better footing, I dragged the water filled boat a few feet on to shore; a quarter of the boat stuck out of the lake on to the ledge rock.

The contents of the Duluth pack called to me. The olive green canvas held food, shelter, and clothing. I anxiously untied the straps that held it in the canoe, then heaved the heavy, water-laden bag out of the boat. It dropped like an anvil on the ledge rocks. I unlaced the top flaps right where it plopped down. Plenty of water filled the inside of the bag, but the sealed plastic liner looked promising. I rolled the pack over and drained it. Then, I worked the plastic wrapped cargo from the saturated canvas. It didn't come easily from the pack, but when it did, contents packed underneath rolled out behind it. The first thing to show was my tent, wrapped tight in its water proof satchel. Underneath that was rainwear, fishing tackle, a first aid kit, and finally another sealed plastic container with the food.

I didn't know where to start. The sky to the south west looked dark and ominous; I wondered if the rains would return. I grabbed the tent and hustled to the rain fly. There was enough clearing behind the fly, away from the lake, to set up the tent. I had it up and secure within twenty minutes. It opened right into the area covered by the rain fly. It would give me room to store and keep dry gear from the packs. I knelt in the open door of my tent, looking out through the rain fly vestibule. The lake appeared calmer. Kinder. Less of an adversary. I suddenly realized how tired I felt. I wanted to lay down inside the tent and sleep.

But I couldn't.

I still had a lot to do.

I carried the large plastic bag up under the rain fly, then returned for my rain gear. Once that was under shelter, I tore open the seal on the plastic and found that water had seeped in, but that most items remained dry. The wettest items were towels and kitchen gear. I could deal with that. My clothing was wrapped in its own plastic wrap. I had a clean dry shirt, a wool sweater, pants, socks… It was nirvana! I peeled off the cold wet clothes that clung to my clammy skin. I rubbed down with the driest towel, then with a spare t shirt. Then, feeling as though I slipped into luxury, I put on a flannel shirt. It was noticeably loose. I donned dry underwear, then a clean pair of jeans and the sweater. The wool was warm instantly, and the warmth amplified as I zipped up my windbreaker raincoat. I sat cross legged under the rain fly, dry and warmer. Dry socks felt lovely. I rubbed my water shriveled feet inside dry woolen socks until they tingled and smarted.

Life was good. I reveled in the moment. I lay back, grabbing my damp sleeping bag to bunch up and pad my head. I was asleep in a moment.

Warmth is wonderful for rest. But it does nothing for hunger. Hunger wakens the most tired of souls. The most sleepy, and the weakest of souls. I woke shortly after a brief nap.

I rummaged through the side pockets of the Duluth pack. Martha had packed essentials, goodies, and special treats. I found two 12 ounce cans of ham, another three of beef stew with potatoes and carrots, and two containers of hard tack—that unfortunately took on some water. They were mush. I set them off to the side and unstrapped another side pocket to find cans of uncooked oats, a tin of maple syrup, a bag of creamed wheat, also wet, and another of pancake mix, a mushy mess. In the front pocket of the pack, she had stored candy bars, a big supply of jerky, and, God bless her, a tin of my favorite oatmeal chocolate chip cookies. Those had escaped the damage of the lake water. I ate four immediately. There were another half dozen apples and as many oranges.

In a sealed packet wrapped inside the larger plastic bag were the main meals: Dehydrated rice and chicken; spaghetti, mushrooms, and cheese; a curried vegetable and rice meal; sirloin and rice; scrambled egg omelets, and several containers of desserts. Dehydrated cheese cake. Tapioca. Chocolate, lemon, and raspberry puddings. There were cans of dried sugary drink powders. And more. There was coffee!

It was too much. I looked at my portable pantry and realized I'd have left overs, since half the trip I'd been caught short and forced to starve myself. I felt a relief from a burden I was unaware of. Just the site of my stores restored hope that had evaporated to worries over the past several days. Life, again, was good.

Few embers remained from the fire, but they were hot and rapidly spawned new flames from the kindling I fed them. I opened one of the cans of stew and set it near the flames. I gathered my cup from the shoreline where I dropped it this morning as I spotted my canoe, filled it with water, and set it on the grate above the fire to make a cup of coffee. Coffee! A real cup of coffee! Oh, my God!

I fed the fire as the stew cooked and the water heated. The clouds rolled overhead and started to spit small drops that splatted on the fire grill, sizzling and dancing before they evaporated or fell into the fire. Before small bubbles started swelling in my coffee water, a steady rain threatened to squelch the blaze. I fed it more small pieces of firewood, building up the heat. The steady, mounting drumming of the rain pattered against the rain fly, dripping steadily from its sides, forming rivers that coursed across the campsite. One stream worked its way directly to the fire pit and the blaze hissed and steamed. I diverted the flow with hunks of wood, rocks and loose dirt and gravel from the edges of the camp. The rain added to the steam coming off the flames.

I grabbed the hatchet and cut long sticks from the branches I'd dragged into camp. I peeled strips of bark and lashed the sticks together to shape a shelter over the fire pit. I'd lost most of the blaze; smoke and steam fizzed from the embers and mucky ash. I cut green fronds from cedar and pines around the campsite and leaned them above the frame. It helped. The fire held on, and I fed it more small kindling to get it to blaze up again.

I ate the stew. It was warmed through, not altogether steamy hot, but it was comforting and tasty. My improvised shelter for the fire worked well enough that by the time I'd finished eating the stew, the water boiled. I doled out a portion of coffee grinds into a webbed filter and poured steaming water through. I collected it in a small pan, then poured it back into my cup. I drank it under the rain fly where I could sip it at my leisure.

Rain belted the ledge rock campsite. Gusts carried sheets of water across the lake. Pings sang from the rain fly pelted with golf ball sized drops, the ledge rock and the surface of the lake screamed cacophony. The rain held steady. I huddled in my tent, wrapped up in my bag and looked out through the roof of my rain fly to the haze of gray that swallowed the lake in rain.

And then, the rain abruptly stopped.

The wind kept blowing, and the clouds didn't break. They did get lighter. But the rain quit.

I crawled out on the ledge rock. The fire was drenched under the grate. At the water, the canoe held maybe eight inches of lake and rainwater, and I had dragged it only a third out of the water. The paddle was still strapped to the thwarts. It would be a ball buster to empty.

I turned to the fire first. While the sky lightened, the day was late. It would be dark in an hour. Sooner if the sky remained over cast. A glance west told all. Dark, rolling skies. As the sun dipped, it would set behind dense clouds. I didn't want to make a fire in the dark. But it would be burning nicely for me after I emptied the canoe, if I tended it first.

My stack of kindling was wet. The larger pieces held the best chance of lighting, if I whittled core wood out from under the damp bark. I used the hatchet to skin a long dead pine branch. Then I shredded it. The pile of chips started well. I kept the fire heating the damp twigs and smaller branches until the ember core was hot, then it graduated to heavier kindling. I got the fire good and hot. The fire would offer both ember and flames by the time I got the canoe right.

I wondered, as I had sat here during the past several days, how long it will take to paddle to Isle of Pines and drink root beer. Now that I had my canoe, I'd find out tomorrow.

# Chapter 55

# A Bad Break

I had 45 minutes to get things in order. Maybe an hour at the most until dark, and it would be ultra dark tonight. Too-dark-to-see-your-hand-before-your-face kind of dark. The cloud bank rolling in was thick and ominous. It was moving quickly. I wanted to be back under the rainfly, watching the fire and cooking dinner before that cloud bank and more rain arrived.

The canoe was as heavy as I thought. It rocked when I heaved up on one side at the center thwart. I wondered whether lifting the bow would be best; the ledge rock was wet but not submerged and the footing was better. But the boat held several hundred gallons of water. It was heavy. Rolling would be easiest, even if I got wet. So I grabbed the gunnel at the midline and lifted hard and rocked the boat. Water spilled out the far side, and I pulled back on it to get the water to slosh first this way, then away. I pulled hard, but it didn't come close to rolling over and emptying. The weight of the water rolled the canoe back, catching my leg. My foot slipped on the wet ledge rock, but my heel caught where the rock had cracked. My canoe, with hundreds of pounds of sloshing water, caught me as my ankle rolled. The water laden boat smashed into my leg from the side and I heard it crack, POP-POP, like reports from a double barreled shotgun. Instantly, I felt the pain of my bones snapping above my ankle. I crashed to the ledge rock, and I felt my head bounce off the rock. My leg curled underneath the boat when it rolled again.

Pain skewered me. I screamed.

I turned to lay my leg flat, anything for relief. My heel was still caught in the cleavage running down the rock into the water. I lay back.

"Jesus," I cried.

And then the winds hit with a force that scattered sparks and embers from the fire pit down to the lake. The fire was directly above me in camp, and I was showered with flying sparks. Before I could react, a wall of rain pounded me, the campsite, my tent and rainfly, and the lake. The impact of mega-drops splattering the ledge rock and the lake's surface thundered like a million drummers. I turned to get a grip on the gunnel of my canoe, and my scream was drowned out by the pounding of the rain.

I looked up into the black shroud of sky. Rain pounded against my face, forcing my eyes closed. I wondered what on earth I could do. I felt panic surge in my gut. I puked my gut empty. I gagged and swallowed and the bile stuck in my throat. I leaned my head back, eyes forced closed, and opened my mouth to the storm. The cleansing of my mouth was delicious.

It offered a note of hope. I rinsed my mouth, then turned my head back and drank heartily.

I dug my elbows into the hard rock and tried to drag my legs out of the water. My scream was reflexive.

"Christ!" I yelled into the wind and rain.

I fell on my back. My head pounded against the rock.

In the pounding symphony of rain on rock and water, I heard a voice. Words. Distinctly. I heard David.

*"Be calm."*

Calm. Be calm. Try to stay calm. I heard. It was my twin's voice. Immediately, I inhaled evenly, fully. And exhaled. Again. And Again. And Again.

*"Always have faith."*

I heard him as I inhaled. I looked into his eyes above me before the blackened sky.

*"Always. Semper Fi."*

His gaze faded into the dark.

Semper Fi. Crazy fucking Marine.

The pain wasn't going anywhere, but I thought it subsided, maybe. I breathed more. The rain beat against my face.

I breathed again and thought, *What should I do? What can I do?*

I couldn't move my leg. I wondered, could I move my leg if it was maybe on something. Like my jacket. Or a board, or something. Yes! I thought. Yes! A splint. I looked around, but all was dark. So dark that I couldn't even see the rain splashing on my face as it rebound from the rock.

But my extra paddle was strapped under the thwarts in my canoe. I'd left it there as I tried emptying the boat. I'd grabbed it as I heave up on the weighty canoe. It was an arms length away. I reached and the pain shot like an electric surge in my leg. The boat was in the dark. I didn't know how far it was beyond my reach. I slowly nudged myself to my left as I scooted slowly inched across the ledge rock to reach for the paddle. It took forever. It was like adjusting in a yoga pose. Every motion was purposeful and precise. Inches. I didn't want to hurt. As I moved my hip the least amount possible, I reached out with my arm, finding, finally, the gunnel. My hand felt the shaft of my paddle and I followed it to the ties.

I placed the paddle next to my broken leg. I could see neither the paddle nor my leg. I felt the blade of my paddle rest gently against my leg.

I moved slowly. Everything about moving was slow. Except for the pain. Pain was lightning. I worked the blade of the paddle under my broken leg.

Face to the rain, I dug my elbows into rock, sliding on my backside, carefully gripping the paddle to keep it under my leg, I slowly hitched myself toward my tent. Time and again, I pulled myself across rough rock, dragging my leg on the paddle, rubbing my elbows raw.

∞

The rain let up. As I got alongside the fire ring, the rain stopped altogether. The clouds brightened. They cast a colorless hue. Dawn slowly brightened the gray morning clouds.

As I got to my tent , blue sky broke through. With it, cool air flooded the campsite.

I had dragged myself for hours toward the tent. I debated shedding my wet, cold pants. My legs were cold. I wondered if that would help contain the pain. Like icing bruises. In the light growing stronger from the morning sky, I saw my leg bent oddly; my foot dangled off to the side at an ungainly angle.

I didn't know how I could get wet pant legs off my leg. How would I reach the lower pant leg to cut it.

I dug my knife from my pocket and slit the leg of my jeans from the crotch to the cuff. I made a cut around the leg at hip high. The cut denim pulled out from underneath my leg in a long rectangular strip.

My shoe remained on my ankle, and was tight due to swelling in my leg. I remembered wrapping sprains to contain swelling, and I remembered that Martha had included long ACE wraps in a first aid kit in the Duluth pack. That pack was almost within reach out under the rain fly. I cut straps from my old pant leg and tied them around my foot inside my shoe and up my leg. I shifted around, reached out to the Duluth pack, and dragged it in. I found the ACE bandage and wound it carefully, not too tightly, to limit the swelling in my leg.

Under my rain jacket, the wool sweater was damp a third up from my fall at the shore, but the shoulders, chest and sleeves seemed dry. It was warm, at least.

My sleeping bag was where I left it in the tent. I wrapped in it and set my leg carefully up on the thick Duluth pack. I closed my eyes and wondered, *Will I sleep?*

242

# Chapter 56

# The Challenge

Sleep was not easy. One minute, I'd be deep in a troubled dream. The next, spasms in my calf twitched the broken bones in my leg and the jolt of pain surged through me like electricity. And then, I'd fall back into a stupor. I gave thought to being in shock. I was certain that I was in shock. But what could I do? I was exhausted. I pulled my bag around me for warmth. Sometimes, I awakened, wondering, *had I passed out? Or was I asleep? Did it matter?*

Through the tent door, I saw the sky clear and millions of stars spill across the blackness beyond. Then, gently, slowly, a new day was born; a blip of light emerging in a half sphere on the horizon at the end of the lake. I watched it grow. I fell asleep, jerked, cried out, and noticed day had grown. The stars were swallowed by the dawn. Last night's storm had cleared. Sunrise was silver and clean.

I examined my foot in the light of the sun as it streamed through the tent door. My toes were red and swollen, but not dark. I thought about Jenkins, a team mate who played defensive end at CU. He'd badly sprained an ankle in practice and wrapped it up to keep down the swelling. He wrapped it too tight and his toes ballooned like plums during the night. He almost lost them. I wondered if he ever made it back onto the football field.

I wished I had ice.

I had to take a leak. I didn't want to move. I held it while I thought about how to approach the day. I rolled slowly to the tent door and sent a stream of dark urine flowing down the ledge rock under the rain fly. It was dark. I was dehydrated. I was thirsty. The notion of shock again worried me.

The day unfolded in the mildest of manners. No wind followed behind the violent storm from last night. The lake settled as I watched. The sun peeked above the ragged pine horizon to the east, then slid above the land and looked like a gleaming silver medallion over the forest. It's rays felt good.

My gear lay where I had left it scattered across my campsite. The pack with my clothing and some of the food was in the tent. But the kitchen satchel was where I unpacked it yesterday. I'd spread out the pan, a bowl and a pie tin shaped dish from my kitchen pack as I took inventory yesterday afternoon. They had caught rain in the storm. They lay a mere six feet from the door. I knew what it would take to reach them. I set off, hitching and dragging myself slowly out of the tent. My raw elbows sparked with pain

The rain that had been so wild during the night was a drink of salvation. I sipped it from the rain filled bowls and cup and felt it wash the taste from my lips and mouth. It loosened my parched throat. I sipped more. It was heavenly.

Birds canvased the campsite and shoreline for tidbits. I listened to their birdsong. It was soothing.

I knew I faced a challenge I had never imagined. I was injured badly, alone, and realized that my family knew only approximately where I was. I tried to recall the plan for this trip. When was I to meet Teddy on Moose Lake. Day 14? When was that? What was today? I didn't know. It was a blur. I tried to reconstruct the route to this point. I couldn't recall. I looked at the water filled canoe. What good would it do me? How could I empty it? How could I get into it even if I was able to empty it?

How could I paddle? Could I even sit up in the canoe, much less control it?

I watched gulls flying about the islands across the lake. They swooped and frolicked, as if their place in the sky marked ecstasy and joy. I followed their flight until they disappeared over the south shoreline, heading perhaps to warmer waters for the winter.

I thought of David. What would David do? I recalled during the night as I lay by the boat hearing his voice. "Be calm." Right. Calm. I looked at my twisted, crooked broken leg. My foot dangled to the side, my toes pointing south, where as I sat facing east. It was not good.

I heard nothing from David. Did I really expect to hear him again? Did I really hear him during the night? To have him somehow be here with me in my time of need?

A banded wooly caterpillar crawled along a path across the ledge rock near the fire pit. I watched it move its many legs in a rhythm of its own. Oh, to have so many legs! It worked with such internal harmony, it's body bunching and rippling as it march stepped over the campsite.

A jay fluttered down to the fire ring. It cocked its head at the caterpillar. It dropped down with a flare of its wings, hopped once and had the critter in its beak.

*Lotta good all those legs did ya,* I laughed. *I'm better off with the one good leg I have.*

I best get on with it. I found several webbed straps to reinforce the paddle splint on my leg. I dug the role of duct tape from the Duluth pack. Crawling to my store of wood, I selected a couple of branches, both about the length of my leg. Gingerly, I sat up. It wasn't going to be easy. I'd been injured and bruised and significantly hurt in football. But never like this. I had learned, though, the the first thing to do after an injury was to slow down. Assess the damage. Work around the pain.

That would be a tall order now.

My back was stiff and sore from laying on the hard campsite surface. I stretched it slowly. I needed more flexibility to reach the length of my leg where I could fasten a better splint. I practiced yoga. Pranayama first. I got my breathing under control. Then, as slowly as a sloth, I bent forward. I worked at the pose for minutes. I worked my back gently, getting it to soften and flex in increments, gasping and breaking the rhythm of my breathing as I moved my leg, or twisted my calf, jolting the bones above my ankle.

Beads of sweat streamed down my face, and their taste was sharp and salty. I was dehydrated. I sipped rain water collected in my kitchen ware. I stretched. I made myself extend, and slip the straps under the paddle and around the two additional strips cut from my pant leg, clicking the plastic clamps into place and snugging the ties to make the splint effective.

I nearly passed out; the worst was when I fixed the strip around my leg, just above the foot. Then, I reached back down over my braced leg and tied a final strip around the paddle and over my foot.

The sun had slipped to the south and west during my first aid session. It was afternoon. I was spent. I dragged myself back to the tent. The effort went more quickly now, but was still slow. I gulped rain water from my kitchen pan. I inched myself back into my tent, wrapped in my bag, and slept the troubled sleep of the wounded.

# Chapter 57

# Deliriously Desperate

When I woke it was dark. The sky was bright with stars. The night was more quiet than a shadow.

My mouth was parched. I dragged my leg out under the rain fly to the Duluth pack and dug through the kitchen stores. I found Lynn's cookies. Like manna. I ate four, then finished the rain water that had collected in the bowls.

My canoe sat idle on the shoreline. How was I to empty the water and ready the canoe to get me home?

A sliver of a moon sliced like a germinating seed though the tops of the pines lining the eastern horizon. I watched it idly until it hung fully in the sky. Then, with the pan in one hand, I dragged myself back across the camp to the canoe. The moon climbed higher into the sky; soon it neared the dangling tail of the Big Dipper. I lay alongside my boat, trying to stay dry and not slip into the shallow lake water. It wouldn't matter. I reached into the canoe and scooped a pan of water. I dumped it out along side me, hearing it splash back into the lake, feeling it soak my tattered pants. I scooped out water until I noticed the sky turning light at the end of the lake. Dawn. David's favorite time, but not mine. At home, in our youth, he would be heading out to his cows in the barn. I'd roll over, tucked in the warmth of my blankets, and sleep until I was called. Not here. Not today. I lay back, looking into the depth of the stars still bright above me and rested. Then, I baled water from my canoe. I wished I had a bigger pan. But it was what it was.

I didn't realize I was shivering as I bailed the boat. It registered only when I felt the warmth of the rising sun. I rested again, letting the rays soak my chilled body. It concerned me that I had not noticed the trembling of my arms, or the chugging gasps of my breathing. I was cold. I was tired. I drank water that I dipped from the lake. I wished it was warm. Tea, or coffee. I was hungry. But my food was up by the tent. And the fire was out.

Most of the water was out of the canoe. I tried tipping the boat. But I was spent. I would try later.

I dragged myself back to the tent, stopping several feet up from the boat. I grabbed the bow lead and pulled it snug. The canoe didn't budge. I crawled on to the tent, trying to balance a pan filled with water and not spill along the way. I was half successful. I would need it for later. On my next attempt, I would be certain to carry along a water bottle.

∞

Exhausted and in pain, I watched the afternoon pass like a lazy butterfly flitting above a field of daisies. Perfect mid-October weather; intense, clear blue skies, a gleaming sun, the lightest breeze wafting from the south. I propped up against my Duluth pack, my sleeping bag cushioning my butt, and my battered, splintered leg elevated in its splint on the kitchen pack. The sun had dried my one legged pants, which I'd soaked in my effort to empty the canoe. I watched geese and ducks, heading south, the geese in valiant skeins, the ducks in groups of three, four or even a dozen flying low across the waters. A moose and her calf, now nearly as tall as its mother, appeared along the shoreline, wading into the water at the point of a small bay. They swam the gap to the eastern rim of the bay and lumbered out of the water before disappearing into the forest. Nature was going about its way.

I wondered how Nature was handling my aching, throbbing leg. I wondered if infection was going to be a problem. The swelling was bad, but not like I'd had when I sprained my ankles playing football. Nonetheless, my leg was red; my skin was tight and stiff. I'd left my shoe on at first, but the swelling bulged out over the tops, and the low cut shoe worked its way off. I left it lay where it dropped off between the rain fly and the shoreline.

I wondered if I could get up on one foot. I thought maybe, until I moved or jarred my ankle, which was tantamount to shooting myself in the leg each time I overextended my self. I'd wait. It would get better, I told myself. I was nuts to think otherwise. Delirious.

I went back to watching the day develop. It was gorgeous. The hillsides framing the lake were mottled with golden bursts of aspen leaves among a field of evergreen. They shimmered and glimmered in the sunlight. The sun heated and dried my clothing. I took off the rain jacket and let the sun and air dry my bulky woolen sweater. I felt warm.

I listened to the quiet. I found peace in the quiet. It seemed to quell the throbbing and aching radiating from my lower leg. I could ignore it.

I thought of Lynn. When the pain increased with movement, I resorted to thoughts of Lynn. I clung to my mental image of Lynn.

I wondered if she could sense my troubles. See them, the way she could see power mulling on warps in the shield of time. I imagined that she probably had no idea of what I was going through. It reminded me of my ignorance of David's death. How could I have not been aware of my twin's death? How could I possibly have known? How could I not see?

How could Lynn possibly know the magnitude of my crisis? How does that work?

I wondered.

A squall rained bolts of angry lightning in a storm cell passing quickly south of Knife. Then, clouds broke in the dark of night, and the clear black of space revealed our galaxy. I trained my view on the north star. I held it tightly in my eyes.

I listened.

What was it was like for David to die? To enter the void of unknowing? Did all the thoughts and feelings registered by the formations of molecules floating around the body or lodging in brain tissue become a non-factor, once the brain and blood and body lived no more? The thought was chilling.

I pondered that thought. I remembered once when my yoga teacher in Boulder talked me through the steps of breathing. She had me think back to early memories. When I was a teen. Or before I left David and Mom on the farm. Or even earlier, when we were little kids. She had me think of occasions, like Christmas, or our birthday, and told me to listen to my thoughts. To hear my voice. And she would take me back to even younger days, as young as I could remember. She said to hear that voice, my voice. And she told me to listen to and recognize what I heard as mine. My voice in the stillness.

And then, she told me to quiet the voice that I was familiar with listening to. That voice that is mine. The voice I knew. She told me to hear only what I heard in my being. She told me that what I heard was me. And then, she told me to be still. And when I was still, absolutely still, and time stood still, she whispered in my ear, "You are here, now. Remember."

I remembered, now.

I remembered where 'here' was again, as she helped me increase the clarity of my meditations. And go beyond. I remember finding that spot, that moment, again and again. The *'now'* she called it. I loved to find it in the midst of a football game, when everything evaporated around me and time warped and bent and fell apart before my eyes, and things like the ball passing through the air took on properties not expected but leading me to that moment when all was complete. And then, I would find myself grounded again, by the jolt of a linebacker or the roar of a crowd.

I found that moment at times of being alone. So very alone. Like on the Trail, the hillside overlooking Allentown, moments before Georgia figured out I was David's brother. David's twin.

Those moments often carried me through time as it normally traveled through space. Those moments became the now moment.

I fell quiet. I was still. I listened.

# Chapter 58

# Those With Me

The sun was setting over my shoulder. I tracked it as it inched it's way down behind the bluff. There, seated as though studying me, sat the wolf. He tipped his head, intrigued, curious, when our eyes met. He sat unfazed. He was watching.

I looked back across the lake. It had calmed to mere ruffles. Occasional rings spread from points where fish broke circles on the surface in chase of a meal. I wondered how long my companion had been keeping watch on the bluff. I turned to view him again; he was gone. I looked around as best I could; the stab of pain that shot up my leg dictated my limits. But there, to the right and just outside the bounds of my campsite, the wolf stood. Nose hovered low above the ground as if reading the scents in the air wafting above the ledge rock, it eyed me warily, then stepped forward to the camp. I felt alarm. And then, I just watched.

He turned out to be a she. She squatted and peed, all the while locking her eyes on mine. She took several steps along the campsite's perimeter. She sniffed at items left in disarray, my t-shirt, a wet towel, but was unimpressed. She seemed wary but bored by me. She wandered up the slope to the forest and disappeared.

∞

I sat, listening, my mind clouded with unknowing.

Lynn was on my mind. I felt her looking into my eyes, but I saw nothing before me but the blue October sky. I felt her, inside me. I heard her voice.

She said, *"You have children to raise. You have a son. And a daughter."*

"YES!" I cried, awake with a start. I hadn't realized I'd been sleeping. Dreaming.

I felt as calm as the still waters reflecting the forest and hills that bordered the lake.

David had told of the calm, the joy, he'd known during the time he'd fallen into the beaver dam back home. I wondered whether it could be any more calm and beautiful than here now.

From across the lake, a voyager in a canoe caught my eye. He paddled in a straight line making good time toward me. In a moment, I felt recognition nagging my mind. *I know this traveler*, I thought. In little time, with bold, strong strokes of his paddle, he halved the distance to my island.

I did! I knew this traveler!

Teddy! The paddler was Teddy!

Strange. I watched as he paddled to the landing. He neither smiled nor called out. He glanced at my canoe as he pulled his own along side on the ledge rock. He walked with certainty as he crossed the camp site. He spoke words I heard but did not understand.

"Hello." I greeted him.

"Good to see you. Got yourself into a bit of a mess here, it looks like." He knelt down and gently removed the wrap around my toes to inspect the swelling. "Been dancing with the loons?"

"Nope. They are gone. Flew away. South." I thought I was being such a smart ass. "The wolves, though. Been dancing with a wolf. She's beautiful." I motioned to the side where she had sniffed at my t-shirt.

Something where I pointed caught Teddy's eye. He walked to my discarded t-shirt, bent over and examined tracks in the sandy grit along the edge of the undergrowth. He turned, astonished. "A wolf?"

I nodded. "She-wolf. Like Lynn."

He smirked. I was truly a wise ass.

He returned to look more carefully at my leg.

"The ankle?"

"The bones. Above the ankle."

"When?"

I thought. *Yesterday? No. Before yesterday.*

I shrugged. "The other night. I lost my canoe."

He glanced again at the cedar strip canoe laden with lake water.

"It's here," he said, checking to see if I might be imagining things.

"It came back."

He nodded. "You're in trouble."

I thought, *does Lynn know?*

Teddy strode around the campsite. He dumped the water from my canoe, pulled it up under the rain fly and left it upside down. He quickly packed one of the Duluth packs full, and half emptied the other, throwing what he left inside the tent. He glanced around the campsite, shook his head, and said, "You're a mess."

I shrugged.

Then he positioned my packs in the front of his canoe, the full one upright agains the thwart, the half empty pack flat on the bottom of the canoe. He made them into a bed for me. He turned the bow to face the lake, and pushed it into the water until just a quarter remained on land. He tested the footings alongside the canoe, his shoes slipping on the wet granite. He pulled the entire canoe back out of the water.

He paced toward me, determined. I watched. I knew what he planned. I knew it would hurt.

Squatting along side, he slung my arm over around his neck. "Hang on," he said, slipping his arms under my legs and just below my shoulder blades. "Ready?" he asked.

I nodded.

He took in a deep breath, strained, moving slowly and deliberately, he lifted me as carefully as he could. He steadied himself, keeping me as level and still as he could. His face turned deep red, and blood vessels bulged on his forehead and neck as he strained to lift me.

The movement of my leg made the throbbing intense. I refused to yell. I couldn't help moaning. I sounded to me like the wolves gnarling on doe behind camp.

"Are you growling?"

I glanced into his face. Now he's the wise ass.

He set me gently as a baby upon the packs, my legs elevated on the front wicker seat. He covered me with my sleeping bag.

He looked to the sky. Overhead, it was clear. To the south, clouds mounded in wooly tumbles, lit by a flash of lightning. Too far to hear, and well to the south. Squalls, dumping more autumn rain on the forest to the south. He glanced to the west. The storm tracked from the far plains, but Canadian skies remained clear.

"Let's go," he said, pushing off and taking his seat in the back of the canoe.

# Chapter 59

# The Isle of Pines

I was grateful for quiet waters, and fascinated at how straight Teddy paddled the canoe. The whisper of his even, strong paddling soothed me.

I had nothing to say. I kept quiet. So did Teddy. He was usually quiet. He paddled like he was worried.

"What did you say?" I asked, "back there?"

He paddled on.

"A blessing."

"Sounded like it. A prayer. All garbled up."

"Words of Sami."

I still didn't understand him. I let it go.

Only the swishing of his paddle in the water marked time. I watched the trees and shoreline as we glided past. We paddled until the sun perched near the southwest horizon. We passed an island, then another. He turned the canoe into a sheltered little bay and paddled the bow right on up to a landing. Stepping out into the water, he carefully shoved the canoe forward on to land.

"Don't go anywhere," he ordered.

Such a wise ass.

In a moment, he returned. A gray haired woman, rugged and weathered, followed, her eyes flashing, inspecting, assessing everything about me. She glanced at my face and I could see she was measuring the pallor of my skin. She leaned over and lifted the sleeping bag from my leg. Her eyes narrowed.

"Can you bring him in?"

Teddy nodded. He took hold of the bow and slowly, carefully dragged the canoe across the landing to a cabin. Then, picking me up like he had back at camp, he carried me into the cabin.

"You are a lug," he muttered.

Inside, the lady instructed him to set me on a bed inside the entry way. She followed him and sat beside me. She put the back of her hand to my face, her lips curling down as if surprised.

"Not too warm."

"Are you Dorothy?" I asked.

"Yes. I'm Dorothy."

"Can I have a root beer? I'm so thirsty. I'm Patrick."

Teddy's not generally boisterous. But he hooted like a loon. Dorothy smiled broadly and said to my friend, "There are bottles in the cooler."

In a moment, Teddy returned with a couple opened bottles. I took a sip; the brown syrup melted across my tongue and slid down my throat. It was dark and rich, and had a bite. I wanted to guzzle it, but after a couple gulps, Dorothy checked my hand as I raised it again to my lips.

"Pace yourself, young man." She handed me a cup of water.

She went about removing the wrappings from my leg, carefully cutting with her scissors. Teddy held my leg up for her to work on. I tried at first not to growl at him again. But I did, just to give him shit.

"Wimpy growl," he said.

I shrugged.

My leg was deep scarlet. The skin looked tight and stretched. My toes looked like worts on a football. I thought, suddenly, of one of David's young heifers who had just calved. Her udder was swollen and distended. My toes looked like her teats. Swollen and pink. But healthy. *Silly*, I thought. *Where did that come from?*

Dorothy glanced at Teddy and left the room. He followed.

They talked in quiet tones. I listened.

"He could lose that foot," Dorothy said. "Or worse. The swelling's bad. It could shut down his circulation. It could go to gangrene."

Teddy grunted affirmation. "Is there anything you can do?"

The concern in her voice carried through into the bedroom. "Nothing better than what you know. The only thing we can do is get him to help. He needs more help than we can give him in this little cabin. And he needs it fast."

Again, Teddy grunted. He agreed.

They streamed back into the bedroom.

"Verdict?" I asked.

Teddy looked me in the eye. "You're a sorry ass."

Dorothy grinned. And shook her head.

Teddy asked, "Got any leeches left?"

Her eyes flashed. "Should. Some, anyway. In the bait tanks." She walked quickly out of the room. I heard the cabin door close tight.

Teddy came along side. He slipped his hand around mine. It cracked me up. I know I have pretty big hands. Teddy's wrapped around mine like a blanket.

"We got a bad break here," he said. "You ready for it?"

I nodded. "Been practicing for it," I replied, trying again to be the wise ass. But the word I had heard, gangrene, stuck in my throat like a dry chicken bone.

"Right," he muttered. "That's good. Cause this is fairly new ground for me."

The door opened, closed, and Dorothy returned carrying a bait bucket that sloshed and dripped. She ignored the water falling on her floor.

They held the bucket between them, viewing the content she'd brought.

"Oh, these are healthy ones," Teddy smiled, dipping into the bucket to snare a leech. "And hungry, too. Look at how hungry they are!" He was much too enthusiastic.

"What are you gonna do with that?" I asked, looking at the slimy annelid. I felt my lips curl in disgust.

"Maybe save that leg you've got there?" He squared off his gaze. "Maybe even your life. Speak well of leeches. They are friends."

I looked away. "I preferred the wolf."

Teddy's eyes flashed. "Blessedly so. Perhaps the wolves brought you to these leeches. Perhaps it is so."

I closed my eyes. What was he saying? "You brought me to the leeches. Can I have another root beer?"

My wish was granted. Dorothy left the room and I heard her bustle about. When she returned, she handed me a cup of hot tea and a full bottle of root beer. "Drink these. Slowly. Sip them both. We're busy."

They huddled over the end of the bed.

Teddy placed a leech on each side where my leg should have revealed the classic ankle bumps. Now my leg looked more like a thick summer sausage, brown and red and swollen, and my foot was a dark lump. Dorothy placed a couple leeches carefully across the bridge of my ankle, holding them in place until they latched onto my skin. Teddy set three more along the front of my toes

I tried to tell them what my toes looked like, but somehow it got lost and garbled. They looked quizzically as I tried to explain David's heifer. Teddy looked sharply at me, like he was gauging my sensibility. I gave up. Forget it.

The leeches attached, and soon I could see them thicken.

"Did you ever do this before?" I asked. "Use leeches."

"Once," he admitted. "In the Nam. A marine brother was hit and we were not going to be able to extract. His wound was a mess. Full of mud and shit. It became infected and his leg swelled like a balloon." He glanced at my ankle, then returned his gaze. "One thing we had in the Nam was leeches. So I stuck a few on him. Worked great." He smiled in a way that made me think he was bullshitting.

But he went on.

"My grandfather used leeches. Used them on his dogs if they got a swollen hind quarter. He used them on us kids, if he thought they would do any good. He stuck them on a shiner I got one time. Imagine me, big old shiner with a couple leeches hanging off my eyelids." He laughed. "They filled up like pickles. My brother thought they looked like penises. He called me Dick Eye for years. Still does."

How could he be making me laugh? I couldn't help it.

"You're going to call me Dick Leg, I suppose."

He leveled his steely eyes on me again.

"Only if you keep that your leg. That's the only way."

Dorothy inspected the skin around my foot. She gently pressed her finger on to my flesh. It dented like bread proofing. She glanced up to Teddy and her eyelids flickered. He nodded in return. The leeches seemed to be helping.

I grew drowsy. Their voices drifted into a distant mumble as I snoozed. I don't know how long I slept. In the distance, I heard thunder, and rain pattered against the windows in Dorothy's cabin. I fell deeper into dreamless sleep.

And then Teddy awakened me. I looked about, surprised at my surroundings. My leg ached, but I was generally comfortable. When I glanced at my ankle, the dressings were clean and neatly wrapped around my leg and foot. I thought I spotted dark green matter sprouting from beneath the crisp white wrap. Like lettuce in a sandwich. My toes had lost some of their plumpness, but remained discolored. By reflex, I tried moving them. The attempt got lost somewhere in the vortex of pain in the leg. Dorothy noticed.

"You can move your toes," she stated rhetorically.

"It hurts."

"I expect so. But that's good. Less damage than I might have believed. Here. Finish your root beer." She handed me the bottle I had sipped earlier. It was warm now, but still good. I took a sip and put it down. She handed it back to me and motioned with her nose for me to drink up. Okay, I thought, and took another swallow.

Teddy set his ponderous hand on my shoulder.

"You ready?"

"Huh?" I glanced out the window. All was dark.

"We have a paddle ahead of us. It's time to go."

I didn't want to. I was sleepy. I frowned and fidgeted. "Why? It's not even daylight?"

His broad, assuring smile crept across his face. "It's later than you think. You've slept. We've rested. Now we have to get you someplace where you can get help as fast as possible. It will be light in a couple of hours. It's calm now on the waters, but squalls are blowing through. We may get winds and rain. We have the boat ready. Dorothy has a motor for her canoe. It's time to go."

He didn't ask any questions. He picked me up again, like I was a rag doll. Dorothy held a lantern so he could see his footing as he carried me off the porch and down the path to the boat dock. He had arranged the packs as he had before in his canoe. He set me on the packs and covered me with sleeping bags and rain ponchos.

Dorothy's canoe was longer than Teddy's, and wider. He sat in the bow, with me just behind the center thwart facing Dorothy in the back. She ran the motor. Teddy watched ahead with the lantern and flashlight, sometimes pushing off a submerged boulder with his paddle.

I dozed. The ride was smooth and I was lulled by the hum of the motor. Eventually, I noticed that dawn was already breaking. A blink later and the sun had risen and was climbing the eastern sky when we reached the first portage. That was rough. And long. But we met a group of young campers at the portage who were on their way out. They left their canoes and packs on the trail and helped. Teddy took off the engine and the guys picked up the canoe with me in it. They carried me across the portage and went back to get their own canoes to help us through the next three portages. How would we have done it without them? God sent. Amazing.

By then, I was fully awake. The throbbing ache returned to my leg. I wanted out of the canoe.

Dorothy noticed.

"Feeling pain?"

I nodded.

"We'll be there in half an hour."

Okay, I thought. I wondered where there was.

"Where?"

"Moose Lake. The outfitters."

Okay. I was okay with that. It looked like I was headed home. Home to where I belong. Where I need to be. Home, with Lynn. With my family.

Had I known I would not see home for another five weeks, I'd have protested. But what could I have said that would have mattered?

Book Five

# Lynn North

*…Be smarter every day
by listening to your intuition,
looking at the world with your forehead…*
*— María Sabina*

# Chapter 60

# Blind Sided

The early October morning sky held subtle portent, I felt as Martha and I picked our way among the birch and cedar along the shoreline. Mist lifted lazily above the looking glass surface of Burntside. Clear to the east, with still waters under calm winds, the shelf of high clouds sliding in from the west suggested change from the recently turbulent weather. A series of fronts from Canada met humid low pressure systems from the plains, mixing wildly, with many squalls of heavy rain passing through our northlands. The wind during the night woke me from an unsettled sleep. My thoughts were of Patrick's well-being. His journey was marked by lovely fall weather interrupted by dazzling storms. I saw clouds nested over him, or sunshine beaming down upon him. The rains were heavy and powerful, but they passed quickly, leaving calm in their wake.

The showers, however, had been good for late season mushrooms. We searched the shoreline and woods north of North Star for crops of fungi and greens that we foraged for medicinals used to ward off ills that threatened us. Some were just good eating.

We looked for chaga. Martha's supply of extract from the fungus was running low and getting old. We found a crusty chunk of the coarse looking fungus clinging to the white skin of a birch and Martha made note to harvest it after deep frost. She'd make do with her dwindling store of chaga to treat the cold that Omie had shared with Ingie. The two snifflers had been under the weather for a couple days. Martha's remedies kept their symptoms in check.

This morning, we searched for fungi that popped through the turf, like lobster mushrooms, or rushed from windfall and branches of aspen like angel tooth. Martha spotted autumn mugwort, a green leafy herb growing among the rocks near water's edge.

The kids were in with Ingie when we got back to the lodge. Omie isn't generally too boisterous, but Ingie and Ally were hooting like geese. It sounded like an Ingie party. All noise, bluster and laughter.

The kids helped get oatmeal and eggs ready for Ingie and Luther, and we had our breakfast like a picnic on the porch where Ingie most enjoyed holding court. The morning calm gave way to warming breezes from the south, sweeping the lake mist away. After breakfast, we laughed and played imaginary 'what-if' games, wondering aloud how it would be to soar like eagles so high and wide above the lake, and be able to spot the finest of movements by the red squirrels and mink along the shoreline, or the smooth back of a Northern sunning in the bay under the clear October sun. Even Luther was touched with the mood of the moment, laughing at the kids' wild imaginations and adding his own somewhat eccentric ideas.

"My oatmeal is steaming. An eagle would see steam from far above," he said. "Eagles eat oatmeal. They like it with maple syrup." He spooned a lavish pool of rich golden syrup into his oatmeal. "Eagles eat oatmeal," he repeated.

Omie studied his grandfather, wide eyed, believing all Luther said. I could see his little head spinning at the image of an eagle perched on the rim of a bowl filled with his favorite breakfast.

"Dad, you're going to make me pee for laughing," Ingie burst into hearty chuckles. "Eagles and oatmeal. Jesus!"

Luther nodded, holding a spoon laden with sweetened oatmeal aloft as proof of principle. "Wolves, too. They like oatmeal even more."

"Wolves," Omie muttered, his eyes bright, but distant.

"Grandpa, are you teasing? Wolves don't eat oatmeal!" Ally protested.

"I heard a wolf," Omie offered.

"Was it eating oatmeal? Sure. They do," Ingie defended her father. "Grampa is witness to the fact. Eh, Dad?" Luther waved the dripping spoonful of oatmeal high, baiting any stray eagle visitor. Omie watched intently.

"I don't know," Ally said with doubt.

"Better fuckin' believe," Ingie winced. She'd been trying hard to not be a potty mouth around the twins. She started again. "It's better to embrace your dreams with all the fun you can whip up than to doubt and deny yourself the joy in those dreams." She spoke deliberately, sounding each word carefully, as if delivering an edict."Dammit," she added.

Ingie reigned like a queen, slurping up maple syrup with the last spoonful of oatmeal, then conjuring fantasies with her spoon as through it was a wand. She egged the children on; she was remarkable in the restraint she'd developed in limiting the profanity in her comments to the children, and her everyday chatter. She credited Teddy for that; I was grateful for all the work he put in the tide pool, life mentoring, yoga, motivation and all around discipline for my sister. But I treasured his encouragement for her to train her unbridled speach.

Ingie sniffled, fighting the cold Omie shared with her. Pushing her breakfast tray away, she blessed us, then, bewitched, hung the spoon on the end of her nose where it swung like a door knocker. Dad noticed, and tried hanging his spoon of oatmeal upon the pinnacle of his long nose. The oatmeal was too soupy to cling and the spoon clattered to his tray. I reached across and wiped the gooey cereal from his face. Ingie snorted her amusement.

"You may go," Ingie said with a wave of her spoon. "I am ready now to meditate. If you see the rascal Teddy, tell him he's been derelict. AWOL. Summoned to an adventure, I suppose. I need him." With a thin, taunting smile, she tipped her nose toward the horizon out across the lake, closed her eyes, and ever so softly, hummed.

So we disbanded. My chuckle came as a snort as I gathered her breakfast dishes and Dad's, reminded the kids to bring along their own, and our morning magic hour settled to the pleasant calm of routine.

I carried Ingie's tray into the kitchen with the kids in lock step behind me, toting their own breakfast plates. Martha worked at the counter, straining the remains of her old chaga extract next to where I put the tray and piled the plates the kids handed me.

The phone rang as I walked by and I nabbed the receiver in stride.

"Hello. North Star Resort."

"Lynn? Lynn North?" The voice was muffled and broken by a soft static. But it was familiar. I leaned into the receiver to recognize the caller.

"Yes, this is Lynn. Can I help you?"

The line cleared, and a voice came through loud and clear as if she were here in the kitchen.

"Lynn, it's me. Elle." Her timid reply suggested she wasn't certain I'd remember her. "Patrick's mother."

"Elle! I can hear you better now. It's so good to hear you!"

I listened as her voice wound up with confidence.

"I'm so glad I am able to reach you, too, Lynn. We have good news!" She said, pausing, then clarifying. "Eva and I, that is. Eva's immigration papers came through. She can go to America!"

"Wonderful! Eva's wait is over. Does she have travel plans made? When will you be home?"

She paused before responding, and her voice sounded little again, like she was inside a seashell. I didn't know whether it was a bad phone line or simply Elle.

"We don't know quite yet. We just found out today that her visa was issued." Elle spoke with softness and pauses, as though she was filtering her response and talking in tones that others might not overhear.

"Well, Patrick is not here today. He's on a canoe trip. But when he gets back, he'll be elated to hear about Eva. And the twins. This is really good news, Elle! Thank you so much for calling to tell us."

"Yes. I had to. I couldn't wait," she said. "We'll let you know the details as we make plans. Eva said she wants to finish the semester with her students. But we will see. By Christmas, no doubt." Her voice dropped to almost a whisper. "Or maybe even Thanksgiving." She left her hope dangle a moment. "Maybe."

"I'm so happy for you and Eva both, Elle. I'll let Patrick know as soon as he returns."

"Thank you, Lynn," Elle said, timidly. "Good bye."

"Good bye for now. Looking forward to seeing you when you return." I put the receiver back in its cradle and stepped around the counter to share the news with the family. But the phone rang almost immediately and I had little time to explain more to the kids.

I reached for the phone as I briefed them."Yes, your Grandmother is coming home to America. And Eva and the twins, too," I said, tossing Omie's hair and glancing at Ally's beaming smile. I put the receiver to my ear.

"Hello. North Star Resort."

"Lynn, it's Teddy."

A shadow. I saw shadow.

"Teddy! We've been wondering where you've been." The kids heard me talking to Teddy and stayed close, Omie wrapping an arm around my leg. We had missed our friend. Nobody worked Ingie harder than Teddy when he got her in the therapy 'tide' pool. She preferred no one's care as her Teddy's.

I had been worried due to his absence.

"Lynn, it's Patrick," Teddy blurted. His tone was firm, somber and urgent. His voice conveyed more than his words; by every measure, what he was to tell me was significant and ominous. "He's hurt. Broke his leg pretty bad. We have him here at LaTourell's. We're getting a van ready to bring him into the clinic. It's not good, Lynn."

Martha read the concern on my face. She set her chaga aside and stepped close, touching my elbow and then gathering the kids in a hug.

"What do you mean, not good?"

"Both bones just above the ankle. Some compartmentalization. It's been a few days at least since he was hurt."

My thoughts whirled. My concerns. I'd seen troubling turbulence as I peered out in my moments alone in the early mornings since Patrick left. I had summoned those who could watch with me, but until Teddy's call, I knew nothing.

"We'll have him in the van in a few minutes and should be in town in half an hour. Can you meet us at the clinic?"

"Yes! Right. I'll be there. Thanks, Teddy. Tell him I'll be there" I heard him click off.

Martha waited. Dependable, reassuring Martha. My mother's finest gift to me. The wise one. I have grown to value her love and friendship more than most everything. She peered into my eyes with her calm, wise understanding and I felt myself cling to her stable peace.

My voice was caught up in my thoughts. I didn't really know much, so I just repeated what Teddy said. I couldn't convey his urgency. I heard my voice sound uncertain. My calm was weakened. Fractured. Frail. Is there nothing more frightening than the state of not knowing?

I didn't want to alarm the kids with what little I knew about their father. I put my hands gently on their heads, my fingers sifting through their hair.

"It's your father," I said. The kids stirred. "He broke his leg. Teddy is with him. He'll be okay," I assured them, but my voice wavered and broke. *Compartmentalization. Two days…*

Ally searched my eyes for more; Omie looked in the distance out toward the lake. He leaned closer and mumbled, "wolf." I tipped his chin up. He met my gaze and repeated, "Wolf." I felt the burden of leaving him without understanding what he was thinking.

Martha drew close, laying her hands on mine.

"You'll be all right."

"I have to go."

She knew loss of loved ones. Of her husband. Of my mother. She knew my fear of losing Patrick. We had spoken of just such loss. Just this fear. Of the years I endured not knowing whether I would see him ever again. And of the joy that flowed after he found me here in Ely.

"We'll be fine. The kids and I will be just fine," Martha said. "Go now."

I felt the burden of leaving her with my children.

And Ingie.

And Dad.

She saw. She shook her head and told me not to fret.

"Go." She repeated. "Boldly" She held her hands, fingers spread, like a basket. She drew her fingertips together, forming a ball. "Bring all together," she prayed. "Wield powers."

I nodded. I hugged the kids and kissed them.

"I'll be back."

I left my family. As I raced along the Echo Trail toward town, I felt an old, previously abandoned sensation. I felt fear of being alone. I knew the emotion of despair peering at me from the tree line along the road. Time filled with the loss of someone I loved. I worried about Patrick. Teddy's tone told me how serious Patrick's situation was. I drove too fast. The bright October sky was overshadowed by the blinding fear I saw in the threat of losing him again.

Teddy sat in a chair near the ER room in which Patrick waited. He looked toward me as I walked down the hall and rose to meet me outside the exam room.

"You okay?" he asked.

"I think so. Is he badly hurt?"

He nodded. "He's in shock, and he's on morphine now. It was a rough trip in from the Knife."

Teddy looked weary. He brushed his thick black hair back from his forehead and rubbed his eyes. "We came in from the Isle of Pines this morning. I'll tell you more later. But first we have things to consider."

"What things?"

"Doc Mehran saw him earlier. He wants to see you as soon as you arrived. He's going to suggest taking Patrick to the Cities to have a specialist for his leg. It's pretty busted up."

I frowned. "How?"

"I don't know exactly. Something about slipping on rocks and his canoe being full of water. I think he rolled the canoe over his leg. I don't know. He's been kind of out of it since I found him. I'll tell you more later, but you'll want to be thinking about how we should move Patrick forward with this."

I didn't know any orthopedic specialists in the Cities. I winced as I drew a blank.

Teddy shrugged. "Doc is going to suggest finding someone who is really skilled with this type of injury." He left the thought at that and glanced back into the exam room.

"Patrick's waiting." He said, taking my elbow and leading me into the exam room.

The thoughts in my mind swirled like aspen leaves caught in an autumn breeze. I searched for something secure. I didn't know the issues with Patrick's broken bones. Entering the exam room, however, hit me like a jolt of electricity. Patrick lay flat on his back, his legs elevated on pillows, under a white sheet and warming blanket. His face was blanched, white as the linens. His eyes moved restlessly, but remained closed even as I approached his bedside opposite Teddy, who circled around to the far side.

Something innate, something very personal gripped my heart. The bright lights of the exam room brought clarity and crispness to my vision. I felt energy stirring from deep within. Patrick rested quietly, not knowing I looked on his pale, thin face. Except for his rough, unshaven beard and matted, dull hair, he looked like an angel napping. He looked in need. I felt my call to that need.

I touched his shoulder, then his cheek. His eyes fluttered and focused, and his face opened into a smile that could grow a field of sunflowers.

"Lynn."

"Patrick."

Our eyes exchanged the uncertainty of the many questions we knew we were about to face. They would come. We could answer them as they shuffled themselves into some sort of order. We basked in a moment when we could just breath, watching, feeling our touch. I ran my fingers down his arm to meet his hand reaching toward me.

"I'm sorry."

I pressed his hand. "Sorry? For what? I should be sorry for urging you on into the Boundary Waters."

He wagged his head in a slow, drugged objection.

"No," he said. "No, no. It's not the trip. I loved being out there." He winced as he lurched trying to reach and hold me. "No. I don't want to make more for you to do. More to have to take care of." He fell back, lay his head flat on the exam mattress, exhausted. His eyes teared. He looked straight up toward the bone white perforated tiles on the ceiling. "I wanted to be help. Not be more work for you."

Teddy leaned in over the bed, looking squarely at Patrick.

"Hey, bonehead," he smirked. "You got more work ahead of you than all the rest of us combined. Get up for it." He grinned.

Patrick focused on him, a grin of his own sprouting across his face. He shook his head. "Numb nuts" he muttered.

# Chapter 61

# Medevac

I heard footsteps and low voices in the hallway and looked up in time to see Doctor Mehran bustle through the door followed by Mary Styer, an E.R. nurse. Mary glanced my way, her kind eyes concerned. Dr. Mehran paced to the bedside next to me. He lifted a dressing set loose on top of Patrick's leg. The ankle was swollen, but I have seen worse. The skin was deep burgundy, more red than black or blue. His toes looked like pegs stuck on a log. His foot lined up maybe two inches higher, alongside his healthy leg. Maybe just above the anklebone. It cant toward the side. It wasn't right.

John glanced quickly to me, then turned his gaze toward Patrick. "How are you doing?"

Patrick nodded. Shrugged. Winced. "Ok.".

"We have to find some options. And make some decisions." Dr. Mehran said, facing me.

"Ideas?" I asked.

John had no poker face. He was adamant.

"We move him as soon as possible. Ambulance. To the Cities. I know Frank Gronkowski in Duluth is up to this, but I called and he's in Oregon. His son's wedding. Won't be back until after the weekend. I don't know that this should wait. I don't think it can. I think Patrick needs to go to the Cities."

*Okay,* I thought. *Then what?*

"Do you know an ortho in the Cities?," he asked candidly. John was a young physician, and good. But he had only two years experience here in Ely. He went to school and trained in Helena. He wanted to return to northern Minnesota after practicing two years in Montana, and chose Ely, just forty miles from his home. He was well trained and confident, and he knew his limits. He didn't know any colleagues in the cities who could respond to Patrick's needs. He knew I had lived much of my younger life just west of Minneapolis. His question was valid.

I thought, but recalled no one. I knew just one orthopedic specialist, but he lived and worked in Chicago. At Northwestern. My used-to-be husband. Dr. Barry North. One of the best surgeons anywhere.

∞

John gave me use of his office in the clinical building to make calls.

I called Northwestern and asked how I could reach Barry's office. I didn't expect him to answer directly, but the first voice I heard was the familiar busy tone of my ex.

His greeting was succinct. "Dr. North."

I felt a wave of shock at the sound of his voice. The pause before my response seemed eternal; fearing he might hang up, I blurted, "Barry, it's Lynn."

His pause was distinctly longer.

Then, his voice softened. He abandoned his work tone.

"Lynn! What's happened that you are calling?" He sounded surprised, startled, but above of all things, kind

"Oh, Barry. It's Patrick. Patrick Joyce. He's hurt and I need to find an ortho specialist for a severe leg fracture and possible compartment syndrome," I blurted a report on Patrick's injury. Barry asked several questions about the break and how long it had been since the accident.

"We think it's been several days. Patrick's not certain himself. He was off alone in his canoe," I explained. "What I am hoping is that you know of someone in the twin cities who might have experience with this type of break."

I could hear Barry thinking on the end of the line.

"Hmm. Nobody comes to mind, Lynn. I can make a few calls, but I can't say I know anyone with a practice in the Cities. How far are you from Minneapolis?"

"Five hours. Over 250 miles."

"Hmm," he was thinking again. "That's a long drive. Ambulance?"

"Definitely."

"When would you get him going?"

"I don't know. As soon as possible. We just got here to our community hospital."

"Time is important with compartment syndrome, Lynn. I can call to see if I can get you names, but you may want to get him moving as soon as possible. He needs to get there today."

"Yes, I thought so, too. I'm just starting to figure out how to go about this."

"Can you fly him to the Cities?"

"It's complicated, but maybe."

"Do it, if you can."

"I best get going."

"It's a shame you aren't close by. Alan, Dr. Reimer, my…partner…you know, is as fine a trauma orthopedic surgeon as there is. We would be glad to help. I'll make some calls. Is there a number that works best for reaching you."

I gave him John's desk number, but told him the number at the Lodge as well.

"Thanks, Barry. I know you must be busy. I am so grateful for your help."

"Let me know what you decide as you get Patrick to the cities. I'll be in touch with names."He paused. "Lynn, I'm glad to help."

He clicked off and I dialed Martha.

"It's worse than it looks," I told her about Patrick's break. "And it doesn't look great. We need to get him to a specialist. Fast."

A thought came to me.

"Martha, you mentioned Walter Sukki flew back from their fishing camp in Canada this week, didn't you?"

"He did."

"I wonder if we could fly Patrick to the Cities? I'd like to ask him. Do you have Sukki's phone handy?"

She did and I wrote it down.

"Let me know what Walter says."

"I will," I replied, clicking off and dialing up the Sukkis.

Martina answered and in a voice filled with alarm, I blurted out my need to see if Walter could fly to the cities. Martina cut me off to fetch her husband.

"Walt's in his garage. Just wait a moment. I'll call him."

She set down the receiver with a clunk and I could her that patter of her steps as she hustled away. A door opened and she hollered to her husband. Then she pattered back to the phone.

"He'll be here in a moment," she said. "This is a bad break?" She asked.

"Very," I assured her, filling in details as we waited for Walter to get in from his workshop.

In a moment, I heard the door and the heavy footsteps of a man in boots.

"'Lo," Walter said."Lynn?"

"Yes, Walter, I've got a problem." I explained briefly about Patrick's need to get to the cities and asked him if he could help with his plane.

"Sure," he said, his tone guarded. "It could be complicated, though. I have the pontoons on the plane. We'd have to clear a landing someplace in the Cities. And then there could be problems moving him from the plane to an ambulance."

"But it would be faster than driving from Ely, wouldn't it?"

"Oh, sure. Much. A bit over an hour. Less than two."

"Okay. Let me figure out where we'd be going in the cities. I have to find an Orthopedic specialist and the hospital to take Patrick to."

"Let me know," Walter said. "I'll get ready to fly."

I hung up and found myself standing still. I didn't know where to take Patrick, or who he should see.

The phone on John's desk rang. A receptionist said the call was for me, from Dr. Barry North.

"Lynn, I contacted several associates in St. Paul. The one firm name recommended is not available. He's at a professional meeting in New Orleans until next week I have another name, but it came with reservations. I'm not confident in passing that person's info on.

"Well, thanks, Barry. If you hear more, please call the Lodge number. Martha will answer and can get info to me as soon as possible. I did take your advice, however. I think I found a way to fly Patrick to the Cities. We just have to find a lake we can land on that is relatively close to the hospital where we will take him." Saying it made me realize how much key data I did not yet know.

"Land on a lake? What do you mean? A seaplane?" Barry asked.

"Well, yes. One of the resort owners here has a pontoon plane. He flies fishing clients into Canada."

"Lynn, could he fly here to Chicago? Meigs Field is just blocks away. We can arrange to bring Patrick here from the airport."

I thought about it. "Let me call Walter, the pilot. I'll see how long the flight would be. This may be a good idea, Barry," I said. "I'd be most confident with you handling Patrick's injury." I added.

Barry was touched, but frank. "I'd be glad to watch over Patrick's case, Lynn. But I would delegate it to Alan. He's the best. Handles all the Bears athletes. And the players from the new basketball team, the Bulls. Patrick will fit right in."

Barry's sentiments were kind. He sounded happier than I'd ever known him.

"Let me get on with figuring this out. I'll be back in touch." I said, adding, "Barry, thank you."

"Of course, Lynn. Of course. Delighted."

We hung up and I set to work.

# Chapter 62

# The Windy City

We landed in Chicago at sunset. The Windy City greeted us with unusually calm skies for October; the western sky was aglow with reds and orange as the top third of the sun dipped beneath the horizon. Though he was heavily medicated, Patrick rolled his head to the west and smiled as he noticed the sunset.

"I always liked Chicago," he murmured

Walter set his plane on the surface of the marina protected by the peninsula on which Meigs airport was built. While Martina chatted with the control tower, pointing toward a dock on the lee side of the breakwater, Walter taxied to a lengthy pier where an ambulance was parked and white clad attendants scurried to receive us. Barry monitored the busy paramedics as he stood near the edge of the dock.

"You made good time," he said as Walter helped the airport officials tie down his plane.

"Tailwinds, and my co-pilot is a good navigator," Walter replied, indicating Martina, his flying partner. She busied herself with tying an anchor line.

"We had some good winds pushing us across Wisconsin. We have some bad weather following us. I'm glad we got here for this bit of calm before it changes tonight." Walter said. He helped me out of the plane and on to the loading platform alongside the dock. The ambulance crew hurried by me to go to Patrick's aid. Loading him had been a real effort from the dock in Ely; I observed as the team considered how to remove this tall, large patient from Walter's sea plane. They moved swiftly and with confidence. I backed away, giving them room to do their job.

Barry's eyes were kind but concerned as he watched the emergency team work. He glanced toward me, a smile of encouragement flickering across his face. He had aged, but pleasantly. His hair had thinned and greyed in these five short years since we had divorced. In some ways, however, he looked younger. More relaxed. Definitely happier. His gaze stayed with me for the moment. I hugged him.

I was near tears, and he sensed my worry.

"We'll have a look at Patrick's injury shortly," Barry said. "He'll be in good hands. We'll do all we can for him." He paused. "And you."

His gentleness broke the reserve I'd been holding all day since first seeing Patrick, white as a sheet, thin from dehydration, shocked, trying to cope with his pain. Tears welled in my eyes, dripped down my face, my breath heaving raggedly, just short of sobs.

Barry's hand pressed kindly on my shoulder.

"It will be all right, Lynn. He'll be fine" His smile was concerned and authentic. I trusted he would do all he could for Patrick. I worried, however, that Barry didn't yet know the extent of Patrick's injury.

∞

As a nurse, I often considered the gnawing angst and loneliness of helpless family members left in the waiting rooms while their loved ones were prodded and positioned, turned and tested by professionals. I understood the demand of the varied tasks medical treatment posed on both the patient and the professionals in attendance. Now, sitting, waiting for any next bit of information about Patrick's well being, I felt the trial of those left waiting during times of trauma and emergency. It was desperately lonely. Then, Barry found me sitting alone in the waiting room.

Barry was comforting. However, I knew he was drawn to the medical questions at hand, and would normally prefer to be in with the team at the side of the patient. So I was not surprised as he inched near his team, taking me with him into the exam room. He had handed the lead to Alan Reimer, and I was grateful for his comfort and company as we watched his colleagues analyze and discuss best practice for Patrick's gruesome injury. I reflected on Barry's bedside manner as he worked with his partner. I had never observed him at work before. I was taken with his sincerity and concern. I was grateful.

As I watched him, I noted an expression of contentment and pride for his departmental staff handling this emergency. He watched Alan particularly. I wondered how often he had this opportunity. Funny, that it would be Patrick and me allowing Barry this opportunity. Surely, he took pride in his clinical teams. But his thoughts for Patrick? And me? We had been swept up together in an affair that none of us expected.

∞

By 8:30 that evening, all the diagnostics were complete. The doctors huddled just outside the room in which Patrick lay, restless with pain, numbed by drugs, watching me. As they moved him about, rolling him to X-ray rooms and carefully positioning his leg to softly palpate and examine the extent of the swelling and the condition of his flesh, Patrick followed me with his eyes. At times, he teared up with pain as they moved him. At other times, tears welled just for the meeting of our gaze. He would smile, a little, kind, grateful smile

"Would you ever have thought?" I asked when we were alone and could hear the muffled rumble of discussion from the docs outside the room.

"Nope," He said. He tipped his head, thinking. I could see he was struggling with his thoughts. He'd been in such pain for so long, and medications did as much to muddy his mind as to control the intensity of his

270

suffering. I wondered which of these many situations he had experienced that he was now considering. We'd been together the entire day, but we'd not had a chance to talk with each other. Alone.

"Did you…see? Did you know I was in trouble"

I tipped my head. "I don't see that way. I don't see the details as they will play out. I sense…movements,"I explained. "Auras of forces. Sometimes they clash and crash like a storm. I did see that. Turbulence. Troubled powers."

He was befuddled.

"Life for me doesn't unfold itself like a magic show. Life is natural." I said. "Nature is life expressing itself on this cutting edge of creation. It doesn't need to be more. It is my prayer. My way of praying. I seek the quiet. Then I see with intent. With gratitude. With hope. I try to clear myself so as to see how this instant of creation is. It's not supernatural. It is not magic. It just is. Life is the flow of grace in time. A force. Life is grace."

I watched a tear well in his eyes. A tear of love.

"You are a force, Patrick," I went on. "I know the power of your force."

He nodded comprehension.

"I could see you were in for a fall. A stumble from being out of step with that instant of creation. Like you were denying that which is, while hoping for something other. I could see you falling. I didn't know how it would be. Just that it was to be."

He considered it. A shadow passed over his eyes. He looked at me with concern.

"I'm sorry," he said. It was what he'd told me when we first were together this morning. I had tried to assure him then; I listened now, taking his hand and gazing steadily into his eyes. *Why?* I wanted to ask. Instead, I listened.

"I failed you," Patrick said.

I thought. *Failed me? Why does he think so?*

He rolled his eyes toward the lights of the darkened city. We were in a room on a fairly high floor. The windows faced south; we could see the tops of the taller skyscrapers light up the sky. Beyond and to the east, the dark pool of Lake Michigan contrasted with the bright illumination from the city. I thought of our time together along the shoreline to the south. In the Dunes. We are here, I thought, because of those times.

"I want nothing more than to dance with you in the light of the moon," he whispered.

Was Patrick dreading the worst outcome from his injury? Did he know what the worst actually was?

He looked into my eyes. "I wanted to give you the best. I fall short of the best."

I knew his mind was thinking harder than the drugs allowed.

"Think so?" I asked, trying to inflect a grain of humor into the conversation. "I'd say it isn't over regarding all you have given to me. To us. The twins and me." I left his hand rest on the bedding and reached for the water glass on the bedside tray. I offered the straw and he took it and sipped.

"The moon will give us plenty of chances to dance in its silver light," I said. "I expect we will be grateful for the grace the moon shines on us and shares with us."

He smiled weakly. He was tired. A tear trickled down his cheek. Quiet prevailed in the room; even the discussion outside the door settled. In a moment, Alan Reimer and several colleagues filed into the room and stood at Patrick's bedside. Barry, I noted, stood behind them, toward the side of the room at the end of the bed. He glanced over to me, nodded, and focused then on the physicians.

"Patrick, you have a pretty serious challenge ahead," Dr. Reimer started. "We are going to get you ready for surgery soon."

"When?"

"Soon. Within the hour."

Patrick shrugged. "Okay. What then?"

"We are going to place your leg bones where they belong. One, your tibia has a clean break. The other, your fibula, is broken in two places, about three inches apart. It's a bit more of a problem. But we should be able to right them.

"You're challenge is after surgery. You have a lot of tissue damage. Circulation problems from so much swelling. Considering, it's a good thing you could keep the swelling down as much as you did."

Patrick nodded. He'd kept his leg elevated as much as he could. And then Teddy and his leeches…well, Teddy did what Teddy could.

"You went into this injury in excellent shape. That helps. But it's going to take a lot of courage and determination to make it right again. And there is the chance of infection. It's good that this break didn't come through the skin. But it remains a challenge. Are you up for it?"

Patrick considered the question. Was there any choice? He looked first at Alan Reimer, then to me. Locked into my gaze, he asked, "Will I be able to dance when this is all over?"

Alan let a smile slide across his face. He glanced over toward Barry, then to his team.

"Depends," he answered. "Could you dance before this accident?" The doctors chuckled; this was a question they had enjoyed before.

Patrick started. He frowned, considered it, and admitted, "Well, not much. Can't say I ever did much dancing at all."

The docs laughed aloud.

A look of surprise captured his face. He looked at me. "We've never danced before, have we?"

Barry approached the side of his bed.

"Patrick," he said in calm, gentle tones. "You're going to be able to run like the wind again. You just have to be ready for the work you are going to need to do to get there." His gaze held Patrick. "Patrick, this is a serious injury. Okay? Are you prepared for this?"

Patrick nodded. "Okay. When?"

"The surgery? Now. In a few minutes. We're getting a surgical team ready as we speak. You ready?"

Patrick nodded with greater certainty.

The doctors filed out, except for Barry, who stood by my side.

He squeezed my hand gently, and then placed mine upon Patrick's. Bowing, he backed away from the bed. "The best that I can do for you is to put you in Dr. Reimer's care." He turned and walked from the room.

# Chapter 63

# An Extending Network

Martina and Walt found me in the surgical waiting room. It was almost 11:30 p.m.; Patrick had been in surgery for two hours. I'd heard nothing about his status.

"You look exhausted," Martina said. She handed me a warm bag. They had brought soup and a sandwich from the hotel. "Have you eaten?"

I hadn't. The thought of hunger was eclipsed by my concerns for Patrick. I opened the bag and caught the aroma of the soup. Chicken noodle. The sandwich was a simple grilled cheese. Comfort foods. After a timid test bite, I devoured the sandwich. The soup was warming and delicious. We chatted as I gulped like I'd never eaten before.

I briefed them on what Patrick's condition was going in to surgery and what they intended to achieve in setting the bones and addressing any tissue damage he'd have from compartment syndrome. It was all still up in the air.

"Where are you staying?" I asked.

"The Hilton," Walter said, with a grin. "Dr. North had it all arranged. Had his office staff line up reservations. It's right down the street. And it's a tad finer than the fishing camp I left two days ago."

"I'm so grateful," I said.

He nodded. "Glad you asked us along on this trip. So is Martina. She's been hankering for a trip to this city for a long time. Years. Now she's here."

Martina chuckled. "We certainly are. Happy to help you and Patrick. But I'm not going to pass up the opportunity we have since we're here. Seems we left Ely in quite a hurry. I didn't pack much to wear here in the big city. Looks like I have some requisite shopping to do while we're here."

She set her hand on my shoulder. Her reassurance was more welcome than the food they brought to me.

"I hope you'll find time to show me around Chicago while we're here," she said. I had told her on the flight down of my short-lived career here, and of living in the Dunes where I met Patrick.

I nodded, realizing that I had brought less in the line of clothing and incidentals than she. I had my purse and a satchel that Martha whipped together in the minutes we had before leaving the resort. I was wearing a sweater and had a light weight wind breaker. I really hadn't thought about staying in Chicago very long. I had my twins to consider. I hadn't thought of it until this moment and I could see my friends reading my expression.

"Dr. North reserved a room for you, too," Walter said. "Same floor as us. We look out over that lake. Amazing view. Nice room, too. Got a TV and a bed as big as a tennis court. You'll be comfy. Beats a tent. Or even any of our cabins at the camp."

Martina shushed her husband. She went into mother mode, picking up my empty food containers and tidying the table where I'd eaten my meal.

"Walter's in culture shock. He's never been in the Windy City. He's like a little boy going to the ball park for the first time."

"It's bigger than life," Walter agreed.

Their chatter was comforting and distracting. But Patrick's situation was like the elephant. Always there, never to be ignored.

"When will you be flying back to Ely?"

Walt shook his head. "Not tomorrow. No way. Those winds that helped us get here so fast are crossing Wisconsin right now. Big storm from LaCrosse to Green Bay. I have to get the plane fueled and fit for the return trip. Even if I get that done tomorrow, the Commander here," he nodded toward Martina, "indicates she won't step on board before she's done her shopping. I'm here for the duration." He grinned.

"It's good timing," Martina suggested. "We are here to help. We'll be here until you know what you have ahead of you. What your plans turn out to be."

They watched my shoulders tense. I considered the time they intended to remain in Chicago. My intent was to return to Ely as soon as possible. I thought we would be heading back tomorrow. I shrugged, and smiled. "I can't tell you how grateful I am for your help. I'd like to be with you when you fly back to Ely. My children...," I left it hang.

Martina smiled like a mother. She asked if I would like more supper. But I had eaten all I could. I realized how little I knew about what the next days would bring. I felt numbed by the intake of food, and fatigue slipped into my awareness.

They sat with me, chatting, comforting, until after midnight. I encouraged them to return to the hotel, but they declined

"We're here with you," Walt declared, "and there's no debating the issue."

∞

At 12:30 a.m. precisely, Barry and Alan strode into the lounge.

Alan spoke first.

"He's coming out from anesthesia," he started. He followed with a report on the surgery. "Patrick injured himself several days ago. It wasn't like it was yesterday," Alan observed. "His tibia split clean. But the break was almost four inches long; the parts of the bone realigned closely but not

275

perfectly. We opened the callous healing, cleaned it up and inserted seven screws to keep his bone in place and heal right.

"The fibula was a different matter. He tore a number of ligaments holding the bottom end of his fibula into the ankle compartment. The bone broke once an inch above the outer ankle knob. It broke again three inches higher into the shaft of the fibula. We repaired that fracture. We used another seven screws as well as two small plates to put the bones back where they belong. Orthopedically, Patrick's in good shape. We cleaned up the breaks, engineered the callous development so that the bones will likely heal in place and in good time.

"His soft tissue around the ankle, however, required more extensive repair," Alan said. He looked to Barry to explain the more serious implications of Patrick's surgery.

"Considering the breaks, Patrick sustained relatively moderate soft tissue damage above his ankle," Barry started. "I would expect more damage from this injury. However, compartment syndrome can be deadly, and he has evidence of serious tissue degeneration as expected with this type of injury" He looked squarely in my eyes. He could see I was focused, hearing what he was saying.

"The possibilities include neural damage. Connective tissue damage. Vascular shut down," he listed. "For the time he spent in the wilderness and the time it took for you to get him here," he paused, nodding to both Walter and Martina, "no matter how quickly you were able to bring hime here, I would have been concerned."

However, he went on to describe the hemorrhaging and damage of surrounding tissue that were virtually starved for lack of circulation during Patrick's wait for help.

"I am amazed he is not in worse shape," He looked over the top of his glasses. "Or even dead. Honestly. Compartment syndrome leads to gangrene in short order. We know he's a remarkable athlete, but what he went through could have caused even more substantial damage.

"We noticed," he said, shifting tracks, "There are a number of little triradiate lesions, it would look like, on the skin around Patrick's ankle, foot, toes and lower leg. A couple dozen, of these lesions, actually. Can you tell us anything about those cuts?"

Teddy could tell us more, but he wasn't here. He had mentioned his use of leeches on Patrick's foot. I repeated what Teddy had told me.

The surgeons' eyes widened, and they glanced to each other with raised eyebrows.

"Erythromycin?" Dr. Reimer suggested.

"Doxycyclin," Barry responded. "Safer."

Dr. Reimer nodded, then hurried away to arrange for the IV antibiotic for Patrick.

"Leeches!" Barry exclaimed. "While they may have introduced a risk for infection, it may well explain why Patrick's leg is in better shape that either Dr. Reimer or I expected. To be on the cautious side, we'll give him antibiotics to ward off any chance that those leeches left something behind while reducing his swelling. Remarkable," he said. "Leeches. If all goes well from here out, Patrick will have his friend's savvy to thank. It might well be the leeches that saved his foot—or even his life. Simply amazing."

"Teddy's a nurse," I said. "He was a corpsman in Vietnam. His grandfather was a Finnish healer. A shaman, really."

Barry nodded in wonder. Then, he leveled his gaze toward me.

"It is time you get some rest, Lynn." He stated. It was an order more than a comment. "Let's go see Patrick. You can tell him good night. Then you both need rest. We can talk again in the morning. He has a lot of healing ahead."

∞

I slept well, but not long.

I called home as soon as I got up the next morning. Ally beat Martha and her brother to the phone.

"I hoped you were calling," she said when she heard my voice. "How's Dad?"

Her reference to her father was striking. In his presence, Ally preferred to address him by his name.

"He's okay," I said, hearing my voice tail upward for the benefit of the doubt. "He had to have surgery to fix his broken leg. It was late last night. I saw him afterward, and he seemed okay." I wondered how he was this morning and felt anxious to get to the hospital. But first, the kids…

Ally chatted about their activities after we left in Walt's plane. She helped Martha dry the herbs and medicinals we'd collected in the morning, before we got the call from Teddy.

"I got to separate the seeds from the Solomon's Seal that we found yesterday," Ally said. "Martha said it's good for bones. Daddy will need it when he gets home." She described how Martha encouraged her to learn about the plant and several others that we had collected earlier

After our chat, Ally handed the phone to her brother. Conversations with Omie were generally more direct and definitely succinct.

"When are you coming home?" he began.

"I don't know yet, darling. I'll know more after I talk with the doctors who are taking care of your father," I told him. "I'll go see them in a little while."

277

"You flew."

His vision made me smile.

"Yes, I flew. In an airplane."

"Was it good?"

"Yes, Omie. It was."

"Okay." He paused. "Why don't we take care of him?" he asked. "We take care of Auntie Ingie."

"We do take care of Ingie. And it's good care, don't you think."

"Yes,"

"Well, when Patrick gets home, we'll take good care of him, too. I think he will heal fast and well if we give as good care to him as we do Auntie Ingie."

"Okay. Here is Martha." He set the receiver down with a clunk. He was gone. In a moment, I heard Martha's gentle voice asking him to take juice in to his aunt. Then, she took up the phone.

"And all is well, I hope?" She greeted me.

I assured her Patrick was fine and shared with her all that I knew about his condition.

"And you?" She asked. Sometimes, I thought, conversing with Martha was as frugal as chatting with my son. But I knew what she wondered; how long would I remain in Chicago. I didn't know.

"I'm fine. Tired. More in shock, really. Everything's happening so fast. Hard to believe I'm in Chicago. With Patrick. What a day it was."

"How was it, seeing your ex? Did that go well?"

"Yes, very well," I said, and related Barry's comments and graciousness.

"Oh, my," Martha commented.

"I don't know what we would have done without Martina and Walt," I said. "They have been wonderful." I described how supportive they had been, and how they stayed with me while Patrick was in surgery until late.

"All I'd expect of them," she replied.

"They intend to stay here in Chicago for at least the weekend. Walt wants to take in the Vikings game at Soldier's Field. Martina wants to shop. They are making the most of it as long as they're here."

"Remarkable, Walt and Martina," she said. " A couple of spitfires. Bet they loved helping get Pat to Chicago."

"They did. And they are loving the opportunity to see a bit of the City"

"Real people," Martha said. "You can count on them."

"Well, I don't know if I can ask them to stay for as long as Patrick will be hospitalized."

"How long will that be?"

I explained that I didn't yet know. Barry and Alan were satisfied that his surgery went well and that the bones should heal well now that they were set and pinned. Infection was their primary concern. They suggested I arrange for post-surgical care for Patrick near Northwestern where the surgeons could monitor his health.

"It wasn't compound, was it?"

"No, but it was complicated. A lot of tissue damage. And then, there is concern about the leeches Teddy used to get the swelling down."

"Yes, Teddy told me about the leeches. He said he made a poultice of elk mint and comfrey over the leech bites to fight infection. Maybe a couple other plants he had with him. Might have saved Patrick's leg.," she said.

Yes, I agreed. If there is no infection…

"Ally said you harvested Solomon's Seal? Was it ready? I didn't think you wanted to take any of it for another year or two."

Martha sighed.

"Well, I thought we might need it for Patrick. I'm extracting it now. We should have a good tincture when he returns," she said. "Ally helped me dig up some of the rhizomes. I was pleasantly surprised how the roots had spread. There was a lot more in the soil than what we saw above ground. I did show Allie how to harvest the berries and prep the seeds. Perhaps we can get more plants started. But the easiest may be dividing the roots again next year."

Martha had been tending and babying the Solomon's Seal she got from my old friend and mentor Ixchel.

The plant tends to thrive in more temperate zones, but Martha has a way with growing anything green. She had prepped the soil in advance of one of Ixchel's summer visits, knowing that what brought our friend to the northland was the opportunity to search for things of the forests. Martha and Ixchel hit it off like sisters when I introduced them four years ago. Every summer since, I joined Martha and Ixchel as they harvested medicinals in our boreal forest. They gathered wild flowers and green plants, as well as mushrooms and fungi. Martha was keen about the power of northern woodland plants. She'd taught me so much, and I was pleased to hear that Ally was intrigued with Martha's craft as well.

"You know," she started, "Ixchel is near Chicago." I could hear Martha thinking. "Not so far from where you lived in Indiana. Near Lafayette."

I knew Ixchel, my old friend and mentor, was back in the U.S. We had kept in touch since I first met her in Oaxaca years ago when I traveled there with Ingie. I left my family home address with her when I fled from Oaxaca to keep up with Ingie. But that she actually looked me up was a surprise. And, perhaps more so, a blessing. I was pleased when Ixchel stayed with us during three past summers. I was delighted to learn she was now an internationally known folk medicine resource, just as I had been surprised years earlier to learn she was a college educated nurse practitioner. And a world respected anthropologist, stewarding, she said, keepsake of the traditions and culture of her native Mayan heritage. She was the real thing.

Martha keyed into the potential in Ixchel's profession.

"I'll give her a call." Martha said.

We chatted a few more moments. Ely was expecting snow, and the wind had just picked up while Martha and Ally were out harvesting late season herbs. Dad was fine. Ingie was concerned about Patrick and frightened at my being away. She had grown so dependent on me. Our trip to Munich had been a trial for her. Without Teddy's help, Martha would have had a terrific challenge with my sister. Now, however, Ingie could worry about someone else's well being—Patrick's—which helped her negotiate my absence a bit better.

"And Teddy's here," Martha mentioned.

Teddy is almost always there, I thought. Except when he disappears for a couple days with no known reason. Like to save Patrick. I wondered about that. Why had Teddy gone into the boundary waters after Patrick?

We hung up and I hurried to get ready to see how Patrick was doing this morning after his surgery.

# Chapter 64

# Prognosis and Plans

He looked aptly like a post-op patient. Pale. Sleepy. Heavily sedated. His leg hung in a sling from posts above his bed. It was bound in dressings and a partial cast to minimize movement. He didn't stir when I approached his bedside.

I placed my hand on his cheek.

His eyelids fluttered, then opened in a narrow slit. He looked at me and his lips curled into a tired smile.

"Can I have this dance?" he mumbled.

The grip of stress and fear that felt like a belt around my heart broke like a dam and my tears flowed down my cheeks and onto his as I kissed his eyes, his nose, his mouth

"We will dance in moonlight forever," I promised.

"Good. I can wait. Now, go home," he said. "You have our children to raise."

I was stunned. He noted the shock on my face. While my intent was to return to Ely as soon as possible, I hadn't mentioned that to Patrick. He may have been counting on my remaining with him in Chicago. I don't think he appreciated how long he might be healing his injury. He took in my expression and continued assuring me to leave.

"I need you. You are everything to me. I will do everything it takes to be back with you as soon as I can. But our children need you more, and they need you now. They need us. But I have this to deal with now. You have them." His shoulder sagged, relaxing, fatigued. "You told me that. You told me I have to raise our son. Our daughter. It's what kept me going. " He described feeling me with him as he lay on the rock in his campsite after breaking his leg. "You were with me. I heard you. You helped me see."

His eyes focused on mine as he related how that moment kept him going when he had everything working against him in his camp on Knife Lake. When he finished, he lay his head back against his pillow, his strength spent for the moment, but his gaze remained trained on me. "I'll come home. I'll be there. As soon as I can."

"You're right. I need to be with our children. But let's see what Barry has to say about when you can leave, and what you can expect in order to go home." I suggested. I looked at his pale face and glanced down at his surgically repaired leg. I didn't want him to think he wasn't important to me. He always has been. But our children, I thought, came first. "We need more information before we know how we'll handle this."

He shook his head. "He was in early," he said. "First thing I asked was when I could go home. It's going to take some time, Barry says. A week. Maybe more. He's concerned about infection setting in. He wants to see how the wound heals, and how the bones stay in place once I start moving around. I'll be here a week, minimum. Probably longer."

Patrick was exhausted from his ordeal. And groggy from anesthesia and drugs. Talking was demanding. I watched him fall back asleep. Sleep, I thought, was healing. Patrick needed healing. I sat by him as he slept, wondering how to leave him behind when I went home.

∞

Barry wore his most professional expression of concern as he walked up to Patrick's bedside. He looked first at his foot, gently moving the dressings to gain view of Patrick's surgically repaired leg. Satisfied, he glanced first at Patrick, then me. His smile was kind and reassuring.

"Looks good," he said.

I agreed. Swollen from surgery, discolored to a deep scarlet, almost black, but firm and relatively healthy looking.

"He tells me you recommend he stay in Chicago to heal."

"I don't see much choice. He shouldn't be moved until those bones knit. And more importantly, after the risk of infection subsides."

I nodded. We both returned our eyes to the sleeping patient.

"How long will you keep him in the hospital?"

"For several days as we watch his progress and watch for signs of infection. We want to be on top of it if there is any sign of inflammation."

I watched him take a closer look at Patrick's incision.

"There are good alternatives to keeping him here," Barry continued. "Rehabilitation facilities. Some are private and exceptionally nice. Clean. Like being at home."

He looked at me with a raised eyebrow. "But perhaps pricey. Do you still have your Trust? You may need to dip into it."

No, I didn't. I explained briefly Ingie's needs, and Dad's dementia had consumed the trust.

"Patrick is financially sound, I think. I don't know if he has insurance. We haven't talked about it."

Barry raised his eyebrow even higher.

"Barry, I only recently got back together with Patrick. In July, really."

I didn't know where to start.

"Patrick didn't know where I have been since we left the dunes. You know of Ingie's accident?"

He shook his head.

I told him about Ingie's injury and coma, and the long road she's taken toward recovery. And of my father's condition and having to sell the house in Minnetonka.

Barry sighed.

"It's been rough, hasn't it?"

I nodded. "Yes. But good. We have a good home in Minnesota. My mother's home. A place where I spent the summers growing up. We have been happy there." I looked down at Patrick, sleeping soundly. "And now Patrick is with us. To help raise our children."

His eyebrows settled quizzically.

"We have twins. A girl and a boy."

A smile rose on Barry's most analytical face. He was happy for us. For me.

"You have had quite a go of it, haven't you? And now this," he said, gesturing toward Patrick.

"It's been good," I said, my voice carrying my confidence. "I've been grateful. But now I have to get back home to my children."

Patrick stirred. His eyes fluttered open and he trained them on Barry.

"Ah. Dr. North. How am I doing?"

Barry let his smile flood his narrow face. "Good. The incision is good. You haven't moved so I assume your bones are all still in place and knitting well. All we have to do is get you healed."

Patrick looked my way.

"Is he going to hold me hostage?"

"He is."

Barry addressed Patrick.

"It's early. But your incision looks fine. No signs of infection, I'm pleased to say. We're going to watch it like a hawk, mind you. And we have to start getting you up and about. Have you ever used crutches? It's not good to just lay there. We have to get you up and moving to make progress.

"And I do think it best for you to stay in Chicago until we are certain that your healing is on course. Lynn and I were just chatting about that. There are good rehab facilities. Are you insured?"

Patrick nodded. He looked at me. "Part of David's Trust." He shrugged. "David thought of everything."

Barry asked, "David? Your brother?"

Patrick nodded.

"His Trust?"

Patrick nodded again.

Barry glanced toward me.

"David died. In Vietnam,"

A shadow crossed Barry's face. He looked back to Patrick.

"'I'm sorry, Patrick." He shifted his gaze between us. "You two have been through a lifetime since I saw you last, haven't you."

Patrick returned Barry's gaze.

"We're just starting, really."

"I'm glad for you." he said.

Barry reviewed his recommendations with Patrick. He'd offer options for an extended stay once Patrick left the hospital. We would do best to find nursing care and residence. His office could provide us with lists of people and numbers to call to arrange for Patrick's convalescence. He paused, then before he returned to his work.

"Patrick," he started, "and Lynn." He gathered his thoughts then turned his gaze to me, then to Patrick.

"Patrick," he continued. "I owe you an apology. And a debt of gratitude."

Patrick frowned, confused. Barry continued.

"I spoke poorly of you back then," he began. "In the Dunes. I admit I certainly slandered you. And I apologize."

Patrick looked perplexed and started to protest. I, too, was surprised.

"Please," Barry forestalled him. "May I say more? I need to say more. To you and to Lynn, both.

"I am forever grateful to you because you, with no bad intent, became an interloper in my life. In my visions and plans. You stepped in the way of the direction I was taking myself." He turned toward me. "And taking you, Lynn. It was unfair. I just didn't know.

"When you two fell in love," he smiled, waving his fingers toward me as I started to protest, "no, no let me finish, please. You see, you freed me. Liberated me, so to speak. You two, and Dr. Reimer. I witnessed your love. I could see it happening. You know, I was jealous. Not of you, Patrick, because you loved my wife. No. Because you knew her love and you were happy for it.

"And then, Alan came into my life."

He paused, his face showing peace. He reached over and took Patrick's hand with one of his, and with his other, gently held mine.

"I am happy now," he said, confidence flowing with his words. "I know joy. And peace. You took part in all that I went through to find happiness. I'm at peace with myself. I hope you both always have as much."

He let this gaze linger on us both, then turned to go.

Patrick watched him leave, looking out the door for a moment after Barry had disappeared. Looking back at me, his face reflecting his puzzled , pain-killer muddled thoughts, he said, "What do you make of that?

∞

We called home after we got a grip on what lay ahead.

Ally answered. "It's snowing!" She bubbled. "Auntie Ingie says we are going to get a foot of snow!"

I gulped. The storm that had followed across Wisconsin brought rain to Chicago, but the colder border temperatures delivered instant winter back home. I thought about the impact of that snowfall had Patrick still been on his island campsite on Knife. Now, it was irrelevant. Just another delay in getting home, I thought.

"Is Patty okay?" Ally asked. Back to his first name. Unlike her twin, she had yet to fully adapt to the notion of having a Dad.

"He's right here. Want to say hi?" I winced as I asked; she may well pass the phone on to Martha or Ingie rather than chat with Patrick. But she accepted my suggestion.

"Okay."

"Here he is," I handed the phone to Patrick.

He took a deep breath and his voice sounded strong when he spoke.

"Hi, Ally. I sure miss you." He held the phone open from his ear and looked up to invite me to listen. I moved close to hear. The combination of medicines and sterile bedding mixed with the musky odors of a well traveled camper and an injury stressed patient were pungent.

"What happened on your canoe trip?"

He thought for a few seconds before telling her of the wonders he discovered on his journey.

"Every day had something beautiful, Ally. Sunrises. Sunsets. Big storms with lightning and pounding thunder. It was so exciting! I saw an eagle swoop down from way up in the sky and catch a big fish in the water. It was magnificent."

Ally took it in for a moment. Then she asked, "Did you catch any fish?"

"Not many. I didn't fish much. I had all the good food we packed to keep me fed."

"Oh. Okay. Gramma's coming home. Auntie Eva too. Want to talk to Omie? He's here."

"What? Gramma Elle? Coming home?" Patrick turned his surprised gaze toward me, mouthing "What?" He paled as he spoke. I could see the effort was tapping any reserves he had. He looked up toward me, I reached for the phone, but he held it away.

"Yep. Gramma's coming home. Ask Mom. Here's Omie."

285

He listened for our son while I verified Ally's news about his mother, Eva and her twins.

"Eva got her visa!"

Patrick's eyes widened.

Omie's voice came over the phone and he was very direct with Patrick.

"Are you okay?"

"Yes, Omie. I will be alright."

"Are you coming home?"

"Yes. Later, when I can."

"Okay. Good bye."

And he was gone.

Patrick smiled at his son's dismissal. As he handed the phone back to me, Martha's voice came over the receiver.

I told her of Barry's advice and the plans we were developing. We had lots of details to arrange, but I described what we were intending.

Martha listened quietly, but when I had finished, she offered invaluable information.

"I spoke with Ixchel. We discussed Patrick's situation and surmised that he'd be needing care in Chicago for some time. Ixchel offered to care for him if he remains there for any length of time. She said she would be able to stay in Chicago and help in any way Patrick needs to recover.'

Ixchel's offer was like the rain after a drought. I was aware she was a registered nurse, but knew her better for her interest and experience with medicinal and nutritional herbs and mushrooms. When she visited the resort just last summer, the twins and I had helped gather baskets of chanterelles and lobster mushrooms and many types of green leafy plants that she used both for nutrition and in her home practice. She made a return visit to search late last fall with Martha for chaga. A wizened little woman of immense energy, she was a wise and ancient sage.

Martha hung up and Patrick settled the phone back in it's cradle.

"Tell me more of Mom and Eva?" he said.

I told him how Elle had called just moments before I got the emergency call from Teddy.

"I totally forgot about Eva's visa once we got working on helping you. I really don't know much from what your mother told me. Just that the visa came through and they were starting to make travel plans."

He nodded. Understandable.

"Well, I've gotta get back on my feet before they come home," he said. His determination was tangible.

∞

Ixchel's offer to help was among several remarkable gestures that came together to assure that Patrick's rehabilitation would be optimal.

The next came from Alan Reimer, who stopped in Patrick's room to check on his patient's recovery. By the time Dr. Reimer arrived, however, Patrick had used his energy to face his first post-op day. His eyes drooped, and he rolled his head back on his pillow in attempts to stay alert and hear all Alan had to tell us.

After checking the surgery site and expressing his satisfaction, Alan summarized his evaluation. Patrick's leg should heal just fine. It looked good. It needed time.

"We did find some fragments of leaves and other debris packed in between your toes and on the skin of your foot. I knew the hospital in Ely cleaned your leg up before you flew to Chicago. I was just wondering what this matter was? Do you know?" Alan asked.

Patrick shook his head. "No. Not specifically. I thought maybe Teddy had used some herbs to treat me after he took the leeches off." Patrick glanced toward me. "We can ask Teddy the next time we call home."

"It was elk mint," I said. "And comfrey." I nodded as though these wild plants could be expected as treatment of injuries on a normal basis. "Maybe some other medicinal plants as well."

"Curious. His efforts were helpful, it seems." Alan took a last look at Patrick's incision, nodding to express his satisfaction.

Then, abruptly, he directed the conversation to me.

"Barry tells me you are going to place Patrick in rehab here in Chicago. It is really the only option for his near term recovery," he said.

"But let me suggest," he continued, pausing to measure his words. "I'd like to suggest that you take Patrick to my apartment. I'd be more confident of the environment there. It is immaculately clean, and I don't use it anymore. I don't even know why I keep it, since, Barry and I live together. My home of record, I suppose. I would be happy to have you use it until Patrick is healed enough to return home."

The offer was astounding. In the years since my divorce, I had never once met Alan.

"Is this something Barry suggested?" I asked.

"No. I thought of this option during my surgery this morning. The idea of having you use my former home simply materialized in the spare space of my brain." His smile was a mix of cleverness and self-deprecation. "I had to put it off until I'd finished the surgery. I did mention it to Barry when I ran into him after surgery. He said, 'Make it happen.' Think on it. It's yours if you want to use it."

Nodding, glancing one last time at Patrick's injury, Alan gave us a gracious smile and left.

# Chapter 65

# Farewell Again

By the next day, everything was arranged. When Patrick was stable, he would be transported to Alan's apartment. Barry concurred with Alan that barring any setbacks, they preferred Patrick to be in residence at Alan's apartment as soon as possible—most likely within three or four days.

"And it's great that you have someone you know and trust who can care for him," Alan stressed. "You'll be less concerned and worried knowing he's in trusted hands."

"We can monitor him at Alan's almost as easily as here," Barry added.

Alan gave me a tour of his apartment; his vacant but lovely home was located a block closer to the lake than the hotel in which I stayed.

Ixchel arrived in town the following morning to assure that all the preparations for Patrick's stay were in place. When she arrived, I was packing my bag with the few belongs I had with me and preparing to head north to Ely.

I said my good bye's to Barry and Alan, and gave my heartfelt gratitude to all. We reviewed the plans for Patrick's recovery one last time, and they assured me they would care for him fully. I knew they would.

Then I said goodbye to Patrick.

I felt strange as we side our goodbye. We were resigned to what we knew were our responsibilities. He knew that he was not my responsibility, and I agreed. I knew that the twins, my father, and my sister were among my responsibilities, as well as my work at the Ely hospital. Patrick was aware of that, and urged me again to return to Ely with no reservations or regrets.

"I can't say I want to stay," I admitted. "I feel a great desire to be back with you and the kids."

"Rightly so. Your family needs you. I understand."

"I have total confidence that you will get well. Completely."

He nodded. "So do I."

I took his hand.

"I know you'll be home soon."

"I know it, too."

"I love you."

"Always." He smiled. "Go."

∞

I left to meet Walt and Martina for our flight back to Ely. By 10:45 this morning, we were taxiing on the protected waters of the Miegs Field marina. As he read the gauges and instruments in preparation for take off, Walt sputtered and moaned disgust over the Vikings' loss to the Bears on Sunday. Martina said he'd complained more about the Vikings than about any of the shopping trips he'd made with her.

"He even bought himself a leather jacket and some dress shoes," she said, teasing her husband who kept his focus on the plane's instrument panel.

The little two-engine plane battled the gusty breezes of the Windy City as we climbed from the protected marina over the deep gray waters of Lake Michigan, I looked forward to being home and wondered when Patrick would join us.

Book Six

Patrick Joyce

# Conjured Healings

# Chapter 66

# Healing Sleep

Ixchel was there when I woke. She usually was. If she wasn't immediately at my bedside, she was nearby, in a chair, studying a book. In a yoga pose facing east across the lake. In the next room. Settled with her knitting in Alan's arm chair looking out the windows. Quietly just being there.

I slept a lot after I was settled in the makeshift rehab unit in Alan's library. It was the only room large enough to accommodate the gangly but comfortable hospital bed on which I spent most of my time. The mechanical bed sat prominently centered in the room, facing a wall of window that looked out over the roofs of nearby buildings along Lake Shore Drive. The view of the lake was stunning. Sunrise each morning varied from a scale of grays to the brilliant emergence of a fiery globe rising across the span of Lake Michigan. It was an entirely different sunrise than those that greeted me in the days of my canoe trip in the Boundary Waters.

David would have loved this view, I thought, watching the red disc of sun slide from the waters, turning bright orange, then yellow until it's golden brightness verged on pure white and was too strong for my eyes. David was such a morning person. A sunrise like this might have made him pause on his way to answering the calls of his cows in the milk line.

Ixchel noticed within minutes of when I wakened. Often, she said nothing. She'd look up from the magazine she was paging through, and if I caught her eye she simply nodded and went back to her reading. She understood that my waking process was gradual. I took my time. When the sun grew bright, she would bring my cap over to the bedside, plop it on my head to shade my eyes, and let me continue my ritual. Sometimes she'd ask how I felt, or more often, whether the pain in my leg was controlled and if I was generally comfortable. I generally was, and she'd resume her reading and let me be.

But then, at a given moment, she'd go into action.

"Here. Drink your water first. Then take these, and drink some more."

I complied.

"Let's get you up."

One of my favorite parts of the day. Standing up on one foot alongside my bed, taking a good healthy leak into a stainless canister that looked like a tumbler for mixing cocktails, and unfolding my body to an upright position. A new start. A new day.

She'd strip off the wrinkled hospital gown that was my sole option for bed clothing. With me standing at the bedside, gripping the shiny chrome railings that I relied on for our morning cleansing routine, Ixchel washed—

no, scrubbed—my backside. Then she'd spread an ointment of some sort with a gentle scent of lavender on my skin and rub it thoroughly until it dissipated into my flesh. She rubbed always in a pattern, like a *flour de lis*, moving up along my spine, her left hand rotating in ascending counter-clockwise circles, her right mirroring the motion in clockwise precision. A little woman, no taller than just above my elbow, she reached high to complete her healthy skin regimen at the base of my neck. Her fingers were strong and precise, searching and probing points of soreness and knots of stress.

"There," she proclaimed when she had finished the morning ritual. "Your skin looks good." She spoke softly, with an accent of Spanish grounded in a tongue more ancient and fundamental.

I'd stand there buck naked, finishing my bath, until she fetched a clean gown. Every day, a clean gown.

"How come I have to wear these things," I asked the third day in Alan's apartment. "Can't I get some real pajamas?"

Ixchel was generally frugal with her chatter. I detected, however, a flash of humor in her response.

"Punishment," she quipped. "For doing stupid things."

∞

All my efforts were toward healing.

This afternoon, when I woke, she was sitting at Alan's desk, which had been pushed against the shelving along the wall to make room for my bed. The entire room, except for the full wall of windows, was lined with shelves filled with books and magazines. Ixchel consumed all she could from Alan's library as I slept. I was her main distraction. But I slept much of the first four days since I'd been here.

"Remind me again," I asked, interrupting her study. "Why am I here?'

"This is a good place to heal," she repeated. She'd answered exactly the same way each time I'd asked her that question when first I woke up here, confused as to where and how I'd come to be in this room of books with the sky close outside the windows. "A good place to sleep. Sleep is healing."

I glanced at her. "How come there are no shades on those windows. I could sleep a lot better if we could pull shades and darken this room when I slept."

"You need the sun in the east each morning. It reminds you to live," she said. "And the light softens as it dims in the afternoon when the sun is in the west. Reminds you to relax. Sunshine is your ally."

*My ally,* I mused as I prepared for the routine Ixchel enforced each time I awakened from my healing sleep.

But my need for sleeping waned and my body ached to move and work out the stiffness that inactivity fosters.

# Chapter 67

# Ixchel's Extensive Rehab

Soon, I was moving more. Exercising. Stretching. We did yoga. Ixchel did yoga. I did some limited issue yoga.

"I do yoga," she explained. "You do yog, maybe. Or just yo. You do what you can. No more."

A wide smile spread across Ixchel's round, wrinkled face. Her dark eyes gleamed when I first told her I was experienced in the practice. She added two and sometimes three poses in our brief sessions. A bit of mountain. A modified tree in which my casted leg pretended to bend and tuck against my good leg. Bends. Twists using chairs and pillows for floor work. It felt good to set a pose and adjust it in slow, graceful steps. It felt useful. Even if it was just yo.

∞

On Wednesday, Omie called. Ingie taught him how to dial the call. He made his calls at his whim.

"Hi. It's snowing."

"Are you staying warm."

"Yes. The chickadees are gobbling sunflower seeds."

"They must be hungry."

"They are. They fill their bellies. Then they fly away."

"Where do you suppose they go?

"Home." He paused. Then, "when are you coming home?"

"Soon."

"Today"

"No. Not today."

"Not soon enough."

Click.

∞

Ixchel sensed that I was having a bad go of it this afternoon. Her demanding therapy involved the yoga stretches and poses, which I generally enthusiastically embraced. Some mornings, however, soreness and pain left me less then willing to do the extent of her plan.

She stuck her pointed finger between my shoulder blades.

"Tuck. Bring your shoulders down. Open your chest."

I wasn't willing to perform at my best. I couldn't get beyond trying to enter mountain pose while propped with crutches.

"Place your head on top of your spine. Do not dangle like lazy turtle."

She set her pose directly in front of me, first in mountain, then sweeping her arms in wide arcs until her hands met above her head, she assumed a salutation position that should normally be easy to reach. For me, today, it was agony. The easiest of things yesterday was a bundle of agony today.

"Not today, Ixchel. Not today."

"You quit today, you will not reach tomorrow until next week."

*Poff,* I thought. Not today.

I eased into Alan's easy chair, set my leg and its heavy cast comfortably in front of me, lifted, and moved an ottoman with my healthy foot to prop up the injured leg.

Ixchel rummaged through her basket of herbs and weeds and whatnot. She selected several dried sprigs from different bunches. She wrapped together several of the dried stems and brittle leaves, tying them tight first at one end with a fine string that she spiraled up the sprigs and cinched several times to form the bundle. With a mischievous smile, she held the bundle like a wand, tipped toward my nose. "Today we beckon help from our Peruvian friends," she said, chuckling. "Huacatay. Mint. Chincho. Llanten. We cleanse your soul. Cola de Caballo. We build your bones."

The humor of her expression transitioned to serene, humble sincerity. From deep within, she uttered a mantra: "Pachamama…Pachamama… Pachamama…"

She took a match from a box in her basket and lit the end of her herbal wand. The fragrance was like mint incense. She waved it gently about, shuffling in a rhythmic two step around me as she sang, "Pachamamma…"She repeated her chorus softly, watching the white smoke waft through the apartment. She held the bundle with it's smoldering end in front of my face and fanned the smoke toward me.

"Breath in," she advised as she circled around me, bathing me in the savory smoke. "Pachamama, cleanse this soul," she hummed. "Pachamama, birth peace in this soul. Pachamama, love this soul. Pachamama… Pachamama…Pachamama…" She softly sang as she shuffled in the circle path about me.

After her third trip around me, she set her smoldering bundle of dried herbs in a cup on Alan's desk. Ixchel returned to her yoga mat and set a relaxed mountain pose before me. She brought her hands together before her chest. Eyes like slits on the face of a happy laughing Buddha, she beckoned me to rise.

"There is no tomorrow. There is now. And now doesn't know quit, or there would never be tomorrow."

My body felt as light as a feather as I lifted from Alan's easy chair. It felt good to stretch.

∞

It was getting late. I dialed home anyway. Luther answered. Luther never answers.

"Hello?"

His voice distracted me. I didn't expect a man's voice.

"Hello Luther?"

A pause.

"I think so."

"I think you are right. I recognize your voice."

Another pause.

"You do?"

"Yes. You sound good."

"Who are you?"

"It's me. Patrick. You know, me and Lynn."

"Are you the guy who knocked up my daughter?"

I sighed. We had been through this so many times.

"If I say no, will you believe me?"

"I believe whatever you say. It doesn't matter. It blows away like snowflakes in the wind. The wind is strong. It's a storm."

"Are you getting snow?"

"Yes. It is all white."

Click.

∞

Perched on Alan's desktop, Ixchel remained in pose, not a tense muscle on her frame. Her eyes sharp, but distant, she lifted a knee, tucked her foot and was in Tree pose. She held Tree for what seemed a long time. Then, with defined, deliberate movement, she slid her foot around her calf while twisting her arms into Eagle. She held a moment, then smiled as if she pondered a joke. The morning sun above Chicago was bright and streamed full force through magnificent windows, highlighting Ixchel's bronze face. The wrinkles of her years accented her childlike joy and the humor she effused.

"The eagle flies over the waters and glides on the wind," she said. She released her pose, and sat on the edge of the heavy wooden library table.

"You move like a child. You flow."

She glanced from the windows toward me.

"I am just a beginner. Always a beginner." A smile spread across her copper face. "You move like a bull. Like an old bull. You fight through every movement.

297

We gazed toward one another. I felt my lips curl, and soon I too had a grin like a jack-o'-lantern.

"Teach me how to not use my muscles when I move my muscles."

"It is easy. Be a beginner. Then think of the Eagle. And fly."

"I am not ready to do Eagle. I need time."

"Think. Not do. Then when you do, all you need is to think."

∞

Such were my days with Ixchel.

One evening, as purple darkness covered Michigan's waters from the east, she had me perched on pillow bolsters with my legs straight out, gently twisting my spine and working my neck. She sat beside me, her legs folded, her tiny body expanded, her shoulders light and straight, her arms resting on her legs with her palms open upwards. She moved her head on her neck, rolling her skull on her spine. Her head looked like a balloon loosely twisting in a gentle breeze, light, as if filled with helium. Again, I noticed there was no tension in her body.

I considered my own body. I was stiff and tight. I sat on the bolster that allowed modified floor work while protecting my leg and accommodating the heavy plaster cast that ran from thigh down to foot. My shoulders were knotted and bound. My spine clinched in a tether of sinew and shortened muscle bundles.

She motioned for me to be still. Walking in a circle around me, she viewed me from all sides. She moved around my left shoulder, examining my neck and looking at my posture. She stopped behind me. I could not see her, but I imagined her sharp eye examining my back.

She place a single finger between my shoulder blades. Her touch was light, but exact. I reflexively arched my spine, drawing my neck up and lifting my head. She increased the pressure on the point.

She stuck another finger at the nape of my neck. It felt as though her finger was sliding directly into a bundle of muscle. Suddenly, like a spark, a jolt of energy surged from the tip of her finger through my muscles and into my spine. I barked like a dog, loud and startled. The charge spread from my neck to the point pinned by the finger she had placed between my shoulder blades.

She withdrew her fingers in a smooth, casual movement.

She slowly paced, examining everything about me.

"Strange," she said. She looked deep into my eyes. "You should rest."

I slept for 11 hours.

When I woke, she was there.

"Where are you from?" I asked as we did our morning routine. "Your home?"

298

"In reverse order of time, I am here now. This is home. I am home. In the past, I lived many places. I started in Guatemala." She carried the wash water to the bathroom. When she returned, she added, "San Marcos, by the Lake."

She brought a book from Allan's library. An atlas. She opened to a spread of Central America.

"Where is Guatemala?" She asked.

I followed the curve of the horn of Central America like a funnel from the border below the Rio Grande. Below Mexico, I spotted Guatemala.

"I am from people who lived here in northern Guatemala. The jungle. Tikal. But that was many years before me."

She shifted her finger across the land to a blue patch nestled in hills and mountain highlands to the west.

"I am from here."

She said no more.

I wondered how her life had been in those mountains near Lake Atitlan.

# Chapter 68

# Calls

Our phone calls with the kids were the highlight of the daily routine. By the time I was up, fed, exercised, and back in bed, exhausted for the first part of the day but not sleepy, I called home. I sensed the rings from my call were like the starting gun at a track meet. Ally was often the winner.

"'Morning, Patrick."

"Hi, Ally," I greeted her chirpy little voice. "How did you know it was me calling? Could have been somebody else, you know."

"It was somebody else, a little while ago," she laughed. "Mom's boss at the hospital called. I called her, 'Daddy'." Her giggles gathered like little bouquets of dandelion. "I said, Hi, Daddy," and Mrs. Chambers asked me when she had become my Daddy!"

I joined in her laughter. "What did you tell her?"

"I didn't tell her anything! I just handed the phone to Mom and ran into Ingie's room. Ingie laughed till she peed!'

We laughed and chatted for a moment until Ally was ready to pass the phone on to her brother.

Omie's time on the phone remained frugal. Direct. Laden with import.

"Are you better?" he started.

"Every day," I assured him. "A little better every day. Progress, Omie. It's called progress."

Satisfied, he turned to a report on his doings.

"I collected pine cones before the snow." His tone was earnest; his work was meaningful. "To start fires. They burn fast and help get the wood burning."

"Good kindling," I replied.

"Yes." He fell quiet for a moment. "Like birch bark. When are you coming home."

"Depends on my progress, Omes." I said.

Another pause.

I asked, "Is your mother there?"

"No," he said. "She went to work. Mrs. Chambers asked her to go in."

"Okay. Tell her I called, please."

"Okay. Bye."

"Bye."

"I'll draw a picture for you."

"Thanks. Bye."

∞

At best, morning chats with Lynn were brief. Either she had the twins at her elbow, asking for a chance to talk with me, or she called them to take the phone while she turned to tending other matters. The morning was a busy time for her.

The best time for talking with Lynn was late, when the night brought a lull to the day, the kids were tucked in bed, Luther had fallen into the stillness of his hollowed dark nights, and Ingie stood watch from her bedroom overlooking the lake.

"Hi," her voice melted me when she called for our late evening chat. At times, it was all I needed to hear.

"How you doing?"

"Good. Got a lot done today. How about you?"

"Okay. Same old same old. The slow pace of healing."

"Yes. It's slow."

"Ixchel had me sit up longer this morning."

"Still making you soak up the sun?"

"Not until she makes me try a sort of yoga. She calls it 'yo'. She lets me use the bed as a bolster. And if it's sunny, I can go right into pranayama while soaking rays."

"Ixchel loves the Sun Goddess."

"Pachamama?"

"No. Pachamama is from South America. She's the Goddess of the World. Kinich Ahau is from the Mayans, a sun god.

A stillness filled the pause between us.

"How do you know this stuff?"

"How do you know which phase the moon is in? I listened. To those who know. A lot from Ixchel. More from Martha, who gets it from Ixchel. But I heard it from my mother, too, though I didn't realize how important it was when she told me about the goddesses. And her focus was more on Gaelic and Scandinavian folklore. I thought she was just telling me tales. Entertaining me. She was really teaching me."

"Who is Ixchel? How did you find her?"

Lynn took a moment before she explained,

"I told you once about Ixchel. I met her in Mexico, when Ingie and I traveled. I didn't find her. She found me."

I remembered Lynn's telling of the old woman she met during her time in Oaxaca, the lady that took her in and watched over her. Protected her, was how I recalled Lynn describing her experiences.

"I thought you met some sort of peasant lady."

I heard Lynn take a breath.

"Ixchel is so humble. I thought so, too. Comes across as just a little Mayan woman. But I found out differently. She told me at first her name was Maria. Now I know that is a name for many older, wiser women in Mexico. I would not have understood what her Mayan name meant. To me, she was just 'Maria.' And she watched over me.

"You know, before I left Oaxaca, Ixchel ask for my address. I wondered why at the time. I thought I would never see her again. And then she contacted me. The year after the twins were born. She was in Minneapolis, at Augsburg University, teaching a seminar on nursing in Oaxaca. And she's an R.N. I was stunned. I didn't know she was a nurse. I didn't know she could speak English. She never spoke any English while I was in Oaxaca."

"She didn't? Why not?"

"She told me she thought I would listen better if we left ourselves open to the world without constraining anything with words. She is a powerful one, Ixchel. Do you know she has a Ph.D. in anthropology? She's an expert in Central and South American culture from before Columbus."

I shook my head. "Holy mackerel."

"Yep. And a Shaman."

"A Shaman? Like a priest?"

"No. Priests wield power by telling people how they should be. Shaman's invoke the universe to draw power from the eternal. In a sense, it's their way they participate in the creation moment. They tell the universe what to do."

"Huh?"

"That's why she's such a powerful healer. You'll see. Well, anyway, when she was in Minneapolis, she looked me up. She couldn't find me at first since I since I had given her my Dunes address. She had Ingie's address from the people we stayed with in Oaxaca. She found me just as we were getting ready to sell the house in Minnetonka. We kept in touch. She's visited here in Ely three times now. One fall she stayed for two months. That's when she and Martha became such close friends."

"I didn't know."

"There is much you have yet to learn."

She did that. Lynn. She kindly reminded me of what lay before me. Alerted me. I never resented hearing that there was much to discover and encounter, much to experience, that I had missed while getting my formal education as a student athlete at the University. It was inviting. Hearing Lynn's kind voice remind me of what lay ahead made me realize how fortunate I was that she had waited for me. And that I hadn't totally fucked up looking for clues about life while I was klutzing around on my own.

She shifted subject. "Doing better with your crutches?"

"Piece of cake. I told Ixchel we should tape a garbage bag around my thigh and I could take a shower. Man, do I want to take a shower."

"I can imagine. What did she say?"

"She won't consider it until I get some endurance and energy that gives her confidence that she won't be lifting me off the floor. She thinks I'm a wimp."

"Rightfully so, Wimp."

I pursed my lips. Yes. I had a way to go. But it was just short of two weeks since my surgery.

"Yeah. I suppose. How about you. What's keeping you busy?"

"We finished tiling the new shower in Number 5. Martha grouted the tiles we set yesterday," she said. "We cleaned up all the construction mess and scoured the entire cabin. It's set for winter guests now, and we have a a number of regulars with reservations. It's our best winter cabin. It's getting cold here. We had a fire going in Number 5's fireplace all week as we lay the new tile."

"The kids said you were called into work again."

"Just for the morning. Jill Anderson's daughter got sick in school so Amy asked me to help out. I was back home by 2:00. Martha was just finishing the grout and we were done cleaning by supper."

Life goes on, I thought. Man, Lynn does a lot.

"What were the kids doing?"

"Omie was with us. He had his chalk board. Luther got into his head about your leg. Omie reveres Luther. Believes so much of what he says. You know how he draws. So explicit. What were you telling him when you talked this morning?"

I tried to remember. "The usual, I suppose. Just that I was getting better. I think we talked about making progress. Yeah. That's it."

"Well, between you and Luther, Omie got a notion that your leg was growing back. Luther had him thinking you had gangrene and the doctors cut your leg off. He drew a series of you with your leg getting longer each time!" Lynn was laughing heartily.

"I so often want to save his art, but he erases it as soon as he finishes whatever his idea is at the moment."

"You ought to take a picture of it."

"I have, on occasion. But most of his work goes to his eraser. He needs a fresh slate whenever he thinks of something new."

"Too bad we can't get him to work on paper."

"We've tried. But he likes chalk so much. And he really likes working in white on black."

She detailed some of the drawings he made until she drifted on to other ideas.

Then, another pause settled over us. After a moment, she said, "Whatcha thinking."

"'Bout you. Us. About being alone again. Seems to me that I spend a good portion of my life away from those I love and want to be with the most."

She listened. I continued.

"I was watching the waves coming in on the Lake today. Made me think of the Dunes. Our time in the Dunes. I look down the beach and see where the Dunes are. The Dunes where we used to lay and watch the lights of Chicago."

She uttered a "hmmm."

"I was figuring that back then, in the Dunes, we had about maybe 45 days together. Maybe 50, before you left on your travels with Ingie."

"Yes," she agreed.

"And maybe another month after you got back."

"Uh huh," she agreed again.

"And now, since I found you in Ely, we had the summer. July, August, September. And then I set out on the canoe trip. So just a part of October. A hundred fifty days, all total."

She listened. After a moment, she asked, "And?"

"Just amazing. Seems like my whole life is about you. And haven't even had a half year of time together."

"We can fix that."

"Yes," I agreed.

"Patrick, you're right," she said. "And really, it is all just one big day. It seems like my whole life is about you, too. One big day meant to be with you. Even those years we were apart, I always thought about you. You and our children. You have given me meaning."

I thought about that. Meaning.

"You know what I discovered on my canoe trip?" I asked.

"What?"

"I don't ever need to go canoeing without you in the boat. Ever again."

She chuckled. "Right."

"You give me purpose." I said. "Meaning to my purpose."

"I love you."

I nodded. "Yes. I love you."

# Chapter 69

# Jack's Back

The weekend was quiet. Ixchel tended me. We read. I was awake longer each day, reading, looking through Alan's great collection of photography books and photojournalism collections. Alan appreciated the difference between portrait photographers like Leibovitz, Newman, Arbus, and pure art such as Ansel Adams, or the photojournalism that reflected culture, society, humanity. Maybe Arbus was in that genre. But certainly Steiglitz. Alan had beautiful images in books he'd collected about all the great photographers, American and international. I spent hours feeding off the beauty of that photographic art. It fed my healing.

On Sunday in my third week after surgery, Ixchel got me up and helped me dress in loose fitting workout clothes. A sweatshirt. A pair of workout pants that she slit down the side to wrap around my cast as I learned to used crutches and gain the endurance to be safe on one leg. Ixchel wrapped tape loosely around the open legs to keep the pants in place and allow me to travel, if only in the apartment and hallway. It was a significant landmark in my path toward health. Ixchel enforced a gradual increase in my efforts. Light duty, but more reps every day. I was amazed at how weak I had become in the weeks since my injury.

After the workout, we watched the Packers play the Bears. The Pack was lackluster under their new coach, Bengston. Nothing going. Couldn't score. The Bears had Sayers. He ran all over the Pack. Boring game. Oh, Lombardi! Why have you forsaken us?

The doorbell rang and Ixchel got up to answer it. A moment later, Jack walked into my room just as half time started. I turned the game off.

"Whoa! What have we got here?" He inspected the dressings on my leg. "Fancy footwear."

Jack. He always seemed to know how to put a smile on my face.

"Jesus!" I laughed. "What are you doing here?

"Not Jesus. Just an admirer." Jack quipped. "Your girlfriend told me you are holed up here." He looked around the library and turned toward the view out the windows. "Wow. You can pick your place of refuge, can't you?"

I shook my head. Jack. He kills me.

"My girlfriend, is it?"

"At the moment, I suppose. Just one of those things I presume you are taking advantage of this little vacation to consider more fully."

Ixchel raised her eyebrows and looked between Jack and me.

I ignored them both. Lynn was my topic to consider. We had to move on. But all I could do was shrug. And try to deflect their interest.

"You've met Ixchel?"

"On the way in. Again, your girlfriend told me all about her. Lynn, and Martha, both told me about Ixchel. You are such a lucky man to have such a wise healer in your service. You know she's a healer, don't you?"

∞

Well, observing her meticulous care and concern, I was witness to her healing powers. Seemed to me that she was always present every time I opened my eyes from the many naps I'd had during my recovery. Often, she'd be reading at Alan's office desk, or in the comfortable stuffed chair facing the window view. Or knitting. She was in the chair more often in the afternoons; she had me sitting in it in the mornings when the sun streamed in and baked me to the bones. "Healing rays,' she contended.

She quietly tended my needs. She never used the phone. She seldom asked me anything not related to my leg. She answered my endless questions about her childhood in San Marcos by Lake Atitlan. She told me about learning to use plants in healing. We chatted about some of the unusual tinctures and compresses she had applied to my leg.

She spoke more to Alan when he stopped by to check on me, although Alan plied her with a much pointed slate of questions about the ointments, tinctures and medicinal herbs she used in my care. He wanted to know how she thought those herbs worked.

Alan was enthusiastic about my response to Ixchel's care. He questioned her about each measure she had taken, and interrogated her thoroughly about her rationale for the grapeseed oil, lavender, dill oil, fenugreek, neem, moltkia lehm extract and other exotic mediums my nurse brought with her. Their dialogue held a distinctly professional tone, both in vernacular and content. She and Alan had lively discussions about the antibiotic, anti-inflammatory or analgesic properties of the medicinals that she gathered in the field or received from fellow healers that she knew from other lands. Alan was awed.

Barry came along with Alan on his last visit, as much, I think, in response to things Alan may have told him about Ixchel and her practices rather than for any I need I might have. He asked her about her basket of medicinal herbs and ointments as he checked the status of my leg. My skin looked healthy and pink, much better than when I arrived in Chicago. The incisions on the sides of my ankle and leg looked fine and well on their way toward healing. Barry asked her specifically about several of her therapies. He mentioned his concern and that he'd phoned Lynn to check whether she was aware that the nurse she had called in to care for me was using less

306

than conventional means of healing? Lynn was totally supportive of Ixchel's practice. Barry raised his eyebrows as he ran his fingers gently up the clean, supple lines of healing along the incision site, Alan's work.

Barry may have doubts, but he had no objections and clearly approved of the condition of my healing flesh.

"She has you doing yoga, I hear," was his only question for me as he inspected my healing tissues. "Really? No problem?

None, I assured him. It was only yo. Or maybe even a little bit more like yog by now. But it was good.

∞

Jack, too, was intrigued with Ixchel's healing prowess.

Before Jack had taken off his coat or had asked me about my progress, he was entranced with Ixchel's methods. He and Ixchel delved into an excited discussion of the medicinals. Jack asked about several extracts or compounds he had been introduced to in Afghanistan, Iraq and Iran. He was familiar with the moltkia and had helped gather leaves and the spindly but beautiful blue flowers from the powerful herb.

Jack's knowledge of something grounded in both science and the practice of folk medicine fascinated me. In this case, however, his insight seemed more practical than literary. Listening to his comments to Ixchel, it was clear his familiarity with some of the medicinals was from seeing their use in the remote areas in which he worked. They, too, like Ixchel and Alan, conversed at a high level of mutual understanding, although with Jack, the discussion was more practical and experiential.

I was weary, however, and their discussion was lost soon on me. Lulled by watching a half of a rather boring Packer game and sitting up for a good portion of the day, I found myself dropping off. Soon, their chatter softened, and became a backdrop for vague, exotic dreaming.

In my dream, pine needles dropped in clusters from above in the trees. I looked up to see a squad of little red pine squirrels gnawing at the boughs above, trimming the clusters like little green broom heads, and dropping them from the trees, tumbling down onto a carpet of scented pine needles. The carpet covered the ground and ran up a gnarled, broken red pine trunk, a tree still growing but old, having lost a worthy portion of the once tandem-bole tree, now reduced to a single spire with a throne at it's base formed from the stump of the broken off trunk. Pine needles showered the throne along with crimson and blaze colored leaves falling from maple trees, and golden almond shaped aspen and birch leaves.

I was in a forest that had no end, no paths, under a ceiling of leaves with few windows to the sky. I looked up to the light above. The canopy of

307

pine and birch allowed entry to just peek holes with speckles of brilliant blue sky above the forest.

The snatches of blue broke off and fell like tiny blossoms down through the holes in the canopy, landing on my shoulders and head and showering me with a fresh, light scent. The little blue flowers drifted in a dance with the needles and leaves that flowed in currents of breeze wafting its way among the trees.

When I looked below, I found Lynn had taken the throne. Her eyes kindled amber; her face placid beneath a crown made of a wolf's head that flowed back over her shoulders and back. Its white fur was mottled in gray and black streaks. In her hand, Lynn held a fine paddle of polished wood, little bigger than a baton, with a ruby embedded in a hole through the center of the blade and a garland of watercress around its face. On her lap lay a bouquet of dried greens and blossoms. On her left, a pine martin perched on the arm of her throne. A doe stood alongside to her right, its eyes dark and dreamy. It started when I met it's gaze. Lynn shifted the baton a smidgen, and the doe settled, and instantly, they evaporated before my eyes. Their disappearance was so unsettling that I awoke from my sleep like rising from the depth of turbulent water.

When I awakened, Jack was watching me. Ixchel stood alongside my bed. She waved a bundle of dried lavender above my face. She had done that a number of times during my convalescence. This time, the subtle sweetness of the lavender aroma drew my focus. I turned my eyes to her, and a thin, pleasant smile spread across her wide dark face. Her eyes glistened and flashed.

"You are ready now."

I looked at her, fully awake. "Ready? For what?"

"New beginnings."

She took her bouquet and her basket and left me with Jack to watch the waning rays of the day dissolve into blues and grays of Lake Michigan.

"Powerful," Jack proclaimed.

I was befuddled. Vestiges of my dreams floated elusively behind my eyes, someplace in my brain. I reflexively shook my head.

Jack laughed. Then he asked, "Do you remember?"

"What?"

"Your dream? What were you dreaming."

I looked into my hands folded on my lap. How did he know I was dreaming.

"Yes. But no. It's fading."

"It will come again. Nice, isn't it? Sliding around without the chains of time and space?

What was he talking about?

He explained what he had observed while I slept.

He had asked Ixchel about the progress of my healing. She tipped her head, looked at him, then turned to rummage in her woven wicker basket. She pulled out several items. An ointment that she dabbed on my temples and the bridge of my nose as I nodded off to sleep. She crumpled dried leaves and folded them into a loosely woven cloth. She waved the aromas from the leaves under my nose. Then she took the lavender and held it over my head.

"She did all this in just that last couple of minutes before you woke. She said she was helping you conjure a dream. Did you? Dream?"

I certainly did. It was vibrant. I told him fragments of what I remembered. Lynn with the wolf hide crown. The ruby embedded paddle.

"What do you suppose it means?" he asked.

I shook my head. It was vibrant, but unreal. Like magic.

"Why did Ixchel say I was ready?"

He shrugged. "She said she was asking your source if you had healed. Whether you were prepared to go home. When you woke, she said you were ready."

"Whew. Crazy."

"What's crazy?" he posed rhetorically.

# Chapter 70

# A False Start

Jack steered our chat to more mundane events. He explained how he heard from Rosie about Eva's visa. So he called Mom to find out where their travel plans stood. They were planning to travel right before Christmas, after Eva finished tutoring at the end of the semester. They were due to arrive at O'Hare on the 21st. When he discussed plans with Paddy, Jack had discussed picking them up. He'd offered to take them to North Freedom since Paddy had his herd to milk. Rose wanted to greet them at the airport, but decided that Jack's offer was not only convenient, but that his vehicle would be more comfortable for Elle, Eva and the two babies.

"Your vehicle?"

Jack nodded. "Yep. The bishop didn't want his Caddy back, even after I had the window repaired. Damaged goods. He bought himself a new car. A Mercedes."

I laughed. Jack's brother had his own concept of poverty. So did Jack, and I let him know about it.

He looked down his nose at me as though my criticism was unwarranted.

"Well, what are you going to do with a shiny new Caddy?"

"I'm going to drive it to Guatemala." He held his chin up in a stubborn pose filled with justification and reason.

My jaw dropped. "Now you're crazy. You're dreaming, and it's crazier than my crazy dreams."

"Not in the least," he explained. He reminded me that he had contacted his friend, a Maryknoll, who'd worked for years in Guatemala. His friend assured him that there was plenty of priest work awaiting Jack in Central America.

"Even if you don't have the support of the Church? The financial support or the ecumenical sanction?"

He shrugged. "Ecumenically, I do believe the Church has given up on me. I was a little disappointed at first. I felt like a little kid who had his balloon taken away. But then I understood. They have given me my freedom."

"Right. But they took away your job. What you going to live on?

His eyes blazed. A smile spread from one ear to the other.

"Your brother saw to that."

David! My twin had taken care of all those he loved. Rose. Paddy. Certainly Mom and me. His dairy enterprise—the milk line and his genetics business—continued to make more money than all of us together were spending. I knew of David's will, and I was aware of the provisions he had left Jack.

"Will it be enough?"

He nodded.

"I have, you know, taken a vow of poverty," he said wyrly. Then he grinned and laughed. "And, I have a Caddy! It will take me to Guatemala! I'll drive the Pan American Highway. And, we can use it to get you home to Ely! Ixchel thinks your ready. Now isn't that a grand idea!"

∞

On his next visit two days later, Dr. Reimer did not agree with Ixchel or Jack that it was time that I head home to Ely.

"You're not ready." His demeanor was absolute and professional. "Your bones have started to knit, but bone healing is minimally a six week event. Your break, longer. My recommendation is for you to bide your time and wait until we can replace this cast with a walking cast.

"Besides, I want to be certain you have no infection whatsoever in that leg. I'm not totally confident of that at this point. Two more weeks. Give it two more weeks. Then I'll feel much more comfortable sending you back out to your wilderness."

Ixchel stood next to Alan, her steely gaze telling me that I should be listening and not thinking. I shrugged. A simple smile crossed her bronze shaded face.

∞

I called Lynn after Alan left. I thought I could rally her support for my early exit from Chicago. I stated my case. I could heal in Ely as well as here. I would benefit from the home environment and be close to those I love the most. It wouldn't delay or interfere with my progress.

"Alan called me this morning. He and Barry agree. You should stay until all risk of infection is gone. Two more weeks."

I felt as if an anchor was hung around my neck, a ball and chain attached to my broken leg. I looked out the windows at the angry gray Lake Michigan. I settled back in my reading chair and picked up a copy of Joe Rosenthal's war photos. I was here for the duration.

∞

Two weeks later, the week before Thanksgiving, I felt strong. Fighting pain is exhausting. Becoming increasingly more pain free is liberating. I was feeling freedom. I was getting stronger.

Ixchel took advantage of my progress. She pushed me in the restricted yoga poses I could take up. She emphasized the need for balance. One legged mountain was her go to. We would start with mountain and she'd work me through a good twenty minutes of adjustments to the pose.

311

"You will always be a beginner," she advised. "Start each pose in beginner. Find the need to make adjustment. Learn the adjustment. Do the adjustment. Remember it for the next time and it will go more quickly. Then search for new adjustment."

She urged me to remember balance in spite of my leg being virtually useless to practice balance. She would lead me past mountain into tree.

"Plant the seed of your tree and let it grow strong," she repeated daily. "Let it grow limbs. Think of your leg in its cast, hanging there. Then imagine it in position, knee wide outside. Think of your foot planted firm above your knee. Think of it, but do not do it. When you heal, it will do what you think now as you practice."

She'd catch me rolling my eyes and her pumpkin face smile slid joyfully across her face.

∞

"Hi, Ally."

"Hi, Patrick."

"Heard you got some snow."

"Lots. Made a snowman. He looks like you."

"Like me? A snowman looks like me! How did you do that."

"We've got him on sticks, like crutches. Mommy says you are getting around on crutches."

"I am. Doing pretty well, too."

"Does that mean you are coming home?"

"It means I'm getting better and will come home soon."

"Omie says you don't know what soon means."

I laughed aloud. "I think Omie is right. I thought soon would be last week. But let's just say, sooner than later."

"When's later."

I sighed. "Oh, I don't know. After sooner, I suppose."

"Patrick, you are goofy. Here's Mom. She wants to talk to you."

"Bye, Darlin'.

"Bye, Patrick."

"Hi."

"Hi. So I've been immortalized in snow, eh?"

"Certainly have. 'Til it melts, anyway," Lynn chuckled. "Barry called this morning. He said Alan is satisfied with your progress."

"Yeah. I was real pleased to hear him say so. He's going to put on a different, heavy duty cast. Says I can't bear weight for another couple weeks, but I can plan to travel."

"What a relief!"

"Yep. I talked to Jack this morning. He's going to pick me up on Tuesday. We'll head to the farm. See how I travel. Spend Thanksgiving there. Wish you could join us."

"So do I. It would be fun."

"Another time. That's a four hour drive from here. Alan thinks I might find that to be enough for the first trip out. We'll see."

"It's a good start. I think he's right."

"Me too!" I agreed. "I will be bringing a surprise! Ixchel is coming along. She said you may need the help with me."

"Yes. We discussed it. I think she wants to see Martha and me as well. She says you are limited only by your sense of caution. Maybe that's why she decided to come along."

"Ha! No surprise there." I laughed. "I'm going to have to demand more of myself if that is how she thinks. She is whipping me into shape."

"Where is she? Isn't she listening?"

"Yes. As usual. And she knows we are talking about her. She's smiling like the Cheshire cat."

"Uh-oh! Better watch out! She'll be sending you through the looking glass!"

I shook my head. "I'm not worried. I spent enough time on the other side of the looking glass on the Knife. I know what's there."

"Here," she corrected.

"Here," I agreed. "Now."

# Book Seven

# Thanksgiving

# and the Ebb of New Light

*…Jump, dance, sing, so that you live happier. Heal yourself, with beautiful love, and always remember … you are the medicine.*
*— María Sabina*

# Chapter 71

# Thanksgiving with Family

When I was ready, complete with the double imprimatur of Drs. Reimer and North, Jack loaded me up in his Caddy and we headed north.

Barry and Alan saw me off on the morning of my departure. All smiles, they examined, for the last, time my incisions, and watched as Ixchel put me though some of the routine that helped me with stiffness and pain.

"Very impressive," Barry said as much to Ixchel as to me. "You've made remarkable progress. And your wound looks like it is completely free of infection."

Alan chuckled. "Due in great part to the care and interventions of your nurse." He turned to Ixchel and offered his hand. "A worthy job of care-taking, Ixchel. I've learned a lot. Thank you. You've done well for our patient."

Ixchel beamed, her eyes closing to happy slits, and bowed.

"You'll be off now." Alan said. "Take your time. Be diligent. You remain in healing mode."

They joined in detailing all the steps awaiting me on this healing journey. They had built a heavy duty walking cast on my leg, but I was not to bear weight for another two weeks. I was to carefully watch the health of my skin. I was to have the cast removed after another six weeks. I was to be very, very cautious about falling or stumbling and putting sudden force on my healing leg.

I nodded at everything they said, and when they finished, I tried to convey my thanks.

"Think nothing of it, Patrick," Barry said, shaking my hand firmly. "It is a privilege. I'm grateful Lynn thought to bring you to us." Alan concurred, and they both excused themselves to return to their work at the hospital.

∞

Ixchel bundled her basket and weathered travel satchel to join us for the trip to Ely.

"I'm going to see Martha and Lynn" she announced with certainty. "And to make sure you don't do anything foolish." She wagged her finger at me. "And I want to see Ingie."

Okay, by me, I thought. Both Lynn and Martha shared their enthusiasm for Ixchel's plans. I thought she might be sick of being just around me, having shared our one room existence for the most of a month.

Jack knew all about it, but hadn't said a word. He just shrugged. "I'm all for it. Ixchel knows a lot about where I'm heading. She knows lots that I need to understand."

So we piled into the Caddy and headed north to Baraboo. After sipping a cup of Ixchel's herbal tea, I snoozed most of the way. Jack shook my shoulder at a rest stop north of the state line.

"Want to stretch? Take a leak? We've stopped."

"Huh?"

"We are in Wisconsin. Welcome home!"

I woke up enough to follow his lead. We snacked on sandwiches Ixchel had packed and rolled on north after the rest stop. I didn't make it far before I fell back asleep, lulled by Jack's questions to Ixchel and her soft voice in reply.

I heard the tires slow and felt the turn off the exit. Another twenty minutes, and we turned into the driveway at the farm.

Rosie and Paddy were all smiles as they welcomed us home. Jack introduced Ixchel as they pulled us inside from the breezy November day. There was no snow yet on the ground, but the air held a biting chill. Paddy and Jack went out to the car to gather our travel bags, while Ixchel and I followed Rosie into the kitchen.

The house was warm and inviting. A fragrance of hickory nut cake hovered over the rich scent of roast beef that filled the air.

"You're moving well," Rosie commented as we hugged. It was good to feel her in my arms. "Healing well?"

"Seems to be so," I said, nodding toward our guest. "Thanks to Ixchel's help. She made sure I was doing all I should to get better."

I let Rosie slip from my hug and she turned to greet Ixchel. I was amused by how Rosie seemed to tower over my tiny nurse. The two dark skinned women exchanged gazes that instantly established a bond of respect and admiration. They were like family reuniting.

We ate dinner. We chatted afterward over coffee and the cake. We listened as Jack uncharacteristically dominated the conversation. Jack was always good at steering the discussion and leading topics of interest, but he did so artfully without imposing his thoughts on others. Now, however, his mix of enthusiasm and perhaps fear propelled him forward, repeating things I'd heard him discussing with Ixchel earlier regarding his upcoming work in Guatemala.

"You're going to Guatemala?" Paddy asked. "When?"

Jack's brow scrunched as he considered that detail. "Soon," he said. "After the New Year. I'm free, really, once the semester is done. And after I deliver Elle, Eva and her twins home." He beamed at that idea.

"This isn't a snap decision," Rose said. "You've been considering this for a while, it sounds like."

"He told us about it in Munich," I said. "Back then, it seemed like just a spur of the moment idea. Mom scolded him for even considering it. I think Jack's as good as on his way, after listening to him pump Ixchel for everything she knew while we were driving today."

"Jack has simply brushed the surface of the situation in Central America," Ixchel said calmly. "But he'll know more by the time he gets there."

"Which will be when?" Paddy asked again.

Jack looked at him curiously. "Are you asking a specific date? I haven't set an agenda yet."

Paddy chuckled. "Have you ever? No, I'm wondering." He glanced at Rosie, who totally registered this conversation. Paddy continued, "We are wondering , Rosie and I, whether you'll be staying with us for the holidays after you bring Elle home. Elle and Eva and her twins."

Rose nodded once and leveled a critical glance at Jack. He felt her gaze and startled.

"Bringing Elle home is the last official item on my calendar," Jack said. "After that, my plans are not firm about anything. I expect I'll know when to leave shortly after New Year. Is there something I'm missing?"

Rosie continued to look at him. Paddy fumbled and stuttered, but once he got going, he finally got to the point. "Well. Umm. We, Rosie and I, well, we want you to marry us. Will you do it over Christmas, once Elle is home?"

All of us burst into smiles and cries of joy.

"Uncle Paddy! And Rosie," I said, looking at her smiling, confident eyes. "Aunt Rosie! How wonderful."

Ixchel clasped her hands together, catching a bit of the joy spinning out from the rest of us. She glowed.

Jack beamed. He nodded enthusiastically. "Oh, this is perfect, Paddy. My prayers have been answered! Spectacular!" He reached down and wrapped his brawny arm around Rosie and lifted her in a warm hug. "This is wonderful, dear Rosie! I'm so happy for you both!"

He reached around Paddy's shoulders and pulled him into the hug. The three of them came out of it with joyful tears about their smiling eyes."

Jack found me in his laser vision. "Now I have you to focus on."

I shrugged, and we returned to celebrating. We had much for which to be thankful.

∞

We stayed through Thursday to give thanks with the Joyce family.

On Friday, Jack, Ixchel and I packed up and got the Caddy rolling north. I rode in joy, heading home to my Ely family.

# Chapter 72

# Twin Dreaming

J ack stayed in Ely no longer than to drop Ixchel and me at the resort, and rest for the night. He spent the evening, laughing and playing with the twins until they slept. Then we adults chatted until late. I don't think Jack had more than three hours sleep when he appeared in the lodge kitchen pleading for coffee and hustling about in preparation for his trip back to Milwaukee. He had classes to teach the following Monday. There was no doubt that he would have preferred staying with us in Ely. He bid us each goodbye, promising to keep in touch, and asked Ixchel when they might next get together. He was soaking up as much background about Guatemala from Ixchel as she could deliver.

"After the solstice," she replied. "We will meet again when the light grows longer. Maybe when the New Year sprouts."

With that assurance, he headed south to complete his final weeks as a college teacher.

I was spent after the travel and the night of discussions. Uncomfortable, feeling the pain, I slept off and on, listening to the sounds of my family living the day. That by itself was healing.

∞

By mid afternoon , I rebounded enough to pay better attention to my children. Two little people, our twins, watched me with renewed curiosity. Ally wondering what I needed, what she could do to make me comfortable, less thirsty, more whole. Omie, looking at me with his eyes wide, wondering endlessly about my plight in the boundary waters.

"You look different. Skinny."

"Yep. I've lost a bunch of weight."

"Hmm," he murmured. He climbed carefully on my lap, inspecting my face.

"You saw the wolf," he asked.

I nodded. "How did you know?"

He shrugged. "How do you know such things,?"

Ixchel, who sat quietly nearby, caught my eye with a twinkle of her own.

"One knows because one listens in quiet." She nodded toward my son.

Omie smiled shyly in return. Ixchel had quickly found her spot in his heart in the few hours we had been at home. She drew Ally like a magnet.

"If you don't hear anything, how can you listen?" Ally asked with a teasing smile.

Ixchel took Alph's hand and drew my older twin onto her lap.

"It is when you don't hear that you listen best."

"I heard the wolf." Omie said. "She called your name."

*How did he know the wolf was a she*, I wondered.

"When did you hear the wolf call my name?"

"When you were camping. In the night. When I slept, but was awake."

A shiver jolted through my core. I looked into his earnest eyes. He spoke truth. It was unreal to me. I felt it fill me from inside. I couldn't comprehend it.

"Ah, a dream listener!" Ixchel said. "Do you sometimes travel in your dreams?" she asked.

Omie pursed his lips and tilted his head.

"Nope. I'm just here."

Ixchel's watched him with fascination.

"Sometimes he travels when he sleeps, "Ally said. "He comes and visits me in my dreams. He wants to play. My brother is funny," Ally grinned.

Ixchel met her glance. "It is his prayer. He listens. He knows his place."

I was baffled. *How could my little son know his place? Did I know my own place in the mix of things?*

# Chapter 73

# Luther and His Daughter, Ingie

Winter was not a good time for Luther. He felt confined. When he could, he would meander about the resort grounds, but he seldom left the driveway or took the road up the Echo Trail. Confined to the lodge, he found comfort around his daughter Ingie. He stayed by her as if it was his duty to watch over her. They didn't chat much. When he did share his wayward thoughts with her, she responded kindly, simply. She put him at ease.

In the morning, with the wind blowing snow like darts parallel to the ground, Ixchel led me through a series of exercises as Ingie and her father sat nearby, watching like an audience. At a break from Ixchel's routine, Ingie gazed, amused at my effort to make simple movements with my healing leg.

"Gonna make it?" she asked.

I nodded. 'Think so." I looked at the massive plaster encasement around my healing leg. "A setback. But nothing to keep me out of the game, now that I'm living a non-contact lifestyle. I'll be fine. You?"

She held a smile short of a smirk.

"I got my will back. What else is there?" she asked.

I searched her face. She made light of her response, but it cut to the marrow at the same time. Her eyes beckoned that I take a step toward understanding the meaning of her words.

"What's with getting your will back? You leave it someplace?"

Her eyes flared and she lifted her eyebrows.

"Parked it. Left it behind. Didn't need it where I was." She leaned into her chair's padded arm. "I surrendered."

She drilled holes right to my soul with her brilliant blue eyes. She watched, waiting, inviting a worthy retort.

"Do you remember anything from the accident?" I unleashed a question I had considered many times. About the accident that took my cousin's life, and left Ingie crushed and damaged.

"Everything."

I felt my eyes widen.

"Really? Astounding! I'd have thought the opposite. You might have forgotten all the trauma."

"I've forgotten nothing about the accident. I saw it all. Felt it, every swerve of his car as he lost control and the impact of the wheels on the ditch and into the woods. The noise. The metallic roar as the car tumbled through saplings. His scream as gravity launched him from the car and threw him into the path of our tumble. The sudden thud as that damn Volkswagen came down hard on top of him. The silence that smothered all as the crash clinched into a tight, crumpled ball of broken metal. I remember it. All of it. I had never been more alive. The absurdity of hanging upside down, tethered by the belt I had clicked tight as I watched him lose all control. I put on that seat belt as he pumped the gas to the floor. Probably the first safe, sane thing I've done in my life.

"See? I must have wanted to live. Right?"

I shook my head. It was hard for me to grasp. How could she remember details of such a devastating crash?

"Were you in pain?"

"Not at first. I felt nothing at first. Nothing but awareness. I knew it had been an accident, but I hung there trying to figure out what had happened. And then I started to notice. My eyes covered with blood flowing from my head. I couldn't say anything there was so much blood in my mouth. My arms didn't respond to free me from that harness that trapped me upside down. I struggled to breath. It was as though my lungs were crushed by my insides.

"I called out for your cousin, but I knew. I saw it all happen so slowly, unfolding like a long, slow movie. I knew he was dead. I called for him, but it was really that I acknowledged him leaving."

She turned her head to face me. Her eyes were dry and fearless. I saw no pain. No regret.

She read my surprise and said, "It all just happened. And I was there to see it unfold. I recognized with awe what I had just lived through. And I felt a tug on my soul. I felt as if your cousin, in departing, was reaching back for me. Like he wanted to give me something, a glimpse of something he already knew. He wanted to help me get through the pain, to go with him to a place of no pain. Not to take me, but to let me go along. Not to harm me. But to keep me from pain. And when he was gone, I felt it like a hammer. And then, I remember nothing for a long, long time."

She snickered.

"It was a real mind-fucker."

Her joke cut the tension of her story and we laughed aloud.

"Don't let Teddy hear you say that!"

She shook it off. "Teddy asks that I focus, and use discretion in how I expend my energy. He says I need it to heal." She shrugged, and let a soft shadow pass across her face. Then she continued.

"So really, I didn't suffer much. I was absent from all my later pain and suffering," she said as she watched through the great room windows as Lynn lead the twins through the snow outside.

"I left all the suffering for my sister," she said, her eyes suddenly wet and shining. "I put it all on Lynn, just about the time everyone else dumped their loads on her back." She turned a knowing eye toward me. "Even you. Just like me, or Luther. Not a thought in our heads, we dumped our worst magic right on my sister's crystal pure heart."

She nodded. "She's done well with it, I'd say. Family. My mother's family. And now it's my turn to do well with it. Love. Family love. I owe it to her. And to Teddy. Those two have been my best friends all my life. I want to share what they have given me with them for a lot longer. So I found where I left my will and I'm training it to do what must be done. How's that for intent? I'm going to do right by them, so help me God."

She trained her steady blue eyes on mine once again.

Ixchel had quietly joined us. She listened as Ingie described her life. She stepped over to Ingie. She craned her neck forward and leveled her gaze at her. She shifter her scrutiny from Ingie's left eye, then her right, and back again.

A smile graced Ingie's face. Her eyes shone, reflecting Ixchel's inspection. Everything about her beamed.

Our tiny friend nodded and a smile spread across her wizened face.

"Everything," she replied. "It is all here to be."

Ingie chuckled. She reached out with a forefinger and tapped Ixchel on her nose. "You know, you'd be scary if you weren't so right."

Ixchel patted her hand. "There is nothing to fear, is there? Fear is something we need not will."

"Yes. Nothing to fear. Especially once you've lost it all."

They turned their gaze toward me. It was as through they were delivering a gift to me.

"What is 'it'?" I asked.

Ingie answered. "The baggage of life."

Ixchel nodded. "All of life's precious and ponderous nuances."

"I have lost my baggage," Luther chipped in, his face a mask of misty confusion, his eyes slits of fear.

It was as I expected. Their understanding of how to live without fretting the instant. *But,* I thought, *What's left? What else is there.?*

As if hearing my thought, Ingie trained her blazing, probing gaze at me.

"We shed the extra. We assume our essence now. That's all there is to magic."

# Chapter 74

# Patrick and Lynn

The short winter day slipped into evening's dark mantel as the kids settled and we turned our thoughts to personal reflections. The busy ones, Lynn and Martha, finished their kitchen work and the tasks of family care. On her way through the great room with an armload of folded laundry, Lynn flashed an inquisitive eye at me. What she was saw was a tired wimp on the verge of fatigue, feeling pain that rumbled in a rising crescendo..

"You're ready, eh?"

"Huh," I muttered. "For what?"

"Bed. You look weary."

Ixchel, who was buried beneath a blanket of twins, piped up. "Want me to get him going?"

Lynn beamed. The kids looked at her with prohibitive glares. They snuggled in closer to the person who was not much bigger than either of them. All that was to be seen were three little heads hiding behind a book cover.

"You are in demand, my dear."

Ixchel beamed back.

"We are comfy."

Lynn shifted her gaze to me. "I'll be back in a moment."

∞

Martha cared for Ingie. Luther idled about with the two women, humming and uttering undirected questions and observations.

Ixchel kept the kids mesmerized.

Lynn came back and turned her attention to me. We were to have time together. Alone. Seldom did we have time alone. We slid seamlessly into the dimension of our own.

She helped me undress and she washed my back and arms, my neck and chest with hot wash clothes. She cleansed my legs, washing carefully above the casting protecting the healing breaks. I propped myself up with both hands on the sink.

"You smell like a patient."

"You scour like a nurse."

She nodded. "As it should be."

She rinsed the wash cloths and turned to my privates. With her, my privates were not just for me, but unexpectedly, her thorough attention prompted my arousal. Taking me quickly to a point of no return, she made me come.

I gasped. I felt my eyes role in my head. I braced myself on the porcelain sink. She beamed like she'd just scored a touchdown.

"What was that?" I uttered.

"We'll talk. And we don't need any testosterone driven distractions and nonsense. Okay?"

I shook my head.

"Yeah." I said, catching my breath. "Wonderful."

∞

We talked for hours.

My weariness dissipated like lake mist rising in morning sunlight.

She asked about my canoe journey.

I told her the details. The wolves singing in the night. Meeting them on the portage. The calm of Eddy. My restlessness to move on. The windy trip to the island in Knife. And all the details of my days there. The wind. The lost canoe. The eagles fishing and the loons fleeing from the oncoming winter. The deer on the ridge to the north of the lake, and the pursuit of the pack. The carnage. Pilfering the carcass of the dead doe. The welcome taste of the venison. The wolf visitor to my island campsite. Teddy's arrival.

We shared all that we'd held back since Teddy brought me back, broken and lost, nearly two months prior. It was our first chance to live through with one another all we had been through alone.

She listened, stroking my neck and cheeks with her fingers as she asked questions leading up to my accident with the canoe. It was like she was taking measure of the forces that led to that moment. I told her all I remembered. It was really quite simple. I rocked a heavy, water filled canoe onto my leg and smashed my bones.

And I survived.

That was the first thing she noted.

"You made it through all of that," she swept her fingers over my eyes and down my face. "You are a survivor."

I felt my lips purse. I tasted the bitter flavor of having fallen short of my expectations. She read my face and knew my mind.

"I'm grateful you survived."

I nodded. "I live for you. You mean the world to me."

She smiled. "It was close, though. Frighteningly close."

"But I made it. Thanks to Teddy," I said. "And his leeches."

We chuckled.

# Chapter 75

# Shaman

"Teddy's a healer. He learned so much traditional medicine from his grandfather. I knew Samuli. He was a small man, dark and quiet, and always kind," Lynn said. "A *tietaja*, Finnish shaman, you know. Even as a child, I could see his deep, personal spirituality. Everything he did had meaning. Teddy loved him.

"He got his size from his grandmother," Lynn added. "Elin. She was a giant of a woman. Teddy tells me she was a *trollkjerringer* with her own powers. Her gift was to bring humor. Always jolly. She died when I was a kid. But I remember her well. But Teddy is more like his grandfather Samuli. Quiet. Powerful, but subtle. But his grandmother's joy of humor is deeply embedded in our friend. We have much to be grateful to Teddy for in our lives. Not only for saving you. I think he's saving Ingie as well."

Lynn and I sat in silence for moments. Then, she reflected her understanding of Teddy.

"I see Teddy's love for us. He protects us. He heals us as a family. He watches out for us. Always has, even as a young person. I used to wonder if it was just because of the bond he and Ingie had, even as children. He adored Ingie. It troubled him as Ingie got older, in her teens, when she became so wild. Now, his purpose is focused foremost on her. When he went out after you, she missed him terribly. She seemed to know he had purpose in being away, yet it worried her."

∞

Our thoughts swept us into a moment of quiet. My head resting on her shoulder, I listened to her heart steadily, quickly pumping life throughout her strong, wiry body.

"I saw that you had fallen. Hurt. I knew you were being challenged."

I looked at her, puzzled.

"I see," she said. "Not the details. Not like I am watching a movie, or seeing what is there from a distance." She tucked her shoulder under my arm and lay her head on my chest. "Nothing like watching replays of your football injury."

"What do you mean?"

She tipped her head back, looking.

"Now, I see forces. Energy. Auras. I see the power of forces flow. Sometimes, forces meet and play havoc on the web of matter that we see in the time we travel." Lynn's hand scooped up space; her fingers waggled, forming space with the kneading of her fingertips. She held the shape of an invisible globe she'd formed and turned upon her palm before me.

"Yours was not the only force with you on your island in Knife." She turned her eyes from mine and looked into the swirling space cupped by her fingers.

∞

I was drawn into the laden space above Lynn's palm. I saw my brother; he looked as through he was watching for me. His brow furrowed, worried, concerned. He gestured as though to warn, alert me. And then the image evaporated, its colors reshaping to form a familiar scene.

A wolf sat upon an outbreak of ledgerock, watching silver moonlight glistening on the ice blanketing the surface of a lake. I saw the wolf from behind as it sat like a sentinel. It's gaze captured all under the sky. It watched as a form hovered above the lake. A woman knelt, her back bent forward, her arms grounding her in her space. Her head tucked down between her forearms.

The wolf's ears twitched to listen, but the sound was silent and tension released from the she wolf's head and ears. She watched.

The woman prayed like a child. She lifted her head and hands; her arms turned dark and fluttered like feathers. Her head swooped black and her eyes were like beads. She flew into the sky above the lake, landing at the waters edge below the promontory where the she-wolf joined her.

∞

Lynn swirled her hand; her fingers slowly curled up around the image.

I held her tucked against me. I could feel my heart beat through my chest up into her ear. Her lips formed a smile. Her eyes turned toward my face.

"You knew? I don't see how."

"It is not yours to see."

Not mine to see, I considered.

"What is mine, if not to see?"

She whispered into my chest, toward my heart, into my inner being.

"To be you. To feel. To be true to your feelings."

Our silence blanketed us, keeping us warm like woolen wraps in winter.

I listened to our breaths. I asked, "Isn't that what I've been trying to be, always, all this time? Me?"

I heard her voice vibrate through my ribs.

"Sometimes it is easier to not try."

The thought snagged my focus.

I turned away from how I felt.

∞

I thought of Lynn lying beside me.

She wore an impish smile. Her eyes twinkled, and she whispered so explicitly that I heard every word.

"How can you be you?" I asked.

"How can I not?"

"No," I laughed. "I mean, how can you be so intense, yet be calm. You never seem to get tired. Look at today. Look at every day. You go go go. But you never tire. Not like I get weary and tired. You're working all the time, and you never seem tired."

"I'm healing, like you. Somewhat like you, but not so much physically. And my healing is here," she touched above her heart, ' and is long in progress. I've been getting stronger all this time we have been apart. I shed those burdens that I need not carry. However I must be careful with the energy, the grace, which comes to me. I choose my struggles, avoiding the battles that would exhaust me to no meaningful end.

She sighed. "Oh, I get tired. I'm ready for the end of each day. I fall into sleep in a breath, and I sleep until my mind is clear, and I wake and I live the day."

The tips of her lips turned up and her eyes shone.

"And I don't even try."

Again, I laughed.

"What are you, anyway?"

Her eyes turned down.

"I'm me. I'm a woman. A mother." Lynn looked up into my face, searching my eyes. "I see. I see forces and I shape them. Train them. Use them. Harness them. The shapes that move through all that is are there to feed upon. To fuel my soul. I am given enough to meet my challenges, and no more. I can not afford to use my energy in anger or in wanton thought. It's something my mother shared with me. Her life was short, and she showed me how important it is to accept grace from all that is, and to honor that grace. Forces give me energy to see through the day and find an ending to the day that brings well being to my family."

She tweaked my nose. "That means you."

She sat up on the bed. She tucked her feet and perched upon her crossed legs, her knees just touching my side.

"I am a survivor. I heal, but I'm not a healer. Even though I am a nurse, I am not a healer. Not like Ixchel is a healer. Healing is just one of Ixchel's powers. One she has honed keenly.

"I am a lover. I love with my whole heart. But I am not a peace bearer. Martha bears peace. She holds ample peace within her heart that we may all find peace when it escapes us even for a moment. Martha gives us peace."

I examined her face. She looked innocent, but as bold as a wolf. I saw our son in her expressions.

"When I was on the island and the wolf sat nearby, I thought she was you." My confession sounded naive, childish. "I felt peace from her. She leveled her eyes at me, and I felt so relaxed. So peaceful."

She gave a quick shake of her head.

"Oh. I was delirious. That makes more sense."

"No. She let you see her. But that was not me. It was no one, but a wolf."

"But how...."

She tilted her head, looking straight into my eyes.

"Omie."

"Huh? Om??"

She nodded.

"I am a mother and a lover. I see, but I am merely learning to see what the powers of my vision means. My powers are to see what is and accept it as is. I shed my burdens to conjure from the essence and see more clearly. But Omie hears and he travels and sees and learns more quickly than I can imagine. He is innocent."

She looked at me and waited.

"I don't understand, Omie? How?"

"I don't know how. I just know he can. Omie sent the wolf to help you find hope."

After a moment, she added, 'I think he learns from Teddy. Teddy guides him. Teddy is a guide. He is also a healer."

She shifted, then moved to my arms. We sat, listening to our breaths for a long while.

∞

A thought tweaked my imagination.

"So, what's Ingie's to do? Her role?"

"It's neither a job nor a role. It is a state of being, that's all. Ingie is broken, of course. She needs all of her powers, her reserves, to heal. But the Ingie you knew, who you met in the Dunes, is a knower. She knows time and the present. She comprehends why now is the way it is based on its past. She knows how the universe functions and flows. She was so wild because she felt so confined that she rebelled against the forces that held her so. She understands the absurd.

"But then she got hurt. And she survived. And in an ironic sort of way, her accident was a blessing. It contained her, slowed her down. And she knows that she must exert all her powers to heal. She knows the saving grace of Teddy. She will heal. She is healing all the time. Her time is just slowed."

"Hmmm." I noted. I thought of the words of Derek, her physical therapist. Ingie is strong of spirit, he had said. But fragile. So very fragile that her battered body could turn on her with the slightest of infections or illnesses. Strong, but weak, I pondered.

∞

Lynn's quiet invited my next questions.

"How about Jack?"

"Father Jack?" She chuckled. "He's a priest. A shepherd of souls. Tough lot. Kind of like a shaman, but fettered by all the ritual and tradition religious priesthood tags on to the powers of shamanism. Restricted by regimentation of thought. Jesus, he's a Jesuit! He's feeling it, too. Kind of like Ingie was. He's set for a rebellion. He's taking himself to it. A dangerous up-taking, for one who is a seeker, and Jack seeks. He's questioning all he accepted as dogma, or should have accepted. Jack's gift is that he thinks about it. About things. And how the things of faith and dogma can be. How he can find truth in those things, and the things beyond."

"Crazy," I joked.

She nodded against my chest. "Crazy."

"Hmmm." I reflected. Then I asked, "How about my mom."

"Elle's gift is that she is of no religion. One who rebelled so thoroughly that she freed herself from the shackles of the regimented, the dogmatic. It was hard for her, and it took her to her insanity. But she survived. She has powers now, but those graces are select and limited. Now she is a minor shaman of her own order who gives thanksgiving."

I looked to Lynn to see if there was any humor intended in her appraisal of my mother. She was earnest.

"Eva?"

"She's a goddess who wields her powers impeccably. I love her like a sister."

I nodded.

"Ally?"

"A witness."

"A witness! What is she supposed to witness?"

"That which we all conjure in our moment of time."

"Come on! What are you saying?"

"That is a common gift that we all share to some degree. Ally is just stronger in that mode than most."

We thought on that for a moment, then she added, "You can learn from Ally, really. Father/daughter. She's a lot like you. She has a child's innocence, so you can see her witness clearly and candidly.

She raised her eyebrows.

"She doesn't have the layers of earth time growth that you have. She doesn't carry much around, so it is easy for her to witness clearly. She's young. She's never been wounded. Just loved."

"Hmmm," I grunted again. I wondered how wounded I was? Wounded, yes, from my canoeing accident. And on the gridiron at Boulder. And the loses of those who I loved. My mind flashed to a moment in the barn at home in North Freedom, when the world of my family disintegrated before my eyes. I could feel the anger that rose in my chest, and David's image appeared again before me. I remember not being able to bring words to my lips. And just surrendering to an impulsive hug of my brother. I forgave him then. And I forgave him for leaving me in Nam. And on Knife. I forgave him, because I love my brother and all the gifts he gave me.

I glanced up from my introspective thoughts. Lynn watched me rise from within. She understood.

"The forgiver," I muttered.

Lynn nodded. She was looking at my forehead, inside me.

"The great forgiver. You must turn your powers loose."

∞

We slept, awakened gently in the morning by a pair of dark, probing eyes at our beside. Omie. Such was our life in Ely

# Chapter 76

# Ely Rehab

It was another day.

For me, the rehab got intense. The cast I had lugged since leaving Chicago was gone. We had cut it off per Alan's instructions. Yoga was no more the stand alone standard for exercise. Instead, Derek took me on as a special project when he came for Ingie's scheduled appointment. He showed me some ankle and leg movements designed to extend the progress I'd made under Ixchel's disciplined therapy.

"You're on the right track," Derek encouraged, once I traded my heavy walking cast for a removable brace. "And you'll do well to hop into Ingie's pool as often as you can. It's working marvels for her, so you'd do well to follow her example."

So I did, although Ingie made as to be a bit put off at sharing her special pool with me. I clearly imposed on the time she spent with Teddy, who regularly attended to her when she undertook her daily hydrotherapy. Within a couple days, however, she found the hydrotherapy time I shared with her in the warm waters of the pool to be more of a party than a therapy session.

"Isn't this wonderful," she said a week into our workouts. "Now I have both Teddy and you to help me walk again."

Her assessment of her progress was a bit overstated. While she had gained both strength and flexibility since Teddy put her to the task once the pool was completed in September, she had miles to go. She could now stand for moments with the aid of a walker, but she had yet to take more than a couple steps at a time while supporting all her weight without the buoyancy of her pool. Her workouts demanded that Teddy or Lynn be present. I could help her with balance while I worked together with her in the current of the pool, but she'd be in peril, I thought, if I had to help her with my leg so weak. Our workouts tended to be a group affair, with either Teddy or Lynn standing immediately ahead of her, supporting her balance and strength, and me following behind in our march in place water trek.

We spent more time together healing in the great room of the lodge, a fire burning in the massive stone fireplace, the kids playing, drawing, or simply passing time nearby. Luther was present, at least in body. He was drawn to our company. I expect that he was drawn more to the presence of his daughter. Ingie and Luther remained remarkably close in spite of his waning moments of clarity. The same was true with Luther and Ally. She was on his lap reading the simple tales told with pictures in the hard page children books that they shared routinely.

I asked Ingie one day how she had come to speak with almost complete absence of the profanity that had laced her vernacular so heavily before we left for Munich. She astonished me by reverting to a prime vulgar adjective when relating the influence Teddy imposed on her.

"Teddy," she said, a sly grin spreading across her face. "Ask that loving prick about it."

Which I did the next time we were in the warm waters of the treading pool.

"Whaddya' do to get Ingie to talk without her sailor's speak?"

Teddy glanced at me, then hoisted Ingie up by the webbed belt she wore during her hydrotherapy that helped us keep her upright. With a satisfied smile, he explained that he would not subject himself to her foul mouth if he was to regularly work with her for her benefit.

"I'd had my fill of foul mouth. So I gave her a little baptism of sorts."

Ingie screamed and splashed him with a swipe of her hand across the top of the pool. "Baptism! You tried to drown me!"

Teddy's smile fleshed out to full bore grin.

"Washing the dark spirits out is all."

"Yeah, well, I was reborn about twenty times with your zealous baptisms!"

He smiled from his eyes.

"Slow learner."

Ingie fumed. She muttered and moaned. Her words were garbled, but I heard no swearing, cursing, profanity or other foul mouth harangue.

"Show him," she demanded.

He took her in his giant hands and gently lay her down beneath the surface. Her arms and legs floated, unrestrained and relaxed. Bubbles surfaced from the breath she vented.

She watched him calmly from beneath the water. She surrendered to her trust in him, hovering in his grasp.

"She asked for help with this," Teddy told me, his eyes locked on Ingie beneath the surface. "She is ready to heal from within."

Then he lifted her from the water like a baby from her bath.

Ingie wrapping her arms around Teddy's neck. She clung to him.

"Oh, you!' she cried. "You, you, you!"

We laughed. We cried. We shared her therapy pool as we healed.

But I felt, at this moment, that perhaps I was the extra in this equation. At least this time. I mumbled something about having had enough and climbed out the ramp to the deck. I grabbed my robe and towel and headed back to the lodge.

Later, Teddy found me reading in the great room.

"You didn't need to leave," he said.

"Oh?"

"Really. You didn't."

"I wanted to." I left it at that. But then I asked him again, how had he managed to clean up her language.

He looked into his hands, turning his palms up, then down.

"It wasn't me. I meant what I said, though. I didn't want to hear her talking that way," he leveled his gaze toward me. "I know her. Always have, since she was a baby and I was just a kid. I know her heart. I know the pain she came back with. I just wanted to help her find a way to shed all that pain from her heart."

He looked again into his hands. "And, she asked. She wanted help. She asked me to heal her. I told her I couldn't. Healing was for her and God to work out. But she cried. She begged me to do something that would help. So I dunked her. Truly, a baptism. It worked. She accepted it. She started to listen. With her heart. We've made progress, eh?"

I nodded. And grinned. "I see. Yeah. You have."

∞

He didn't have to dunk me to help my progress. He worked with me, and added the techniques that Derek shared during his appointments with Ingie. I needed no walker or crutches, but kept a cane close at hand while I continued my rehab.

Ixchel worked with Teddy to restore circulation and repair innervation to my leg and ankle. She applied a bit of acupuncture to my legs, spine, neck and shoulders. But she used her fingers more effectively on muscle bundles and tendon connections during massage sessions. Often, Teddy worked with her. He might ply his gentle touch with his big strong fingers on muscles in my calves or feet while she tended sites in my neck and shoulders. Often, she'd waft smoke from bundles of sage leaves or dried cedar fronds about as she applied her skills to my healing body. They worked with Ingie, as well.

And, interestingly, Ixchel found ways to reach Omie. Often, as we sat in the great room after our therapy sessions, Omie would make his way to her lap where he drew shapes and scenes on his blackboard. She listened to him say what he meant with his shapes. They spoke so quietly I rarely could hear their conversations.

∞

"She's amazing, don't you think?" Lynn asked, although she knew my response.

I nodded. "Unbelievable. Did you see her take Omie's chalkboard and draw her design today?"

Lynn hadn't. She'd been in and out of the great room while the two shared their art with chalk, but was taken up with the business of the day and hadn't homed in our her friend and her son.

I related the scene. Omie had offered his cleaned board to her after she had interpreted a drawing he had made of a wolf watching the stars cross the winter night sky. She worked the chalk in patterns of lines and shapes, drawing what from a distance looked like a maze with a heart in the center.

Omie watched as the picture unfolded. She offered him the board when she completed her art. He studied the lines. He tipped the board over and looked at it upside down, and from the sides. When he had thoroughly viewed her work, he set the board aside and wrapped his little arms around the tiny woman's neck. He set his ear to her chest.

"I hear your heart," he said.

She smiled.

Lynn, too, smiled at the anecdote. "She has great reach." She said.

I nodded.

"We have her to thank, you know. Both of us." Lynn said, dimming the bedside lamp. "Ixchel heard my heart, too. Twice, really. She listened. She heard my heart when I tried most to not hear. I was trying to still my heart, I hurt so badly."

I peered deep into her eyes, listening. She went on.

"The first time, she reached me during our travel. Ingie and me. When I met Ixchel. She has this way of hearing without listening. Seeing without looking. She saw me for what I was. She heard me with my troubled heart, trying to forget you. To get you out of my life."

She leaned up on her elbow and set her hand on my chest. "I was trying to survive you by being away from you. Being over you." She smiled. "Ixchel showed me how my intent was all folly. I am meant for you."

I listened. Lynn had me in her spell and I let her take me.

"When was the other time? The second time she 'heard your heart'."

Lynn looked into her hands. Then to me.

"Here. In our home. When we first moved back to Ely. I will always be grateful. She came and found me. I was in despair. She heard my heart, and showed me how to heal myself. From within."

# Chapter 77

# On the Ebb of Light

December skies opened in a crystal brilliant blue on the morning of the solstice. I bundled up after breakfast and limped my way through the snow to help drag firewood to the pile we stacked for the evening's bonfire. The twins and the women of the house had chatted enthusiastically about solstice fire almost the entire month since I returned home. It was tradition. It spearheaded winter festivities here at Lynn's North Star Resort.

Martha's tale of the tradition started years back with Lynn's mother after Martha was widowed. The young, independent women marked the solstices together each December and June for more than 30 years.

"Are your nephews going to be here for the bonfire?" I had asked Martha as we bundled up to gather wood and prepare for the evening's folly.

A shadow of regret passed over Martha's face.

"I don't know. Sometimes I think the boys can't bring themselves to participate in our doings," she said. "I may spook them off, I suppose. And they can't plan for hoot. But we can hope. They are, if anything, unpredictable."

"Oh," I said. "Well, I thought it'd be fun if they're here. They could detonate the fire." I pulled on my coat and headed out to help the twins, snickering at the memory of Gully's tiddlywinks greenstone flipping over the roof of the sauna and landing in Jack's Caddy.

We had a good wood pile stacked before lunch. I moved, slowly. I knew I had enough strength to lug myself around the yard today, but for how long? I didn't know. I'd be testing endurance. This was my first real challenge without naps after therapy. I was going to move wood. In the snow. Hunting with David was probably the last time I'd worked or played in snow.

Ixchel had knitted thick warm stockings, large and bulky, to keep my feet and legs warm in the evenings. They worked well for outside walks when I strapped on a furry deer hide chap that Teddy fashioned to fit over boots. It kept me warm and dry. But it was heavy, and the snow was pretty deep, up to my shin. I worked to stay on paths others packed down, but sometimes I found myself wallowing in the deep white blanket that covered the ground. Yes, I'd healed well over the past six weeks, but I recognized my limits. I did what I could.

The twins were my partners for dragging slash and branches to the wood pile on the snow covered beach. They broke paths to the stashes of cut and windfall limbs that we had pruned during the summer months and stored in convenient piles away from the beach and cabins along the shoreline. It was a workout for their little legs and my gimpy leg.

"Here, Patrick," Ally offered me the end of a limb of cedar protruding from a pile of snow. She pulled for all she was worth, and wiry as she was, she was little more than 40 pounds. The snow laden limb was probably 60 pounds. The snow pile may have been a three foot drift.

"Can you reach?" She called as she tugged.

Omie stood on the beaten path, assessing the problem.

"We need a sled dog," he ventured. "We could hitch it to that branch. That would work."

"We don't have a sled dog," Ally said

"We should."

I chuckled. "One sled dog, Omie? You couldn't pull a sled with just one dog, could you?"

"Aren't pulling a sled."

"We could get a sled!" Ally cried. "Then we could get lots of dogs!"

My chuckle swelled to a guffaw. "That's what we need, Ally. A herd of dogs!"

"Pack," Omie stipulated.

"We have no dogs at all, so help me with this firewood," Ally demanded.

I moved to help. I took one step in the soft snow toward her and was suddenly in a drift over the knee of my good leg. My weaker leg kind of floated on the snow. I looked to my son, who was now at eye level with me.

"Now you're sunk."

Ally left her firewood go and offered me a pull. It was useless. As hard as she yanked, I was stuck. Omie came to help, getting behind me and pushing. Still, useless.

"You're a lug," he said.

"Let me try something else," I said. I sat on our path and rolled over onto my back.

Like puppies, the twins were on me. Omie climbed on my belly, standing with both feet and jumping carefully up and down. His care, I thought, was more for the benefit of not falling off the pinnacle he'd claimed than any concern for me.

Ally, on the other hand, perched firmly on my chest, a leg straddling each side of my head, vigorously washing my face with a handful of snow.

"He's not going to like that," Omie said.

"You bet I'm not," I laughed, rolling again, dumping them both off the path into the deep snow. They squealed, whipping around and climbing back on before I could gain footing. I grabbed them both around the waist and tossed them back onto the snow. I had them down, threatening face washings in retribution. Their squeals turned to shrieks.

"No, Daddy, no!" Omie protested.

"I'll get you," Ally fought back, reaching for handfuls of snow to smear on my face.

I growled like a bear, laughing and wrestling with all my might when I noticed a pair of black boots before my face on the path. I craned my neck to look up. Teddy. Grinning from ear to ear, he shook his head. He stepped with one foot carefully but fully on to my back, pushing me face down into the snow.

"You bully my friends, do you?" He laughed.

The twins screamed their gratitude and were back on me in a flash, both of them dancing on my back.

"Uncle!" I cried, but it did no good. I sagged, gave up, let them wash my face with their chorus of laugh and taunting.

When he decided they'd had enough, Teddy grabbed the twins by the back of their jackets, one in each hand, and held them aloft, their boots kicking, their arms pumping air. He pulled their faces close to his and placated them softly.

"Think he's had enough? You might want to save a bit to give to him later." He held them down so they could see me, helpless in the snow. The three of them beamed.

"Rise, Wimp!" Teddy's deep voice boomed above me. "Your redemption is granted. You are called in by the wise one. It is time."

He set the kids down and they all helped lift me out of the snow and on to the path.

"Ixchel waits. I'll be right up," he said. "Come on, kids. I'll help you with this limb." He tugged at Ally's cedar branch and it slid, begrudgingly, from under the snow cover. "Then you can help your mom tramp the circle around the fire ring."

Off they went, lugging the kindling. I trudged my way to the lodge. I knew what awaited me.

# Chapter 78

# Healing Therapy

What awaited me was Ixchel. She proved in her weeks with us that she was forceful. A tyrant, I believe, is what I had called her in my reports to Lynn after one of our sessions. Her discipline hadn't surprised me. Just like in Chicago, but more.

Our sessions included yoga, calisthenics, and stretches that I believe she inserted into the day's itinerary to address what she observed in my gait or posture. She directed me to move this way, then that, sticking her finger, sometimes with force, always with precision, finding knotted muscles, calcified tendon bundles, and stiff scar tissue. She probed around the atrophied muscles on my injured leg; she paid attention to knots in other parts of my body where she gauged tightness or swelling. My shoulders. My neck. My other leg. Never content, she demanded I do each exercise or pose to the fullest, adjusting for flaws or shortcomings, taking me to the limits, and beyond, of endurance. Always adjusting.

She planted her finger deep into muscles running from my shoulder down along my triceps. How she found key pressure points, I don't know, but it was like her fingers had sensors and just by kneading and probing, she could free passage of energy through those blockages.

Teddy had watched a couple of our sessions the first week I returned. Thereafter, he made himself present most times Ixchel worked her muscle-bending magic on me. He joined in. In one particularly vigorous session, the two of them worked over the back of my right shoulder.

"Are you doing that for my benefit," I complained as Ixchel probed deep into my torso next to my shoulder blade, "or are you teaching Teddy."

"Both," she said. "Efficiency of effort." That was all the more explanation she offered.

Teddy chuckled, then stuck his much bigger finger into the dent that Ixchel tapped, homing him in on the target. I roared as he pulverized the bundle of my muscle.

"First, we care for those scars from all the nonsense of your past. Now, we do yoga." She said, making me stretch out the pulverized muscle groups she had just worked over. Yoga I liked. It was gentle. Usually.

This morning, on the solstice, for whatever reason she saw fit, Ixchel's routine proved extreme. She teamed with Teddy to make it so. Even Ingie critiqued my posture to the extreme as I walked into the porch.

"You walk funny," Ingie sniped.

"I just got a cast off my leg. I'm not done healing."

"You walked funny before you ever took your canoe trip."

I gazed into her stubborn expression. I was stunned. "What do you mean?"

"Stiff. Like Ed Sullivan."

"Hmmm," I grunted.

"We will see," Ixchel said. She sat on the lounge where she worked the cords of muscle along the spine from my waist up to my skull. At sites particularly sore, she set a finger and rubbed deeper until she felt the knot subside. She found another hard knot between my shoulder blades and indicated to Teddy that he should work that trigger point while she moved higher along my spine.

Teddy melted the knot with his thumbs.

"Jeeze!" I cried. His touch was not brute strength. It was measured. He addressed a bundle of muscle, sinew and nerves. He prodded forcefully at a small area as though squeezing juice from a grape.

It may have seemed sharp at the point of his finger, but he didn't let up. Instead, he shifted the angle of his probe, moving the lumpy knot against the vertebrae in my neck, rolling it, reducing the muscle lump to pulp. Sometimes, his finger tips seemed to separate sticky soft tissue anchoring on rough boney spurs.

With his other hand, he reached down and found a point on the front of my leg, directly between the scars that ran in parallel down the sides of my legs to the bony knobs of my ankle. He traced a line along my shin up to my knee, then further along my femur. When he reached the top of my thigh, he angled the route of his finger around the side of my leg, to a point in the very small of my back where he found a knot alongside my spine. He held pressure above while working the spot in my lower back.

Ixchel, at the same time, slid her little finger gently into a spot near the base of my skull. It felt as though her finger reached up into my spine, prying apart the vertebrae.

I heard a 'pop,' and I barked like a hound. A flash of white occluded my sight. It was like looking into a flash bulb.

In synchrony, they both slowly released the pressure points they held on me. The tightness in my shoulder and neck softened; the spasm that held the knots in place was gone.

I felt weakened, but totally relaxed.

Ixchel peered into my eyes and nodded. Teddy took a look and grinned.

"It is not just what you put into your work. Your efforts," she said "It is also what you hold back. What you conceal. There is always more. You have to account for all. Be meticulously responsible for all.

"Reach down. Bring to your memory that which your Grandfathers and Grandmothers knew in their time of being. Invite that which is braided into your essence to come forth and be part of your healing now."

She stood me up and brought me into yoga. Full fledged yoga, not just yo. She talked me gently into mountain. Then, my modified tree.

Munich flashed in my recollection. I thought of Mom. Of what she knew, and how she came about her awareness of now. I stretched my arms higher, and spread my chest open. I imagined my healing leg folded up, the flat of my foot planted on my thigh.

In my mind, Mom's smile beamed love. And now, she was nearing home. She was bringing Eva home. Eva and her babies.

Ixchel led me into child's pose on the padded mattress of my bed. And then to total recline.

"You will sleep now," Ixchel said. "You will be ready for our Solstice dance tonight,

She was right. I could not keep my eyes open. I fell into a deep, restful slumber. The last thing I remembered was the feeling of a quilt being spread over me. I didn't even know who placed it there. I knew I was home.

∞

I slept for three hours and awoke to the aroma of warm rich soup and Lynn's touch.

"Hi, sleepyhead." Her voice was quiet and assuring. She called me gently from my dreams. I felt her fingers slide across the skin above my eyelids. I realized I was dreaming. I was in the midst of a dream that had started before, in another sleep. Lynn was there. On her throne, she wielding a scepter of lavender blossoms. I rose through the visual images of my dream quickly, seeing Lynn, robed in pelts, bobbing a blade of wood embedded with a ruby oval orb alongside my ears. I heard her voice, calling, calling calling...

"Wake up, sleeping beauty. It's time for the birth of a new day. A time to feed our needs. And then, we'll have the bonfire and song and dance!" Her voice rippled with excitement.

I woke. Her eyes smiled into mine as she waved a wand of dried lavender above my face. The dried fragrance wafted from the crisp purple petals. She took me by the hand and helped me from my bed.

I followed her through the lodge. I was struck with how comfortable I felt. I felt no pain.

# Chapter 79

# Lynn North

# North Star Solstice

We nurtured the flames with tinder and care. Tongues of golden heat lapped at the sky. Our bonfire was majestic; we fed the blaze aggressively. It forged the shape of a great lion's head, the flames like a mane, flickering and full about the face of the blazing feline. It reminded me of Jack. I sent Jack thoughts from my heart, wishing that he could have been with us.

We circled it, Patrick, next to me, then Omie, followed by Teddy, who carried Ingie, their arms wrapped about one another, then Luther, the Bass brothers, one with Martha, the other with Ixchel, and finally Ally, whose little hand reached warm and tender to my own. We formed a ring. We clasped hands, with our arms spread outstretched around the fire. Family. Family and fire. Warm, blazing. The tongues flashed and flourished. We reached out, stretching the circumference we held around the flaming lion until it's heat pushed us back, radiating upon the skin of our faces, flashes sparkling off the gleaming surface of our eyes.

We hummed. We sang. Our tone was primal, kind in harmony, and creative. The blend of our individual voices formed a resonance that softened the crackle of the flames. As a flash of a brilliant spire of fire burst into the dark above, Teddy invoked a guttural cry; we broke our chain of hands, turning to our right, moving about the flame in short, shuffled uneven steps. Our arms extended, we dipped and raised our hands, our fingers fluttering as we teetered around the blaze. We danced, but for Teddy, who held Ingie in one arm a step away from our path, batting rhythm on the stretched face of deer hide drawn across his drum of cedar. Luther, then Patrick, set our pace. With a high, waning cry from deep within Teddy's chest, we stopped our march and turned again to face the flames of the lion.

It had tamed. The tongues of fire climbed not as high, but the core of embers burned hot and nearly white.

Teddy took Ingie to her lounge and wrapped her in layers of wool blankets and set her on skins of deer fur and covered her under a blanket of beaver. He took up his warp and tapped it with the heel of his hand in a rhythm that set our feet to moving again. He maintained a pace that tested our endurance, and soon Luther withdrew into a recliner, then, Patrick took a chair, with Omie settling on his lap.

We danced about the fire equally far apart our faces flashing with the golden and red hues of fire.

Teddy took up his drum, jingling metal jangles, waving the frame so that it's bangles and feathers floated among the rays cast by the fire. His pace picked up and sent us faster about the fire.

We danced on.

Ally moved before me, her feet light, wrapped in mukluks laced to her knees, lifting off the snowpack like flakes flaunting their freedom in a breeze, skipping in joyful leaps. Her fingers fluttered on hands that winged like doves in flight. I watched her head lean back on her thin, fragile neck, looking above, deep into the stars, her eyes dark and fathomless. My eyes turned upward, searching the heavens, seeking Ally's vision.

Ahead of her, Martha swayed gracefully, measured, her steps soft, her arms moving like the wings of a crane; slowly, evenly and balanced. She tipped her head right, then left, gazing into the deep glowing embers. Her nephews followed, moving low, as if they held high the train of their Aunt's veil.

Ixchel kept her pace between the Bass brothers and me. We shamanka, the women, spaced ourselves equidistant about the fire, dancing and singing, humming, chanting. Teddy kept the pace, sometimes hurried, sometimes slow, on his deer skin drum.

I saw as my eyes swept down to our fire, and Patrick stood, retrieved wood from a pile nearby, and placed a heavy branch upon the fire. And then another. And a third. With the bulky fur wrappings about his legs, he moved with a rhythmic shuffle; his pace slow as he picked his way between Ally and me to kindle the flames, his every move in time with the beat. I caught a glimpse of my lover's eye cast upon my face as my head leaned back to better see the heavens. Dancing near him, I felt him, first in my head, inside my brain; then, in the depth of my heart. I danced around the fire, I saw Patrick sit again, and that Omie was on his lap. His eyes were locked with our child's. Father and son then watched with awe at the dance of their daughter/sister. When they turned their eyes to me, their awe poured into the power of my soul.

∞

We danced until we were three. Ally, whose energy was infinite; me, whose energy was driven by the love of those about me, and Martha, who danced with the determination and instinct of a female whose duty was nearly complete. Maiden, mother and sage. We moved in synchrony to the sound of the night about us.

Ixchel had joined Teddy. She stood across the fire singing as he maintained the beat of the night. She matched his rhythm with sounds of her voice. Hummings. Mutterances. Cries. Her song was a refrain, a mantra, an invocation of different tongues repeating the message of many cultures and many peoples, calling into the skies. I felt her prayer. Our dance persisted; we stepped our way around the fire.

Many times, the flames waned, and Patrick coaxed it back to brightness.

And then, when the deepest darkness closed in, and our mother Earth's poles tipped, the hope of a bright morning was closer, Ixchel cried out in a voice plaintive and sure of rebirth, of new days and of the new year. Her song called the men to their feet, Teddy with Ingie in his arms, Patrick with Omie in his. The Bass Brothers together. We danced again together, three times around the burning fire.

We joined together alongside the embers of the quelling fire. We gathered, our arms around each others shoulders, our heads huddled cheek to cheek, our breaths meeting and mingling in vapors of prayer.

"I love you!" I sang.

"I love you!" Ally and Omie echoed.

"I love you!" Their father added.

"I love you!" We all sang together. We sang our chorus, our mantra, with joyful voice.

"I love you. I love you. I love you! "

*I love you, my family.*

# Lynn Joyce

*North Freedom, Wisconsin*
*Mother's Day*
*May 11, 1969*

At first light, I felt the covers shift as Patrick stepped out of bed. He leaned over to me and kissed my temple. He snugged the bedding around my shoulders and neck. I barely woke. I heard him quietly close the door as he left. A few moments later, I heard the muffled drone of the compressor in the milk house. Paddy and Rose had started milking. The image of Patrick helping with the milk line waffled around in my head until it took over my dreams. I heard nothing more until later, after I noticed the aroma of coffee filtering up from the kitchen.

∞

The twins slept. I wrapped in a robe, freshened up, and joined Elle in the great room where she sat in her rocker, watching out toward David's barn.

"Good morning, Elle."

Elle's smile was seldom more than modest, and it was so this morning. Her lips curled at their ends; the smile drew upward, spreading to her eyes. Her glimpse was often fleet, but most always soft. Sometimes, it hardened, or flashed, and her fear or anxiety quickly overshadowed her normally joyful outlook. But that occurs seldom now. Not like when I first sat with her in this kitchen five years ago, and her expression was fixed, weak and sheltering. She flows outward now, toward those her gaze lingers upon and to whom she registers love and trust. She smiled at me in just that way now, as I joined her in her the great room.

"Patrick's up on David's ridge," she shared. "He told me he was headed there." Her gaze shifted out the window to where rays of the rising sun spilling above the woods and hills to the east, lighting the the high rooftop of the barn. Her eyes rested peacefully on the barn. Partially silhouetted by the rising sun, the backline of the barn's lofty ridge line intersected the ragged treelike horizon of her son's hallowed ridge beyond.

"He's up there, now," she mused. "With his brother."

I wrapped myself in an afghan as I curled up on the cushions of the old family couch. It was built for young, strapping men. Patrick had been comfortable in it as a teen. He has told me about it. His favorite couch ever. I sunk into its cushions and pillows. I trained my eyes out the windows, searching where my mother-in-law trained her gaze. Toward David's ridge.

Where my husband now walked among the trees, looking across forest and marsh, seeing the new day.

∞

*In the twilight of this morning's dawn, as I trudged through the brambles of David's ridge, I thought I'd lost my way. More than once. I knew if I kept the budding light above the trees to the left of me, I would come to the bluff. I did, finally, after wandering about for a bit. I was grateful for my cane; the woods were littered with windfall and rough terrain. My cane has become a part of me since my Boundary Waters accident. I pressed on, searching. The marsh below the bluff was dark in night's fading shadows, and dawn had yet to slip her early rays into the wet lands below when I stepped up to bluff's edge to look across the marsh. Then, like a beacon, a sliver or two of sunlight cut through the mist hanging above the cat tails and marsh grass below. I knew this ridge. I knew Davey's tree was further on, right on top of the bluff, just above the cliff's steep face. I plodded on. I'd find it. I had to find it. I felt that there is where to find David close by.*

∞

"Was Ixchel awake when you came down?" I asked.

Elle startled, her face turning from the window.

"Yes. I saw her when she went out to the barn. She was awake before Patrick left for the ridge. Does she ever sleep?"

I saw her stir back and forth, almost in a shiver.

"Probably as much as you," I teased her. Elle seldom slept. But she mastered resting.

She got up from the chair as she rocked forward. Breaking her gaze from the ridge outside, she turned her attention to the kitchen.

"Time to kneed dough," she said, glancing over. "Ready for a cup of coffee, Lynn?"

The scent of rich coffee wafted lazily in the air.

"Oh, yes. Please," I said, pulling the Afghan snug about me as I climbed from the depths of Patrick's couch.

"Stay," Elle encouraged. "I'll bring it. You keep watch. And stay warm."

*So like Elle!* I chuckled. *Keep watch, she says.*

She brought me a cup, then returned to work on the great table in the kitchen.

"They should all be coming in," she said, "in a little while,"

Across the garden and the alfalfa field beyond, stepping out from the tree line and over the fence into the alfalfa, Patrick appeared in the morning light. He stepped carefully, leaning on his cane, as he plod through the greenery with intent. With purpose. He'd be here shortly.

As he made his way, I noticed the hmm from the milk house go still.

346

They, too, would be in soon, Paddy and Rose. And Ixchel. I got up, sipped my coffee as I headed back to our bedroom. It was time to get dressed.

∞

I peeked into the twin's room on my way to dress. They hadn't made a peep so far this morning. I expected them to be still sleeping and was surprised to find their bedding turned back and their pillows abandon. I took a few more steps toward my bedroom when I herd chirping and soft giggles from down the hall. Eva's door was ajar, and I found my twins cuddled on each side of Eva as she nursed one of her babies. Ally, propped by pillows and tucked in close to Eva, carefully held Eva's other sleeping child.

Eva caught sight of me in the doorway and softly greeted me.

"Good morning, Lynn," she smiled. "Your little ones are here to help with their cousins." Eva's accent carried tones from her years in the French orphanage, but I couldn't help notice how far her fluency had come in the half year since she arrived in Wisconsin. She practiced her English as passionately as she did her music.

"Good morning, Eva. Hi, kids. I hope you didn't bother Eva and her babies too early this morning."

Ally held her gaze on the baby in her arms, mesmerized by the face of her young cousin. Omie looked up, his face a picture of awe and wonder. He shook his head to assure me that he and his sister had been discreet.

"Auntie Eva was up already," he calmly explained. "The babies were already awake. They were hungry."

"How about you," I asked him. "Are you ready for breakfast?"

He shook his head back and forth. "Not yet."

It was early for the twins to be up, but we were away from home and I accepted they might be breaking from their morning routine.

"Okay," I replied. "I'm going to get dressed, then go help your grandma get breakfast ready. She's making coffee cake."

Omie tipped his nose up and sniffed. "Smells good."

"It will be,"I promised. "How about you, Eva? Do you need help here before I go out to the kitchen.

Like Omie, Eva shook her head. "We are good. Your darlings are help. I am fine."

I looked at the cuddling cluster on Eva's bed in the new morning's light and wished I had my camera in hand. I lodged the scene in my mental file of absolute photogenic masterpieces never to be recorded on film. It warmed this mother's heart to see my children with their aunt and cousins. Family.

∞

The aroma of breakfast lured the children into the kitchen before I finished dressing. I heard them chatting with their father and Jack who sipped coffee as the milking crew came in from cleaning up after finishing in the barn.

"Good morning," I offered to all. "Ally, is Eva coming for breakfast? Does she need help with the babies?"

Ally shook her head. "I don't think so, Mom. The twins fell back asleep. Auntie Eva said she might nap a little longer, too. She asked Omie to take her a glass of water."

Omie's big round eyes flashed his feeling of importance. "She was thirsty."

"I'll take her a coffee in a little while," Elle said. "Give her a few extra moments before her babies call her into action." She topped off Jack's coffee as she talked, and then filled more cups as she heard Rose, Paddy and Ixchel stomp boots on the porch. The door opened and the milkers came in as Elle slid one of the coffee's toward me. I nodded my thanks.

Patrick planted a kiss on his new bride's cheek as I took the chair next to him at the big round table. *His bride*, I thought. It seemed so right. The way he looked at me this morning after our wedding last night confirmed my feeling.

"What's this Jack is telling you? He'll be in Guatemala by when?" I asked.

Jack picked up my question. "Today's the 11th. We leave at noon. If we average 10 hours a day driving and catch the Pan American Highway at San Antonio, we should get to the Mexican border by Wednesday, maybe Thursday at the latest. Right? The highway is complete through Mexico, so we should be able to reach Mexico City by Sunday or Monday. And Oaxaca Wednesday or Thursday later next week. We can be in Guatemala in a little over two weeks."

Ixchel sidled up behind Jack, her lips spread closed in a happy, wide grin.

"You expect miracles, Father Jack." She glided into the chair next to Jack, picked up one of the coffee's, sipped it, and said, "But you don't give magic time enough to happen. We get to Antigua, maybe," she paused, furrowed her brow, her smile spreading again across her cheery face, and declared, "the solstice. Maybe the solstice."

Jack coughed his mouthful of coffee, drips of which flowed down the mane of his beard.

"A month!" He coughed again, reaching across the table for napkins. "What do you think, are we traveling by bicycle? Why could it possibly take a month, no, more than a month, to get to Guatemala?"

Patrick put his chin down to his chest, smiling, as he twirled the coffee in the bottom of his cup. He knew Ixchel's ways of getting what she expected. Rose and Paddy pulled up chairs around the table, grinning, seeing the consternation of their old friend Jack, and knowing that the good priest was about to face a lesson in life. Elle smiled as well, as she walked up behind Ixchel and placed her hands on her friends shoulders. It warmed my heart to see my mother-in-law reaching out to her new friend.

"Are you in such a hurry?" Ixchel asked Jack.

He looked startled. It was a question he'd not considered. He assumed the trip would be forthwith and expedient. He'd decided Guatemala was where he was destined to go, and if he was going to go there, he'd might as well just drive directly there and see what awaited him. It was simple, he thought.

"We need to take time to see miracles happening." Ixchel said.

Suddenly, Jack realized that there was more to consider. He hadn't considered what that more was. And Ixchel was about to tell him. He wiped his beard with a cloth that Elle handed him and held out his cup as she offered more coffee.

"What is it?" He lobbed the softball of a question to his Guatemalan friend.

"We don't drive to San Antonio. We drive to Indiana. I left things in Indiana. We go first to Indiana," she said. It was indeed clear and simple.

"Then we drive to Colorado," she said. "I need to see the Columbine in the alpine meadows. So do you."

Jack blinked, startled by her directions. He recognized them as a mandate. He blinked again, and nodded.

"We will drive through the four corners. I've never seen the four corners, and the route from Gunnison through the four corners will take us to the painted desert. There are plants in the painted desert that I hope to find. We will go to Chinle to visit my sister among the Navajo. She will help us find plants."

Jack stood transfixed.

"We cross the border at Nogales. The west coast along the Sea of Cortez is where we will travel. The coast is beautiful. The sunsets will free your heart."

Jack was mesmerized, his eyes frozen in a thousand yard stare.

"We will visit my sisters in Morelia, and Leon. And Oaxaca. You will like Oaxaca. Good food. You like good food," she poked a finger into his belly just below his ribs. He grunted.

"Then, we go to Guatemala. You will take me home. And I will take you to Antigua, where you will learn to talk Spanish."

He nodded. "You have lots of sisters."

Her eyes flashed and her grin spread. "Sisters everywhere."

Paddy broke the silence that followed Ixchel's directions.

"How long will that route take you?" he asked. "Will you get there this summer?" He joked.

Ixchel beamed. "We will be home on the Solstice."

Jack shook his head. "A month. It's going to take us a month to get to Guatemala!"

"If we hurry," Ixtchel warned.

Patrick held back, but his shoulders bounced to the restraint of his laughter.

"Surely, you've already thoroughly discussed your travel plans with Ixchel. Right?" he asked.

Jack's head sagged forward, his beard coming to a rest on his barrel chest.

"Not in detail," he said. "I figured I was the driver. I chose the route. I am mistaken."

"You are in such a hurry to live your life that you drive like a tumble weed in the wind. I have much to share with you about my home. I will teach you along the way. Guatemala is my home and my home will embrace you. It will absorb you. It might even set you free. I will help you to understand what you see when you are in my country. You will do right by it." Ixchel said. "We will work on that while we drive."

"Right," Jack agreed. "I wouldn't want to be in a hurry. I've got my whole life ahead of me."

"Exactly," Ixchel nodded.

"Jack," Rose piped in. "You've met your mentor. You are ready for your travels."

∞

Elle took coffee to Eva, her other daughter-in-law. Within a few moments, she returned with Eva's son Jacob in her arms. Eva followed, carrying David, the younger of her twin babies. We shared this last family meal, Elle's breakfast feast, chatting about the promise of the day and the joy of last night's beautiful wedding ceremony between Patrick and me. We talked about our lives after we parted, Patrick, the kids and I heading north, Eva, her twins, staying here with Elle, Paddy and Rose. Ixchel and Jack heading south. Paddy talked of his plans for the new barn, and Rose explained their intent for genetic management of the expanding herd of dairy cows. They told of remodeling Paddy's old bachelor quarters across the road, and hiring full time help who would live there. There was a young couple from the reservation near the Dells who had been working part time with the herd;

Paddy and Rose considered them a good solution for managing the farm and herd as they grew older. The envisioned transitioning the dairy business to these younger farmers, helping the younger generation to fulfill their hopes of farming.

"Dairying is a full time commitment. It takes half a lifetime to build a career in farming dairy cows," Paddy observed. "David had vision, and that was just one of his gifts to us," Paddy said. "We think he would like our plans to help others build a career here while working to make David's dreams come to be."

I turned to Patrick. "You have never said anything about wanting to farm. Wanting to see David's dreams come true. Do you?"

Patrick was adamant. "No. I understood David. I knew what he wanted to do here," he said, looking at his uncle and Rose. "It's something I never wanted. Something I felt I escaped from, really," he grinned. Jack and Rose both chuckled at Patrick's remarks.

"No. I'm more interested in the North Star Resort. I see our lives best within the setting of our home. That's where we belong."

Omie grunted like an elder giving consent. "Uhmmn."

His sister agreed. "I love our home! I love our lake. That is where I want to be."

"Agreed," Patrick said, gazing firmly at me. "The resort is our home."

"This will always be your home, too," Rose made clear.

Paddy nodded in agreement. "Even if Eva and her twins move on. And take Elle with them," Paddy said. "This is home for all of us."

"Are you thinking of living elsewhere," I said, turning to Eva.

"No, we are here. We are with family. It is good for us," she said clearly.

Paddy explained his thought. "This is your home, Eva. It always will be. This was David's home, and it is yours. Forever," he looked keenly into her grateful expression. "Every time I hear your music, my heart fills with joy. You play like David played, with your heart, from your soul. Such music is meant to be heard by more than just a herd of dairy cows. You will know if it is in your heart to leave here and find audiences other than me and these cows. But this will always be your home, and the home of your twins."

Eva nodded once, as clearly as Paddy had a moment earlier.

Elle, however, fidgeted. "If you do find it best to go to the cities and find places where you can play your music for others, will you need help with your children?" Her eye's welled in tears.

"Your grandchildren? David's children? I will always need your help raising our Joyce children," she said, her eyes locked with Elle's "Always. But right now, I want to be here. It is our home. I need home. So do my children. Always, thank you."

I watched Patrick as he gazed at Eva with Jacob in her arms. I could see only love and happiness. I felt full and healed.

∞

By late morning, a lull set upon us. I felt the split in our family that was about to take place. Looking at Jack, who was beginning to pump his knee up and down, I knew it was time for goodbyes.

"Jack," I said. "Thank you again for marrying us. I will always be grateful that Patrick and I married under your blessings." He had led us though our wedding ceremony yesterday here in the Joyce homestead. Our children witnessed our wedding, and our family blessed us with their witness.

A smile crept across Jack's face. He nodded. "It was a privilege. And I will always be grateful that you asked me to lead you two into marriage. You are meant to share this time together. And raise your children together. I wish your sister could have been here for you, Lynn, as you are there for her. And your father. And I wish David were here. But that is not as it is. I'm thankful for what is, what we have, that our family is together to see your little family continue life together, as it should be."

He looked at his traveling companion. "Well, Ixchel. It is time. Are we ready?"

"We are."

∞

Patrick hobbled off to our bedroom as we broke company in Elle's kitchen.

"Don't go driving off before I get back," he called to Jack over his shoulder.

We helped as they packed their final travel bags and the basket of sandwiches and treats that Elle handed them. Patrick returned from the house carrying a large, crate sized cardboard carton bound with cord.

"Do you have room for these?" he asked, offering the container to Jack, who looked on with curiosity. "Letters," Patrick explained, "from David."

Jack teared up. "Patrick, how can you…?" He left the question dangle.

"I've read them all many times. I've almost memorized his words," Patrick said. "Thank you, for everything. For marrying us. For being there for David. You're one of us, Jack. A Joyce. These will give you something that only you can appreciate. Take them."

Jack set the box carefully in the massive trunk of his Burgundy red Cadillac. He turned back to Patrick, tears streaming into his mane-like beard. He could not speak, but nodding, reached his arms around Patrick and hugged him as he sobbed.

352

I came along side with Ally in hand and we hugged Patrick and Jack both, and Paddy and Rose joined us. Ixchel gathered in Omie, and Elle with Jacob and Eva with David wrapped arms around us as well, and I felt the familiar reach of our own twins as they wrapped their arms around our legs, snugging into our family huddle.

For moments, we swayed as one, in the peace and quiet under the morning sun. A solemn moment embraced us on the lawn in front to the Joyce family home. We shared goodbyes, hugs and blessings.

"I am grateful," Jack said as we unfolded from our hug. "I will return these to you."

Patrick nodded.

The travelers loaded themselves in Jack's car. It was time to continue their journeys. I walked to the passenger door window and tapped. Ixchel pushed a button inside the door and the window hummed open.

"Thank you," I offered. "For Patrick. For us."

She nodded, and a grin spread like honey across her face,.

"Will you help our Father Jack as much as you helped my Patrick?"

Her eyes widened, and her lips drew in from her broad smile, puckering into a kiss.

"Perhaps," she snickered. "Patrick was an easy fix. He's a seeker. He is driven to find the center," she said. "This guy," she pointed to Jack behind the wheel of his Cadillac, "not so much. He seeks something that he cherished," she peered out the windshield of Jack's Caddy. "Something he lost. Something less than real. Less than authentic. We have to find something worthy to replace his misplaced faith. Something to feed his soul." Her eyes danced. 'We will. Something worthy of family. Of love." She nodded a final time.

I reached my hand through the window and touched her shoulder. A farewell touch.

With Ixchel smiling contentedly and perched on a thick stuffed cushion, Jack started the engine. Before he shifted into gear, he turned his eyes to meet each of us as we watched him prepare to drive away. I felt the kindness and joy, the fear and the uncertainty that his gaze revealed to us. He was leaving on a journey that had yet to reveal its mission.

He looked at us, his expression a caricature of his hope.

Then he shifted his car into gear, slowly accelerating, seeing us all one last time as he headed away from our home.

Also by Russ Vanderboom

*The Good Guy List*

# The Rumble of the Earth

I t hit the moment I'd gone to bed. I'd just glanced at my watch while grappling boot laces. Just after 3:00. Roger had kept me up and out all night. I was still awake, alert from our stirring, intense visit. Bothered, really, by Roger's revelations to his work here in Guatemala.

But overriding my thoughts was growling from deep in the earth. It-mumbled it's curse through the stone in the ground and the adobe walls of the bedroom. It's tone mounted long enough to snap my attention to something portentous. I heard it as I dropped my boot to the tiled floor and tossed my body to my bed.

And it hit, first with a sway of bed and floor that caught me half air-borne. I skimmed the side of the mattress and spun off the bed on the cool tile. The heave continued. I rolled, falling to the tile, and again as I tried getting up. Wedged against the wall, I reached for the mattress as the bed swung toward me. Shards of glass from the window above me splashed off the tiles and bed frame, missing me mercifully as it flew over-head from the window frame. The wall grumbled as the floor heaved in a swell coming from well under the house, deep below the hills around the village. I crawled toward the door; the voice of the quake outside drowning out the grinding from within the wall. It howled like a train. On all fours, I scrambled into the hallway and outside. Seizures from the earth continued, waning, softening in voice. The rumble of the walls in the village gave way to the crashing of dried mud and stone breaking from the walls of our homes. My bedroom wall tumbled as I clamored away from my house's portal. The door swatted down at my heals as it sprang from it's frame un-der the weight of the falling stucco. Our alley filled with the rush of fine, thick dust rising from the street and billowing in over the crumpled wall beside the gate. The dust rose like a mask from within the darkness of the night. It spread, spewed from the grounds of our broken village, obliterat-ing any light coming from the star laden sky above us.

The night surrendered to darkness. For an instant, the quiet was as deep as the shadow of the darkness. But then, a wail pierce the night air, shrill and heartfelt. And a cry of pain echoed in the stillness. Voices reached out among the neighboring families. They grew in number. Cries. Shouts. Wailing.

Fear was rampant in the village. I could feel it in the air. I lifted my watch before my face. Dulled by the dust cloud sweeping over me, the glowing illumination from the markings on my watch stared at me. 3:08. Just a few minutes since I'd gone to lay down.

It was a moment that I'd remember. And it continued getting bigger as the ground vibrated and the calls for help grew louder across the hillside.

∞

In the morning, as the sun burned through the lingering smoke and dust cloud as it arced it's path above the mountains to the east of the village, I could see the damage in it's entirety. The village was destroyed. People milled around the streets, dazed, picking through the ruins of their homes, or wandered for help, water, food, or information. Clusters crawled over rubble, throwing rabble off the heaps, looking for family buried beneath. We knew it was a quake. We know nothing of it's strength, but that it was huge. The epicenter couldn't have been far. We felt random tremor, some very strong. I wondered if any aftershocks would be as devastating. There was little left up right in the village. That which stood vertical was broken and tumbled. Another quake like the one in the night would be dangerous. I wondered what to do? How would we survive?

I wondered. Where was my car?

# Thanksgiving

*June 21, 2024*

This day and age of independent publication of novel literature enables me to offer this portion of the Joyce Family Saga to you, my Reader, and I am most grateful that you took up North Star Resort. It is my heartfelt hope that you have been entertained, inspired and enlightened by the story of Lynn and Patrick, Jack, Elle, and Eva, and the extended members of the Joyce/North family as they strive to grow and heal together amidst the challenges of life in the world.

I am grateful first and foremost to my family for their encouragement, suggestions and perhaps most of all, patience in their support for my work on this story. Catherine, Anne and Michael are my mainstay. Catherine offered critique and advice as a reader—and an avid reader and editor she is. Her copy editing suggestions were invaluable. Annie is the true editor in our family, and her advice on content matter, story line, and character development is essential to my writing. Michael, my son, encourages me with his patience and confidence. My family is my inspiration.

A fictional family saga builds upon facets of life that people embrace daily. I am grateful for the insight into those elements of life that contributors to the Joyce Family saga shared with me.

I enjoy symphonic music and other genres of music, and I listen to and am motivated by the recordings of voice and instrument as I compose. However, the depth of my knowledge of Bach, the Baroque and classical eras of symphonic composition is limited to being a recreational audience. In the early developmental stages of *North Star Resort*, I benefited greatly from the advice and insight of Elsa Nilsson, an eloquent violinist whose career graced the St. Paul Chamber Orchestra. Elsa pointed me to the music of Hillary Hahn, and particularly Bach's Chaconne. Her suggestions lived with me as I listened to the Chaconne and other Bach compositions while weaving Eva's story into the Joyce saga. Music such as Ms. Hahn's motivated me as I produced not just the Munich section of this story, but throughout the trails taken by Patrick and Lynn as they built and cared for their family in the forests of northern Minnesota.

This northern realm of our nation is steeped in the heritage of Finns and Norwegians who immigrated and resettled in these parts. Walter Passi, who contributed in his self-described role as our local neighborhood Finnish Cultural ambassador, informed me about the shamans and healers among the swarthy Mustalaiset Finnish gypsies, and the Laplander Sami tribes, peoples on whom the character and healer Teddy in this story is based. Walter, who contributes to the health of our fellow Elyites as a nurse at our community hospital, also advised me on aspects of compartmental syndrome in leg and ankle fractures.

Our Ely Writers Group has offered extensive improvements and suggestions to *North Star Resort*. The expertise, dedication and skill of my colleagues, who meet the first Thursday of every month at the Ely Folk School, is invaluable. I'm grateful to this core group of authors, Kay Vandervort, Ann Stewart Uehling, Becca Manlove, Linda Sutton, Rachel Brophy, and John Kopp, for all their suggestions, edits and attention to the story line of the Joyces in North Star Resort.

I value as well the edits suggestions that my long time friend and fellow author, Patrick Quinn, contributed to North Star Resort.

I cherish the photographs that our family friend, Gabe Horstman, has gifted to us and that adorn the wall of our Northwoods cabin. The cover image is a work of Gabe's and I am grateful for his permission to display it on this book. Gabe is family. As is Gustavo Estrada, my son-in-law, who masterfully offered suggestions on producing the cover artwork. Chuck Weber's painting of the Joyce twins is a treasure to me. He captured the spirit of the Joyce brothers.

And my friends and early readers. John Bunce, Bob Bluhm, Sue Duffy, and Pat Sieren Frederick, your encouragement has proved to be the nudge that budged inertia and enabled me to bring this story to completion. Steve Schon's advise to consider changing my description of a northern pike was welcomed. Fiction must, after all, depict the natural in ways that reflect the beauty of creation.

To all, I am grateful.

*Russ Vanderboom*

## An apology, or perhaps a boast

I read the acknowledgements and gratitude statements of conventionally published authors, at times with admiration for the assembly of those who advise, edit, promote, represent and help with an well orchestrated publication of the authors story. (Read Richard Osmond's tribute for his colleagues in The Thursday Murder Club. It's exhilarating!) At times I'm just downright jealous of the ability of authors to muster the industrial machinery to achieve their storytelling goals. But then I settle down and get back to work, doing everything from transforming imagination into sentence structured storytelling to formatting, design, and all the logistics of getting my story printed and delivered into the hands of readers. I'm not real fast, and I don't have the resources or connections to publish conventionally. Hence, I'm an independent publisher. My work sometimes takes shortcuts. For example, I depend on Professor Google, the linguist, for translation of languages that I really have no grip on. I am no polyglot. My apologies to those whose mother tongue may be compromised by my usage of 'Dr. Google's' linguistic services. I also extend my experience and talents in graphic display of text and cover art. I admit clumsiness in my command of Pages, the Apple software upon which this story has been displayed. I take liberties in my fictional license that builds upon historical reference. Please accept the limits of my scope of mastery in this wonderful opportunity to self publish my stories of the Joyce Family Saga.

## To Readers

I am grateful to you for your reading of the story told in North Star Resort. I hope you found the story of Patrick, Lynn and her family, and Jack Hanley interesting and satisfying. I hope it touched your heart. I will be even more grateful if you are moved to contribute your thoughts, appreciation, and appropriate star awards to review opportunities at Goodreads, Amazon, or on my website www.pepperseedpublishing.com. Your comments as a reader are fitting tribute to the value of this story. Did the characters come to life for you? Share your copy of North Star Resort with your reader friends. Or send them a copy from IngramSpark print on demand, or Amazon. Feed the Corporate algorithms with data of sales of my books. That promotes awareness of these stories. Thank you.